Surviving the Evacuation
Book 11
Search and Rescue

Frank Tayell

Dedicated to my family

ISBN-13: 978-1974212637
ISBN-10: 1974212637

Other titles:

Post-Apocalyptic Detective Novels
Strike a Match 1. Serious Crimes
Strike a Match 2. Counterfeit Conspiracy
Strike a Match 3: Endangered Nation
Work. Rest. Repeat.

Surviving The Evacuation/Here We Stand
Book 1: London
Book 2: Wasteland
Zombies vs The Living Dead
Book 3: Family
Book 4: Unsafe Haven
Book 5: Reunion
Book 6: Harvest
Book 7: Home
Here We Stand 1: Infected & 2: Divided
Book 8: Anglesey
Book 9: Ireland
Book 10: The Last Candidate
Book 11: Search and Rescue

For more information, visit:
http://blog.franktayell.com
www.facebook.com/TheEvacuation

Part 1
Life & Death

Bill & Kim

Anglesey & North Wales
28th & 29th October

Chapter 1 - At Sea
North Wales, 28th October, Day 229

"I almost wish I was in a council meeting," Bill Wright said as another wave slammed into the cockpit's window.

"Doesn't it make you feel alive?" Heather Jones asked.

"It's making me seasick," Kim said. "I can't believe people used to sail boats like this for fun."

"What's that they say in Yorkshire?" Lorraine said. "Nowt so strange as folk." The young Scot turned back to Bill. "Aren't the council meetings going well?"

That was an understatement, but Bill didn't say it aloud. It was three days since the election, and Heather Jones was one of the newly elected members of the council. Bill had been appointed as Mary O'Leary's chief of staff, and given responsibility for co-ordinating the meetings. Corralling was a more accurate term for his riding herd on the captains, colonels, and civilians who were content giving orders but rarely happy taking suggestions.

"The problem's water," Bill said, opting for the more diplomatic reply. "Or food, or ammunition, or medical supplies, or ships, or oil, or the weather."

"Or zombies," Kim added.

"Or them," Bill agreed. "Basically, there are too many undead, and too little of everything else. Above all, we've too little time."

"The rumour at the docks is that we've got until the seventh of January," Lorraine said.

"That's reached the docks?" Heather asked. The yacht hit another wave. This time, the sleek craft rode up the crest, seeming to pick up a knot of speed with each foot climbed. The sail filled, the ropes grew taut, and Bill was certain that the ship would capsize right up until it glided smoothly down the other side.

"Aye, the seventh of January," Lorraine said. "It's not true?"

"Not really," Bill said. "If the power plant doesn't melt down, that's when it'll be switched off. There's an eighty percent chance that there won't be a catastrophic failure before then, but that still leaves a twenty percent chance there will be."

"That's according to Chief Watts," Jones added. "He trained to maintain the reactor on a nuclear submarine, but those are kettles compared to the facility on the island."

However the problems facing the last remnant of humanity were prioritised, the current crisis stemmed from the power station. Most survivors had found Anglesey by accident. They'd stayed because the island had been emptied of humans during the evacuation and cleared of the undead shortly after the outbreak. After Quigley was finally defeated, and the *Vehement* had sunk the renegade politician's rogue submarine, the survivors had turned the nuclear power station back on. At the time, they'd had food thanks to the Canadian grain-carriers, mains water thanks to the electrically powered treatment plant, and safety thanks to the destruction of the bridges leading to the mainland. What they hadn't realised was how severely the power station had been damaged during the global civil war that had followed the outbreak. The alarms and monitoring systems had failed, and it had required a visual inspection to spot the first leak. Fortunately, that hadn't been radioactive. The second leak was. Two people had died sealing it. Though the power station was still operational, it couldn't be repaired, nor properly decommissioned. That was their current Catch-22. The sooner they shut the plant down, the sooner there would be a containment failure and a leak of radioactive material across Anglesey and into the Irish Sea. If they waited too long, the pile might melt down, giving those survivors on Anglesey a matter of minutes to flee the island.

Objectively, everyone had known that there was no spare fuel for the reactor and that it would have to be shut down one day. No one had thought that day would be so soon. Almost no one. Mary O'Leary and George Tull had known, as had Admiral Gunderson of the *Harper's Ferry*, and Mister Mills, captain of the formerly-HMS *Vehement*. It was two of their engineers who'd died sealing the radioactive leak. They'd kept it a secret from the wider population to avoid panic. The long-promised election had been called. Mary O'Leary had hoped it would prompt a debate into the direction, both social and geographical, the future of humanity would take. Instead, the election had been hijacked by Rachel Gottlieb.

Rachel had manipulated the contest into a three-way race between Bishop, a zealot who'd invented his own religion, Markus, a man who thought he was running to become the official opposition, and Dr Umbert, a psychiatrist who had no interest in leadership at all. Dr Umbert would have made a better leader than most, but he'd died on the Isle of Man. Bill held himself responsible for that, and for not realising what Rachel was doing until it was almost too late.

Under Rachel's direction, Bishop had abducted Bill and Lorraine. She'd wanted Bill and Lorraine to be murdered by Bishop so that their bodies could be found at his campsite. Bishop and his followers would be killed during the rescue attempt, leaving Markus the sole candidate and Rachel the real power behind the throne. Bishop was dead. So was Rachel. The election had still been held. A ten-member cabinet had been elected and Mary O'Leary was asked to remain as mayor. With the election over, the populace was informed of the power station's imminent collapse and the need to leave Anglesey. All that was left was to work out how. That was a task left to Bill Wright, a former speechwriter and spin-doctor who'd had vague dreams of making his way to Number 10. Mary and George had wanted him to stand in the election and take over the island's governance, and now, in all but name, he had.

"If we've got until the seventh of January, we'll get everyone off Anglesey in time, right?" Lorraine asked.

"We're aiming to have everyone off long before Christmas," Bill said. "I've no fears about that. The evacuation itself is straightforward because we have so few options."

"I wish you wouldn't call it that," Heather Jones said. The yacht bounced up a wave. Lorraine grabbed a strap, but Bill nearly lost his footing. Kim kept hers, as she'd had the foresight to sit down. Heather Jones barely moved an inch, nor did the wheel in her own iron grip. "No, after what happened to all the occupants of Anglesey," the Welsh sea captain continued, "after what Quigley did to them, that word has a dark meaning."

Heather Jones had been a student and employee of the University of Bangor, working there to take advantage of the reduced fees. Like everyone else on the island, she'd been evacuated by train, but she'd escaped. Very few others had. Most had been gassed, shot, or poisoned with the supposed-vaccine. Jones was only twenty-five, but she'd become the leader of the town of Menai Bridge, which, over the last few weeks, had grown into one of the largest settlements on Anglesey.

"The *departure*, then," Bill said. "And it's easy since we have so few ships."

"That's truer than most people realise," Jones said. "There aren't many of those sailing boats I'd trust in deep water, and fewer captains and crew I'd trust to a long sea voyage. Did you know two hundred and fifty-nine people have already left? I've got people keeping a record."

"Do you know where they've gone?" Kim asked.

"A lot won't say, but of those that do, most say Ireland and they don't mean Belfast," Jones said. "I tell them to speak to Miguel, to ask him what Dublin was like, but they don't want to listen. They prefer the certainty of the undead to the uncertainty of the power plant's demise. Their ships aren't seaworthy. I doubt they'll survive the voyage. No, we've twenty larger sailing boats, and thirty small yachts I'd trust to the open sea. We've no diesel for the trawlers, and the solar panels on the *Smugglers Salvation* are useless in this weather. There's no time to repair the *Harper's Ferry*. We're down to the *Amundsen* and the three grain-carriers. They'll need a mile to turn and another to stop. We can point them towards Ireland, but we'll be lucky not to run them aground. How lucky do you feel?"

"Which leaves us with the *Amundsen*," Bill said. "It'll leave Belfast tomorrow, return to Anglesey, and collect the last of the children. We'll get them to the container ship, *The John Cabot*, just outside Belfast Harbour. By week's end, there will be around six hundred people in Belfast, and the *Amundsen* will be sailing north to Svalbard where it'll refuel. We'll have to… to *collect* half the people from the archipelago because they were banking on supplies from us to survive the winter. They'll be dropped in Belfast while the *Amundsen* sails down to the Shannon Estuary where it will transfer fuel into Kempton's ship, *The New World*. Hopefully, by then, we'll have found some other ships. If we haven't, we'll have to use those grain-carriers and hope we can beach them somewhere closer to Belfast than Dublin."

"So, no, Lorraine, we'll get everyone to Belfast," Heather said. "Don't worry about that."

"I wasn't," Lorraine said. "I'm worried about what comes next."

"Me, too," Bill said. The boat hit another wave, and again he marvelled it didn't capsize. "Assuming we don't sink the grain-carriers in our attempt to get everyone off Anglesey, we'll be around nine and a half thousand people crammed onto three grain ships and a container ship which were designed for crews of a dozen each. It's going to be unsanitary to say the least. We don't have enough ammunition to occupy Belfast, but we'll have to secure somewhere along the coast. The ships have some desalination gear, but not the capacity to provide water for everyone. We might be able to move more people down to Elysium, but that's the exact opposite end of Ireland."

"About four hundred nautical miles," Jones said.

"The islands of Connemara might be a better bet," Kim said. "When Bill and I sailed through there, we saw a few islands that didn't have any undead on them."

"But there'll be no food, either," Bill said. "None but what we bring with us, and we don't have enough to start with."

"I'd disagree with you there," Heather said. "The greenhouses we've been building are producing enough for a thousand people."

"When supplemented by the fish that the trawlers caught before the diesel ran out," Bill said. "Fish that are currently stored in freezers powered by electricity from the nuclear plant. We can transport some of that fish to *The John Cabot*, but the ship's batteries were designed for a crew of a dozen, not hundreds. Electricity used for the freezers can't be used for desalinisation. I'm sure the engineers could redirect power from the engines, but then we're back to a question of space. Do we transport frozen fish to Belfast, or do we move your greenhouses? Do we use the oil from Svalbard to keep the freezers working, the lights on, or in reserve to move people somewhere safer come spring?"

"We keep people alive today," Lorraine said, "because the dead don't worry about tomorrow."

"Which is fine," Bill said, "except that there's a seventy percent chance that the Svalbard archipelago will become ice-bound this winter. We may have two months when we can't bring any oil from the reserve there. This winter, we have to say that we're starting again, and we're starting with nothing."

"And then comes spring," Kim said. "The zombies might have died by then, but we can't wait. If we're going to settle in Ireland, we need farmland. Do we spend the winter hacking fields out of the turf? In which case, is it in Belfast or Malin Head, Connemara or Kenmare Bay? We have the seeds, thanks to you, Heather, but we can't afford to waste them. We'll need the harvest next year or we truly will starve. We can't make a mistake in choosing where we plant them."

"Now you're sounding as bad as Bill and Heather," Lorraine said. "Elysium has solar panels, doesn't it?"

"How effective do you think they are in this weather?" Heather replied.

"Fine, but it has wind turbines, too," Lorraine said.

"But it's the other side of Ireland," Bill said. "In the long term, we don't have the ammunition or trained troops to hold more than one location against the undead."

"So you think we should go to America, too?" Lorraine asked.

"Only if the admiral can find a truly safe harbour," Kim said. "And if we can find the ships to take us there, and if, by then, we haven't used up all the oil to keep the lights on. We need somewhere we can plant a crop where we know we can harvest it next autumn. Even without the undead, the next year is going to be hard, but we need some measure of hope it won't end in starvation and death."

"America's going to be the same as here and everywhere else," Lorraine said. "Where do we even look?"

"It has to be an island," Captain Annabeth Devine called out from below. She'd decided to sleep during the journey to the north Welsh coast. Quite how anyone could doze while the boat crashed and bounced across the waves, Bill didn't know.

Captain Devine was a U.S. Marine, a military police officer, and the de-facto number-two of the U.S. military contingent. She'd lost her hand to an IED, and had been waiting for a transfer to a proper medical facility when the first outbreak had occurred. That had saved her life. She was on the current expedition to Wales because her professional experience as a law enforcement officer was essential.

"We'll start with Newfoundland," Devine said, "that's closest, but the weather may prove too demanding for long-term settlement. Then we'll make best speed to Nantucket, Martha's Vineyard, and Long Island. From there, we'll go south to the Outer Banks in North Carolina, stopping at islands and bays where we'll see what there is to be seen."

"And if it is as bad as here?" Lorraine asked.

"At least we'll know," Devine said.

"And we do have to find somewhere," Jones said. "America, or Ireland, or the Mediterranean. Somewhere."

"It's going to be a long winter," Kim said, "and it hasn't yet begun."

"You really are starting to sound like Heather," Lorraine said.

"You're right," Kim said. "We're alive today, and we should be thankful. We know what the problems are, and that's always half the battle when it comes to devising a solution."

Bill nodded, but he was more concerned with the other half of the battle. His eyes fell on a loose piece of tape that covered a bullet hole in the cockpit's wall. It was at head height and came from a shot that had killed an undead member of the yacht's original crew.

No, the evacuation was straightforward, but life was about to get immeasurably harder. Water, food, ships, medicine, electricity, zombies. Those were problems, but ones they knew how to deal with. It was the crises that those problems created, and how those were overcome, which would determine humanity's fate.

For the next few weeks, while the evacuation was underway, and while everyone bated their breath against the collapse of the nuclear plant, everything would stay calm. Bill expected it would break as Christmas drew near. Minds would turn to the past, to an idealised version of the family gathering around a table laden with food. They would see what little they had, and order would collapse.

Law and order, peace and justice, those were the real problems. That was what differentiated a society from a collection of barbarous individuals. There had nearly been a riot after the announcement was made about the nuclear plant. The trial had restored a thin veneer of calm.

They had searched Willow Farm and arrested all of Bishop's followers. They had searched Markus's pub, and found the evidence that Rachel had left behind. It was encyclopaedic, and it implicated only one man, Gareth Lenetti. There was an audio recording of him discussing the murder of four people with Paul. After the jury heard it, the trial was effectively over. It had been a swift affair, pulled together in a matter of hours more to soothe the mob than to pursue justice. No one had come forward to offer evidence for the defence, and after the recording was heard, the jury had been ready to give a verdict: guilty. The judges had taken barely longer to decide on a sentence. Throughout it all, Lenetti had claimed innocence. Only when the verdict had been pronounced did he admit some measure of guilt. He'd said there was proof of his lack of culpability in the campsite near Llandudno where Bill and Lorraine had been held prisoner. That claim had been made in open court, in front of a packed gallery.

That was where Bill and Kim, Lorraine, Heather, and Captain Devine were going. The evidence would be searched for because they had to become a society of laws. Guilt would be proven, not assumed. If they found nothing, the sentence would be carried out with all that meant for the future of their fragile, fledgling society. What worried Bill more was what would happen if they did find some evidence. No matter how compelling, he doubted it would satisfy the mob.

Chapter 2 - Evidence
North Wales

Mist hung over the Welsh coast, reducing visibility to a few hundred feet. Heather Jones swung the boat to within a short jump of the concrete jetty. Lorraine leapt ashore, rope in hand. Kim was half a step behind, a rifle in hers. As she aimed her weapon into the fog, Heather and Captain Devine quickly disembarked. Bill clambered awkwardly after them.

At first, he wasn't sure it was the correct section of coast, but then he saw the boat in which Bishop and his acolyte had attempted to flee. Lorraine had sniped at it from their vantage point on the cliffs. Her bullets had found their mark. Water had flooded the craft, but it had been securely moored and those ropes still held it fast to the jetty. As the boat had filled with water, it had toppled onto its side. The mast now floated on water flecked with fragments of bright red fibreglass from where successive tides had smashed the hull into the quayside.

"Our ship's secure?" Jones asked.

"Aye, Captain," Lorraine said.

"You don't need to come with us," Jones said.

"If I leave it to Bill, you might get lost," Lorraine said.

Kim and Lorraine moved quickly towards the shore, Heather close behind.

Captain Devine glanced at Bill. "You don't need to come, either," she said.

"I do," he said. "More than anyone, I need to know." He limped after the others.

His left leg had never properly healed from the fracture he'd sustained at the beginning of the outbreak, but he could now limp almost as fast as he'd once been able to walk. Possibly faster considering how out of shape he'd been after a sedentary decade of parliamentary campaigns. Even so, he couldn't keep up with Kim as she vanished into the mist.

Ten steps and five seconds later, there was a near silent sound of a suppressed shot followed by a sharp crack of metal hitting rock, and then there was silence. It was absolute. Bill hurried down the jetty, Devine at his heels.

Alone among the expedition, the American military police captain wasn't holding a weapon. Her holster's flap was unbuttoned, and her hand was never far from her pistol, but she hadn't drawn it. Bill wondered if that was because she had over a decade of combat experience, or whether she needed the hand free for balance. Her left hand was missing, the result of an IED before the outbreak. That injury was why she'd been taken to the *USS Harper's Ferry*, and why she'd survived when so many others hadn't. Bill decided that the captain hadn't drawn her sidearm because she didn't think danger was imminent. He drew comfort from that until he heard a flurry of bullets impacting against stone and flesh. He turned his quick limp into a loping run, and almost slipped on the slick steps. Devine caught his arm, holding him up.

"Less haste, less speed," she said. "Zombies don't have guns, so don't panic when you hear shots."

Bill couldn't help wonder if he should panic when the shooting stopped, because it had stopped now. He reached the edge of the jetty, and the beginning of the rock-covered beach. Kim stood next to an undead corpse, Jones and Lorraine either side.

"There were three zombies still moving," Kim said. "They must have fallen from the cliffs, and managed to crawl this far."

Splinters of white bone jutted through the zombie's shredded trousers, evidence of the injuries the creature had sustained during its fall.

"That's a military jacket, isn't it?" Lorraine asked.

"So are the boots," Devine said. "British Army, standard issue. He was a soldier."

"Probably infected near the beginning of the outbreak," Kim said. "And after that fall from the cliffs, after wrecking its legs and oozing that... let's call it blood, but leaving a trail of it from there to here, after all of that, it was still... alive."

Bill took the point. He and Kim had seen a zombie die. Once that news had spread, everyone was keen to report having seen others dying or dead with no obvious head wound, but they had yet to find definitive proof. This dead soldier was the opposite. Not all of the living dead were dying, not yet.

There were more bodies close to the cliffs. One that Lorraine had shot, and four others that had landed head first. There was a rattle of stones and a dry rasp from near the base of the steep steps. A zombie in an almost-clean tweed jacket snarled as Bill approached. Like the creature on the beach, its legs were a mangled ruin. Its face was marred by three ragged gashes where a clawing hand had torn through flesh and beard, but its features were discernible.

"I don't think I recognise him," Bill said. "Lorraine, was he one of Bishop's jurors?"

"No. No, I don't think so," she said.

"But he's recently turned," Devine said. "He must have been one of Bishop's people."

Bill brought the machete down on the zombie's skull. "We should call Bran, let him know."

"When we're at the campsite," Devine said.

After Rachel and Bishop had died, a squad of soldiers had travelled to the campsite to ascertain whether any of the zealot's followers had survived. They'd found no one living, and had ventured inland to search the nearest safe houses. The safe house network had been organised by George Tull, and had a grander name than the reality deserved. Flags were hung outside isolated buildings. Food and water were left inside along with a map directing any survivor towards the next safe house and, ultimately, to Anglesey. That squad of soldiers was being led by Bran, though it would be more accurate to say that the British Army sergeant was leading a group of volunteer-fighters. Though they were looking for Bishop's people, they were also leaving a warning for anyone who arrived at the safe houses in the months to come that Anglesey was no longer a sanctuary.

At the top of the steps, the mist was thinner, visibility better, but sounds were still eerily muffled.

"Is that the zombie you thought might be Sorcha Locke?" Devine asked. She pointed to the corpse that Bill had killed while Lorraine had been shooting at the boat. The creature's head was a mangled ruin, but around the corpse's neck was a blue and gold scarf.

"I think so," Bill said. "I mean, yes, I think that was Sorcha Locke."

"Good." Devine bent down, opened her satchel, took out a cloth, and carefully lifted the corpse's hand. "Damn. I was going to take her fingerprints, but they're too worn, too covered in grime."

"Is it important?" Heather asked.

"There's been a crime," Devine said. "The trial notwithstanding, it's a crime in which the victims will not get justice. In the absence of justice, people look for answers. The fate of one of Kempton's lieutenants is an answer they would welcome hearing."

"She's right," Kim said. "You made a big deal out of Lisa Kempton and Sorcha Locke in that account you published, Bill. People now think she's as big a monster as Quigley."

"I thought it better that people focused on Kempton and her people rather than on anyone living in our community," Bill said.

"True," Devine said, "but you've created a villain, and people want to know that she's dead. But I can't take fingerprints from this woman, not here."

"Could you do it on Anglesey?" Heather asked.

"Sure," Devine said. "I'd need a few hours to put together the equipment. We've got prints from the bunker in Belfast. I had Sergeant Conrad take samples a few days ago."

"If you only want fingerprints, you only need the hand," Heather said.

Bill sighed. "Stand back," he said as he raised the machete. As the blade severed rotten sinew, he felt he was also severing another link with their lost civilisation.

13

After another hundred yards along the path, they reached the first of the mobile undead. The dark-haired creature in the shredded remains of a sun dress tore itself free of the hedgerow. Mud caked its legs. Dried blood covered its face. Kim and Lorraine fired almost simultaneously. The zombie collapsed into the hedge with a cracking of branches far louder than the gunshots.

"Call out your targets," Devine said. "We can't waste the ammunition."

Dr Umbert had expressed it best, though others had expressed it before: they were fighters, not soldiers. Umbert's death on the ill-fated expedition to the Isle of Man had proven the psychiatrist's point. Bill blamed himself for Dr Umbert's death, and his own arrogance for not heeding the man's words. Then again, in his darker moments, Bill blamed himself for the death of the entire world.

They came to another undead corpse. Bill didn't remember having killed it. The bullet wound in its forehead was too neat for it to have been caused by Bishop's shotgun. He assumed the zombie had been killed by Bran. He *hoped* that was the case, but dark thoughts were growing as they ventured back to the place of his recent imprisonment. They managed another twenty yards before they heard the next creature. It was alive, and more recently turned.

"Recognise him?" Kim asked.

But Bill didn't, nor did anyone else. Kim fired. The zombie fell, and they continued down the track.

The wind picked up, thinning the fog. The caravans and chalets emerged from the mist, as did the path down which Bill and Lorraine had escaped. From the scores of footprints in the mud, some booted, some bare-footed, more undead had found their way out of the campsite than had died on the beach. The barbed wire that had previously blocked the gap between the two caravans had been trampled into the dirt. Two corpses lay on top of the wire. Again, both had been expertly shot. The caravan's walls were dented, smeared with dark stains of blood, gore, and soot. That last showed those creatures had come from the house in which Bill and Lorraine had been held prisoner, and which Bill had burned down.

The silence was fractured by the tinkling of broken glass. Rifles and machete were raised, but the sound came from deep inside the campsite. Captain Devine's hand was braced on her sidearm, though she hadn't drawn it.

"Once more unto the breach," Bill murmured, "but just this once more."

The caravans were more battered than he remembered, the glass often broken and always smeared with grime. The paintwork was peeling, with white and grey flecks floating in the wide puddles that had gathered after a long night of heavy rain. The steps leading to the caravans' doors were covered in a thin moss. In the drier patches of gravel, leaves of ivy poked upwards. In a few years, the plant would rule the campsite, choking out all other vegetation and swaddling the mobile homes until the ivy's own weight crushed the caravans' rusting metal frames.

More glass shattered, this time far closer. Shards sprayed onto the path as a zombie tumbled halfway out of a chalet's window four feet from Kim. The zombie snagged itself on the glass still embedded in the frame, but its clawing arm brushed against Kim's shoulder as she turned.

"Mine," Devine said, and before Bill could take a step towards Kim, before Kim could finish her turn, the captain had drawn her weapon and fired. The zombie slumped forward. The group froze, and held their breath as they listened, but the only sound was of gore dripping from the creature's head onto the leaf-litter below. Devine holstered her weapon.

"It's clear," she said.

The house at the centre of the campsite was a charred shell. The northern part of the roof had collapsed. On the upper floors, the plastic window frames had buckled and the glass had fallen out. On the lower floors, the boards covering the windows had kept the fire contained. There were some undead corpses near the building that Bill remembered killing, but others which lay on top of the ash. Killed by Bran and his squad, he thought, he *hoped*. That same ash coated the line of cars parked outside the building, but otherwise the vehicles looked undamaged and untouched.

15

"They didn't try to drive away," Lorraine said, indicating the two vehicles with inflated tyres. "Though I think *he* was going to."

The body of a juror lay on the gravel close to the lead car. *Most* of it did. There was no sign of his right leg.

"Even after all this time, I still can't figure out if they are trying to eat people, infect them, or just kill them," Kim said. She shuddered. "That's the house, then?"

"We're unlikely to find any evidence inside," Devine said.

"We've got to look," Bill said.

"Is that the hut where you found the petrol?" Jones asked.

The door to the concrete blockhouse was held ajar by the broken shotgun Bill had used to pry open the lock.

"The petrol's still inside," Lorraine said.

"Lorraine and I will search the cars and gather everything we can salvage," Heather said. "We'll need ten minutes. Will that be enough?"

Out of all of Bishop's followers arrested at Willow Farm, and those detained at the Inn of Iquity, the only evidence they'd found pointed to the guilt of one man, Gareth Lenetti. The evidence was extensive. The trial had been quick. The verdict was unanimous, and only after the sentence was announced had the man changed his defence, claiming that, though he'd worked for Rachel, there was proof that he'd had nothing to do with the murders or abductions. That proof was in the campsite, locked in a safe within the main house. A house that was now an ash-coated ruin.

"Ten minutes will be more than enough," Bill said.

The charred front door creaked as Bill pushed at it with the machete. It moved an inch, and then stopped. Hoping that the door wasn't keeping the rest of the house from falling down, he slammed his shoulder into it. The wood split, cracking louder than a gunshot. A bird took off from the bare branches of a pine tree at the edge of the driveway. Bill watched it fly up and around before it settled back on its perch. It was a raven. They'd seen a lot of those recently.

There was a corpse inside the door, the hands held in front, the fingers missing.

"*Some* things don't change," Devine said.

"You've seen this before?" Kim asked.

"Bodies in burned-out ruins? Yes," Devine said. "I worked a war crimes detail in North Africa under General Carpenter. We had a U.N. mandate, gathering evidence that was never used. It's why the general resigned. He offered me a job when he was made V.P. You can't say no when your president asks you to serve, and even though Maxwell was in the White House, General Carpenter was the man I voted for. I told him to ask me again, but when I was stateside. Before I could get back, there was the outbreak. So it goes. Lenetti said the safe was in the office upstairs."

Bill had only seen a few of the downstairs rooms and the basement storage room in which he and Lorraine had been kept prisoner. With daylight coming through the fractured roof and broken windows, the stairwell was easy to find. The bannister had burned like a candle, leaving the metal support rods exposed.

"Do you think it's safe?" Bill asked.

"There's one way to find out," Kim said, and bounded up the stairs. "Seems fine," she said from the top. "Heather's right, we need to get this done quickly."

"I'll check downstairs," Devine said. "I'll shout if I see any collapsed ceilings."

Bill climbed the stairs. The wide landing at the top led to a dozen smoke-blackened doors. Soot obscured the metal plates affixed to each.

"I didn't ask," Kim said. "Do you think Lenetti is telling the truth?"

"About there being a ledger that proves his innocence?" Bill asked. "I don't think so. The middle-aged woman who acted as Bishop's assistant had a book. I think it contained details of the people that they'd tried and the crimes of which they'd been accused. That might prove the guilt of others, but I can't see how it would prove Lenetti was innocent."

"Maybe that's what he's hoping for," Kim said. "I mean, that audio recording we found in Rachel's room in the pub was pretty indisputable.

17

There was no mistaking Lenetti's voice, or how he was bragging to Paul about those people he killed."

"It's too neat, though, isn't it?" Bill said as he pushed open the first door. It had been a sitting room, judging by the skeletal shell of a sofa that took up most of the space. "I mean that the evidence was there and it only implicated Lenetti and Paul. I think Rachel kept it as a way of claiming innocence herself. Of course, what I really want to know is where the other recordings are. I bet that she didn't make only that one. As for Lenetti, without the bodies, without the murder weapon, without some form of corroboration, it's hard to prove his guilt." There was no safe in the living room. He stepped back out into the hall. "I suppose that's why Lenetti's defence centred on claiming that he was lying on that the audio recording. That he was only showing off to Paul. That's what worries me. In the old-world, would the recording have been enough? Would it even have been admissible? It's that recording which caused the jury to find him guilty. Then again, after the sentence, he did change his plea, admitting to some involvement when he told us about the ledger. Or perhaps he's stalling. Perhaps he thinks one of his old comrades will come to his—" He stopped when he saw Kim's face. She stood in the doorway of the next room along. "What?" he asked.

"You don't need to see," she said.

But he knew that he did.

Whatever *that* room had been used for a year before, he couldn't think of a word to describe what it had become. Cell wasn't enough. Bedroom was only correct in that the room contained an iron bedstead. On it was a corpse, burnt long beyond recognition. The wrists and ankles were still chained, each to a corner of the bedframe.

"We came for the ledger," Kim said. Bill didn't move. "Bill, please. Looking at it won't change anything."

"Her," Bill said. "Not it."

"Yes, probably *her,*" Kim said, "but this isn't the time to think about it."

"She was here," Bill said. "I didn't search the house. I just ran. I started the fire. I killed her."

"No," Kim said. "No, *you* didn't. *They* killed her." She took his arm and dragged him out into the hall, but the room was now indelibly imprinted on his memory.

There was a chance the woman was dead *before* he and Lorraine had escaped. Not a great chance. Bill hadn't considered there might have been other prisoners. He'd been focused on stopping Bishop, but the zealot hadn't truly been in control of the campsite, let alone his pseudo-religious movement. That had been Rachel, acting through her proxies like the man with the spider-web tattoo. The man who'd taken Lorraine from her cell the moment the opportunity presented itself. *That* was who and what those people were, and Bill had no excuse for not recognising it sooner. He didn't know what word described them best. Sadist, rapist, barbarian, thug, they all seemed too tame. Of course, he'd seen it before, Cannock and then Quigley, the kind who saw the entire world as an object, theirs to take.

"It's the office," Kim said, from the next doorway along. "There's a safe. Floor looks a little dodgy. Bill?"

"Is there any point?" he asked, because there was no longer any doubt in his mind about Lenetti's guilt.

"Yes," Kim said. "Yes, there is." She went inside, but emerged a few seconds later. "The safe's door has buckled. It must have been the fire. There's only ash inside."

"Then it's really over," Bill said. "Or it will be."

"Don't tell anyone about the body," Kim said.

"It's proof," Bill said. "Not the proof Lenetti wanted, but it's proof of his guilt. It should be entered into the record."

"Why? He's already been found guilty," Kim said.

"Then we should bury the woman," Bill said.

"You know that we can't," Kim said. "You said so yourself. There are too many to bury. Where would it stop? No, we can't bury her, and we won't be coming back here. Let's keep this to ourselves. There's no reason to tell Lorraine. You shouldn't feel any guilt, but I know you, I know you will. Even so, Lorraine doesn't need to know. She doesn't need to share that pain."

"Did you find anything?" Lorraine asked when they went outside.

"Only ash," Kim said. "The heat buckled the safe's door. The fire burned up all that was inside. There's no evidence here to prove Lenetti's story, and I doubt there was ever anything here that would prove he was innocent. What about you?"

"About twenty litres of petrol," Heather said, "two dozen cans of food, and a few road flares. There's nothing else of use to us. Grab a fuel can, and let's go back."

Back, Bill thought, but not back home. Anglesey wasn't that anymore. They would take the boat back to Menai Bridge, then he would return to Holyhead and report their findings to the judges. After which, Lenetti's sentence would be carried out.

Chapter 3 - Black Cap
Anglesey, 29th October, Day 230

The courtroom was silent except for the sound of Lenetti tapping his fingers on the leg of his chair. There were only a handful of people present. The proceedings weren't private, but unlike the trial, few had come to watch. Sholto sat next to Bill. Captain Devine had a chair at the back. Dr Knight sat in front of her, but other than two clerks and two submariners acting as warders, the rest of the room was empty. Despite it being just after dawn, Bill was surprised. He wondered whether the populace had grown disinterested, or perhaps it was because they knew the outcome.

Word had spread as to why they had made the trip to the campsite. When they'd returned to Menai Bridge yesterday evening, there had been a small crowd waiting to hear what they'd found. There had been a tension in the air, a frisson that could become the spark to reignite the mob, so Bill had told them that they'd found nothing. The crowd had dispersed, and word must have spread. No one wanted to be a witness to the sentence, but Bill imagined the entire island's ears pricking as they awaited confirmation it had been carried out.

Lenetti's tapping grew louder, echoing more in Bill's head than the improvised courtroom. It had been a community hall a year before. The judge's dais had once been a stage. He could imagine the plays that had been put on, the children's parties, the fetes, the fairs, and the public meetings. It had once been a focal point for the lives of those who'd lived in this corner of Wales. With only weeks left before the island would finally be abandoned, the building's swansong was to be a place of death.

Bill wanted to ask Lenetti about the woman on the bed, but there was no point. The man would lie or deny knowledge. If he implicated anyone else, then, as with the rest of his testimony, it would only be the dead. No, asking the man would only have the woman's death entered into the record. It would do no good, but might do Lorraine harm. Kim was adamant about that, and Bill would defer to her. He wouldn't ask Lenetti, nor would he include it in his journal. The woman's death would go unrecorded, though never forgotten, not by him. He just wished he knew her name.

The door opened. The judges came in. Everyone stood, though the two submariners acting as warders had to drag Lenetti to his feet. The judges took their chairs. The room went quiet.

"The court has decided," Judge Nicola Kennedy, a former solicitor from Berwick, said. "Mr Lenetti, you were charged with murder based on the evidence of an audio recording, based on fingerprints, and based on witness testimony. You pled not guilty. The jury found otherwise, and did so unanimously. You then amended your testimony, claiming complicity without responsibility, and offered a ledger as proof. You said this ledger was held in a safe on the mainland in the campsite the man known as John Bishop used. Captain Devine, a military police officer with an impeccable record and long experience in war crimes investigations, conducted a search of that property. No ledger was found. You have been given ample opportunity to produce evidence in your defence, and you have failed to do so. As such, the original verdict stands. The decision is unanimous. There are no more appeals. You were found guilty of murder. The sentence is death. The sentence shall be carried out immediately." The judge banged her gavel.

The sound woke Lenetti from his trance. Finally, he seemed to understand that the trial was over, and his life was forfeit. He began protesting, offering more evidence, more names. Bill tuned him out. The man had nothing to say that they needed to hear.

The two submariners took Lenetti by the arms. They weren't rough, but they were firm as they led him from the room. Bill waited until the judges had followed the condemned man through the door before he stood.

Sholto grabbed his arm. "You don't need to do this, Bill," he said.

"If not me, then who?" Bill replied, and followed the prisoner from the room.

"What's this? What's going on?" Lenetti asked. He had been taken to what had once been a storeroom. A chair had been installed in the middle of the room and had been bolted to the floor. The two Marines pushed Lenetti into it. They secured his wrists, his ankles, and then his neck and forehead into a brace. That had come from the hospital. It was the best they could find.

They had discussed punishments when Rachel had been charged with Paul's murder. There were only three: hard labour, exile, or death. For Lenetti, for the crime of murder, it had to be death. After what he'd seen in that campsite, Bill had no qualms about that. What they hadn't discussed until the jury was deliberating was how an execution should be carried out. Lethal injection or hanging required an expertise that no one had, and it had to be an execution, not torture. A bullet in the head was the only possible method. All that was left was to choose an executioner. Again, they had few options.

"Do you have any last words," the Reverend Ignatius Pasternack asked.

"I didn't do it. It wasn't me," Lenetti said. "I've got information. Useful information. I can tell you everyone we killed. That's something you need to know, right? All the people we— they killed."

Bill was reminded of how he had been in not too dissimilar a situation after he'd been abducted by Bishop. This was different, he told himself. Very different. He looked to his brother. Sholto held out a revolver. Bill took it. He looked to the judges. One by one they shook their heads.

"The sentence has been decided. It shall now be carried out," Judge Kennedy said.

"May the Lord have mercy on your soul," the Reverend said.

Bill raised the gun, pointed the barrel an inch from the back of the man's head. He fired.

Lenetti slumped forward, dead.

In Bill's head, the shot rang long after the echo faded. He waited for the priest to utter a prayer, but the reverend was as silent as the judges.

"You'll see that he's buried?" Bill asked.

"And hope that is the last grave we will dig on Anglesey," the Reverend said. "Your… your jacket."

Bill looked down. Blood had sprayed his coat. He unzipped it, and wrapped it around the gun. He handed it to his brother. "Throw that in the sea," he said. "I don't want an executioner's weapon to become a talisman."

He went outside, and found Kim waiting there, alone.

"I thought there would be more people," he said.

"There were a few," she said. "Not many. They left when they heard the gunshot."

"You're going to tell me that I should have left the task to someone else."

"No," she said. "No, you're right. It can't be the police, or one of the soldiers or sailors. It can't be the judges, or someone on the council. Who does that leave? You, me, Sholto, but few others. No, it had to be done, though I still think the jury should have been made to watch."

"The chamber was too small to get them all in," Bill said, though that wasn't the real reason.

"It's over now," Kim said. "I wish it had been someone else, but maybe, this time, it had to be you. Let's hope it'll be the last."

"It won't be," Bill said.

It wouldn't be the last time, and it wasn't the first. Quigley was the first, or perhaps the first were Cannock and Sanders who'd held Kim captive. There had been many since. Barrett and the others who'd taken Annette and Daisy. Rob. Kempton's follower in Belfast. Bishop and *his* followers in Wales. Rachel, and now Lenetti. The list was growing long.

Kim put her arm in his. "It's been a long year," she said, seemingly guessing what he was thinking. "The hard work is nearly done. The first radio antenna is finished," she added, changing the subject.

"Hmm?" he murmured, only half listening. The streets were emptier than he'd ever seen them. It wasn't just the lack of people, it was the sudden lack of activity. No one was attempting to open a new shop or clear out an old house. No one was wasting the day away on a street corner, or digging over a verge, back garden, or park in the optimistic hope of a spring planting. The heart had already gone out of Anglesey. It was only the people who had yet to leave.

"Yes, we'll have the second antenna finished in a couple of days," Kim said. "Then we've just got to transport one to Elysium, the other to *The John Cabot*. We could get another ten produced before we have to leave. I don't think we'll need that many, but we might as well make use of the electricity now, and we may come to need the spares in the future. You know Elysium is near where the first transatlantic radio broadcast was made?"

"Was it?" Bill murmured.

"Yes," Kim said. "Although they used stationary ships as relay stations."

"We've not got the ships," Bill said.

"No, but I think we could send an antenna over with the admiral," she said. "I'm not sure how reliable the signal will be, but it would be insurance against those satellites being lost. We need to stay in communication with one another. Rahinder Singh has an idea we can power them using a water mill. That's his next project, his and George's. I think… I… I don't know." Finally, she gave up. "Oh, Bill. I still don't know what our dream of happiness looks like, but each day it seems to get further and further away."

They walked in sombre silence back to the terrace. The ground floor had been knocked through, and was now given over to dozens of screens, each showing images of the Irish coast taken by the three satellites. The current search wasn't for survivors but for ships. On one wall, a large map of Ireland had been pinned. Every time a ship was found tied to a dock or adrift in an inlet, a pin was added to the map. There weren't many pins.

A dozen people were there, mostly in their late teens or early twenties. They were those who'd chosen a life of analysis over farming, fishing, or volunteering for one of the expeditions to the mainland. Bill wasn't sure if that was cowardice or good sense. It was always the same faces, though, and he supposed he should learn their names since he was sure most of them now slept in the terrace.

They looked up as he and Kim entered, then buried their faces in their screens. Only Annette came over, Daisy toddling a few steps behind.

"We've finished with Ireland," Annette said with the same brittle cheerfulness Kim had used on the walk from the courthouse. "We were talking about where we should move the satellites next."

"Leave that to the council," Bill said. "They were elected, it should be their choice. Not now, Daisy," he added. The toddler was tugging at Bill's trousers. Kim picked her up.

"I was thinking we could make a start on America," Annette said.

"We'll talk about it later," Kim said.

"You discuss it," Bill said. "I have some paperwork to catch up on." He forced a smile, and went through to the kitchen, and then upstairs to the first floor.

It wasn't really an office, but a room with a table large enough to keep the notes and plans for the evacuation of Anglesey and for where they should settle after that.

He sat down, and listlessly leafed through the notes, maps, and books. It was impossible to know where to begin in his search for the place humanity would call its final home. Each time he found a likely island, he discovered some critical element missing.

There was coal on the Svalbard archipelago that had been mined to power a coal power plant on the islands. They couldn't dig for coal in an Arctic winter, but could they wait in the dark until spring? Possibly. There was a report from the professor who ran that small community. Two ships, both small tugboats, had floated into the harbour. The undead crew had still been on board. That was the first instance of a zombie-infested ship since June, but would it be the last?

His finger tapped against the desk, and Lenetti's face appeared in his mind. Almost instantly, it was replaced with an image of the corpse he'd found chained to the bed in the campsite. He shook his head, picked up a pen and underlined a few words at random.

Even if they mined the coal, what then? According to Siobhan, Ireland had only one coal power station. It was on the Shannon Estuary, and she'd said its chimneys were the tallest freestanding structures on the island of Ireland. He and Kim would have motored past it on their way out of the estuary, and he didn't recall having seen them. The satellite images were inconclusive. There was a building there rather than a crater, but the shadows had seemed wrong. When the sailors went to collect *The New World*, they would investigate, but Bill had little hope they would find an undamaged power station. Even if it still worked, so what? They would have to burn through the scant supplies of oil to bring the coal from the Arctic, and what would they do when the oil was gone? Bring the coal south by sailboat? Besides, did they really want to make humanity's new home on the Shannon Estuary?

He realised his hand was tapping the pen against the desk in an increasingly rapid beat. He stood up, and walked to the window. A middle-aged trio were dragging suitcases along the street. From the way the cases bounced and rocked, they were empty.

Coal wasn't going to work. Water turbines might. North of Ireland, south of Svalbard were the Faroe Islands. A book on his desk claimed they got half their electricity from hydro. That was an Icelandic murder mystery about a crooked banker who'd fled to Faroe to avoid his creditors. Bill wasn't sure how much to believe, though he doubted the descriptions of savage winters weren't exaggerated. Even with the Gulf Stream, the temperatures barely rose above freezing. No, anywhere to the north of Malin Head was a non-starter. The kind of agriculture their community could sustain wouldn't work in sub-arctic conditions. Besides, Faroe had been home to around fifty thousand. Anglesey had been home to almost twice that, but they had already exhausted most of the stores of clothing, chemicals, and other supplies on the small Welsh island. Faroe was too remote, too small, too cold.

His hand was tapping against his thigh. To stop it, he picked up one book and then the next. The admiral had seen Cape Verde, and had reported it full of the undead. Tenerife and Gran Canary would be much the same, though the weather would be infinitely better than in Northern Europe. The Canary Islands had been home to a few million people, that might mean enough old-world supplies to keep people alive, but for how long? A year? Five years? There was always the expectation that, some day, the undead would stop and humanity would return to the mainland, but the nearest landfall to Gran Canary was the Sahara.

Water turbines might be the answer. Or *an* answer. Trying to build them would keep people occupied over the next few months, and that might be the best they could hope for. The problem might be electricity. It might be a lack of drinking water or sanitation. It might be hunger, the weather, or it might be the undead. The upshot would be nearly ten thousand people gathered around the ruins of Belfast. Hungry. Afraid. Cold. Alone. It would only take a spark to bring civil unrest and rioting. To keep order, a curfew would have to be implemented, and that would only make things worse. Rationing, curfews, martial law; it was everything that they had survived, everything that Quigley had relished, and everything that they had rejected. Lenetti probably wouldn't be the last to be executed, but he might be the last one who truly deserved that fate.

Bill sat down again, and cleared away the papers and books, throwing most onto the floor. He began with a fresh sheet. The admiral's expedition to America *wouldn't* be the solution. He knew that, as did anyone who paid attention to how long it was taking simply to move across the Irish Sea. That transatlantic expedition would keep people distracted, but not forever. No, they needed something better, a more concrete plan. He found a mostly blank sheet of paper, and picked up the pen.

"Soup's ready," Annette said, opening the door. "I'd call it lunch, but it's the same as breakfast, and it's going to be the same as dinner, so I'm just going to call it soup. It's got some paprika in it, though. Doesn't taste too bad. Well, it mostly tastes peppery."

"I'll come in a moment," Bill said.

"Okay, it's just… well, you've got a visitor."

"Mary?" he asked.

"No," Annette said. "It's the soldier, Bran."

Bill sighed, and laid down the pen. He'd not found a solution, but he had found a different way to approach the problem. Rather, a different way of utilising Dr Umbert's solution to the problem before they knew that they'd have to leave Anglesey. "I better see what he wants."

Bran, the taciturn Yorkshire soldier, was in the kitchen. A bowl was in front of him, but he was leaning back in the chair, his eyes closed. He jumped to his feet the moment that Bill opened the door. Bran's hand went to his bayonet before he'd properly opened his eyes.

"Sorry," he muttered. "Good habits out in the wasteland turn into bad ones back in civilisation."

Bill sat. "You're just back?"

"About an hour ago," Bran said.

Kim came through the other door, a tray in hand. "Some things don't change. A year ago I was serving coffee, now I'm serving soup." She gave a smile a little less brittle than earlier. "It's good soup," she added, setting another six bowls onto the tray. "What news from Wales?"

"None," Bran said. "I mean that in the best possible way. We all got out alive, thanks to those kids from Ireland."

"You mean Dean and Lena?" Kim asked. "They went with you?"

"They said they'd okayed it with you," Bran said.

"They were meant to be on the ship to Belfast so they could join up with Siobhan and Colm," Kim said. "That was what we discussed."

"I should have asked you," Bran said. "I'm sorry, but they make good recruits. They might make good soldiers. I can't say the same for the rest of the squad."

"Even so, I better go and talk with them," Bill said.

"No," Kim said. "Not now. Not today. For that matter, it shouldn't be you. I'll do it this afternoon." She turned back to Bran. "How bad was it?"

"It was a close fight, but we all made it back alive," Bran said. "I'm going to fail three of those recruits. They can fight, but they haven't got the temperament for the grinding horror of not knowing when or where the next attack will come."

"There are plenty of other jobs that need doing," Kim said.

"What about Bishop's people?" Bill asked.

"We found no trace," Bran said. "We killed eleven zombies in the campsite, but it was clear from the supplies left in those cars by the entrance that there were no living people there. Any who fled did so hastily while the house was on fire. Did you collect those supplies?"

"We did," Kim said.

"There wasn't much, was there?" Bran said. "I took a look around a few of the caravans, but the undead kept drifting in, and we weren't there to fight them. Instead, we cut due south, heading to the first safe house. It was empty. No one had been there in a month. From there we headed northeast in a line that took us up the coast. I can show you on the map if you like."

"Maybe later," Kim said. "There was no indication any people escaped?"

"No. We checked two more safe houses, a dozen farms, and every likely looking cottage we saw," Bran said. "We kept an eye on the mud for footprints and bicycle tracks, on doors for fresh splinters, and fireplaces for newly burned ash. We covered about sixty-five miles and we only found the undead. It's possible that someone got away. If they'd had a go-bag close to hand, they wouldn't have needed to stop to search for supplies. My official report is that none of Bishop's people made it out."

"Did you go into the house at the centre of the campsite?" Bill asked.

"No," Bran said. "There didn't seem any point, and that was too insecure a location for us to linger. Why?"

"It doesn't matter," Kim said. "Is that why you came here, to report on what you found in Wales?"

"Partly," Bran said, "and partly to say that it's a little unclear exactly who I'm meant to report to. I went to Mrs O'Leary, and Mr Tull sent me here. Confused command is never a good thing. Mostly, though, I wanted to talk to you about what you wrote."

"Wrote?" Bill asked.

"I glanced at your journal in the summer," Bran said. "Didn't read it properly. I've heard a lot of stories about people's journeys through the wasteland. On the boat ride back this morning, I looked at what you published before the election. A few names jumped out. George said I should come and tell you."

"Which names?" Bill asked.

"Before you arrived on Anglesey, I went up to Northumberland," Bran said. "We'd heard rumours that someone was up there. I found out it was

Quigley. I was assessing whether it would be possible to launch a frontal assault. I recognised a few of the people with him. They weren't on-the-books infantry. I'd seen them years ago."

"Where?" Annette asked.

"Somalia," Bran said.

"Somalia? There weren't any British soldiers there," Bill said.

"They call it off-the-books for a reason," Bran said. "When I was in Northumberland, counting their rifles, a woman was brought outside. Her hands and ankles were chained. I watched. I waited. I saw where she was being taken. It was a converted barn to the north of the main building."

"That was the old brewery," Bill said. "Though it was used as a guest room when they had people over for a hunt."

"At night, I went in," Bran said. "The woman wasn't alone. There were others. I rescued them. Quigley's people followed us. They found us. They caught us. I was being tortured when an unexpected rescue appeared. A deaf soldier and a teenage boy. I asked the soldier and the kid to come back with us, but they said they had to go to London. The kid was looking for his mother, you see. He'd left a note at their old family home saying that's where they'd gone. The soldier's name was Tuck, the boy's was Jay."

"Jay? That's Nilda's son!" Annette said.

"Rob didn't kill him," Kim said. She met Bill's eyes.

"Rob killed Simon, Will, and Lilith," Bill said.

"Except if we'd known the truth," Kim said, "Rob wouldn't have been with us in Ireland, would he?"

"Except we don't know the truth," Bill said. "Not all of it. How did Rob get Jay's sword?" He looked to Bran.

The soldier shrugged. "We didn't talk for long," he said. "Quigley's people were still on our trail. I don't know the details."

"When was this?" Kim asked.

"The end of May," Bran said.

"Long before I found Nilda on that rock in the North Sea," Kim said. "I could have told her that her son was alive."

Bran shrugged. "It wouldn't have changed what Nilda did. She'd have still gone looking for him."

"Jay told you that he was going to London?" Annette asked.

"It was the one place in the world that he thought his mother might go to look for him," Bran said.

"Ah. That's… that's interesting," Annette said. "Here, I'll take that, the soup's getting cold." She picked up the laden tray from the counter and took it back into the knocked-through room with the screens.

"Thank you for telling us," Bill said. "It's an interesting detail."

"That's not what I came to tell you," Bran said. "Not all of it. The mother, Nilda, left here with Chester Carson."

"Yes, I think so," Bill said.

"You don't read what you write, do you?" Bran said.

"What do you mean?" he asked.

"You've forgotten, but George didn't. You know the name, and you even wrote it in your journal. You found a suicide note left by a police officer who described Chester as a petty thief on his way to graduating as a full-time fence. But you met Chester Carson yourself, more or less."

"A full-time fence?" Bill murmured. "I do remember that letter, though I didn't connect the name with the man. I'm pretty sure I never met him, though I did speak to him on the sat-phone when he was heading to Hull. We didn't have much time to talk."

"No, I meant you met him in London," Bran said. "After Chester arrived in Anglesey, George had him join me setting up safe houses. This was before I met Tuck and Jay on my way back from Northumberland. That's when Chester told me how you and he first met. Not that he knew who you were, of course, or even that you were still alive."

"What did he say?" Kim asked.

So Bran told them.

Part 2
The Soldier and The Thief

Bran and Chester

Wales
2nd - 3rd May
&
29th October

Chapter 4 - The Brigadier
Pontcysyllte Aqueduct, 2nd May, Day 52

"We'll stop for five minutes," Bran said, when they were halfway up the slope. He eased his pack off his shoulders, stretched, and sat on a moss-covered boulder. There was no sign of the undead that had forced them from the road a mile and two hills away.

"I thought I was pretty fit before," Chester Carson muttered, easing himself to the ground. "Goes to show. Still, nice day for it. It really feels like summer is on its way. Yeah, it's a nice day to be alive. Nice place, too, or it would be, if it wasn't for the zombies."

Bran took out the map. "We're ten miles from where we want to be," he said.

"Is that a problem?" Chester asked.

"Time will tell," Bran said.

A boat had brought them from Anglesey along the north Welsh coast to the mouth of the River Dee, near the border with England. They'd hoped to find supplies in the Deeside Industrial Park. Instead, they'd discovered craters and ruins. The damage was similar to that on Anglesey, probably caused by cluster bombs. Who had dropped them and why no longer mattered. Those were details consigned to a history that would never be written. Leaving the sailors to search the ruins, Bran had ventured inland. He'd said he'd wanted to visit Wrexham, and set up a few more safe houses along the way. That was a mission that had begun after he'd met George Tull and Mary O'Leary. Their meeting on a lonely road a few weeks after the outbreak had ended on Anglesey with the discovery that their small band weren't the only survivors.

Their final destination for this trip, though, was Wrexham. A private with whom Bran had once served had worked in the petroleum depot in the city. At the time, Bran hadn't asked for any more details than that, but he now wished he had. It was ten weeks since the first outbreak in New

York, barely seven since the nuclear war that had ended civilisation, and they were already short of fuel.

"How long will the boat stay at Deeside?" Chester asked.

"We said four days," Bran said. "They'll wait, but I want at least a day in Wrexham. I don't know precisely where that petroleum depot is."

"It should be easy to spot, shouldn't it?" Chester said. "We just look for the steel towers and chimneys."

"You're thinking of a refinery," Bran said. "Worst case, we miss the boat and walk back to Anglesey."

"If this morning was anything to go by, you mean we'll be running," Chester said. "Still, all this green makes a change from concrete, though I'm not sure I prefer it. Are you a country lad?"

"I'm a soldier," Bran said and went back to his map.

Bringing Chester on this trip had been George Tull's idea. The old man had said that Chester was a good fit for the safe house network. After two days on a boat and half a day of hiking through the Welsh countryside, Bran wasn't sure. Chester talked a lot, but without ever saying anything important. All Bran had really learned about him was that he'd escaped from London three weeks before. Chester *had* managed to keep up with the soldier's gruelling pace though, despite being very definitely a civilian. Then again, there weren't many soldiers on Anglesey. There weren't many people at all.

Most had arrived by boat, part of the large flotilla of refugees that had set off from the Americas, Africa, coastal Europe, and the British Isles. None had a destination in mind, but the individual ships had coalesced into a ramshackle fleet that had been attacked by rogue and traitorous elements of the Royal Navy. That was how Bran thought of those who'd followed the utterly illegal orders. It was how he thought of the renegade soldiers who'd followed those same orders on land, murdering civilians in the muster points and along the evacuation route.

"Did you hear what that woman on the boat said?" Chester asked, cutting into Bran's thoughts.

"Which woman?" Bran asked.

"Heather Jones. About the trains evacuating people from Anglesey, about how the carriages were gassed."

"What about it?" Bran asked.

"She said it was soldiers who did it," Chester said.

"So?" Bran asked.

"Well, back in London, I saw… I don't know how to describe it. A missile strike, maybe. It was like a civil war."

"That wasn't a question," Bran said, but he thought he knew what the question would be.

"I didn't know Britain had chemical weapons," Chester said, "but I wondered whether they might work on the undead."

That wasn't the question Bran had expected. It wasn't the question that people usually asked. Usually, they asked why it had all happened.

"No idea," Bran said, and decided he should unstiffen a little. He was going to be stuck with Chester for the next few days, and the man wanted to talk. "Just before the evacuation, I was working road clearance. We had two hundred convicts, all curfew breakers, to do the hard graft. Under my command were twenty recruits who'd barely begun their phase-one training and a captain who was three weeks out of officer selection. They were in uniform, but they weren't soldiers. We were clearing a road of stalled traffic. We came to a lorry. There were zombies in the back. The captain emptied an entire magazine into one of them. Thirty bullets into its chest from less than ten feet away. Didn't do a damn thing. The zombie kept coming. Stopping power's a myth, you know that, right? People can be shot, but with so much adrenaline coursing through them, not know they're bleeding out. An entire magazine? That's different. You *would* notice that. The zombie didn't. If the catastrophic destruction of their vital organs doesn't stop them, why should a chemical weapon be any different?"

"Well, that's a cheery thought," Chester said. "Seen the same myself, of course. Bullets only work if you destroy the brain. It makes you wonder. Makes you think." Silence settled for half a second. "So what happened to them?"

"To who?" Bran asked.

"The rest of the soldiers on that road."

"They died," Bran said. Silence returned, and this time it settled. No, there weren't many people on Anglesey, and fewer who would volunteer to search for other survivors. Most of the new arrivals came by boat, sailing up from Africa or down from northern Europe. Most weren't looking for salvation, but simply a bay with a fresh water stream, and instead they found a fishing boat that directed them to the Welsh island.

Bran didn't spend much time on Anglesey. On each return trip, he found more boats in the harbour, but not more people on land. The island was a refuge, but it wasn't a community, not yet. George and Mary were good people, but Anglesey needed a leader. It needed—

"So where are we?" Chester asked, again cutting into Bran's thoughts.

"That river down there, that's the Dee," Bran said.

"The same one we left the boats on?" Chester asked.

"The same, but it doesn't follow a straight path through the hills. Chirk Castle's to the southeast. A couple of miles east of here is the Pontcysyllte Aqueduct. Have you heard of it?"

"Should I?"

"You'd probably recognise it if you saw it. It's about forty metres above the ground. Canal boats used to travel along it. They had it in that 'Unbelievably British' show a couple of years ago. You didn't see it?"

"That's not really my kind of viewing," Chester said. "So you get to watch a lot of telly in the Army?"

Bran gritted his teeth. "I like to see the places I'm risking my life for," he said, "but there was never enough time to visit them all. Eight miles northeast of the aqueduct is Wrexham. The Deeside Industrial Park, and our boat, is about twelve miles due north of that."

"Then we've come completely the wrong way," Chester said.

"Not if we're going to the aqueduct first," Bran said. "There were some people there the last time I came through this area. I want to see if they'll come west."

"This was before you got to Anglesey?"

"After," Bran said. "On my first expedition away from the island. We think, we hope, that the Welsh mountains create a natural barrier against the undead, but that barrier works on people, too. We wanted a line of safe houses running near the border with England, a way of telling people that, if they got this far, they should keep going and not go north. You heard about Scotland?"

"Yeah, it's pretty grim," Chester said. "So who are these people at the aqueduct?"

"There were twenty of them," Bran said. "The aqueduct was partially destroyed, but they'd rigged up some platforms on the supporting columns. Can't say they were very sturdy, but they were out of a zombie's reach. It's not tenable in the long term so I want to persuade them to come to Anglesey."

And not just because they needed people. Anglesey needed a leader, and there was one at the aqueduct, Brigadier Hemsworth. Bran had served with him back when he was a private and the general was only a major. It was that action that had got Bran his stripes. The brigadier was a good man, but he was holding onto too much guilt. There was no time for guilt now. Anglesey needed a leader, and the brigadier fit the bill.

"Wales is different up close," Chester said. "Of course, I've been here before. For work," he added, "but that was usually Cardiff or one of the ports. Sometimes an industrial estate. An airfield, once. You don't notice the hills so much when you're behind the wheel. Less when you're a passenger riding in the back of a windowless van."

Bran was unsure what that last comment meant. The Londoner was a tall man, broad-shouldered, and recently scarred though most people were. His build suggested something in construction, but he spoke as if he'd worked in advertising. His head was shaved, but again that was common on Anglesey among men and women alike. It was easier to keep a bald pate clean than scrub lank hair with cold water, or waste time and wood boiling up hot. There was talk about getting the nuclear power plant turned back on, but there was a lot of talk; about where to go when the undead died; about what had happened to the rest of the world; about when an American aircraft carrier might steam into Holyhead's battered port.

Bran turned his attention back to the map. The border-country with its steep hills, deep valleys, and fast flowing streams was full of places where survivors might have taken refuge. Despite the nuclear bombs, and the conventional ordnance dropped on industrial locations; despite the undead, the murderous evacuation, the hunger, the dehydration, and the disease that must have followed; despite it all, there had to be millions of people left in Britain, clinging on, hoping for rescue. There *had* to, but to find them, he needed help, and they needed proper organisation. That meant the brigadier. That meant—

"I thought of taking the shilling," Chester said, his voice once more a tree trunk across the path of Bran's thoughts. "Years ago, I mean. When I was… well, when I should have been in school. I thought of joining up, but I didn't like the idea of taking orders."

"We all have to take orders from someone," Bran said, folding the map. "It's the nature of existence."

"Yeah, I learned that eventually, but a little too late for it to do me any good. After I got a record, you lads didn't want me."

Ah, he was an ex-con, Bran thought. One who still wore his past as an identity even after his sentence was spent. "When did you see the error of your ways?"

"It's been coming for a while," Chester said, "but what clinched it was when a zombie bit me and I thought I was going to die. I looked at my life and I saw how little it amounted to."

"You weren't an ex-con?" Bran asked. "You're a criminal who turned honest only after there were no laws or police left to stop you from taking all you wanted from anywhere you chose?"

"I wouldn't put it like that," Chester said. "I thought Mr Tull told you this."

"He told me you were reliable," Bran said, "but you're a crook."

"A *reformed* crook," Chester said.

"To reform, you have to atone for your crimes. How can you do that when your victims are dead?"

"I didn't kill them," Chester said. "I was a thief, not a murderer."

"I meant the outbreak," Bran said. "You can't make amends now." He picked up his bag, and walked east.

"Hang on," Chester said. He slung his pack and followed. "Look, I didn't mean it like that."

"Didn't mean what like what?"

"I meant, I thought George had told you," Chester said. "I thought you knew. Now you do, if we're going to have a problem, I'd rather it was over and done with here and now. I may not know much about the countryside, but I fought my way through London, and then out of it. I know what we're facing, and I don't want to worry about getting a knife in the back as well as teeth in the neck."

"A knife in the back? You think I'd kill you? You think I'd take revenge on you for all those innocent lives you ruined? Then you don't know anything about people."

"And you don't know me," Chester said. "Yeah, I robbed and I stole, and I took from those who couldn't afford to lose it. I admit it, but that was the old me in the old world."

"How many?" Bran asked.

"How many what?"

"How many lives did you ruin? How many did you rob?"

"I don't know," Chester said.

"When did you start?"

"When I was a kid," Chester said.

"Twenty years ago?"

"A bit more, but yeah."

"You're saying you've changed?" Bran said. "Overnight, you've abandoned the habits of a lifetime?"

"If anything could bring that on, wouldn't it be the undead?" Chester asked. "Look, for the last few years, it's not like I had a choice. There wasn't anything else I could do."

"Sweep streets? Haul bricks? Can you drive? There're plenty of honest ways to make a living."

"Yeah, yeah, all right. Maybe you're right. Maybe I didn't look hard enough. Maybe I enjoyed it, or some of it, and just enough to forget the parts that I didn't, but that changed when I got bit a few weeks ago. I thought I was going to die. I really did. I didn't want to turn into one of *them*, so I tried to shoot myself. The bullet was a dud. That's when it changed. That's when *I* changed. It was in a Victorian terrace in Sydenham. A bit further down the street was a grand house. It was a massive place, the kind I dreamed of owning. I saw a flashing light. There was a guy stuck inside. We sent messages to one another with bits of paper stuck to the window. His leg was broken, and he couldn't get out on his own so I said I'd help. There were too many zombies outside. I tried leading them away, but I ended up getting trapped. I was stuck for days. When I finally escaped, the guy had gone."

"So?"

"So I went back," Chester said. "I went back for him."

"You helped someone in need? That's what any normal person would do."

"Well, I guess that's my point," Chester said.

"You've a lot to learn about what real life is like," Bran said.

"Like what?"

"If you live, you'll find out," Bran said. "Anglesey's that way, I'm going to the aqueduct. Keep up or go back."

After twenty yards, he heard the crook following him.

The aqueduct had been partially destroyed. Two of the supporting columns had collapsed. Below a banner that hung limp from the aqueduct were a crashed helicopter and a cluster of mobile homes.

"That sign used to read *Safety Here*," Bran said. Now it read *Zombies*. He took out his binoculars. "Zombies is right," he said. "I can see two, no, three near the grey and blue campervan."

"That's where they lived?" Chester asked, taking the binoculars.

"It's where they cooked," Bran said, "but there's no smoke from a cooking fire, which means they're not boiling water. They slept halfway up the aqueduct. Do you see the ropes? The gantries?"

"I… ah, yeah. That doesn't seem sensible. If the zombies came, how would they escape?"

"Climb up to the aqueduct," Bran said. "The ropes are attached to the metal pins that the maintenance crew used to inspect the brickwork. When the undead came, they would have climbed up and followed the aqueduct away."

"And they changed the sign before they left?" Chester asked.

"Looks that way," Bran said. He took the binoculars back. "The general would have known to come to Anglesey, so it must have happened recently. Unless… unless he got word of someone else, somewhere else. A better place to go, maybe? Come on."

"We're going down there?" Chester asked.

"They'd have left a lot of useful gear behind," Bran said. "This is a good spot, with a clear line of sight for miles. We can make sure it's safe for anyone else who comes along."

Halfway down the hill, Bran drew his bayonet and fixed it to the barrel of his rifle. Chester dragged the machete free from his belt with an audible rasp. Bran didn't think it was loud enough for the zombies to hear, but the creatures did notice them approach.

"Go left," Bran said, as he moved to the right, one eye on the zombies, the other on his footing. The ground was uneven, and a twisted ankle would be a death sentence. Two of the creatures were heading towards him, the third towards Chester. He focused on the foe in front as the slope levelled out.

The undead wore matching green windbreakers. They weren't military, but Bran couldn't help think of them as uniforms. A sinking dread set in as he realised who they might once have been. As the zombies drew nearer, their features became clearer. Both had dark stains around their mouths and other stains on their clothing, but they hadn't been undead for long. Bran didn't recognise them, but he wasn't sure even their mothers would, not now.

Twenty yards from the creatures, he stopped. He confirmed there were no other threats before returning his attention to the two shambling figures lurching towards him. Ten yards. Eight. Five. Three. He lunged, spearing the rifle-bayonet forward. He'd done it in training. He'd done it in Afghanistan. He'd done it in Somalia in an action that had gone unreported and unremarked. The blade met the target, sinking deep into the creature's eye. A twist, a wrench, a backward step, and the blade came free as the zombie fell. He marked his second target and lunged again. Again the creature fell. He looked to his left. Chester, gore-covered machete in hand, was already walking towards him. Bran wiped the bayonet clean on the fallen zombie's jacket, and continued towards the campsite.

A door banged open and closed with the wind. There were dozens of corpses close to the caravans, but none moved. The ladders leading up to the gantries had been kicked to the ground. The bulk of those wood and plastic platforms blocked Bran's view of the next twenty feet, but he could make out the ropes leading up and around the side of the aqueduct.

"I thought fixed bayonets was a thing from the movies," Chester said. "You know, those ones about the trenches."

"There might be more zombies," Bran said. "Check under the—" He heard it, and looked up just before the zombie fell from gantry, fifteen feet above, right on top of him. Bran was knocked to the ground, and his head hit it the hardest. Winded, stunned, it was all he could to get his forearm up under the creature's throat. He pushed up and back as the thrashing zombie snapped its teeth inches from his face. And then the weight was gone as Chester grabbed the creature, and hurled it off. The zombie kept flailing as it flew five feet through the air, landing on its back. It rolled to its knees in time for Chester's boot to slam into its head. The zombie fell to the ground. Chester raised his foot again, and stamped down, crushing the zombie's skull.

Bran rolled to his knees, and grabbed his rifle, slipping the safety off as he aimed upward. Chester drew a revolver from his pocket. All was still.

"Watch the gantries," Bran said, as he scanned the river, and then the grassland over which they'd walked. They seemed alone. He rubbed his hand on the back of his head. It hurt, but there was no blood.

"Thank you," he said.

Chester shrugged. "It's what any person would do, isn't it? Help someone in need."

Bran nodded, conceding the point. "Nice revolver. Is it loaded?"

"Of course," Chester said.

"You carry a loaded revolver in your coat pocket?" Bran asked. "Remind me to give you a lesson on gun safety when we get back to Anglesey."

"I'd rather risk shooting myself than be torn apart by the undead," Chester said.

There was a thump, a bang, a clatter. It didn't come from above, but from one of the caravans.

"Sounds like it's trapped," Chester said.

"When I say, open the door," Bran said, detaching the bayonet. He slung the rifle. Unsuppressed shots were dangerous, and bullets were scarce, to be kept for the times when danger was greatest. Bran knew what was inside the caravan, and knew how dangerous the undead could be, but from the sounds, there was only one zombie trapped inside.

"Now!" Bran said.

Chester pulled the door open. The zombie, no longer beating against immovable metal, tumbled down onto the grass. Bran stabbed the bayonet through its temple. As the blade bit into bone, a flash of memory came back to him. He dragged the blade free, and turned the corpse over. He didn't recognise the face, not really, not twisted twice in death, but he recognised the wood and jade cross around her neck.

"Her name was Bernie," he said. "Or maybe it was Bernice."

"She was one of the brigadier's people?" Chester asked.

Bran didn't answer. He glanced into the caravan. There wasn't much inside beyond a few sheets and pillows still in their plastic wrappers. He walked over to the next campervan, took one look inside, and walked out again. "Damn."

"What?" Chester walked up the steps. "Is that the brigadier?" he asked, looking inside.

"It is," Bran said.

"He's been shot," Chester said.

"Obviously."

Chester went inside. "Here, come and look at the wound," he called. "It wasn't self-inflicted. Someone shot him." He knelt down, and rolled up the brigadier's sleeves and then his trouser legs.

"What are you doing?" Bran asked.

"Checking for a bite mark," Chester said. "I don't think I'll find one."

"Why?"

"It's my professional opinion," Chester said. "As someone familiar with crime scenes," he added.

"You said were a crook, not a detective."

"Right, and though I had a few brushes with the law, they never pinned anything on me. Not anything serious, anyway. You know why? Because I know what evidence usually gets left behind. I know crime scenes, and that's what this is. It's a robbery and a murder. There're no bite marks, and that removes the only innocent reason the man was shot. The shelves are empty. The drawers are open. This group was robbed, and this man was killed. How did the others get infected? What did you know about these people?"

Bran took a closer look around the caravan. "I came through here about two weeks ago," Bran said. "The brigadier had been at one of those muster points. When he realised what the vaccine was doing, he stopped people taking it. He led them away, tried to organise them. The undead came. He got some out, and got them as far as here. There were about twenty of them, but I'm not sure of the precise numbers. I didn't stay long, I had a rendezvous to keep."

"What about their routine?" Chester asked, peering under the table.

"They didn't venture far from the vehicles by day, though they were digging up some of the pasture to the west where they planned to put in a crop. At night, they'd climb up onto the gantries above."

"That zombie who fell from the gantry," Chester said, "that must have been someone who was infected but didn't turn immediately. I'd say that the brigadier was shot by someone he knew, someone sitting on the other side of this table. It might have been one of his own people, but then, why did the killer leave? And, more importantly, how did the others get infected? No, I think it was an outsider, but someone the general knew before the outbreak."

"It had to be a soldier, then," Bran said, "because the Army was the brigadier's entire life." He went outside and counted the corpses. He'd assumed they were the undead killed by the brigadier. He moved from corpse to corpse until he was as sure as he could be.

"I think they're all here," he said to Chester. "None of them were shot. They were all stabbed or bludgeoned. Only two were zombies. I don't think any of the rest were infected before they were killed."

"I can't see any weapons," Chester said. "Did the general have any guns?"

"They had a few rifles and sidearms," Bran said, "but no ammunition except for the rounds I gave them. It was knives and spears, swords and axes, and whatever else they could make or find." He walked back to the caravan, and looked briefly inside. "The brigadier's belt is missing. It was brown leather from World War Two, a family heirloom with a gun to match, though that came from the regimental museum."

"There's a few tools lying around," Chester said. "Shovels and hammers that might have been used in a fight, but no swords. No knives. No spears. Whoever came here can't have had much gear, and they took everything away with them."

"I'd say it was about a week ago," Bran said. "Maybe a bit less. Four to seven days."

"I'd say the same," Chester said.

"That's long enough for a survivor of this massacre to reach Anglesey," Bran said. "None of them did, so none of them escaped. There's nothing here, nothing that will help us or anyone else." He looked up at the sign suspended under the bridge. "What kind of sick person does that?"

"Change the sign, you mean?"

"After killing all of these people, yes," Bran said.

"If I'm honest with you," Chester said, "I can think of a few people I knew in my old life who'd do something like that. One person, at least."

Bran sighed. So could he.

Three hills, two miles, and an hour later, they came to a fortified farm. Corrugated metal reinforced the thin fence. Rusting girders had been rammed into a ditch, held in place by poorly mixed concrete that spilled into the ruts on the ill-maintained track. Inside the ramshackle wall were a farmhouse, a long barn, two smaller outbuildings, and a water tower. It was the water tower they'd first noticed and used as a guide-marker to find their way to within a quarter-mile of the property.

"No," Bran said as he gave the farm a closer inspection with the binoculars. "Someone *tried* to fortify it, but was interrupted with the job only two-thirds done. The wall doesn't extend to the western-side. There's a zombie by the tractor that's half out of the barn. Here." He passed the binoculars to Chester.

"Do you think someone tried to drive the tractor outside?" Chester asked. "More importantly, do you think whoever killed the brigadier made it this far?"

"Maybe, but that zombie's proof they're not there now. We're not going to make Wrexham before dark, so we'll stay here tonight and set off before dawn." He slung his rifle and unbuttoned his holster. "The rules of engagement have changed, but our weapons haven't. A rifle shot might save a life, but it'll only bring more of the undead. That goes for a revolver, too." He drew his sidearm and then a long metal tube.

"That's a silencer," Chester said.

"It's a suppressor," Bran said. "You've seen one before?"

"If you mean did I ever use one in my old life, no. It's never a good idea to bring a weapon on a burglary because you might end up using it."

"Huh." Bran wondered if that was meant to be a joke. If so, it was in poor taste. He let it go. "Mr Tull's promised to make me a suppressor for the rifle. Not just for mine. It's hard to run a lathe without electricity. Ordinarily, I'd not want to waste the ammunition for the pistol, but I'm tired. Stay behind me, and on my left hand side. Keep an eye on the rear."

They walked across the overgrown meadow, scattering pollen from the white and yellow flowers interspersed among the vivid green fronds.

When they reached the track outside the farm, the sheet metal blocked everything except a narrow few feet of the yard.

Bran whistled softly, and raised the pistol. "Watch our rear."

They heard the creature drag itself across the mud and gravel. The moment it staggered into view, Bran fired. It fell. After five minutes, the silence remained absolute and no more creatures had appeared.

The barn was empty, as was the house. Empty of people and the undead, but they found a shotgun in the mud by a second, smaller gate just beyond the water tower. Bran picked it up, and broke it open. The shells inside had been spent.

Inside the farmhouse, in the kitchen, they found food on the shelves.

"Wholegrain pasta, basmati rice," Chester said. "Chocolate blancmange. I was never a fan of blancmange, but it's a while since I had chocolate." He opened the cupboard below. "This is more like it. We've got tins of rice pudding, custard, tapioca. It's all low sugar, but still, it'll be a welcome change."

"The people who killed the brigadier didn't make it this far, then," Bran said. "Nor do I think whoever took refuge here will come back. No, this will make for a good safe house. Look for a shovel."

"A shovel? Why?" Chester asked.

"To bury that zombie," Bran said. "We want to make this place look hospitable." He went to find some paint.

It took longer to climb the ladder than to scrawl the words *Safe House* on the water tower. He'd found three flags in the barn, all Welsh dragons, and hung them from the railing running along the narrow platform. With the job done, Bran sat on the platform, his legs hanging over the fifty-foot drop, and watched the countryside. He'd always liked heights. Not planes, not helicopters; those made him feel apart from the world. A tall platform with a view of a wider horizon usually helped put life into a clearer perspective.

He'd half-expected to find the brigadier and his people either dead or gone because the aqueduct was a thoroughly insecure location. That was why he'd suggested the mission to Deeside and Wrexham. He *did* want to set up some more safe houses, and there *was* a petroleum facility in Wrexham, but the government had probably requisitioned the fuel during the period between the outbreak and the evacuation. He'd used that as an excuse to get a ship to come close so he could collect the brigadier and his people. No, he'd half-expected them to be gone, and dreaded they'd be dead, but not murdered.

Below, Chester had finished digging a grave. Bran scanned the horizon. On a hill to the southeast, figures shambled across the grassland, but they weren't heading towards the farm. Not yet. He climbed down.

"I've eaten worse," Chester said.

"Thanks," Bran said.

"I meant it as a compliment," Chester said. "There was a week when we were down to ketchup packets, and there've been days when I look back on that with fondness."

"Hmm."

"Are you sure we can't open one of those tins of custard?"

"Better to leave it for someone whose need is greater," Bran said.

There was silence as Chester gave the next mouthful a thorough chewing. "I don't think they were locals," he said when enough of his mouth was free that there was space for words to come out.

"The killers?"

"I meant the people who fortified this farm," Chester said. He waved his fork at the bags by the window. They had been packed when he and the soldier had arrived, though the contents now lay strewn about the coffee table and floor. "I recognise some of the labels," Chester continued, "but the real clue is in how some of the gear still has the labels attached. It's high-end stuff. Must have left here in a hurry if they didn't have time to take it with them."

"Hmm."

"You're from Yorkshire, aren't you?" Chester asked.

Bran nodded.

"Is that why you don't talk much? Or were you thinking about the brigadier? People came. They stole the supplies. That's what life has become. We're fighting over the scraps of the old world. Fighting to survive just another day. It's not worth dwelling on."

"The eternal war," Bran said. "That's what it's called, but if that's all we do, we'll survive today but die tomorrow."

"All right, so what was the general like?" Chester asked.

Bran frowned. There was no simple answer to that question, and he didn't know Chester well enough to give him a complex one. "I was meant to be on holiday," he said instead.

"When you first met the general?"

"No, you're right," Bran said, "there's no point dwelling on those deaths. I was meant to be on holiday when the outbreak happened. I was going to Australia. Scuba diving off the Great Barrier Reef. Evening flights were cheaper than morning ones, that's why I was still in England when the first outbreak hit the news."

"Do you wish you'd gone?" Chester asked.

"To Australia?" Bran considered the question, and decided on an honest answer. "Sometimes. Some days. Days like today."

"A few hundred quid saved your life, then," Chester said.

"Did it?"

"Yeah, there was a professor I met in London who said that, statistically, humanity was extinct, therefore those of us who were alive owed our existence to every misstep, mistake, and bad decision we'd ever made. That's not quite how he put it, and thinking about it, I'm not quite sure that's what he meant."

"There were many survivors in London?"

"Not now," Chester said. "They're dead. They're bound to be. It's… no, that's not something *I* want to dwell on."

"Hmm. Maybe we'll run the safe houses to London one day," Bran said.

"I wouldn't bother," Chester said. "It's a dark place, absent of hope, of life. I'm never going back."

"Never say never," Bran said.

Chapter 5 - The Captain
Rhosllannerchrugog, 3ʳᵈ May, Day 53

"Not a bad piece of paintwork, even if I say so myself," Chester said, as Bran hung the sheet over the gate. On the sheet were the words *Safe House*. "I just hope those words are true."

"The farm was safe enough for us to spend a night," Bran said. "That's as much as we can promise."

"I was thinking more about the map inside," Chester said. They'd sealed the remaining food in containers, and repacked the bags the previous occupants had left behind. On the kitchen counter, they'd left a hand-drawn map and a short note directing anyone who reached this far to come to Anglesey. "And I was thinking about the people who killed those friends of yours. If they find the map, they'll come to Anglesey."

"They might," Bran said. "This isn't the first time I've come across a killer who survived the chaos of that first month. The day that I met Mary O'Leary and George Tull, I'd fallen into company with a group of mostly normal people and one psychopath. I should have recognised his true nature sooner, and I might have done if it wasn't for the outbreak having changed us all. He would have killed George, Mary, and everyone else, not for their supplies, not for pleasure, but just because. But we can't assume that everyone who might find the map is evil. No, if those killers come to Anglesey, let's hope we identify them in time."

They walked across fields until they found a track. That led them to a road, and that brought them to the undead. Over forty creatures had gathered in a dip, and heard them approach. The zombies began to rise. Chester and Bran began to run, back into the grassland and up into the hills.

After that, Bran plotted a route that avoided the roads. If it hadn't been for the previous day's grim discovery, he would have enjoyed it. Each year he took two holidays. He spent one week visiting his parents, and one week walking the hills and mountains. England, Wales, Scotland. Ireland a few times, the Appalachians twice, and the Great Dividing Range once. That trip to the Australian highlands had been where and when he'd got the invitation to go scuba diving. He'd almost not bought the ticket. After six months, he'd thought the invitation might have expired. It hadn't. The moment the email came in, he'd booked the flight. His only hesitation had been at the price, which was far more than he could really afford. Not going, though, meant missing out on the true opportunity of anyone's lifetime. He'd been a soldier long enough to know that when that particular opportunity came, it should never be passed up. Having bought the tickets, he'd spent a few glorious hours dreaming of beaches and air conditioning, of the Australian summer and blue drinks with umbrellas in them. Those dreams were dashed with the news of the outbreak.

Of course, February wasn't when he usually went hill walking. It was when he usually took his other holiday. His parents had returned to Poland when they'd retired. Sergeant Wojciech Emil Branofski, known as Web at school but Bran to his friends, was a dutiful son. Or he had been. His parents had died at Christmas. Bran had planned to visit their graves, but the last words his mother had spoke had rung in his ears.

"Never give up on a chance of happiness," she had said.

Bran had booked the flight to Australia. A few hours after that, he'd seen the news, and reported to the nearest barracks. By nightfall, he was guarding a supermarket. Two days later, an airport. Three days after that, he was in command of twenty green recruits and two hundred innocent criminals.

"Happiness is a long way off," he murmured.

"What's that?" Chester asked.

"Nothing," Bran said. "Do you think that looks like a railway line?" He gestured ahead.

"Could be," Chester said. "There are too many trees to be sure."

"There's no railway on the map," Bran said. "Not around here. It might be a goods line, or it might be disused."

"Or we're not where you think we are," Chester said.

"No, we are," Bran said with absolute certainty. "It's more likely to be a bad map. Out here, every railway will lead to Wrexham. I'd say it's about five miles."

They followed the train line until they found both sets of tracks blocked with industrial boxcars. While there had to be locomotives in the distance, clustered around the rearmost boxcar were the undead.

"I count seven," Chester said, raising his machete. "Probably double that."

The nearest creature still wore a rucksack, the chest straps still tight. It lurched a step towards them, and was then knocked aside by a far taller zombie in a fluorescent jacket. As the zombie swung around, Bran saw the pack was ripped and shredded, its contents long gone.

"Way more than double," Chester said. He walked off the tracks to the edge of the embankment. "There's at least a hundred. No, two hundred. No, too many to count. The train must have been full."

"Undead evacuees," Bran said, backing away. "Quick now."

And they were back to run-walk-run across the meadows and fields.

The sign read *Rhosllannerchrugog*.

"How do you pronounce that?" Chester asked.

"I don't," Bran said. "I'd call it Rhos."

"The railways around here are impassable," Chester said. "There're just too many undead, and there were too many close to that safe house. We're not going to bring the petrol from Wrexham back to Anglesey this way. What was that place near Llandudno, the one by that road where all of those vehicles had crashed?"

"Dwygyfylchi," Bran said.

"Another name I'm sure is just so the Welsh can make fun of the English," Chester said. "Anyway, we're not going to get a tanker down that road, so if roads are out, that only leaves the railways, and the one back there was worse than any I've seen in weeks."

"We'll worry about it when we find the fuel," Bran said. "*If* we find the fuel."

"I'd always worry about—"

"There's smoke," Bran interrupted. He raised a hand, pointing towards the town. A thin plume of white-grey smoke arose above the treetops. "Looks like a campfire."

"Survivors?" Chester asked.

"Probably." Bran glanced at Chester, then down at himself. "Remember to smile," he said. "We look threatening enough as it is."

Chester looked at his clothing, tattered and covered in mud and dried gore. "Right. Smile. I can manage that."

They stopped in the cover of trees on the western bank of a bridge. On the eastern bank was a restaurant. The sign proclaimed it to be The Worker's Rest, and underneath, that it had first opened in 1757, though Bran doubted it had opened with that particular name. The remainder of the sign listed a string of rosettes and other awards that meant nothing to the soldier. That it still served beer had been relegated to a brief line at the very bottom promising 'The Very Best Real Ales'.

While a wall ringed the car park and restaurant, it was only three feet high. Nothing had been done to reinforce it, though a quartet of trestle tables had been stacked in the gate-less entrance. Another trestle table had been broken up and set ablaze.

"Four people," Chester whispered. "They look like soldiers."

"The uniform doesn't make the man," Bran said. "And they *are* all men. Five, not four, one's lying down. No rifles that I can see. Some knives. An axe. Two shotguns. Here." He passed the binoculars to Chester.

"Why would a group of civilians dress up in military uniforms?" Chester asked. "There are other clothes available in every house. For that matter, why would a soldier wear a uniform? You don't."

"Good point. Give me the binoculars." Bran took them back, scanned the group, and then passed the binoculars to Chester. "Look at their feet."

"Some are wearing boots, some are wearing trainers. What am I looking for?"

"They don't clean their boots or maintain their gear," Bran said. "Those uniforms are the very definition of ill-fitting. Look at their stance, their walk. They're civilians dressed as soldiers. Never in the history of the world has that been a good thing."

"A couple of them are drinking," Chester said. "I'd say that's another bad sign. With that fire, it looks like they're settling in. Do we go around them?"

"You tell me," Bran said. "If that was you, what would you do next?"

"Probably get killed when those zombies who were on the railway line arrive here," Chester said. "That river isn't deep. The undead will be able to wade across. That wall's no protection, and I don't think they've even barricaded the windows around the restaurant."

"Maybe they don't plan to stay here for long," Bran said. "If they want supplies, Wrexham is the logical place to look, unless that's where they've come from. There's an old Army barracks in the city that was used for officer training. Maybe that's where they got the uniforms. If they've come from the east, and keep going west, they'll reach Anglesey. Either way, this is a confrontation we can't avoid, so it's best to get it over with."

"You mean you want to fight them?" Chester asked.

"No," Bran said. "Not if we don't have to. Most likely this is just another group of survivors who donned the uniform because it's more hardwearing than denim."

"What if they're the people who killed the brigadier?"

"How would we ever know?" Bran asked. "I doubt they'd freely admit it to a pair of strangers. No, we'll talk to them, but we won't mention Anglesey. We'll say we're from a community in Ireland. We're here seeing what's happened to the country. That's all."

He unslung his pack, took the holster off, and put that and the suppressor into his bag. He tucked the pistol into his belt at the small of his back.

"Gunfire's the last resort," Bran said. "If I start shooting, you start running. The zombies will hear the shots."

"This isn't my first fight," Chester said.

"Fine. I want you to do the talking. Let them focus on you so I can concentrate on them."

Halfway across the bridge, Chester raised his hand and waved. It wasn't until they were at the far side that they were noticed. There was a shout. The man on the ground stayed there. Three of the others stood and walked a few steps away from the fire. The fifth ran into the restaurant. That wasn't a good sign. Either they had more people inside, or better weapons, or both.

"It's good to see people," Chester called, stopping on the road near the restaurant's sign. "Haven't seen anyone for a while, not alive. Did you come from Birmingham?"

"Birmingham?" one of the men carrying a shotgun asked. "Is that where you're heading?"

"We caught a snippet of a radio broadcast," Chester said. "There are meant to be survivors there. We're going to see if it's true."

"Just the two of you?" the man asked.

"We didn't want to send too many more in case it was another will-o-the-wisp," Chester said. "You hear so many rumours, don't you? So you're not from Birmingham?"

"We're from a lot of places," the man said. "What did they say about Birmingham?"

Before Chester could reply, there came a yell. It *was* a yell not a scream, and it was angry rather than afraid. It came from inside, was definitely female, and was followed by a woman running out of the door.

"I said get your hands off," she said stumbling out into the daylight. She came to a halt when she saw Chester and Bran. The woman's accent was Scottish. Her hair was bright red, and her face was young. Bran placed her in her early twenties, if that.

"Afternoon, ma'am," Chester said. "I don't suppose you've come from Birmingham?"

"You're not with them?" the woman said. She took a step across the car park towards Chester. One of the faux-soldiers stepped between them.

"We've come from Ireland," Chester said, leaning to the side to address the woman. "There's a settlement there with people from all over. We heard a radio signal from survivors in Birmingham and we're on our way to check it out. What about yourself?"

"I'm…" She took a step towards Chester and Bran. The nearest uniformed man tried to grab her, but she ducked under his arm, stamped on his foot, and jabbed an elbow into his side. As he doubled over, she ran out into the road, and stopped near Chester and Bran, though not quite at their side. "Ireland? That has to be better than this."

"This is a military matter," the man with shotgun said. "She's under arrest. We've got to take her back to central command where she'll face trial for murder."

"That's a lie," the woman said. "I had the misfortune to be passing, that's all."

"You need to step back," the man with the shotgun said.

The door to the restaurant opened again. A figure stepped out. This man was also dressed in uniform, though it was far better fitting. Despite the captain's insignia on the man's shoulders, Bran recognised the man instantly. More than that, he knew where the man had recently been. Bran might have been mistaken about the World War Two gun belt at the man's waist, but not when it was taken with the ivory pipe between his teeth.

"What's going on out—" the man began. He stopped. "Why, if it isn't old Web. How are you, Sarge?"

"Barclay," Bran hissed. "Run," he added, as he dropped to a knee and drew the pistol from his belt. He fired three shots at the doorway. Barclay ducked back inside as Bran emptied the rest of the magazine at the man's supporters. There was a roar of a shotgun, but the pellets went nowhere near. Then came a sharp crack from Bran's left as Chester fired his revolver.

"Run! The bridge!" Bran snapped. The woman had already set off. Bran slotted a fresh magazine into place, and pushed Chester after her. Bran fired as he ran, not aiming at the group, but just wanting to keep them from realising they had the upper hand.

Another shot came, this one the more familiar crack of an SA80. Stone flew from the bridge's balustrade as Bran ducked behind it. He dropped the pistol and unslung his own rifle.

"Do you know him?" the woman asked, snatching the pistol from the ground.

"That man's name is Barclay," Bran said. "He's a soldier, but he wasn't a captain, not the last time we met. You saw the belt?"

"Can't say I did," Chester said.

"World War Two, standard issue back then, but very un-regulation now. You'd have to hold serious rank to get away with it."

"Like being a brigadier?" Chester asked.

"A lot higher than a brigadier unless you had a reputation that went with the rank," Bran said. "The brigadier smoked an ivory pipe. Another antique. The man was obsessed with them. A leather belt, an ivory pipe, do I need to draw you a picture?"

"You might want to draw me one," the woman said. "Are you really from Ireland?"

"Actually, we've come from somewhere a little nearer than that," Chester said. He half stood and fired over the balustrade.

Bran pulled him back down. "Save the ammunition for when they're closer, and they *will* get closer if we stop firing. What was that stuff about Birmingham?"

"You said I should do the talking," Chester said. "I thought it was a plausible reason for us being in this part of the world."

"There wasn't a radio broadcast?" the woman asked.

"Sorry, no," Chester said, "but there is a refuge not far from here. I'm Chester Carson."

"Lorraine."

"And this is Bran," Chester said.

"That man called you Web," the woman said.

"Long story," Bran said. "This isn't the time for it."

A bullet hit the road, followed by a shotgun blast that sprayed pellets into the bark and leaves of a willow ten yards further down the bank.

"Nice to meet you, Lorraine," Chester said. "You're from Scotland?"

Another bullet hit the bridge.

"He's right," she said, "this is *not* the time for small talk. Where's this refuge, and why are we waiting?"

"Anglesey," Bran said. "Though we've a boat on the coast."

"And why aren't we sprinting there now?" she asked.

"I want to make sure we're not followed," Bran lied.

The bridge had stone balustrades at either end that were far older than the iron bridge over the river itself. That looked like a temporary structure installed when a more ancient bridge had been washed away. More importantly, the bridge was open-sided. They were safe behind the stone balustrade, but only until the undead came, and they *would* come. They'd seen too many zombies in the last few days not to know that this area would become infested with the creatures. They weren't going to reach Wrexham. It was time to go back. First, though, he had a score to settle with Barclay.

"Chester, on my word," Bran said, "I want you to fire a shot over the top. One shot, and then you both run to the other side of the bridge. Now!"

Chester fired, and Bran swung out around the far edge of the balustrade. He found a target, a man with the shotgun. He fired his rifle, and his bullet found its mark. He shifted his aim. There was no sign of Barclay, so he fired his next round at the window close to the door. Then he saw movement, a rifle barrel in the window next to the door. He fired. The shadow fell, but a shotgun blast came from his left. He ducked back into cover.

Chester and the woman were halfway across the bridge. Bran rolled to the other side of the balustrade. There was no clear target, so he shot the windows, hoping the sound of falling glass would distract Barclay's men. Another blast came from a shotgun. The pellets didn't come close. Whoever Barclay had surrounded himself with, they weren't soldiers. They weren't even raw recruits.

Bran aimed at the corner of the building from where the gunfire had come. A figure appeared in the doorway. It was Barclay. He held an assault rifle in one hand, his other hung loose by his side. Barclay pulled the trigger. The weapon was set to fully automatic. Bran ducked back into cover as Barclay emptied the magazine.

The shots came out too fast to count, but Bran knew how long it took for a magazine to empty. When the last shot came, while Barclay was still pulling the trigger on an empty chamber, Bran swung around the stone abutment and fired. Barclay staggered back into the restaurant. There was another shotgun blast from an upper window, but Bran didn't waste ammunition returning fire. Barclay was dead, and Bran could see what the bandits in the restaurant couldn't. Coming up the road, summoned by the gunfire, were the undead. It was time to get away.

He ran to the far side of the bridge where Chester and Lorraine crouched together in the scant cover of a willow.

"Zombies! Move," he snapped. It was ten minutes before Bran slowed the pace to a brisk walk.

"Did Barclay tell you anything?" Bran asked.

"Like what?" Lorraine asked.

"Why he was here. Where he was going. Where he'd been," Bran said.

"Not really," Lorraine said. "Nothing I believed. They said that the government was running things from Northumberland. They were scouting for supplies, chasing looters, trying to get survivors to go back there."

"That's a lie, isn't it?" Chester asked.

"Probably," Bran said. "It's probably no more true than what you were saying about there being survivors in Birmingham. No, we need to get back to the ship, then back to Anglesey."

The mission had been a failure. The brigadier was dead. Anglesey would have to find another leader.

Chapter 6 - Signs and Prints
Anglesey, 29ᵗʰ October, Day 230

"That was Sam?" Bill asked. "Chester Carson was Sam? The guy in the house in Sydenham? I wonder why George never told me."

"He'll have had his reasons," Bran said. "He usually does."

"So that was how Lorraine came to be on Anglesey," Kim said. "You know she won't tell us because she doesn't want it to go in Bill's journal. Did you ever get to Wrexham?"

"Not yet," Bran said, "but that wasn't the end of the story. Barclay survived. I don't know if he'd really come from Northumberland, or if he'd only heard about it, but that's where he went. Maybe he died when you and your brother confronted Quigley, but why assume that he did? You survived, didn't you?"

"Only just," Bill said. "Was Barclay a portly guy in his early fifties?"

"No, he was thirty-eight, with greasy-black hair. Broken nose, close-set eyes. Olive skin pockmarked on his left cheek."

"I don't think I met him," Bill said. "Perhaps he was already dead."

"Why assume it," Bran said. "Why assume that only the good people survived? Didn't you write something like that?"

Bill raised his hands. "What I wrote was really just what I thought at that particular moment in time," he said. "Usually it was at the end of a long day limping away from the undead. I was tired, hungry, and scared out of my wits. I wouldn't take any of it as a philosophical treatise."

"My point," the soldier said, "as much as I had one, is this, we talk a lot about us being the last people left alive, but we don't know that we are. We don't even know if we're the largest group left on Earth. I agree that we have to act as if we are, but for that we need a leader. Mary and George have done a good job as far as it goes, and maybe they were the leaders we needed, but they're not the leaders for the future. We need a strong mind and a steady arm. There was a time I wanted it to be the brigadier. There was a time I thought it might be me. There were a lot more times when I thought I'd return to find this place nothing but ash and bone. We need a leader. Like it or not, that's you. I heard about the execution. Everyone did, but no one's talking about it. You know why? Because they have nothing to say. You did what they expected would be done. You did what *had* to be done. You made the hard choice, and that makes you our leader in everything but name. Thank you for the soup." He stood up. "*I'll* have a word with Lena and Dean. If they want to be soldiers, they need to get used to a dressing-down from their sergeant."

"The hard choices?" Kim said. "How on earth did we end up here? But he's right, you're the one making them."

"*We* are," Bill said.

"Hmm," Kim murmured.

"George and Mary wanted me to be the candidate in the election. Sholto wanted you. I think they both got their own way in the end," Bill said.

"Do you think Barclay is still alive?" she asked.

"I don't know," Bill said. "If he is, or if any of Quigley's people are, they know about Anglesey, but they haven't come here. Until or if they do, we have enough problems to worry about."

"Speaking of problems," she said, taking her coat from the hook. "I'm going to find Dean and Lena. They might be over eighteen, and they might have fought their way across Ireland, but they told me they were getting on the boat to Belfast. I don't like them lying to me. I don't suppose I can stop them going to the mainland with Bran, but while they're on Anglesey, they'll sleep under our roof. That way we can make sure they get off the island if we get the signal to flee."

She left, and Bill was alone. The kitchen seemed suddenly large, yet somehow too small. He was about to return upstairs when he caught a few words from the front room. He opened the door and found that everyone was gathered around one set of screens.

"Have you found a ship?" Bill asked.

Almost as one, the entire group spun around. All wore a matching guilty expression.

"Oh, hi, Bill," Annette said, sounding as guilty as she looked. "I think we're there."

"Where?" Bill asked.

"London," Annette said.

"You moved the satellites?" Bill asked.

"Well, it's more that we're *moving* one of them," Annette said. "I watched Sholto do it. It's not hard."

"That's not the issue," Bill said. "You shouldn't have moved it without permission."

"There wasn't time to ask," she said. "We'll be leaving soon, won't we? And when we get to Belfast, we might not have the electricity for all the screens. We need to get the images now, and find any people in them before winter because they might not be alive in spring. Anyway, I didn't use much of the propellant. Oh, and we've got some pictures of France," she added, giving the lie to her previous statement. "At least I think it's France, but I'm sure this is the Thames."

There was a general murmur of agreement from the group. Bill opened his mouth, but closed it. In a month, if not in days, all of these people would be living in a world without electricity, without screens, without an excuse *not* to spend a day hacking at a field or at the undead. He let them have the moment.

"Why London?" he asked.

"Because of Nilda and Jay," Annette said. "That's where Bran said they were both going. Maybe they got there."

They wouldn't have, Bill thought, but he didn't say it aloud. Nor did he voice the real reason he suspected Annette had decided to move the satellite. London had once been her home, too. She didn't talk about London much, or her parents at all. That told Bill she spent a lot of time thinking about them. She was looking for a way to say goodbye, and he wouldn't take that from her.

"Fine," he said. He peered at the screen. All he could see were clouds. "It'll be getting dark soon," he said. "We can work out where it is come dawn. Why don't you all go outside and get some fresh air."

"This is *important*, Bill," Annette said.

"Fine, fine, but go outside as soon as it's dark," he said. "You're right, we'll all be leaving soon, and when we do, it might be a long time before we can safely walk through the night-time streets again."

He went back upstairs to his study. He opened the laptop and spent a few minutes looking at the screen, imagining a time when they would forever be without technology.

"One problem at a time."

He opened the template for the newssheet. The double-sided document barely deserved the name, but he'd been trying to get an edition out every day. He hadn't published one that morning. He didn't know how to write about the execution. In fact, he wasn't sure *he* should be the one to write about it. The execution was an unpleasant job that'd had to be done, but he felt the account should be deeper.

After another minute staring at the blinking cursor, he turned his attention to what he thought of as filler, beginning with the weather report. Tomorrow's prediction was much the same as today's, mostly cloudy with the possibility of rain. He added a few paragraphs on Chester Carson, on Nilda, Jay, and Tuck. He didn't mention Lorraine, or Barclay, but finished with a postscript on how communication was more vital than ever, with a plea that everyone get to know their neighbours.

That gave him a moment's pause as he thought about the people gathered downstairs. He still didn't know their names.

Thirty minutes later, the section on the execution still blank, there was a knock at the door. It was Captain Devine.

"I'm sorry," she said. "Am I disturbing you? Annette said I should come up."

"She's still down there? No, you didn't disturb me. I was struggling with a way to describe the execution for the newssheet," he said.

"You don't," Devine said. "You state the criminal's name, the crime, the jury's verdict, the judge's sentence, and that the sentence was carried out. No more, no less. Here, let me."

She sat at the keyboard, and tapped away one-handed. Four sentences later, she stopped. "There. Done." She turned to face him. "You won't forget about Lenetti, so there's no point me telling you that you should.

There's no point me telling you he'll be the last, because he won't. There are hard times ahead, and those need hard people. I won't say that you have to decide whether you want to be one of those people because you don't have a choice. You *are* that person. That burden is yours. It will define you. Just don't let it *become* you."

"Bran said much the same thing about an hour ago," Bill said. "It's been a rather grim day all round."

"Mine hasn't been much better," she said. "That's what I wanted to talk to you about. I managed to get some readable prints of that hand."

"The hand?" he asked.

"From the zombie, the one that we thought might be Sorcha Locke. It wasn't her."

"Oh. Oh, right," Bill said. "That hardly seems to matter now."

"It probably doesn't," Devine said. "You need to make sure it doesn't become important this winter when there are fewer distractions for all these people."

"You think Markus will try to make use of it?"

"I think Markus is up to something," Devine said. "Kim makes for a good investigator. Her log of Markus's associates makes for interesting reading. Even without his pub, even *with* the cloud of suspicion hanging over him, he still has his supporters. He will always be dangerous. More so when everyone is in Belfast."

"George had a plan for dealing with Rob," Bill said. "He was going to send him to Svalbard. We could do that with Markus."

"Someone else will take his place," Devine said. "At least with him close, you know where trouble's going to come from."

"Another problem to add to the list," Bill murmured. "It's a shame that corpse wasn't Sorcha Locke's. I suppose she's just another one of those people whose fate we can guess at, but never know for certain."

"There's still the gravedigger, O'Reardon," Devine said. "We've got Marines in Elysium. We could send a team north, and they could find her in two days, maybe three."

"To what end?" Bill asked. "What could O'Reardon tell us? Did you get the report from Elysium today? I think I missed it."

"More zombies came. They killed them," Devine said. "If we want to hold it through the winter, we'll need to send more people. At the very least, they need another twenty civilians to free up all of the Marines for defence."

"As soon as we can spare the ships," Bill said.

"I propose we send the *Vehement*," Devine said.

"It'll sink," Bill said.

"It'll be lost if we leave it here," Devine said. "We should send the *Vehement*, and have her tow the *Harper's Ferry*. We need the medical gear, but there's no point offloading it here. If Belfast isn't going to be our permanent home, there's no point moving the ship there. They can anchor in Kenmare Bay, try to repair the engines this winter, and they can offload the medical gear into Elysium. We can power the equipment using the wind turbines, and that farm can become our hospital. That will give us a reason to keep sending a large ship there, and knowing that there's a chance to be treated if you get sick will be good for morale. It'll help keep order in Belfast."

"If the *Vehement* doesn't sink," Bill said. "Mister Mills seems to think it will.

"The admiral is confident the *Vehement* can make it to Elysium, and then out into the Atlantic where she can be sunk in water deep enough she won't trouble us again. We'll have the hospital ship anchored off Ireland, and Elysium will have another fifty personnel."

"I'll take it to the council," Bill said.

"But you agree?"

"I do."

"Then I'll tell the crew to prepare for departure," Devine said.

A pro-forma protest about following the necessary procedures died on Bill's lips. There wasn't time. If Elysium fell, if they lost the equipment on the *Harper's Ferry*, if any one of a thousand other things went wrong, the chances of humanity's survival would be diminished, and they were already so low.

"I better tell Mary," Bill said, "and get her to sign off on it."

He glanced at the screen with its oh-so-brief statement of Lenetti's execution. The story of Bran's encounter with Tuck and Jay filled the page, but he thought there should be something more.

"Is it worth mentioning Sorcha Locke? No, I suppose not." He saved the file onto a flash-drive and shut down the laptop. "There's nothing to say, and better to say nothing than to lie. Still, I do wonder what happened to her."

Part 3
The Last Conspirator

Sorcha Locke

Anglesey to Birmingham
May - August

Chapter 7 - Beer Today
Anglesey, 8th May, Day 58

Sorcha Locke wearily climbed aboard the single-masted boat with the red fibreglass hull docked in the harbour at Holyhead. They'd only been in Anglesey for two days, but if they were going to stay much longer, they would need a more permanent home.

"You're back late," Sean O'Brian said, opening the hatch from the cabin and coming out onto the deck. He glanced left and right, checking the quay was empty before he spoke. "Bring any news?" he asked, his voice low.

"Only the bad kind, though I also bring fish," Locke said, handing him the plastic bag.

"What's the bad news?" O'Brian asked.

"A ship returned last night from an expedition to Deeside. The industrial estate near Wrexham?" she added.

"Ah." O'Brian looked up and down the quay again. Theirs wasn't the only boat tied to a precarious mooring in the Welsh harbour. Yachts with tattered rigging, motor launches without any fuel, and battered skiffs with no chance of surviving the next storm were tied to every jetty. Anglesey was full of boats, and each boat was full of survivors, but no one seemed interested in the two newest arrivals.

"There was a Claverton warehouse in Deeside, wasn't there?" O'Brian asked. "Did they find it?"

"Worse. They found craters," Locke said. "I don't know if our warehouse is intact, and there's no way of asking without arousing suspicion, but it's the most logical target."

"You think Quigley did it?" O'Brian asked. "It must have been him."

"Probably. It hardly matters now," Locke said, "but it does mean we've got to change our plans. Is there any hot water?"

"There's a saucepan's worth on the stove," Sean O'Brian said. He sniffed. "It's all yours."

"That's a day gutting fish for you," Locke said. "It'll be a week before I can get rid of the smell. For an entire day's work, I only got two fish and some soap. They say there'll be bread tomorrow, but I'll believe that when I can bite into a loaf. What about you?"

"I got a far better haul. Some hot chocolate, coffee, sugar, and some fuel for our stove. There was no diesel, though. At least, there's none that anyone's willing to trade." He followed her down into the cabin, checking again for eavesdroppers before he closed the door. "Did you find out where they store the fuel?"

"For the fishing trawlers? Yes," Locke said. "It's kept in an underground tank in a boatyard on the other side of the harbour. There's no official guard, but the trawler-folk sleep in a shed next door. We'll have to wait until they've gone out to sea before we can take it."

"Which brings us back to the question of where we should go," O'Brian said. "This isn't a large yacht, and we don't have a powerful engine or a large fuel tank. We could carry enough fuel to get to Deeside, but if we can't refuel and resupply there…" The boat rocked as a wave swept under it. "As long as we don't go back to Belfast, I don't mind."

"Amen," Locke said. She took one of the wind-up LEDs from the hook, and the saucepan of water into the small boat's small bathroom, balanced it on the sink, and stripped off her clothes. They, at least, were relatively clean. The fishmongers had provided her with a set of overalls to use while gutting the plaice, haddock, skate, and other fish she hadn't recognised.

She peered at herself in the mirror. Her face was lined, and seemed a decade older than it had mere months before. Some of that was a lack of sleep and food, but most of it was that she'd led a dozen lifetimes in the hectic nightmare since the outbreak.

"This *is* better than Belfast," she murmured as she took out the liquid soap she'd been given in part payment for her day's labour. "It's just not as good as it could have been."

If it hadn't been for the outbreak, Lisa Kempton's plans would have changed the world. Locke's employer had predicted and planned for a nuclear war, but no one could have prepared for the undead. Even so,

Locke had held Elysium against scores of zombies and the arrival of Quigley's troops. There had been three glorious days when they thought all would be well, but then the undead had come in greater numbers than before, greater numbers than she'd ever imagined. Elysium had fallen, and Locke had barely escaped.

She'd found O'Brian at his post in the bungalow in Pallaskenry. Of course she had. Sean was nothing but loyal. No one else had made it to that rendezvous. Together, they'd gone to the warehouse on the Shannon Estuary, and found Captain Tamika Keynes and Kempton's ship, *The New World*. The ship's crew had already come ashore, heading to Elysium while Locke had been fleeing from it. They were almost certainly dead. As Lisa wasn't on the ship, and she hadn't made it to Elysium, Locke and O'Brian had continued north, going to their location of last resort, Belfast and the bunker hidden beneath the warehouse. Lisa hadn't been there, either. Finally, Locke had accepted that her mentor's plans, like the world, were in ruins. O'Brian had gone looking for a boat. Locke had stayed behind, hoping against hope that Lisa might arrive. She hadn't. When Sean didn't return, Locke began to believe that she was the last person left alive on the entire planet. She was well beyond the edge of despair when Jasmine Cotter had arrived. Locke had been so grateful to discover she wasn't alone in the world, she hadn't realised how badly the outbreak had warped Jasmine until it was almost too late.

Finally, Sean *had* returned, and just in time, having found the yacht abandoned in an isolated inlet. They'd left Belfast to Jasmine, though the woman had seen them off with a barrage of gunfire. The waves were steep, and Jasmine had never been a good shot. They had sailed away from Ireland, and into the Irish Sea. The boat had a small engine, but virtually no fuel. It didn't matter, they knew how to sail, Lisa had insisted upon it.

Their original destination had been the warehouse in Deeside. Like the house in Pallaskenry, the bunker in Belfast, and so many other locations strategically located around the world, there was a cache of supplies hidden for members of Lisa's inner circle unable to reach a rendezvous. Among those supplies in Deeside, were two hundred gallons of diesel.

First, they'd had to find potable water, and so they had sailed towards the Welsh coast with the intention of finding a stream. Instead, they'd sailed into a giant fishing trawler who'd towed them back to Anglesey.

That was two days ago, and now Locke had learned that Deeside had been destroyed. She had no proof Quigley was responsible, but she'd never liked the imperialistic Englishman who acted as if the Easter Rising had never happened. It would be true to form for that superannuated politician to take this last petty revenge if he'd realised that Lisa Kempton had betrayed him.

Locke sighed. She'd run out of water long before she'd run out of body to wash. She towelled off, dressed, and wrapped the blue and gold scarf around her neck. That had been a gift from Lisa, and was Locke's last link to her old life. She smiled. It was typical of the billionaire to give a gift emblazoned with her company's logo. She went back to the cabin where O'Brian was frying the fish.

"There're no chips, no vinegar, and no way to clean the frying pan," he said, "but I threw in some of the flour we ground last night. Since we *can't* clean the pan, I'm going to season it with a little sugar. Do you remember that seafood restaurant in Temple Bar?"

"The one we went to for your birthday? I remember the bill."

He grinned. "You'd just got a pay rise. Didn't you think I'd take advantage of it? They had tuna seasoned with cocoa."

"Don't even think about it," she said. "You can experiment when we've got food to waste. Even then, I'd like to see a recipe book open in front of you. It's a shame about Deeside."

"Do you want to go there anyway?" he asked. "If it was an aerial strike, maybe something's survived."

"I don't think so. Have you heard about Scotland?"

"That it got the brunt of the nuclear warheads? Yes," he said. "Scotland, Cornwall, and the south coast. Possibly Norfolk and East Anglia, too. That's what I heard."

"The south coast as well?" Locke asked. "I didn't hear that. Maybe we *should* go to Deeside." She sat down. "But if we do, and if we've just stolen some of their diesel, we can't return to Anglesey. We'll have to follow the

Scottish coast north, then south again before we could cross the North Sea. Even if we fill the boat until it's about to sink, we'll be out of fuel before we reach Thurso. Assuming there's any diesel left in Deeside."

"So we'd have to rely on sail, but be further north than we are now," Sean said.

"And be out of supplies before we reach Denmark," she said. "If our goal is Portugal, we'd be better cutting due south from here. On the other hand, if we can't go ashore in Cornwall or along the English south coast, even with all the diesel in the world, we'll die of thirst before we reach the continent."

"There are other Claverton warehouses, aren't there?" O'Brian asked.

"In England? A few," she said. "Not many, and no others near the coast. Because of Quigley, the plan was for everyone to leave England as expeditiously as possible."

"You're still thinking of Leif Erikson?" O'Brian asked.

"It's never far from my mind," she said. "We could head back to the Shannon Estuary and hope that Tamika is still there, but she was only waiting on Lisa. She won't wait there forever."

"You know what Lisa said, if the problem has no good solutions, change the parameters of the equation," O'Brian said.

"You mean steal a larger ship?" Locke asked. "They never leave them untended, and the rumour is they have a Royal Navy submarine on hand. We'd get blown out of the water, but I don't think they'd waste a torpedo for a few gallons of diesel."

"Eat your fish," O'Brian said. "Let me tell you about my day, and how we might have an alternative after all."

"Oh? What?" she said.

"The sun was high," he began in a singsong tone, "and the air was clear when Sean O'Brian set out on his quest. His pockets were full of gold, his head full of questions, and his heart—"

"Sean, please."

He grinned. "There's a pub in town that's become a bit of a trading post. I took the gold, but no one was interested. Everything's sold for barter, and they take about twenty percent as their cut."

73

"That's where you got the hot chocolate and sugar? What did you trade?"

"My time," he said. "I spent the day sorting through suitcases. Someone had been through the empty houses in the town, throwing in anything and everything that they could. Most of the cases went into a shed, but some were left out in the rain. They wanted someone to sort through them and work out what could be salvaged and what couldn't."

"For that, you were paid in a few sachets of sugar?" Locke asked.

"And the fuel for the stove, and…" He reached under the table and into a small bag, and pulled out two bottles. "Beer. It's a pub, after all."

Locke peered at the label. "Hopvar? Never heard of it. Even so, it's a finite resource. It's worth more than a couple of hours of light work."

"That's where the story gets interesting."

"You always save the important part to the end," she said.

"A story has to be told in a certain way, otherwise it's just a list of facts, and what fun is there in that?"

"So what's the fun part?" she asked.

"That would be in who's running the pub." He paused for dramatic effect. "Rachel Gottlieb."

"Who?" Locke asked.

"Rachel Gottlieb. From the office in Guildford? The one who found out about the redoubts?"

"Oh, her. She's running the pub?"

"She is, and she's the one who gave me the job and paid me in beer."

"She doesn't bear a grudge?" Locke asked.

"Not against me," Sean said. "I think she enjoyed bossing me about, but I also think she was grateful to see a friendly face. There's a group of mercenaries who've camped out in the pub. This guy, Markus, is leading them, and he hasn't exactly taken over, but she thinks it's only a matter of time."

"Ah. She wants to us to get rid of him?"

"I think so. Reading between the lines, I think she invited Markus and his people in to secure her hold on the place, and now they're pushing her out."

"Can't she go to the authorities?" Locke asked.

"I asked her. She says there aren't any real authorities. There're a dozen different factions that pay lip service to the old couple who administer the grain and run the school and hospital. The crew of that submarine and a regiment of French Special Forces mean that no one can pull themselves to the top, but at the same time, they're not willing to offer her a hand up. Nor does she think anyone will stop her getting rid of these mercenaries."

"Beer today, blood tomorrow," Locke said. "The more things change, the more the violence stays the same. Are they armed?"

"Sure, but not as well as us," Sean said. He tapped his foot against the floor, and the compartment in which their own weapons were stored.

"So what's your plan?" Locke asked.

"Simple," Sean said. "We take over the pub."

"And Rachel?"

"She's one of us. Or she could have been," he said.

Locke leaned back. "She's not. She wasn't. She never would have been. She was doing something in accounting, wasn't she? That was it. She was meant to be auditing the effectiveness of our charity work, but instead she looked at where the rest of the money was going. She found out about Claverton Industrial Supplies and *The New World*, and tried to blackmail her way into one of the redoubts. We had to buy her silence. No, we can't trust her. But, okay, let's say we did this, what's your plan for after we've killed the mercenaries?"

"I don't mean we should kill to take the pub," Sean said. "Think of it more as a hostile takeover. Once we've got the pub, we offer to help the people running this island. After all, we ran a multi-billion-dollar business with more employees than there are survivors here."

"We helped run a small part of it," Locke said, "and there's a difference between a company and a society."

"Except there isn't, not really," Sean said. "We trained for this. We prepared. We could make something of this place, of these people. Like you said, there's still Claverton. Maybe not in Deeside, but there are other warehouses, and there's Portugal, if it wasn't destroyed. And, of course, there's Belfast. Rachel's problems are with mercenaries, but what do they ever want except to be paid? We can pay them with what's left in Belfast, and use them to get rid of Jasmine."

"When have you known a mercenary to accept payment tomorrow for work today?" Locke asked. "How many people does Rachel have that she can rely on?"

"Two or three, I think," Sean said.

"How many mercenaries?"

"About twenty," Sean said. "Though it's hard to be sure."

"So six against twenty, or possibly two against twenty-four," Locke said. "Once it's done, we'll be pitting ourselves against the crew of a nuclear submarine, and a detachment of French Special Forces. All for what? Control of a rocky island at the wrong end of Europe?"

"What's the alternative?" Sean asked. "What's the *real* alternative? We might reach Greenland, but we'll never make it to America, not now. The mission's over, Sorcha. Lisa's dead."

Locke knew that Sean was probably right. Ireland had fallen, as had so many of Lisa Kempton's plans. After Belfast, Locke knew it was time to make the best of their terrible situation. Even so, she couldn't give up all hope.

"How did you leave it with Rachel?" Locke asked.

"I said I'd consider it. She said to come back tomorrow, and she'd find some more work for me."

"Then I've a day of gutting fish to think about it," Locke said.

Chapter 8 - Blood Tomorrow
Anglesey, 9th May, Day 59

"Another day, another dollar," Locke said, dropping the bag on the table. "Or another fish, at least."

"I can top that," Sean said. "I have the option on a house."

"A house?"

"With a chimney and fireplace. It's next to the pub."

"But it's only the option?" Locke asked.

"We get the house if we take the job with Rachel Gottlieb," Sean said. "Both of us. We're to become bar staff."

"Really? I haven't pulled a pint since I was at Trinity, but I don't suppose that's what Rachel really wants us for."

"No, she hinted as much," Sean said. "You're the boss, so it's your decision, but I know where they keep the canned food they get in trade. So, if you decide we should leave, I know where we can steal supplies."

"You've changed your tune," Locke said.

"Yeah, I have," he said. "I guess Rachel didn't think I was being sufficiently enthusiastic. She dropped a less than subtle hint that she might start telling people who we were, and what Ms Kempton knew."

"Rachel doesn't know anything, not really," Locke said. "She only knows that Lisa built a few farms with high walls."

"She knows enough to rouse a mob," Sean said. "I'd rather slink away than get chased out of here."

"And if she's willing to threaten us today," Locke said, "she'll be more than willing to do it a few months from now. There is an alternative, because I've revised my own opinion, too, at least as far as the authorities here are concerned. They seem a bit more organised than it first appeared. It is very ramshackle. I've still got my doubts. What little structure there is could evaporate in the first crisis, but when the old couple give orders, people listen even if they don't immediately obey. Forget Rachel, her pub, and those mercenaries. We'll tell the old couple about the Claverton

77

warehouses, though it would mean telling them about Lisa. If *we* did it, rather than have Rachel blow the whistle on us, we'll get a hearing."

"How sympathetic do you think that hearing would be?" Sean asked.

"That would depend on what we told them," Locke said. "There's no escaping that Jasmine is in Belfast, or that, sooner or later, a ship is going to sail there. Perhaps that's how we approach it. We take them a warning of a mad woman with a bunker and guns holed up in that city. We could tell them of Deeside."

"And Elysium? And what about *The New World*?"

"I suppose we'd have to," Locke said. "It's an alternative to slinking away, as you put it, and you're right, we're never going to make it to America, but we did prepare for this. If this is to be our new home, then it's best that we're the ones who shape it. How did you leave it with Rachel?"

"That you were the boss, so it was your decision to make," Sean said. "She's expecting us in about an hour."

"Then I'll meet her first, and make a decision afterwards."

"Sorcha Locke! Welcome, please," Rachel said warmly.

"Rachel, I'm glad to see you're alive," Locke said, and gave a smile she'd practiced on prime ministers and presidents. She took in the dimly lit pub. "This is a nice place you have, though it's quiet for this time of night." There was only one customer. A blond-haired man sat at the bar, a coffee cup in front of him.

"We're more a trading post than a bar, at least at the moment," Rachel said. "After all, there's little for people to sell, and not much beer for us to trade. I'd like to change that before the nights shorten."

There was still a trace of the last light of day streaking through the windows, supplemented by a score of candles on a shelf behind the bar.

"What do you use for currency?" Locke asked.

"Mostly candles and batteries," Rachel said. "Come through to the back, it's more comfortable there. Paul, give a yell if Markus returns."

"Who's Markus?" Locke asked.

"Muscle," Rachel said. "A role he *volunteered* for." She led them into a small kitchen behind the bar. "Please, have a seat," she said, indicating the padded chairs around the scrubbed pine table. "I'll get us a drink."

Locke sat. The kitchen was so clean that it was obvious no cooking took place in it.

"You don't want a barmaid, do you?" Locke asked.

"Oh, I do," Rachel said, "but that's not what I'd like *you* to do."

"And what is it that you want *us* to do?" Locke asked as if she couldn't guess.

Rachel placed three glasses and a bottle of clear liquid on the table. "It's vodka. Well, no, technically it's moonshine, but we call it vodka."

"Why am I here, Rachel?" Locke asked.

"You were Lisa Kempton's number-two, yes? Her deputy?" Rachel asked.

"Not quite," Locke said. "I oversaw her operations in Ireland, Britain, and some parts of continental Europe."

"You knew about the refuges she was setting up, yes?" Rachel said. "You know where they are."

"I know where one of them is," Locke said. "The one in southern Ireland from which I escaped. It was overrun by the living dead."

"But there are supplies there," Rachel said. "Enough to keep people alive for years. What I'm proposing is that we go and get them."

"Oh." Locke looked at Sean. He shrugged, and looked as nonplussed as Locke.

"I don't know whether I should first ask *why* or *how*," Locke replied.

"Anglesey is a temporary home for a temporary community," Rachel said. "There's talk of turning the power plant back on, and talk of digging over every patch of grass, but that's all it is, talk. When the submarine goes out, no one knows if it will return. The French soldiers are already planning a mission to Paris. Without them, there's no strength behind the weak throne. Without strength, there's no government, only a veneer of peace while the knives are sharpened. Once those soldiers are gone, the knives will come out. Anglesey could become the future, but it will have to change, and change from the top."

"When you're in charge?" Locke asked, wondering whether it was Rachel who was sharpening the knives.

"Someone has to be," Rachel said. "You know it. Lisa Kempton knew it, didn't she?"

"How do you see the redoubt in Ireland fitting into this?" Sean asked.

"It has the supplies we need," Rachel said. "Ammunition, food, fuel. Whoever can bring that back can show everyone that there's a different way, a better way, that there's treasure to be found out there in the world. Treasure that's there for the taking, and of far more value than the rotting trinkets we can find in terraced two-up two-downs."

"I'm sorry," Locke said. "I'm sorry, but there isn't. There *was*, yes. There *were* enough supplies for a few dozen for a few years, but before the undead came, so did some locals. We offered them sanctuary and they used up our food. The ammunition was expended keeping the zombies back, but there weren't enough people or ammunition, and far too many of the undead. They got inside. Everyone died. There might be a few hundred rounds left, a few cans, a few bottles, but less than we'd use clearing the place of the living dead."

"What about Claverton Industrial Supplies?" Rachel asked.

Locke kept her expression blank. "We used those to store the composite components for rocket fuel, fertilizer, and other chemicals," she said. "There truly isn't much need for them. Not now, not yet. They are what we'd need in a year or three after our immediate survival had been secured, but we didn't plan for the undead. We thought it was going to be a limited nuclear war that would see either North America and northern Europe destroyed or the only places left. No, I'm sorry, I can see what you want to do, but I don't think there's anything we can offer which will help."

Rachel opened the bottle and poured a large measure into each of the glasses. "I had to ask. I should have expected it. If there were supplies in Ireland, you wouldn't have left."

"The idea is sound," Sean said. "Perhaps there's a military supply depot in Wales."

"There isn't," Locke said. "Not that anyone has found intact. We heard that Dublin was overrun, but what about the rest of Ireland?"

"I think it's the same as Britain," Locke said. "What little wasn't consumed has been lost to the weather and the undead."

"I thought there might be a shortcut to success," Rachel said. "I suppose that's as unlikely now as it was a year ago. It's the hard way instead, then. Cheers." She downed her glass. Locke did the same, as did Sean. The fiery liquid burned.

"Wooh!" Sean hissed.

"We've still got a ways to go with that," Rachel said. She put her glass on the table. "The thing is, Ms Locke, I know that you're lying. I know that you purchased a food canning business in Salford, and that you dismantled the factory and shipped the entire thing away two years ago. Why do that unless you were canning supplies? So where are they?"

"The factory was sold to Saudi Arabia," Locke said. "One of the royal family wanted to try his hand at being a food baron. He didn't want to… to start from the ground up."

"I don't believe you," Rachel said.

"Then I'm sorry we… we can't help," Locke said. "Thank you for the drink." She tried to stand, but found she couldn't. Her legs were like concrete.

"It was in the glass," Rachel said, as she opened the bottle and poured herself another shot. Locke and O'Brian passed out.

Chapter 9 - Chalets and Caravans
Wales, 10ᵗʰ May, Day 60

"Sorcha? Sorcha?"

Someone was calling her name. Her mother? Was it time for school? The haze of dreams faded to memory. The present returned, and she remembered to whom the voice belonged.

"Sean?"

"You're awake, good," he said.

Sorcha tried to raise her hand, but couldn't. Her arm was tied at the wrist. So was the other. Her legs were secured at the ankles. She was tied to a chair. Tied or chained? She couldn't see, as the room was almost pitch black, but it felt like rope.

"Where are we?" she asked.

"Don't know," Sean said. "It's a room about twelve feet square. Looks like a wooden cabin. There are two bunk beds opposite me, a sink to my left. There's a window above it, but it's mostly blocked. There was a ray of light coming through it earlier, but that's gone, so it must be night."

"A wooden chalet with bunk beds? Some kind of holiday camp, then?" Locke asked. "Why?"

"Rachel drugged us, remember?"

"I'm starting to," Locke said. "Has she said anything, asked anything?"

"Nothing," Sean said. "I haven't seen her. I haven't seen anyone, but I've only been conscious for an hour or so."

"And it's night now, but there was daylight?" An entire day must have gone by. With that realisation came another, how thirsty she was. She licked her dry lips with a dry tongue. To distract herself, she tried to raise her hands. "Are you tied to a chair?"

"Which is tied to the back of yours, and bolted to the ground," Sean said. "I saw fresh splinters around the bolt pinning it to the floorboard, so it was recent."

"Done for our benefit?" Locke said. "Great."

"So, boss, any ideas?" Sean asked. "Because I'm all out."

"Give me a minute," Locke said.

But before the minute was up, the door opened. The blond man who'd been sitting at the bar came in. He had an electric lantern in one hand, a small leather bag in the other.

"Evening," he said. He grinned, showing a mouth of overly white teeth. "Please accept my apologies for the conditions." He placed the lantern on the counter by the sink.

"Why are we here?" Locke asked.

"Why are any of us?" the man replied. "I guess the answer depends on whether you believe in God or not. I'm a little uncertain on that topic myself, though I've a friend hereabouts who'd be more than happy to discuss the eternal verities."

Locke thought back, dredging up memories of the previous evening. "You're Paul, yes?"

"I am," he said. He opened the bag and took out a bottle. "It's water," he said, and held it to her lips.

She took a mouthful and almost gagged.

"Moonshine *is* mostly water," Paul said. "Don't worry, you'll get water soon. More than enough."

"What do you want?" Sean asked.

"Ah, the pit-bull speaks," Paul said. "Good. What I want is some answers. The questions are pretty simple. Where did Lisa Kempton keep her supplies?"

"What supplies?" Locke asked.

"Don't play games," Paul said. "There's no point, and no point in stalling. No one's going to help you, no one's going to hear you scream, and you *will* scream, believe me. Kempton built redoubts, yes? Refuges across the world."

"They were overrun," Locke said. "Why do you think we left?"

"Kempton planned for that, didn't she?" Paul said. "She had caches of supplies all over the world. Rachel saw the purchase orders. She knows about the canning factory, so where is it? Where's all the food, the weapons, the medicine? Your redoubt would have kept you safe for the first couple of months, right? What was the plan after that? To put it another way, where were you going?"

"We weren't going anywhere," Locke said. "Just looking for somewhere safe."

"You're lying," Paul said. "That's okay. Everyone lies at first." He opened his bag and pulled out a pair of pliers. "I learned from the best," he said. He gave another wide grin. "Do you like 'em? Every single tooth was pulled out by the root. Yeah, I learned from the best, I learned from personal experience precisely how much pain someone can take. I know just how much and for how long. Right now, you think that you can escape." He put the pliers back, and took out a thick leather strap, ten inches long, weighted at one end. "I have to disabuse you of that. Then I'll really start hurting you. I'll make you understand what pain actually is. The incentive of making it stop will get you to tell the truth." He ran the leather strap down her cheekbone. "Sorcha Locke. You were in a car crash ten years ago. You had plastic surgery, and Lisa Kempton paid for it. It was just after you were promoted. One of the perks was a car with a driver, but the driver had five too many the night before, hence the car crash and a need for a new face. Yes, Rachel did her research. She knows *exactly* who you are."

Locke jutted her head away from the strap. "There was a court case," she said. "The car drove straight into an empty shop. It was all over the papers. That's not research, that's just reading the news."

Paul grinned. With his face in shadow, it looked like a hollow mask.

"As for you," he said, walking around to Sean. "Rachel doesn't know anything about you. Fortunately, we've got plenty of time to get acquainted."

There was a soft whish as the leather strap sliced through the air, then a meaty slap as it hit Sean, but no sound from him. Paul hit Sean again. Again. Again. A rhythmic slap of leather hitting flesh filled the cabin.

Locke closed her eyes, forcing herself to say nothing. Sean managed to stay quiet for over a minute. Finally, a soft grunt of pain escaped from his lips.

"Ah, good, now we're getting somewhere," Paul said. He began beating Sean with renewed enthusiasm, but was stopped after ten blows when the door opened. A young man stood in the doorway, an older woman just behind him.

"What's this?" the man asked.

"Nothing, Mr Bishop," Paul said. "Nothing for you to worry about."

"You can't torture them," Bishop said.

Those words ignited a flash of hope within Locke. The man wasn't as young as she'd first thought. Perhaps thirty, though it was hard to tell. His clothing was plain, simple, and dirty. His hair was short. When she looked in his eyes, though, all hope faded. His eyes were wild, betraying a madness that was confirmed with his next words.

"A confession gained under torture would be inadmissible in any court," Bishop said.

Paul sighed. "I told you, it doesn't have to be. If you write the book of laws, then you get to decide what the rules are."

"In the extremes of pain, at the limits of endurance, a tortured soul would sell the world," Bishop said. "We would be unable to believe their words as truth, and isn't that why we are here, to learn the truth?"

Paul growled. "Fine. Yes, fine. Go on, ask your questions." He walked around the chair and raised the bloody leather strap to Locke's face. "I can wait." He walked over to a bunk bed, and sat down.

"My name is John Bishop," the man said. "This is Ms Frost."

Ms Frost was around forty-five, her hair done up in a tight bun, but with the same madness in her eyes that were in those of the man.

"Water?" Locke croaked.

"Ms Frost?" Bishop said.

A bottle was held to Locke's lips. This time it *was* water. "Sean?"

The woman walked behind her. There was a short gasp of pain as Sean drank.

"What's going on?" Locke asked. "Where are we?"

"*I* will ask the questions," Bishop said. "The answers will illuminate the past, thus bringing light to our future. In that you are an instrument of divine intervention, a gift. The question is who gave you to us? Did you come from above, or from below? You will be judged upon what you say. Yet even if you were sent to us by that tormenting demon, your confession can save your soul, your salvation can become a beacon from which a new world will arise."

"You want us to confess?" Locke asked. "Confess to what?"

"Speak, let your words be recorded in the ledger, then they will be weighed against your deeds," Bishop said.

"And then you'll let us go?" she asked.

"Indeed," Bishop said. He glanced at Paul. "It is not us who will punish. It is not us who will judge. It is not us who will kill. That is left to a higher power. No, you shall be released, but your words shall determine the manner of your release, your honesty shall dictate your survival in this life and the next."

Locke was still no clearer on what their fate would be, but she now knew what would happen if she stayed silent. Their only hope, their only *real* hope, was in buying some time, and doing it without Sean's blood.

"Fine. I'll talk," she said. "I'll tell you about Elysium." So she talked. She talked about the redoubt in the southwestern corner of Ireland, though without mentioning any specifics of where it was. She talked about Quigley and the soldiers he'd sent, though not about when she had first met the politician. She talked of the people who were there, and how they had died, but without mentioning their names. As she spoke, Ms Frost scrawled note after note into her ledger.

"That's useless to us," Paul said, finally growing irritated. "We don't care about that."

"We care about the truth," Bishop said. "The whole truth. We agreed to let you assist, Paul, but do not forget who is really in charge. Go on, Miss Locke."

"Stick to what happened before the outbreak," Paul said. "Where're the warehouses?"

Locke began talking again, this time beginning with when she was first hired. She told them about when she first met Sean, when she first met Lisa Kempton. She dragged out every little detail until Paul grew bored again.

"This is pointless," Paul said. "She's stalling."

"The truth can not be rushed," Bishop said. "But it *is* late. We shall reconvene in the morning." He leaned forward. "And then we shall test you on what you have told us. We shall test your memory. If it is found wanting, even in one word, you shall regret it." He opened the door, and left. Ms Frost followed.

Paul lingered for a moment, then picked up his bag. "You can't get the help," he said. "You really can't." He leaned forward and took the gold and blue scarf from around Locke's neck. "I think I know someone who'd like this, but she wouldn't like it so much if it was covered in blood. I'll be back in five hours, and then it's your turn. I'll leave the light. Don't want you to get too much sleep."

"Sean?" Locke asked, after Paul had left.

Sean grunted in pain and anger. "Fine," he mumbled. "I'm fine."

"We're getting out of here," Locke said. "We're getting out, and getting away. We're going to leave this benighted corner of the world and never return."

Sean grunted again.

Locke braced her feet on the floor, rocked forward, pulling her feet out and her hands up. As Paul had beaten Sean, and as her friend had rocked back and forth in the chair, the ropes had remained taut, but the arm of the chair had loosened. She strained, pulled, stretched. There was a sharp creak of wood, but not a crack.

"Sean, lean forward," Locke said. "Lean forward with all your weight."

He did. She leaned back. The bolts pinning the chair to the floor creaked. She rocked forward as she pulled her arms up. The chair's right arm cracked, coming free from the support.

"Good job, Sean," she said, sliding wrist and rope off the chair's arm. "Sean?"

A moment later she had her other hand free, and then her feet. As she stood, the two chairs, now unbalanced, toppled over.

"Sean?" She hurried to him. His face was a bloody mess. His eyes half closed. His lip split and bleeding. "Sean?"

"I'm fine," he groaned. She undid the ropes, and went to the door, regretting not having checked for a sentinel-jailor before untying Sean. No one had come in when the chairs had fallen, and she could hear nothing outside but the soft chirrup of a grasshopper. Cautiously, she tried the handle. The door was unlocked. She opened it an inch. There was no one there.

"Sloppy," she murmured. "There's no guard." Sean groaned again as he pushed himself to his knees. Locke took the water bottle from by the sink where the middle-aged woman had left it. "Drink," she said. "Drink. That's it. Okay, listen, you've got two minutes, then we're leaving."

She opened the cupboards under the sink, then the ones attached to the wall. The cupboards were empty. The pipes were plastic.

"I think Rachel was telling the truth about needing help," she said. "I don't think there are many people she can call on. Paul, and these… I don't know who or what that Bishop guy was."

"Religious," Sean muttered.

"It's not any religion I know," Locke said. "He's not a diligent jailor, and nor is Paul. There's nothing we can use as a weapon. It doesn't matter. We're not going to fight. We're going to run, okay? We'll keep going in a straight line until we get to a road. We'll follow it back to the town, get to our boat, and we'll get out of here. Okay, Sean, it's time to go." She helped him to his feet.

"I'm fine," he said. "I'm fine."

"You're not," she said, "but you will be as soon as we get away from Anglesey. First we have to get away from Paul and Bishop."

Outside were steps leading down to overgrown grass. There was a familiar scent in the air. It wasn't the smell of fish, or unwashed bodies, or cooking fires fuelled by varnished furniture. It was something else, something with which she'd grown familiar during the weeks in Ireland. It was the smell of decay.

Immediately in front of them, about two hundred metres distant, were lights. She counted five, but they were the only illumination except for the stars and moon.

"This way," she whispered, helping Sean away from the lights. At any moment, she expected a shout. With every footfall, she expected a shot. With every breath, she expected it to be her last. They staggered on.

They'd had training, but not for this. Lisa Kempton had organised survival courses, firearms practice, and self-defence exercises. They'd had classes in navigation, vehicle repair, plumbing, wiring, cooking, and farming. They'd learned how to turn the land into something they could live off, but they'd not prepared for torture. Even so, Locke was surprised there wasn't a guard. It confirmed her earlier suspicion, that Rachel really couldn't find the help. That amused her, but she knew the smile that wanted to turn into a laugh was born of hysteria.

Behind the cabin were dozens of others. She picked a route that kept the blocky chalets between themselves and the house. Get away, she thought, they just had to get away.

The cabins ended in a scraggly hedge on the other side of which were caravans. They were in a campsite. She kept going, avoiding the path, until she found a line of razor wire between two caravans.

"I can't see how it's attached," she said.

"Then leave me behind," Sean said. "Go on. Go and get help."

"No," Locke said. Memories of Elysium came back to her, of the deaths of all those she'd recruited. "I'm not leaving anyone behind, not again. Never again." The razor wire was justly named, but it wasn't deep. "I'll be a minute."

She left Sean leaning against the caravan's side and went to the nearest door. It was unlocked. She grabbed the mattress from the first bunk she saw. Outside, she laid the mattress on top of the wire. "After you," she said, and helped Sean over. She followed, but paused on the other side, staring into the dark campsite. No alarm had sounded, and no pursuit had begun. Hardly believing their luck, they slipped into the night.

"We're heading east," she said after twenty minutes, finally deciding they were far enough from the campsite that she could risk talking normally.

"Are you sure?" Sean asked, he sounded better. Though she walked beside him, he no longer needed help staying upright.

"Do you remember the celestial navigation course Lisa took us on?" she asked.

"I remember being taken out to the desert for what was meant to be a meteor-shower party," he said.

"We're heading east," she said. "I'm certain to within sixty degrees."

"That's the wrong way. Our boat's near Holyhead, so we want to go west."

"Right now, I want to get away," she said. "At best, we've got until dawn. When they find we're gone, they'll go to our boat, if they haven't gone there already. It's what I would have done. Move the boat in case people ask where we've gone. It's not like Rachel would have been aware we *didn't* know our neighbours. But if they have already moved the boat, they didn't find the weapons hidden in the hold. Someone like Paul would have carried one to taunt us as well as to intimidate Bishop."

"Small mercies, right?" Sean said. "So if we've lost our boat, what's the plan?"

"I'm working on it," Locke said and she still was when they came to an old stone bridge over a small stream. They climbed down, and drank water out of cupped hands.

"Now I'm starting to feel more alive," Sean said. "Do we have a plan?"

"We *could* go to the authorities, such as they are," Locke said, "but between Bishop, Rachel, and those mercenaries in her pub, there *would* be a fight. People would die, and I couldn't guarantee we won't be among them. At the end of it, we would be asked the same questions that Paul was asking. I don't think they'd use the same methods, but nor do I think they'd let us escape so easily."

"Is there any alternative?" he asked.

"Yes. We could take one of their fishing trawlers with as much diesel as we have time to grab."

"What about the submarine?"

"We'll take our chances," she said.

"And go where? Portugal?"

"No," she said. "We have to assume they faced the same fate as Elysium. We'll do what we should have done months ago. We'll return to the Shannon Estuary, and to *The New World*. We'll cross the Atlantic."

"What if Captain Keynes has gone?" Sean asked.

"We'll manage," she said. "We'll find a way. Remember Leif Erikson. We'll take our boat north to Greenland, and then to Newfoundland. We'll hug the coast until it's time to head inland." Even as she said it, she knew how desperate it sounded, but these were desperate times.

"Good enough." Sean straightened and stretched. "Then if we're going, let's get gone. I'm ready. Do you think the ranch will still be there?"

"Oh, it'll be there," she said. "The question is whether anyone else is."

They climbed up the bank, and back onto the road. Memories of her first visit to the United States came back to her. Except for a school trip to London, that was her first time overseas. It had been three months after she'd started working for Lisa Kempton's company. Some papers had to be taken from Dublin to Chicago, and they were too valuable to be entrusted to a courier. Her boss had given the task to her. That trip was the first time she'd met Lisa Kempton and Tamika Keynes, and it was the first time anyone had shot at her.

She'd delivered the papers, and been told to wait. Kempton was in the building and came to speak to her. It transpired that the papers were highly confidential, containing a list of dozens of properties that the billionaire had purchased. They were meant to be delivered by Locke's supervisor in person. The man had tickets for a cup final he didn't want to miss. For palming the chore off on a junior employee, he was fired, and Locke was put up in a luxury suite in a five-star hotel. Years later, she learned that the room was bugged and that she was being kept under observation in case she tried to tell anyone what was in those papers. It hadn't mattered. She'd not looked at the documents, nor had she called anyone except her mother, and only to brag about the splendours of the room.

The next day, she'd joined Kempton and her bodyguard, Tamika Keynes, on a tour of a construction site. That was when they'd been shot at. Locke's instinct was to push Kempton to the ground, covering her with

91

her body while Keynes returned fire. The assailant had died. There was no report of the incident on the news, and Locke never learned what happened to their attacker. She didn't ask, and she didn't dig.

Five years later, Locke walked into a meeting room and found the assailant sitting next to Kempton. The whole incident had been staged. It was an exercise in trust and she had passed. The fake attacker was Sean O'Brian, and he'd been appointed as Locke's number-two. Their friendship had grown, and together they had joined Kempton's inner circle. Together, they'd learned of project Prometheus, and of Archangel, the super-vaccine. Together they had learned of Kempton's own plans to use both to change the world.

She shook her head. Now wasn't the time. They were far enough east of the campsite that it was time to head for the coast.

"We'll take the next turning we come to," she said. "Maybe look for some bicycles if we find an empty house."

"We're more likely to find them in an occupied one," Sean said. He sniffed. "Can't smell any wood smoke, but surely someone lives around here?"

Ahead was a stalled coach. The windows were broken. The wheels on the right-hand-side were buried in a ditch. The coach looked as if it was about to topple over.

"If they don't move that coach," Sean said, "the ditch will fill, the road will flood, and it'll be washed away. Pity. I—"

"Shh!" There was a rustle from inside. "Foxes?"

Sean shook his head. He mouthed something that Locke couldn't quite make out, but she could guess. Someone was living in the coach. Perhaps it was just another survivor, someone who couldn't face living in a house after all that had happened to them. More likely it was one of Bishop's people. She wasn't confident in her navigation, nor in how straight the road was. They might have simply been walking in a wide loop around the campsite. The coach might well be a sentry post.

Sean had reached the same conclusion. He braced a foot on the up-jutting tyre, and hoisted himself onto the tilted coach. The vehicle rocked with the sudden addition of extra weight. There was a rustle and then a bang from inside, but there wasn't a voice. There wasn't a shout. There was a rasp, a hiss, and before Locke could call out, a figure lurched through the window. Its hand clawed out, catching Sean's shoulder. Its mouth snapped down, once on his face and again on his neck. Warm blood arced out, spraying Locke.

"No!" she screamed. She grabbed Sean, pulling him free. "Sean? Sean!" But he was already dead.

The zombie flopped onto the road and began thrashing to its feet. Locke kicked its legs from under it, and stamped on its hand, its forearm, its knee. Bone broke, sockets popped. She slammed her foot into its jaw, kicking it down to the ground, and then brought her heel onto its skull. The creature died, but she felt no better. Sean was dead. There were people she'd known for longer, but none she'd held so dear.

She walked away from the coach, following the road, her mind lost in memories of past happiness. It was only when she came to a road sign that she stopped.

"Anglesey, fourteen miles."

She wasn't on the island. She was on the Welsh mainland.

Chapter 10 - The Warehouse
Birmingham, 14th May, Day 64

Sorcha Locke stabbed the improvised spear forward as the zombie staggered across the courtyard. The butcher's blade plunged into the creature's eye socket, but the cord tying it to the broom-handle broke. She let go, backed up a step, and pulled the hammer from her belt, waiting for the rest of the undead to come outside.

It was four days since Sean had died. Four days of walking, cycling, running, and hiding from the undead. Many times she'd thought of giving up, but she'd finally reached Birmingham only to discover it was worse than anywhere she'd seen in Ireland, and far worse than her worst expectations.

A zombie in a firefighter's jacket staggered out of the door, tripped on the steps, and tumbled down to the dusty concrete loading bay. Locke jumped forward, swinging the hammer before the creature could stand. Its skull cracked, the zombie went limp. Again Locke skipped back, this time shaking the hammer to loosen the wad of scalp caught in the sharpened claw. There had been five zombies immediately inside the door, crouched on their haunches as if they'd been waiting for her. Two were now dead, but the third staggered outside, with the last pair of the creatures immediately behind it. The lead zombie wore a bobble-hat, a scarf, and a quilt jacket too warm for anything but the early days of the outbreak. The last two were more recently alive, wearing thin trousers and thinner shirts, with faces less desiccated, gums less receded. Even so, Locke was sure she didn't recognise them. That begged the question of why they had come to the warehouse, but the answer would have to wait until they were dead.

She thought they'd trip on the stairs, but they didn't. The bobble-hatted creature stumbled, but managed to keep its feet. Locke swung wide, a great sweeping blow, but the hammer hit the zombie's arm. Bone broke, but the zombie kept moving, its snarling mouth kept snapping. Locke ducked under its grasping hand, and scythed her leg at its knee. The creature toppled, but the other two had staggered down the steps, managing to keep upright by bouncing off one another until they reached the flat expanse of the courtyard.

There was a rasp from near her feet as the bobble-hatted creature reached for her ankle. She stamped down, breaking its fingers, swung the hammer wide at the face of the nearest shirted-creature, then spun backwards, looking for a better weapon. There was none. Whoever these people had been, they must have left their gear inside.

She darted forward, swinging the hammer at the nearest creature's thigh. Its fingernails caught against her cheek. A bright-white heat surged across Locke's face. She turned her swing into a charge, barrelling the creature over. As it fell, it knocked the bobble-hatted zombie back to its knees, and that meant only one upright creature to fight. As that zombie lurched forward, Locke grabbed its arm, twisted and pulled it around. Bone snapped as she forced the zombie to its knees. She slammed her heel into its spine, and it sprawled to the ground. Hammer up, hammer down, and she split the creature's head. Locke pivoted, spun, putting her entire body into an extended-arm hack that brought the hammer into the skull of the bobble-hatted creature. The hammer's claw stuck. She let go, clutched her hands together, ducked low, and slammed them into the last zombie's knee. It fell. She stamped her foot onto its neck, and then its skull.

She breathed out, allowing herself one more short breath before she ripped the hammer free. She turned left, then right, then a full three hundred and sixty degrees, but the courtyard remained empty. It was over. She allowed herself to relax, but only fractionally. The immediate threat had been dealt with, but that didn't mean she was safe. From the way they were dressed, it was unlikely that the survivors the zombies had once been had arrived at the same time. There could be more inside. Even so, she would have to go in. She would have to search the building. She had no choice. There was nowhere else to go.

She walked back to the entrance. Dirt and leaves had gathered in the runners of the sliding gate. She had to fish them out before she could slide the gate properly closed. It squeaked after months of inattention, but the street beyond seemed free of the undead. It wouldn't remain that way for long, but she didn't need long, just long enough to get to the vault.

After Sean had died, after she'd discovered that she was on the Welsh mainland, miles from Anglesey, she'd realised that she couldn't return to the island. The bridges had been destroyed. She would be stranded on the coast until she could signal a fishing boat. By the time she returned to Anglesey, her own boat would be long gone. She could probably trust to the kindness of the island's authorities, but saw no point in taking the risk. Rachel had been right about one thing, there was no future on Anglesey. Everyone would leave there soon enough. Besides, returning to the island risked being killed by Rachel, Paul, or Bishop, because she was determined she wouldn't be caught again. No, Anglesey was doomed, though the people there didn't realise it yet. Locke had turned her face to the east, and kept walking.

At first, she had tried to reach Deeside, but there were too many undead and they had forced her to take a route more south than due east. As hunger grew and pickings in farmhouses remained scarce, she knew there was only one possible destination, Birmingham.

Locke had supervised the design of the warehouse, though not its actual construction. It was built in a U-shape with no outward-facing windows on the ground floor. Those on the upper level were small and thickly reinforced. Natural light came from the large windows on the interior that overlooked a courtyard that was, ostensibly, a loading bay. There was a rainwater recycling-system that, with a few hours work, could be turned into a filtration plant for the pump hidden in the cellar. That pump was the real source of water for the warehouse. It was attached to a highly illegal set of pipes that drew water directly from the Edgbaston Reservoir a few hundred metres to the west. To the north and south were construction sites, owned by Kempton, but on which nothing had yet been built. To the east was the old canal, acting as a breakwater against hordes of starving people coming from the city.

It *wasn't* one of the Claverton warehouses, stocked with fertilizer and other chemicals that would help a group of survivors hack a new life out of the barren earth. It was a backup to Lisa Kempton's backup, a final redoubt if every other plan failed. A last resort if the Russian intercepts were wrong or deliberately faked, and the cities weren't their target. If their retaliation for Prometheus was a destruction of the countryside and then an invasion, and if the only chance of survival was in the urban centres, then they had the warehouse in Birmingham. It wouldn't be a place to rally survivors to their cause, nor was it a place from which they would rebuild. It was simply a place to hide. Except the world hadn't ended in nuclear fire or invasion, but with tearing, rending, infected teeth.

Many buildings on the city's outskirts were bomb-damaged. Others had been burned down. More still had been broken into and looted. There had been no evidence of living survivors before she'd reached the warehouse, but she'd only been through the very western edge of the sprawling city. The thin clothes of the zombies she'd just killed suggested there had been survivors alive in Birmingham recently. That was reassuring. Her dread on seeing the shattered buildings had been that the city was radioactive. That the zombies had been recently alive suggested otherwise, but she wouldn't relax until she had a Geiger counter in her hands. That device was in the vault, and that vault was hidden below the cellar. There was only one way into the complex from the road, and only one way into the warehouse from the loading bay, and only one way down to the vault from inside the building. She eyed the door, but still no more undead came out. She would have to go in.

Two hours later she was dripping with sweat, but that was only partly due to the frantic battle in the narrow confines of the stairwell. There had been two more zombies inside. Both had found the staircase that led to the basement, and it was there she'd fought them. The walls were too close, the ceiling too low to swing. By the flickering beam of her looted torch, she'd stabbed the hammer, and punched and kicked until the creatures were oozing corpses. She raised a hand to wipe the sweat from her brow, but stopped herself in time. She needed to wash. She needed to disinfect the cuts. She allowed herself a fraction of a smile as she took in the reading on the Geiger counter's screen. It was the first and only good news she'd had since Sean had returned to Belfast. The memory of his death returned her to sombre melancholy.

She shone the torch around the cavernous vault, searching for the shelves with the rechargeable lamps. The vault was the real reason for the warehouse. It had been built below the basement, and was far bigger than the building above. On the shelves were sealed boxes. Collectively, they contained enough supplies for ten people to last ten years. That was the theory, but based on a crude estimate of calorie intake, medical need, and a rough guess at how many people might make it to Birmingham. Close to the door, she found the lamps, and then searched for the medical gear.

By nightfall, she was bandaged, fed on rehydrated curry, carrying a silenced submachine gun, and watching the zombie that had appeared on the other side of the gate. She held her fire. She wanted to see how well the gate withstood its assault. The creature saw her. Its hands pawed against the metal. The gate shook, shuddered, and rattled as the creature pushed and clawed. She raised the gun, took aim, and fired a single shot. The creature fell. She ignored the corpse. The gate would have to be reinforced. That was her first job. The second was to look for more supplies. There wasn't as much in the warehouse as there should have been.

The vault was secured with three mechanical combination locks. She wasn't the only person who knew the code, but she didn't think someone had been here since the outbreak. The weapons were untouched, but most of the painkillers were missing. She was sure some of the food had been taken, but there would be time for a proper stock-take later. That it was the opioids that had been stolen suggested someone had skimmed them, and sold them on the black market. Someone who knew what the vault's purpose was, and knew that, if it were ever used, there would be no one left to hunt them down. It didn't matter. Locke was safe.

Another zombie staggered along the road towards the gate.

Relatively safe.

She raised the submachine gun and fired a shot. The bullet took the creature in the forehead. It fell.

She was safe for tonight, but tomorrow would *not* take care of itself.

Chapter 11 - Bookworms
Birmingham, 15th May, Day 65

Sorcha Locke sipped the instant coffee and imagined it was espresso, bit into the energy bar and imagined it was a croissant, stared at the empty courtyard and imagined she was at a cafe near the Seine with Sean. When her cup was empty, she put all thoughts of him to the back of her mind. He wouldn't be forgotten, nor would those who'd died at Elysium. No, she wouldn't forget, but this wasn't the time to remember them.

She brushed a crumb from the blue jumpsuit embossed with the logo of a golden wave. It was the same outerwear she'd found in Elysium. She remembered when Lisa Kempton had bought the company. Rather, she remembered being woken by a phone call from a business journalist wanting to know why Lisa had bought a company that specialised in clothing for endurance sports. The share price of their publicly traded arm had bounced back and forth during the day as the stock market reacted with suspicious speculation to Lisa's plans. The material was fire resistant, waterproof, and breathable, but could be cleaned with less water than traditional fabrics. It wasn't bite-proof, but that hadn't been a danger they'd considered.

Locke had spent the evening counting the remaining supplies. Aside from the medical supplies, most of the dried pasta and tins of sauce were missing. The crates in which they'd been stored were empty. That narrowed who had stolen it, and when, to three possible culprits. If she'd had access to the company records, a quick search would find which of them had a contact in a low-end trattoria. No records were stored in Birmingham and it didn't matter now. The thief clearly hadn't come to the warehouse since the outbreak and that spoke to their fate.

There was enough food for one person for between fifty and seventy-five years. As she was closer to fifty than forty, that meant more than she'd need in her apocalypse-foreshortened lifetime. Since it was unlikely that all the food would last that long, a better way of thinking about it was that it was far more than she could carry.

"So you know where you're going," she murmured, filling a small bag with spare magazines for the submachine gun. "The question is how you'll get there." She added a water bottle and bowie knife to her belt, a torch to the bag's strap though she had no intention of being outside after dark, and a small crowbar.

Her journey, her *real* journey, would begin at the coast. Precisely where would be determined by where she found a boat. She might find one due east in Felixstowe or Great Yarmouth, but if not, and since the south coast was a radioactive ruin, she might try London and the Thames. Either way, she would need a way of transporting supplies from the vault to the boat, and she'd need fuel for the ship's engine.

"Then you better start your search."

Before she left, she went down the vault, to make sure that the door was closed.

Locke moved slowly through the streets. Haste risked injury, and that meant death. She followed the canal north towards the City Hospital, ignoring the noisome tang of the scum-covered and corpse-filled water. When she came to the first bridge over the canal and found that it was in ruins, she detoured due west. The hospital was an obvious place for a survivor to loot, as was the prison. The zombies she'd found in the warehouse told her that there had been survivors in Birmingham, so she needed to find the places they wouldn't have thought to look.

Tudor Street, Winston Street, Dudley Road. She wasn't lost, not when the fractured tower blocks in the city centre gave her as good a bearing as her compass, but she hadn't seen the streets before. She'd overseen the purchase of the supplies, the land, the vault, and had ensured that there was no trail leading back to Lisa Kempton. They'd known that people were watching their movements, people who'd guessed at what they were doing. For that reason, though she'd designed the warehouse, she'd never visited it, or this part of the city.

Metal clattered from inside the broken windows of a barbershop. She raised the submachine gun and waited. The noise came again, a discordant rattle of a tray being knocked over. She peered into the gloomy interior and there, yes, she saw a figure. She held her fire until the zombie took another step into the light. One shot, and the creature collapsed. Locke's foot crunched on broken glass as she peered through the shattered window, but the zombie was alone. How and why it had ended up inside, she didn't know and didn't care. She kept moving.

In Belfast, she'd found fuel in the tanks of abandoned cars and used that to keep the bunker's generator running. There were plenty of cars parked outside the terraced cottages on the western side of the road, but syphoning petrol an inch at a time would be time-consuming work. She wanted a large haul, but she wasn't the first person to come looking for supplies in the city.

A zombie lay in the doorway to a small pharmacy. It was dead, but what struck her first was that the glass from the broken door lay on top of the creature. What struck her next was how fresh the wound in its head looked. The pharmacy shelves had been emptied, with a good portion of the stock left on the floor. She didn't go in to investigate what was missing, but kept going. Leaving Dudley Road, she headed north and west towards Smethwick. She stopped when she came to a fast-food chicken shop. There were two dead zombies just inside the doorway. Again, the wounds looked recent. The small restaurant had been thoroughly looted. Napkins and paper cups, everything in the small fridge, the soda-syrup from the fountain, the sauces, the vinegar, the box of salt sachets, everything had been taken. There was a smell of rot in the kitchen. Not of death, but a more natural decay that came from the sacks of pre-packaged pre-spiced breadcrumb coating. The contents had turned a near-luminous shade of green.

"Makes you wonder what kind of spices they used," she said, "but it gives me a time frame. Whoever came here did so long after the evacuation."

That gave her pause. Taken with the body in the pharmacy, and the undead in the warehouse, she could narrow it down to within the last month. In which case, were there people still in Birmingham? And if there were, what should she do?

"Be cautious," she said, and left the shop.

A throaty rasp came from down the street. A zombie staggered out of a side road. Perhaps it had heard her approach, and it had certainly seen her. It let out another gasp and lurched an awkward step towards her. It was oddly clad in ski boots and shin pads, a wicketkeeper's jerkin, and an archer's wrist guards. Around its neck was a tight leather stock, and on its head was a catcher's face-guard. That improvised armour hadn't saved it from infection. She fired. The zombie fell, and Locke counted to five, listening. All she heard was a distant cawing of a bird. A raven? She remembered O'Reardon and her talk of ancient Celtic gods. Locke shook her head, dismissing the dangerous thought that would only lead to memories of Sean.

It was two hours since she'd left the warehouse, and she had little to show for it. She decided to head east, find a way across the canal, and then head for the railway. Someone who'd looted shops might not have thought to syphon the fuel from a diesel locomotive.

She was on the verge of turning back when she heard it. An arrhythmic drumbeat of flesh against metal came from the far side of an acre of rubble. Locke picked her way through the debris, narrowing in on the sound. Beyond a small car park was the rear entrance to a row of retail units. Above were flats. For students, judging by the outward-facing posters pinned to the window. The sound came from the ground floor, not inside, but down a narrow alley blocked with bollards and a sign warning against skateboarding and cycling. Halfway along the alley was a metal fire door. Two zombies were beating their fists against it. Locke raised the gun. She fired. Once. Twice.

There was silence in the city again, except for the raven. Locke thought it was following her. Then she turned her attention to the door. There was no handle on this side, just a small sign warning that it was alarmed.

She heard something else, movement behind the door. Another zombie. That had been what had caused the two outside to pound on it. She'd seen that before in Belfast. One zombie mistook an unseen other for the living, each then beat their flesh to pulp in a futile attempt to reach the illusory prey. She was tempted to walk away, to leave the creature trapped in there. The raven cawed.

The memory of O'Reardon came back to her. Like many, the outbreak had changed the woman. Where Jasmine Cotter had turned violent and psychopathic, Phyllis O'Reardon had become obsessed with old legends. She'd refused to believe that the undead would ever die. It was kill until you were, in turn, killed. Their purgatorial existence served no purpose but to relieve the suffering of the living dead, and so relieve one's own suffering. Locke fundamentally disagreed, but solitude was making her superstitious. The door was solid. She wasn't going to force it. She'd have to find another way in, or leave the trapped zombie alone.

The raven cawed again.

"All right, Phyllis," she said. "I get the point."

"Hello?" For a moment, Locke thought it was the raven that had replied, but the voice came from inside the building.

"Hello?" Locke said. "Is there someone in there?"

"Yes." It was a woman, a Birmingham local from the accent. "Just me. I came in here trying to lose them, but the corridor's blocked with rubble, and I can't open the door. You're from Ireland?"

"I was," Locke said, peering at the door again.

"I mean... I meant... you're not one of us. I meant I thought someone would come looking for me, but you're a stranger. I..."

"There are others of you in the city?" Locke asked.

"There are," the woman said. "Can you get the door open?"

"Give me a lever long enough," Locke said, taking the small crowbar out of her bag. She inserted it into the gap between brick and the door's lip. She pushed. The door moved, but only a fraction of an inch. "But this lever isn't long enough. Give me a minute."

She hammered at the mortar surrounding the hinges, pausing every fifth blow to listen. Five hits. Listen. Five hits, listen. She heard them. Zombies. She swung around, dropping the crowbar as she grabbed the slung submachine gun. She took aim, fired, and bent to pick up the crowbar before the two creatures had collapsed. The mortar was loose. She levered, pushed, hammered, and pulled until she heard the hinge straining, the brick cracking. With one final effort, the lock broke. The door swung open.

Locke sensed the movement behind her, and pivoted around. The woman had dived out of the doorway, a homemade spear in her hands. The point stuck into flesh, but not Locke's. A zombie had been in the alley behind her. She'd not noticed, not realised. It would have got her. It would have killed her. The woman twisted the spear deeper into the creature's face. It sagged to the ground, pulling the spear with it.

"Thank you," Locke said.

"No, thank you," the woman said. "Isabella Garcia."

"Sorcha Locke."

"You're really from Ireland?"

"For the most part," Locke said.

"I meant recently?"

"I… yes," Locke said, opting for a lie that was close to the truth. "I came over by boat. I didn't plan to come to England, but ended up here anyway. What about you?"

"I grew up here," Isabella said. "It was our home. Our family have been here for generations. Birmingham won't fall while an Isabella Garcia calls it home. Let me take you back, the others will be glad to meet you."

"There are more of you?" Locke asked.

"At the library," she said. "Words are heavier than water, at least when printed on a page. We have the terraces for planting, and we'd made a start on the City Centre Gardens until the zombies came. They destroyed most of what we'd sown."

"They always come, don't they," Locke said. As if in punctuation, a zombie staggered into the alley's mouth. Locke raised her gun. "The undead always come."

And they had come to the library.

The two women crouched behind a collapsed tree in Birmingham's City Centre Gardens. In front of them was the library. Locke had been expecting redbrick and granite but it was made of glass and steel, four massive rectangles of different widths, stacked one on top of the other, with the upper level overhanging the ground floor. She couldn't decide if it was meant to be a wedding cake or a ship.

"That's the way in?" Locke asked.

"No," Isabella said. "That was our way out."

A thin plume of smoke rose from the roof of the glass and metal structure. The ground floor was plate glass, covered on the inside, with crude concrete and metal barriers outside keeping the undead away. There were no barriers by the loading bay. Locke counted twenty zombies outside, and at least that many shadows inside the loading bay. She turned away, and surveyed the nearby buildings. "There, that car park," she said. "The top floor will have a clear line of fire."

The car park was dark, musty, and almost empty. There were half a dozen cars on the ground floor, twelve on the first-floor, but only one on the upper level. The fuel caps had been removed from all of them.

From the top floor, Locke had a clear view of the library and the road, but only a slim section of the loading bay. "Could be better," she said, propping the submachine gun's barrel on the car-park wall. "Could be worse." She fired. A zombie fell. Out of the corner of her eye, she saw movement. Isabella was waving her arms.

"What are you doing?"

"Trying to get their attention," Isabella said.

"The zombies?"

"No, Gavin and the others."

"Don't," Locke said. "I don't want them coming down. I want the zombies to come outside." Locke fired. Paused. Waited. "They're moving too much. We have to wait. How many are you?"

"Inside? Eight, I hope," Isabella said. "There were more, but we lose a few each month."

"I know that story," Locke said.

"Not all died," Isabella said. "Some just left."

"To go where?" Locke asked.

"That's why we didn't go with them," Isabella said. "They set off with no destination in mind, just with the hope that somewhere was better than here."

Locke fired. "You didn't go on the evacuation?"

"You heard about that in Ireland?" Isabella asked.

Locke had asked the wrong question. To give herself time to think, she fired a hasty shot. The bullet slammed into a zombie's thigh. By the way it fell over, the bullet had broken bone. "Yes, I heard about the evacuation. Not in Ireland, but after I got here. You didn't go?"

"No," Isabella said. "It didn't seem safe. I thought we'd wait, go to an enclave a few weeks later. Then I heard what happened. I made the right choice."

Locke fired. Waited. Waited. She fired. Finally, some of the undead turned away from the building and towards the sound of the falling corpse.

"Watch the ramp," Locke said. "There's always been an Isabella Garcia in Birmingham?"

"For the last eighty years," Isabella said. "My brothers were Hemmings. It's only the oldest daughter who gets the name. My great-grandparents met during the Spanish Civil War. The eldest daughter is named Isabella Garcia after my great-great-grandmother. It's a tradition."

"Ah." Locke aimed and fired. She was taking her time, more time than she needed because she had a decision to make. Birmingham was occupied, but who were these people, and were they like those on Anglesey, or could she trust them? Could she use them? From the open fuel caps, she guessed they'd looted petrol. If they'd stored it, could she trade for it? Or would she have to keep the warehouse a secret, and in which case, what next?

She aimed, fired, aimed, and fired. The undead came out of the loading bay and into the road, and she kept up a steady barrage, killing one after another until there were no more.

"Is it okay if I wave now," Isabella said. "Because they're waving at us."

Locke looked up. From the green branches, she guessed that was the rooftop terrace, and there were people there, waving at them.

Locke slotted a fresh magazine into place. "Let's see if we got them all."

They hadn't.

As Locke stepped around a corpse at the entrance to the loading bay, she heard something slithering along the ground to her right. She raised the submachine gun. She pulled the trigger, but the weapon jammed. She stepped back, let the gun fall to its sling, and drew the bowie knife. Isabella lunged forward with her improvised spear, stabbing it through the creature's brain.

Above, a door creaked open. A man ran out, spear in hand.

"Isabella?"

"Hi, Gavin, sorry I took so long. This is Sorcha."

There *were* eight people inside the library, but only if you counted the baby. Isabella took the infant from the arm of a woman who was at least sixty.

"Sorcha," Isabella said. "Let me introduce Isabella."

"Your daughter? How old is she?"

"My daughter, Isabella, is four months," Isabella said.

Locke did the maths. She was a little uncertain of the exact date but thought it was sometime in mid May. That placed the birth in February.

"She was born before the outbreak?" Locke asked.

"Three days before," Isabella said. "And let me introduce my mother." She took the hand of the older woman. "This is Isabella."

Sorcha gave the smile that she'd practiced on princes and presidents. "Three generations of the same family? That's something. And who's everyone else?"

Dusk was falling, and Locke had found an empty chair among the spindly branches of the roof terrace. Among the profusion of green leaves, and vibrant flowers, she saw few plants that would produce food. The shade was welcome, as was the more floral scent which almost masked that of the city below. There was no hiding from the evidence of her eyes. The city was a ruin. A few tower blocks still stood, and though she didn't know how many had dotted Birmingham's skyline at Christmas, she could see the wreck of three large buildings. No, there was no hiding from it, but, for today, for now, for this moment, she could tell herself that it didn't matter.

Aside from the three Isabellas, there were Phoebe and Damien, two ten year olds. Hazel was twelve and far more timid, having said barely a word to Locke during the day, and that word had been muttered and indistinct. The other three were adults, Gavin, Micah, and Talya. All had lived in Birmingham before the outbreak, though Talya had either been a recent arrival or had spent some time away before returning. Locke hadn't picked up the fine details and they didn't matter. What did was that none of them had been soldiers. They had little experience in survival, for that matter. What they knew came from the library, and if what she could see was anything to go by, they'd been reading the wrong books.

In the raised bed to her left were the familiar wide leaves of a banana plant. In the British climate, outside of a greenhouse, that would never be anything more than decorative. Without constant tending, soon it wouldn't even be that. She told herself that, perhaps, she was being unfair. They had survived until now, and with a newborn, which was a greater feat than most had managed.

There were footsteps behind. She turned, and saw the older Isabella.

"I wanted to thank you for saving my daughter, and my granddaughter," the older Isabella said. "Do you mind if I sit? I'm not disturbing you, am I?"

"No, not at all," Sorcha said. "I was just remembering the last time I was here. It was a meeting in a hotel that I think is that pile of rubble over there."

"I don't know why they bombed Birmingham," Isabella said. "I don't know who did it. I suppose they were trying to get rid of the monsters, though it clearly didn't work."

"It was a global civil war," Locke said. "When orders were given to launch pre-emptive and retaliatory attacks, some commanders and generals disobeyed. Not all did, but many followed their conscience."

"That's how the world died? By accident?"

"It was already doomed," Locke said.

"How do you know?" Isabella asked.

The lie came easily. "I met an American sea captain," Locke said. "She'd sailed her boat across the Atlantic. She heard it all on the ship's radio."

"Ah. So America is gone, too? We were hoping that enough of them had survived that they might come to our aid. We supposed they might go to London first, but Birmingham would have been second."

"The whole world is like this," Locke said. "Not quite like this," she added. "I came through Belfast, and that had suffered some damage around the harbour, but most of the city was intact."

"What about the people?"

"I saw few," Locke said, "and fewer that can be trusted."

"We were a law-abiding people, weren't we?" Isabella said. "I always marvelled at how the presence of laws kept the peace more than the presence of police officers. I always worried what would happen when the laws could no longer be abided. We had our own troubles here a few months ago."

"Oh? What kind?"

"The kind that ended in blood," Isabella said. "That's the past. We must look to the future. Why did you come to Birmingham? I don't mean to pry, but were you looking for someone?"

Locke turned her head away, pretending to be lost in a memory. She decided that the truth, or a version of it, was the best policy. "Two of us escaped from Belfast," she said. "There were so many more at the beginning of all of this, but only two of us made it out alive, and only just. We managed to get to Anglesey, and we found people there. Hundreds of them. I wouldn't call them an organised group, but a collection of different factions, one of which captured us. They tortured Sean. We escaped, but he died in the attempt. I kept walking until I came here."

"Anglesey?"

"I wouldn't go back there," Locke said. "I wouldn't go to Ireland, either. There's nothing there." She thought of the ship, *The New World*. That *might* still be in the Shannon Estuary, and it might represent a way to get far away from Europe, but that was a lot of uncertainty on which to hang one's life.

"You're here now," Isabella said. "You're safe today. We'll worry about tomorrow when it comes. Thank you." She patted Locke's arm, stood, and walked away.

Locke returned her gaze to the skyline. These people would have to do. She had little choice. Her final destination was set, but whether she went via Portugal, or the Shannon Estuary, or due north, she would need help getting supplies to the coast. It would take weeks, and weeks more to find fuel and a boat. These people might well be the only help she'd ever find. Perhaps. It was too early to say.

Chapter 12 - The Vault
Birmingham, 12th August, Day 153

"You've been keeping this from us for three months?" Gavin asked, staring in wonder at the shelves in the vault.

"I needed to know I could trust you," Sorcha said. "After what happened to Sean, after what happened in Belfast, I needed to know that you weren't going to do the same."

"This is where you've been getting all the supplies you've been bringing back?" the younger Isabella asked.

"It is," Locke said.

"Then you cheated," Phoebe said.

"Yeah, the bet's off," Damien said.

There had been a running competition to see who could collect the most, best supplies. They hadn't defined what 'best' was, nor had they decided on a prize. Where others would return with a few tins and an occasional jar, Locke would bring back a bag filled with rations, and her pockets full of loaded magazines. The subterfuge had been difficult to keep up, and Locke had finally decided to abandon it after Phoebe had sneaked out and followed her halfway to the warehouse.

"So how did you get all this stuff?" Gavin asked.

"My employer was a prepper," Locke said. "She thought the apocalypse was actually going to happen."

"So she built this?" the younger Isabella asked. "If you told me that a year ago, I'd have said you were crazy. Actually…" She picked up an oiled submachine gun. "Actually, I'd have said that it made an awful lot of sense, and that you were both very wise people, and then, as soon as I could, I'd have run out of here screaming for the police."

"How much is there?" Gavin asked.

"Enough for about five years," Locke said. "Give or take."

"Any formula?" Isabella asked.

"Sorry," Locke said. "This wasn't a place for people to rebuild or repopulate, it was a place to hide, to survive, to wait. Keeping a child alive wasn't…" She frowned, and decided against the truth. "I suppose we didn't think any children would end up here."

"I suppose your boss didn't really think the world was going to end," Gavin said. "I mean, who would? But Bella seems to like that vitamin powder stuff."

"It's not as good as formula," Isabella said. "But we won't find any more of *that*. We'll make do, we'll have to, and that means our time frame hasn't changed."

Locke nodded. That was another reason for telling them about the warehouse, and the reason she hadn't told them until now. Isabella couldn't breastfeed. The looted pharmacy that Locke had seen on her first day in Birmingham was evidence of their search for formula. With the addition of her silenced submachine gun and its seemingly endless supply of bullets, they had searched the rest of the city, but found most pharmacies looted or their remaining stocks contaminated by mould and decay.

"There's powdered potato, and powdered milk," Locke said, "and she seemed to like the re-hydrated vegetable soup that we pureed."

"I'm not sure it liked her," Isabella said. "No, but this is good. It takes the pressure off."

"It does, doesn't it," Gavin said, visibly relaxing.

"Is there any ice cream?" Damien asked.

"No, I'm sorry," Locke said. "It's only canned, freeze-dried, and dehydrated foods."

"What about chocolate?" Phoebe asked.

"There, I think you might be in luck," Locke said. "There are some chocolate chip energy bars somewhere."

"Cool," Damien said. "Hazel will like that.

"She doesn't like anything," Phoebe said.

"At the end of the aisle," Locke said, handing the children a lantern. "It's a green box. Don't touch any blue, white, or red boxes. Okay?"

"A green box. Got it," Damien said. The two children hurried off in search of chocolate.

"So why are you *really* telling us now?" Isabella asked. "There's something else, isn't there?"

"It's the generator you found," Locke said. "I know you want to turn it on, but we can't waste the diesel. The petrol is a different matter, but I'd rather not use it yet, either. There is enough food here for about five years. Spoilage is a risk, and I'd say the margin of error is two years either way, but my bigger concern are the buildings. There are too many ruins on the verge of collapse. The canal has been breached in too many places. The roads that aren't flooded now soon will be. We need to think of the future, and it won't be in Birmingham."

"Do you have a place in mind?" Gavin asked. "Not Ireland?"

"And not Anglesey," Isabella said. "Not after what you told us about them."

"No, not Anglesey, and that's another reason to leave," Locke said. "We're too close to them here. In Ireland, we had a farm. It was built by my employer, and was another refuge in case the world came to an end, though they ran it as a working farm. That's where I was. We had wind turbines and solar panels, and high walls. They weren't high enough. The farm was overrun, but it wasn't the only redoubt. There are others. The nearest is in Portugal, but there's a larger one in America."

"They might as well be on the moon," Gavin said.

"That's why we need the diesel," Locke said. "We can't waste it to keep the lights on. We'll need it for the boat."

"You know where there's a boat?" Isabella asked.

"No," Locke said, "but we'll find one. We'll find a boat, but not by looking around here. We need to go to the coast. These supplies give us time, but time creates a new problem. You saw what happened to the zombie two days ago?"

"You mean the one that was injured," Gavin said.

"I think it was dying," Locke said. "When the zombies die, the people on Anglesey, assuming there are any people left, will come back to Britain. The threat of the undead was the only thing holding that island together.

When Anglesey collapses, people will come here. When they do, we need to be gone. So, yes, these supplies give us time, but not as much as it might first appear."

"You want to go to Portugal?" Isabella asked.

"Possibly," Locke said. "We'd find more supplies there, and we might find people that we can trust. Reliable people. *My* people."

"Assuming they didn't die like all your people in Ireland," Gavin said.

"Which is why, ideally, we'd go to America," Locke said. "But our final destination will depend on what kind of boat we find, and as I say, we wont find one around here."

"So what *is* your plan?" Isabella asked, more firmly.

"We should go to the coast and look for a boat," Locke said. "A fishing trawler, perhaps. We'll take enough food for six months. If the craft can make an Atlantic crossing, then that's what we'll do, and we'll leave before the winter storms. If the boat can't make that distance, we'll head to Portugal. It would be a better place to spend the colder months than Britain."

"That's all well and good," Gavin said, "but precisely how do we get everyone, and all our gear, to the coast."

"By using the Grand Union Canal," Locke said. "We could use a barge, make three or four trips. It would be noisy, yes, and it would be slow, but it would be safer than a road, and less likely to be blocked by the undead or stalled traffic."

"If we can find a barge," Isabella said.

"I already did," Locke said. "Ten miles south of the city. We can take the canal down to London. Perhaps we'll find other barges that we can bring back here. Ultimately, we'll reach the Thames. We'll go through London and into the estuary. There, we'll find a ship."

"You hope," Gavin said.

"If we don't, we can search up and down the coast. The alternative is staying here and hoping no one comes from Anglesey. At best, we'd survive for four years, maybe five, possibly six, but I doubt it will be that long. The food will run out, and by then, any abandoned ship will have been dashed against the shore, the hull turned to rust, the rigging to rot.

There are risks in leaving, but the only certainty in staying is that of death."

There was a scampering of feet as the children returned, fists and mouths full of silver-foil wrapped energy bars.

"Found them," Phoebe mumbled through a full mouth.

"What do you think?" Locke asked.

Gavin looked to Isabella.

"Think about what?" Damien asked.

"I think," Isabella said slowly. "I think that we should go back to the library and find some maps that show where the canal joins the River Thames."

Part 4
Five Days

Eamonn Finnegan

London and Beyond
September & October

Chapter 13 - Departure
The Tower of London, 26th September, Day 198

The streets of London rang to the sound of ancient metal biting into undead flesh. Eamonn Finnegan dragged his axe free from the zombie's skull. He spun around, raising the weapon above his head. Fine droplets of dark brown gore sprayed from the blade, splattering the rotten clothing of his next foe. Its trousers were torn, its feet so caked in mud and grime that Eamonn couldn't tell if it still wore shoes, but somehow a pair of glasses were still perched on its necrotic head. He slammed the axe down onto its temple. Skin split, bone broke, and its glasses flew off. Eamonn wrenched the axe free as he looked for the next threat, but the fight was over. The zombies were all dead.

Behind him, Jay had climbed onto the roof of one of the coaches. They contained the fruit and vegetables they'd brought back from Kent. There had been too many undead in the streets near the Tower of London to drive the coaches up to the walls. Instead, they'd abandoned the vehicles a few hundred metres away. There hadn't been any pressure to collect the food immediately, but everything had changed in the time it took to pull a trigger.

Jay had organised the expedition to collect the food. Organised wasn't the right word, the teenager had said he was going and asked who'd come with him. Almost everyone had.

Jay waved the all-clear. Eamonn waved back, then spared one last second, trying to find Greta among the crowd hastily rushing to the buses. He couldn't see her, but if he spent any more time looking, he might never leave. Someone had to, and he couldn't allow anyone else to risk their life for him. Not now, not ever again. He turned his back on his newfound family, and vanished into the narrow streets of London.

His pack was light. He had water, weapons, and little else. He needed little else. It was about three hundred miles from London to Anglesey. Three hundred miles of farmland and cities, hills and rivers, zombies and ruins, but he had the maps Chester had created before he was shot. The annotation was a little odd, and it didn't contain a specific route so much as the best areas to travel through. With that as his guide, he would make it to Anglesey, but not on foot. His first task was to get out of central London, find a bicycle, and then find a railway line he could follow away from the city. It was still early, and he hoped he could make at least seventy miles before dark. He'd be beyond Birmingham tomorrow, and into Wales the day after. In four days, he'd be on Anglesey. Five if he was unlucky. *If* he could find a bike. *If* he didn't find the roads and railways filled with too many undead. *If* he could just get out of the maze that was London.

Cartwright, Royal Mint, Leman. He mentally noted each street, looking for one that was familiar. There was a sign for Aldgate East Tube, but he wanted to go west towards Liverpool Street Station. He spied an alley that was too narrow for a car. When he reached it, he found the undead clustered inside. They were standing rather than crouched in that sedentary squat they adopted when no prey was nearby, and they saw him. Arms clawed and thrashed as the creatures staggered out of the alley. For one brief moment, Eamonn thought of his family in the Tower, but fighting these zombies wouldn't save them. Their only salvation lay on Anglesey. He ran.

The towering offices cast deep shadows across the canyon-streets filled with leaves and litter, then steel and rubble next to a fire-ravaged hotel. The building beyond looked remarkably intact. He paused for the briefest of seconds, peering at the grimy windows, trying to discern what had lain inside. A fist slammed against the dust-smeared pane, then another, and a third, a fourth. A score of decaying hands and faces beat against the glass. Eamonn ran, and had made it ten yards before he heard the window break. He didn't turn around, but took one street, then the next, no longer sure where he was going except that it was away from the Tower.

He found a narrow alley, ran through, and found the street outside free of the undead. At the next junction was an upright map-board that displayed the location of nearby landmarks. He was already four hundred metres northeast of Liverpool Street, and close to Brick Lane. That was a familiar name, a place he'd heard of and promised to visit some day. Like so many others, that day had never come and now it was beyond too late.

He'd been running for half an hour, and his legs were beginning to twinge. He reached for the water bottle at his belt. There was a dull thump as a fist hit the glass window of a coffee shop on the other side of the street. The doors had been hastily barricaded with upturned tables and benches, but a figure had managed to squeeze between them and the glass. From the oozing stump on its left hand, the flap of skin hanging loose from its jaw, the rotting clothing barely concealing dried flesh, it was undead. Not long ago, it had been a survivor, just not one that Eamonn recognised. He left the creature there and the water un-drunk, and continued, though at a slower pace.

There wasn't time to fight, nor was their time to stop, not now, not today. Get out of London. Get to the Midlands. Get to Wales. Get help. Get back to the Tower, and then they could all leave. They could begin a new life. Him, Greta, and the children in a house in Wales. A large house, sure. A mansion. A castle. A farm. In three days, he'd be on the island. Four days at the outside. Five if he was unlucky.

He'd left a note for Greta. It hadn't said enough, but there wasn't enough paper in the world to say all that he'd wanted. Words were easy, actions were hard, but they were what mattered, and by his actions she would know how deeply he loved her. Hana, their vet turned doctor, was dead. Chester was unconscious. Realistically, he was dying. By now, he might well be dead. Both had been shot by Graham, the man who'd stolen their food and, in doing so, stamped a death sentence onto their community. It wasn't just a community, not really, though Eamonn hadn't realised it until it was almost too late. They were a family, and one that had doubled in size with the discovery of the group in Kent. Other than the man, Styles, the newcomers were all children, mostly from a remote boarding school. The children had brought their numbers close to a hundred, and they'd changed everything.

While Chester had gone back to the Tower for help, Eamonn and Greta had stayed in Kent. They'd helped the children bag the food from their small farm. Eamonn knew exactly how little there was, and how long it would last: not long enough. There was no more food in London or Kent. The children couldn't travel far or fast. Someone had to go for help, and if it couldn't be Chester, it had to be him.

His foot crunched on glass. There were ominous shadows beyond the gaping hole where the window should be. He returned to the middle of the road and picked up his pace. He reached a junction with a sign pointing to a dozen places. Hoxton Railway Station was at the bottom of that list. Again, he recognised the name, but couldn't place it in relation to the Tower, or to London's outskirts. There wasn't time to take out the maps because, outside a sushi bar, were two ragged zombies. As he raised the axe, a third stepped out of the restaurant. Then a fourth. There wasn't time. Eamonn turned and ran. It wasn't cowardice. Not this time.

The road curved, and he knew he was going the wrong way. There was another map-board at the next crossroads, but a zombie stood next to it. Eamonn had the axe held across his chest. It wasn't a firefighter's tool, but an ancient weapon, a steel war-axe from the Tower's collection. The weapon had been painstakingly restored with a new grip, new shaft, and, judging by how sharp it was, a new blade, but the sign in the museum had said it was a thousand years old, and that had given him comfort.

He swung the axe, cutting deep into the zombie's face. The blade sliced neatly through flesh and bone, and slammed into the map-board behind. The zombie fell, but the axe needed a tug before it was free. The cut and dent marred the map, but he could see where he was, Columbia Road.

"Second left. First right, keep on." Always keep on, and in four days he'd be in Anglesey. Five days at the most.

"It never ends," he muttered, taking the smallest sip from his water bottle. He'd been on the move for over two hours, was still in London, and was close to lost. He was heading away from the river, but no roads ran straight. When he found one that should lead him to a railway line, he'd also found the undead. He was out of central London, and somewhere near Highbury, though he wasn't sure if he was north of it, or south, or due east.

He'd thought he'd known London. In the last five years, he'd spent as much time in the city as he had in Frankfurt or Dublin, but knowing the names of bars and Tube stations wasn't the same as knowing the city.

"Find a bike, find a railway station," he murmured, eying the bridge behind the fire engine. It was definitely a rail bridge, but there was no station on this road. If he could find a way up to the bridge, he could follow the tracks. That would be quicker than navigating through the maze of alleys and roads.

The fire engine had been driven into the front of an office block, demolishing the ground floor. From the way the building sagged, resting on the roof of the cab, the vehicle had knocked down a supporting joist.

"Give it a year, and that building will collapse," Eamonn murmured, and he got a reply. It came from ahead, from behind the rear of the truck. He raised the axe and stepped closer to the fire engine, turning around so his back was against the vehicle. The sigh came again, this time accompanied by the rustle of cloth in what was almost an echo. It *was* an echo, and it came from above.

A zombie fell from the roof of the vehicle. Its arms caught in Eamonn's pack, tearing one strap completely free of his arm. He danced and spun, letting the pack fall as he swung the axe. The blade bit into flesh, neatly severing the zombie's arm. Then came the sound of the other creature, staggering around the side of the fire engine. It wasn't alone. There were three of them. Eamonn backed off a pace, then darted forward, hacking the axe low, aiming for its legs. That was a trick every survivor knew, aim for the legs, knock them to the ground, give yourself time to deal with the others. It worked. The lead zombie fell, but though it gave Eamonn time to plan his next move, it also gave time for more zombies to appear from around the side of the fire engine. Three, then four, then five. He backed off another pace. He needed the pack. The maps were inside. The zombie that had pulled it from his shoulder was standing up, and the others were getting closer.

Eamonn darted forward, risking a high swing aimed at the creature's exposed neck. The blade sunk deep into rotting flesh, and lodged in the zombie's spine. The zombie fell, taking Eamonn's axe with it. He took a step towards the weapon, but the other living dead were lurching closer. A ragged creature with tattered lips and a jagged scar running across its face swiped its arm at Eamonn's head. Its hand hit, just below his ear. Eamonn staggered back as the zombie stepped over the axe still embedded in its fallen comrade. He took another step back as he tried to draw the bayonet from his belt. It wouldn't come free. He took another step, and another, backing away as the zombies came forward. He spared a glance at his belt, saw the clasp on the knife's sheath, and finally remembered to unbutton it.

Sharpened eighty-year-old steel in his hand, he told himself not to panic. He glanced behind. The road was clear. As long as he didn't rush, he could manage this easily enough. He darted forward three steps, slicing the bayonet low, aiming for the lead creature's knee. The blade cut, and then it stuck, but Eamonn dragged it free as he spun and danced back up the road. Had that been his axe, he'd have knocked the creature down. As it was, the zombie wobbled on its leg as it took a lurching step, but then was pitched to the ground by the two creatures behind.

Don't panic, he told himself. He needed his axe, but he needed his pack more. He had to retrieve those maps. He backed away, leading the undead from the fire engine, forcing them to spread out. As long as he didn't panic, as long as he was patient, he could kill the undead and retrieve his gear.

Eamonn heard another sound. It came from the office block the fire engine was partially buried in. A thunderous creak as a girder collapsed. A crunch of metal as the frontage dropped onto the truck. A loud pop as the fire engine's partially deflated tyres blew. A louder crack as the joists gave way. A deafening roar as a cascade of bricks, dust, and mortar erupted from the collapsing building.

Coughing concrete, spitting dust, Eamonn staggered away, not stopping until he was back at the junction. He needed the bag. He needed those maps. Another few minutes, and he'd go back for it. As the dust began to settle, he realised he'd have to dig his gear free. As it settled more, he realised it wasn't entirely coming to rest on the ground. Ten feet away, a dust-covered figure staggered towards him, another two close behind.

"Why won't you die?"

He turned and ran, and this time he didn't stop.

Sweat trickled down his face, running lines through the thin layer of concrete dust. He regretted the waste of water since his bottle was close to empty. The two spares had been in his pack. He'd planned to find a stream when he got out of London, but that was meant to be hours ago. Between the gaps in the dense-packed suburban homes, he could make out the distant and never oblong skyscrapers of central London. They were too close. He couldn't be more than eight miles away. He wanted to weep with the frustration of it all, but that would mean more water wasted. His spirits sunk lower.

He'd deliberately left without any food, but now he had no maps, no water, and no weapons except the bayonet. Eight miles was two hours of good walking, less than half that on a bike. He wondered whether he should go back. Part of him knew that would be sensible, that he could get back there today and leave again tomorrow, but if he did, he wouldn't be able to sneak away. Greta would insist on coming with him. He jogged north.

The houses became a row of shops. The newsagent had been gutted, as had the corpse that lay in the doorway. The deli next to it had smashed windows and empty shelves. The accountant's was, unsurprisingly, untouched.

The door was still locked, but that broke after a second's levering with the bayonet. The air inside was stale, un-breathed and uncirculated for months. It was the smell of a tomb. On the desk nearest to the window were a backpack and an open first-aid kit. Underneath was an unrolled sleeping bag.

Just as he realised what that meant, there came a crashing clatter from behind him. He spun around as a zombie lurched out of a back room. It staggered forward, arms swinging, scattering filing trays and USB-mice from the desks. Eamonn charged, the bayonet outstretched, bellowing and screaming his rage and defiance. The blade hit flesh. A second later, so did Eamonn. Momentum pushed the thrashing zombie back. The bayonet was embedded in its shoulder. Eamonn tugged, but he couldn't free it. The zombie clawed at his throat. He knocked it back, grabbed the first thing he saw, a phone, and smashed it down on the creature's skull. Bone didn't break, but the plastic casing did, sending fragments of wire and circuitry across the room. He grabbed a keyboard, and punched it lengthwise into the zombie's face. Dislodged keys sprayed out in every direction. The zombie didn't notice. It staggered on. Eamonn jumped back, looking for something, anything that could be used as a weapon and saw a Big Ben paperweight. He grabbed it, swung, and his blow knocked the zombie onto the desk. He changed his grip, jumped forward, and stabbed the paperweight through the creature's eye. The zombie was still.

He had to push, pull, and twist to free his bayonet. Exhausted, he collapsed into an office chair, his eyes on the zombie, but seeing the person she'd been. He couldn't guess at her age, not now, but she'd been a survivor, and she'd been here long enough to unroll her sleeping bag. He stared at that for a long moment, knowing it was important, but it took another full minute before he realised why. She'd found something here, in this very building, something that made it worth staying in an accountant's rather than searching for a more secure refuge.

It was water. He found four large cooler-bottles in the corridor between the front and back offices. One was empty, probably since before the outbreak. A second had been opened, probably by the survivor. The other two were sealed. The corridor was dark, and he hoped that meant the water was still potable. He ripped the seal from the top, and then couldn't work out how to get the water out without spilling it on the floor. He drew his bayonet, but remembered the blade was hardly clean. He found a ballpoint pen at the back of the manager's desk drawer. He made two small holes in the bottle's top, and used the pen like a straw to suck some of the wondrous nectar from the bottle.

The woman's gear was mostly useless. He kept the pack, but not the sleeping bag. The matches, but not the clothes. The two label-less cans were the real prize, but there was no weapon. The woman must have dropped it when she'd gone out and been bitten. She'd returned because...

"Because she hoped she was immune."

That left the question of what he should do. Go on, or go back. It wasn't really a question. Eight miles was still eight miles. He had to go on. For Greta, for the children, for his family, but not today. He was exhausted.

The accountant's wasn't secure, but above the shops was a block of small flats. In the hallway on the top floor he found a bicycle padlocked to the bannisters, and the key for the bicycle lock in the second flat he checked. A bigger prize was the box of red liquorice in a cupboard above the sink. All of the other food had turned mouldy. Quite what that said about the ingredients of the liquorice, Eamonn wasn't sure, and wasn't going to dwell on, not when he could concentrate on the wonderfully alien flavour of the sugary treat.

It was a small flat, a one bedroom with a knock-through lounge-kitchen, and wet-room with toilet and shower but no bath. It was small, but not too small. Certainly, it was larger than a lot of hotel rooms he'd stayed in. The flat had belonged to a man who'd lived alone. The walls were covered in posters of star-ships except for the one that was covered in a far-too-large TV. Behind it were windows that could be covered by blackout blinds, though those were currently open, showing a view of dense-packed streets dotted with golden-leafed trees. He couldn't see any landmarks, but the houses seemed to go on forever.

Next to the window was a portable air-conditioning unit. Next to that was a stack of computers and hard drives. Facing the TV was a leather armchair with speakers in the headrest. At the side was a holster for a curving keyboard, and another for a controller with luminous buttons. He collapsed into the chair, wondering if the solitary courier-gamer who'd lived in the flat had been happy with his life. As he closed his eyes, memories of his own life came back to him, of the miserable times there had been in Dublin, and the brief days of happiness since he'd found Greta.

He had to reach Anglesey. He'd get out of London tomorrow, then to the Midlands, and then to Wales. He had a bike, now, so it shouldn't take more than three days. Four at the outside. Five if he was unlucky. In five days, he should be on a ship, sailing back to London, to Greta, to the children, to his family.

Chapter 14 - The Royal Train
East Finchley to Cuddington, 27th September, Day 199

A crowbar wasn't the best weapon to wield while riding a bike, but it was the only weapon Eamonn had found. The tip crunched into the zombie's skull, and he almost lost his grip on the mass of padding he'd taped to the other end. He swerved to the right, then to the left, overcompensated, and almost cycled straight into the four undead slouching out of the fire-ravaged police station. He clutched the length of steel to the handlebars, ducked his head low, and pedalled frantically until the road ahead was empty of the living dead for as far as he could see. He didn't look back. As his fingers slipped on the brain and bone adhering to the metal, he decided no one could fight while riding a bike.

Chester had spun many a story of how he'd charged at the undead, sword raised, while travelling through England with Nilda. Eamonn decided Chester must have been exaggerating. Actually, considering that Chester had never told the story while Nilda had been within earshot, he'd probably been lying.

Another road, another pack of the undead, and Eamonn swerved the bike to the left, up onto the pavement, and across the forecourt of a drive-in car wash.

He was travelling with more gear than on the day before. During his search of the flats for a weapon, he'd found a watch, a torch, and a box of matches, but no food other than the liquorice to add to the label-less cans. He'd eaten one can while waiting for dawn, and packed the other, but most of the extra weight was water. He'd filled every bottle he could find from the canisters in the accountant's. He still had his bayonet, and the radiation-dosimeter clipped to his belt, but there was no way of replacing the lost maps. He'd taken them from Chester's room in the Tower. Though they'd not contained a route north, they'd marked out various different areas that, Eamonn assumed, contained the safe houses. He told himself it didn't matter, that his route was being determined by the undead. All he'd lost was the illusion of a safety net, but he found no comfort in that thought.

Finally, he saw a bridge, a sign for a railway and, next to it, an abandoned bulldozer. It balanced precariously on the edge of the embankment leading down to the tracks. The dozer had knocked a hole in the six-foot-high wall and dislodged the chain-link for thirty feet in both directions. He slowed, preparing to dismount. The bike shook and rattled as the thin tyres failed to find purchase on the rubble and debris.

Over the sound, he almost didn't hear it. The zombie was on the far side of the wall. As Eamonn passed through the gap, the creature lurched forward, knocking him from the bike. He tumbled down the embankment, bike and zombie skittering after him. Brick and stone tore his clothes and bit into his flesh as rolled down the incline, and then to his feet. The bike landed eight feet from him, the zombie two feet from that, but behind the creature were a dozen more. The undead were still slowly rising to their feet, but in another second, they'd be upright.

He took a step back and heard a metallic creak. He glanced to his left. The bulldozer teetered on the edge of the embankment. Dirt and pebbles slipped and fell from underneath the precariously balanced treads. There was a snarl from the undead. He shouldn't have looked. He shouldn't have been distracted. The creatures were upright, and too close to the bike. There was a grinding screech. The bulldozer rolled forward. Spraying gravel and grit as its heavy blade ploughed through the thin topsoil, the vehicle slid down the embankment. Eamonn dived backwards. The zombies staggered forward. The dozer slammed into the pack, pulverising the creatures beneath its massive blade, crushing them under its heavy treads.

For the second time in less than a minute, Eamonn pulled himself to his feet. The zombies were… gone. A few limbs protruded from under the heavy machine, but the rest of the creatures were buried beneath the yellow dozer. The zombie that had knocked him from the bike was still moving, crawling along the ground towards him. As the dust cleared, he realised the zombie's legs were missing below the knees. Eamonn raised the crowbar as the creature pulled itself another few inches. He swung the metal bar down on its skull.

The bike was covered in dust but, miraculously, the tyres looked intact and the chain was still attached. He wheeled it away from the dozer.

"I lost the maps because of a fire engine, but was saved thanks to a bulldozer. Now that's a better story than charging at zombies on a bike. Yes, that's one to tell the kids."

He mounted the bike, and a little unsteadily, cycled north. In three days he'd be in Anglesey. Four days at the outside. Five if he was unlucky.

Distance was hard to judge, but the watch said it was eleven and the shadows told him it was noon when he crossed the bridge over the river. It was his fifth river since leaving London, but the first that truly deserved the name. The others had been little more than gullies filled with slow-flowing mud. This was different, a fast flowing torrent covered in bubbling scum and floating corpses. Or he thought they were corpses until one rolled over and raised its arm.

"That's just rigor mortis," he muttered, though he knew it wasn't. When he resumed cycling, he found it harder to pick up his pace. He needed rest. He needed food. He needed a map.

He'd found a tourist guide to London in the flat, but he'd ventured beyond its last page an hour before. The names of the train stations he went through meant nothing to him. Occasionally, the railway ran alongside a road. Even more occasionally there would be a sign. Mostly, the signs indicated a motorway, and he knew well enough to avoid those.

Other than to Kent, he'd not ventured far from central London since the outbreak, but he'd heard the stories that others had told. He'd listened to the accounts of Tuck and Jay and, later, Nilda and Chester. He'd not believed them at first, but part of that was due to arrogance and the rest was due to fear. That same fear had made him seek the obvious strength in McInery until he realised that her strength was rooted in arrogant delusion. Kent had changed that. Kent had changed everything for Eamonn, though change had been on its way before then. Or perhaps it was meeting Greta that meant he was finally able to let go of the past. It wasn't just Greta, it was the children as well. He'd found his family. He had everything he'd ever wanted, though in a way he'd never imagined, but in a way far better than any dream because it was real. As long as he could reach Anglesey. Three days. Five at the outside, but if he failed…

For twenty minutes, he sprinted along the side of the tracks. The bicycle was lightweight, but the thin tyres were designed for darting through city streets, not for the uneven gravel-coated railway. He was already slowing when he saw the five undead. There was no way he'd be able to cycle past them. To their right were fields, but they were surrounded by dense hedgerows. To the creatures' left were train carriages. He assumed there was a locomotive somewhere in the distance. It was an old train, and oddly coloured in dark paint a shade and style he'd never before seen on a British railway.

Behind him, the tracks were empty. He hesitated. He wasn't sure where he was, but he was certain that he was heading northwest, and that was the right direction. Fighting came with a risk, not just of death, but that he'd lose time. If he was forced off the tracks, or if he lost the bike, he'd lose even more. The zombies were staggering towards him, slipping on the gravel, tripping on the sleepers, but there were still only five.

He leaned the bike against a broken signal box and walked towards the undead. The nearest wore a camouflage jacket. Not a soldier's uniform, but a civilian's cheap coat. Male, Eamonn thought as he stretched his arms. The zombie eight paces behind had been female, wearing trousers, boots, and a shredded blouse. The three behind, he couldn't tell. He swung the crowbar low, ducking as he slammed the metal bar into the zombie's knee. Its hand clawed within inches of his face as it toppled to the ground. Eamonn skipped back a step, and another, his eyes on the four upright zombies. Another low blow, and the female creature was down. He swung, cleaving the metal bar into its skull.

The other three were getting nearer. The zombie in the camouflage jacket was trying to stand, but its knee wouldn't support its weight. It was taking too long. Time was running out, and London didn't have enough time left. Eamonn charged, swinging wildly. The blow smashed into a zombie's temple, but that took the momentum out of his swing. A hand curled around his arm. He jerked himself free. He kicked, stabbed, punched, and cut his way through the creatures until he was standing close to the rearmost carriage, and they were between him and his bike. Two still stood, and a third was dragging itself along the ground. No, two more were forcing their way through the hedgerow near the signal box where he'd propped his bike. Still, he hesitated, until he heard gravel crunch behind him. A zombie was crawling out from between the wheels of the train carriage.

He bellowed a scream of frustrated rage, turned, and ran, hacking the crowbar down on the crawling zombie as he went by. There was no satisfaction in the crunch of bone.

The carriages each had a large crest near the door, but there was no locomotive at the far end. He paused, ten yards from the front-most carriage, looking back at the zombies and at the train. There were too many of the undead to properly investigate it. Far too many. He counted ten, now. Ten between himself and the bike. The bike with his bags of water and his only means of getting to Anglesey in three days. His instinct was to fight, but if he died, then London was doomed.

"You'll find another bike. You'll find more water."

On foot, he headed northwest.

Greta, he thought.

"Greta," he exhaled, speaking her name with every breath. It was a plea, a prayer, an impossible dream. Two syllables that represented all his newfound hopes that were vanishing with every bead of sweat. His foot hit a sleeper. He tripped, fell, and landed face-first in gravel.

"Greta!" He screamed to the unforgiving sky.

He looked back down the track. He couldn't see the train or the undead, but the creatures would follow him, he knew it, and they wouldn't stop. Not now, not ever. He pushed himself to his feet and kept on. He could outpace them during daylight, but at night, when he stopped, they would catch up. He had to leave the railway. The question, then, was whether to go left or right, to head due west or due north. He trudged on, unable to summon the energy to run, eyes open for a sign.

He found it on a hillside house overlooking the railway line. He'd passed many buildings since leaving London, but none with sheets hanging from every window. Some sheets were white, some were pink, two were black, though that might have been dirt rather than dye. One had been caught by the wind, dragged from its window, and become tangled in the branches of a sycamore. It hung like a flag, a herald of safety, and that was what the house had to be, one of the safe houses Chester had set up during the time before he'd returned to London.

"Thank you, Chester," he murmured. The prospect of a refuge so close gave him new speed, a new strength. He hurried up the meadow towards the house. In front of the house was a barn, and it was there that he went first.

From the profusion of bridles, saddles, stirrups and other gear, the house had belonged to equestrians. Behind the barn was a large concrete building with wooden cladding that almost made it look like a shed. Inside was a well. The top had been broken open. A rope was next to it with a kilo weight at the end, a plastic bucket tied three feet above. He dropped the bucket and weight into the well. It fell for only a few seconds before there was a pleasing splash. He drew it back up, and drank his fill.

More alert, he returned to the barn door. From its cover, he watched the train tracks. He couldn't remember when he'd last checked the time, nor precisely where he'd been, but after that locomotive, he'd run for half an hour, he was sure of it. Half an hour of running and at least the same of walking, he had to have covered six miles in total. Maybe eight. Possibly more. He thought he had an hour before the zombies caught up with him. He was wrong. He'd only been standing in the doorway for a minute when the first of the creatures came into view. Another followed a moment later, then four, then ten, then twelve and they kept on coming.

They couldn't have all been in the hedgerows near the train, though that didn't tell him where they'd come from. There were too many to fight. His heavy limbs told him he wasn't going any further today, but even if it took him two hours to retrieve his bike tomorrow, he'd catch up with the undead before nightfall.

He'd followed the railway as far as he could. The only question was whether he'd followed it for far enough. Could he now simply cut due west and into Wales? Where, precisely, was he? The answer would lie in the house. Hadn't Chester said that they left supplies and maps in the safe houses? Although, now he thought about it, Chester hadn't mentioned setting one up this close to London.

He almost didn't have the energy to check every room, but the creaking woodwork made him look under every bed and in every cupboard before he was certain the house was empty of zombies and people. The torn packets in the kitchen suggested that it had become home to mice. There were four tins in the cupboard, so he didn't begrudge the rodents the packets of pasta and pulses. Other than birds it was so long since he'd seen any animal that even mice were something to be treasured. The first can turned out to be spaghetti hoops, and he'd eaten half of it before he remembered to look for a map. It was taped to the granite kitchen counter. One sheet of A4, with the top half a map, the bottom half a brief note that said there were survivors in Anglesey and supplies left in the house.

"Should have told the mice that the supplies weren't for them," he mumbled through a half-full mouth. The map was more interesting. It was a sketch with a rough route that cut due west into Wales, with the ultimate destination being a place on the coast called Llanncanno. More pertinently, another safe house was listed far closer, north of the Cotswolds town of Northleach. There was a brief instruction to travel due west, but to stay north of Oxford, south of Blenheim Palace, and to avoid both at all costs. It wasn't very reassuring. If the note was to be believed, he was near Cuddington.

The safe house in the Cotswolds was fifty miles away according to the atlas he found in the house's large study. Bound with leather, it was a reprint from 1901 to mark the accession of Edward VII.

"How often do towns move?" he asked himself as he leafed through the atlas. "Not often."

Fifty miles? That was doable in one day if he had a bike. Perhaps he should go back and get the bicycle he'd left by that train. Maybe. First, he'd search the house. Perhaps Chester had left a bicycle outside. Although he wasn't sure Chester had ever come to this house. The map and note weren't in the man's handwriting. It didn't matter. Tomorrow, he'd be in the Cotswolds, and perhaps he wouldn't stay at that safe house. With a good bike and clear roads, he could cover the distance in three hours. He leafed through the old atlas, but couldn't find Llanncanno. In fact, Wales was far less detailed than the Home Counties. No matter, he'd be in the Cotswolds tomorrow, Wales the day after, Llanncanno the day after that. Perhaps there would be people there. Perhaps a radio. Perhaps even a boat. They could leave from there and be in London a couple of days after that. Five days, and he'd be back at the Tower.

After making sure the doors were closed, he sat in a chair by a window with a view of the railway. It would have been a great view, once. A view worthy of the house, a view of rolling countryside, of fields and hills, of trees and track, and not one hint of a road. There was a spire in the distance, and a quartet of pylons marching across the countryside, but they only emphasised how little had changed in so long.

His fingers went to the chain around his neck, and to the ring that hung from it.

Everything had changed now, of course. The view was as close to the English idyll as existed last year, but that had never been Eamonn Finnegan's dream.

He unhooked the chain, and freed the ring. It was a wedding ring. *His* wedding ring from his one and only marriage. He rolled it in his fingers. He had told Greta that his wife had died. She had, but that was only half the story.

They'd been married for thirteen months before he realised it wouldn't last. If he was honest with himself, the doubts had set in on their honeymoon, and cemented themselves when they'd returned. They just didn't fit. Not together. They were always in one another's way, neither wanting to give ground on even the smallest of things. Who'd use the bathroom first in the morning, or who'd get the milk on their way home from work, or even who'd get to choose which television channel to watch became the battleground of their marriage. Those battles were never won, but settled with an uneasy compromise. They'd moved to a larger, new-build home with two bathrooms, set up an online daily grocery delivery, and bought a second television. That last was the death knell for the relationship. He should have realised. They had no interests or friends in common, and rather than spending time developing them together, they spent more time apart. She took on more cases. He volunteered for the oversight position that took him from Dublin to Frankfurt to London. They barely saw one another. When they couldn't agree on which set of in-laws to spend Christmas with, they spent it apart rather than together, alone in their house. After that, he decided to end it. Before he could tell her, she got sick.

He couldn't tell her then. Instead, he'd donned a mask, playing the dutiful husband, and he'd found that easy mostly thanks to the support of her friends and family who did most of the work. After the hospital, came the home-care. The savings that hadn't gone on their wedding and honeymoon had been spent on a deposit for a house he was sure neither of them wanted. She had insurance, but it wasn't comprehensive, she was young, after all. With her on sick leave, their income fell. The bills built up, so he'd taken on more work, more overseas trips, and was in Ireland less. Everyone thought that it was all for her. It wasn't. It was for him. He couldn't bear being around her. He'd not let on, but he thought she knew. He thought she'd realised.

In the end, though it had taken an age, she had died. Before the funeral, he'd had a call from one of the partners at her firm. She'd written a letter for Eamonn, one not to be read until after her death. He'd assumed that she'd say that she'd known. That she'd realised. That she'd forgiven him. She hadn't. She hadn't realised. She hadn't known. In her note, she'd simply expressed her love and her thanks for all that he'd done. She'd said that she loved him now and for always, and that she wished him nothing but a long and happy life, and that, one day, he might find love again.

That had almost killed him. It was too much. He'd barely made it through the funeral. Work had kept him alive in the weeks after. It had kept him distracted until he could deal with the emotions. The anger at her for not realising. The anger at himself for not being honest. The anger that, after she died, he could never confess and so never be forgiven.

He rolled the ring around his fingers. He'd worn it as a lesson to himself, a cautionary reminder that he'd forgotten when he met McInery, a lesson he'd remembered when he'd met Greta. He didn't need a reminder anymore. He placed the ring on the windowsill. As the sun set, he finally let go of the past.

Chapter 15 - The Horde
Oxfordshire, 28th September, Day 200

"Where did they come from? Which way did they go?" Eamonn whispered as he stared at the L-shaped scar ripped through the landscape. It roughly followed the line of the hills, snaking back and forth through the valley. A twisted lamppost suggested where a road might once have been, but all was now dust, dirt, and a few grasping hands reaching up to the sky. He knew what had caused it, a horde. A great mass of the undead hundreds of thousands strong. Again, he'd learned of those from Chester and Nilda. Like thirst and starvation, the horde was an axe hanging over the heads of all those in the Tower. Not a day went by that someone hadn't stared north, dreading the sight of an approaching dust cloud. The only clouds above him were those that promised rain, and that gave no clue as to which direction the horde had gone.

Nilda and Chester had seen a horde near Hull. He would assume it was the same one, and that meant the undead were heading to Wales. He didn't know how far the undead had got. He didn't know why they'd changed their course so abruptly. He didn't have any evidence to prove this *was* the same group that had been near Hull. For thirty minutes, he stared at the scar, hundreds of metres wide, and at the arms reaching up, moving as if with the wind.

"It's the valley, that's what caused them to change direction."

He had no reason to believe that, but no better theory to prove he was wrong. He wheeled the bike around, and pushed it back the way he'd come.

He'd planned to go west, aiming for Llanncanno, the beach mentioned in the note in the safe house. Instead, he'd go north. His knowledge of British geography was hazy, but he'd turn west somewhere before Birmingham and follow the northern Welsh coast until he reached Anglesey. Mentally, he reset the clock. In two days, he'd be deep into

Wales. Three, and he'd be on Anglesey. Certainly, within five he'd be on his way back to London.

As he reached for his water bottle, he saw the blinking light on the dosimeter. The reading was higher. A lot higher. It wasn't lethal, but as he stared at the digital display, the numbers beyond the decimal point ticked upward. He mounted the bicycle, and let gravity take him down the hill, and away from the devastation left by the undead.

He'd found the bicycle three hours before, one hour after leaving the safe house. Once again, he was uncertain where he was or how much distance he'd covered, but the bike had allowed him to cycle straight through two small groups of the undead. There had been fewer than ten in each pack, and that suddenly seemed like a very small number, but he didn't want to fight them, not now. There wasn't time.

After half an hour, he slowed for long enough to look at the dosimeter. The number had stopped rising. What he didn't know was whether the device recorded total accumulated exposure, or exposure at that very moment. He cycled faster.

When he saw a tattered-coated zombie on the road ahead, he didn't slow, but sped right past, kicking his foot into the creature's chest as it lurched at the bike. Eamonn almost fell off, *almost*, but the zombie went flying into the hedgerow.

"Maybe Chester wasn't lying after all."

Ten minutes later, he came to another one of the living dead. He tried the same manoeuvre, but this time, wasn't so lucky. His foot hit the zombie, but the creature was like a wall. It kept coming. The bike slid out from under Eamonn, and he tumbled to the ground.

He rolled to his feet as the zombie changed direction. Its face was a patchwork of red, as if it had been steamed off. As it snarled a mouth of broken teeth in receding gums, Eamonn swung his leg low. It was like kicking a tree trunk. He rolled again, drew the bayonet, and slashed it at the zombie's face. The blade sliced through the creature's nose and across an eye. The zombie staggered on, heedless of the wound, and walked, eye-first, into the blade. With a push and a twist, Eamonn plunged the blade deep into its brain. It collapsed.

Teeth gritted against a hysterical laugh at the brutal horror, he dragged the bayonet free, picked up his bike, and cycled onward.

Eamonn hesitated by the wrought iron gates. On the one hand, there were at least another two hours before darkness, he was making good time, and had no need to stop. On the other, the gate was closed and there was no sign of the undead inside. The road was empty, but his pack wasn't, not entirely. When he'd found the bicycle, he'd discovered half a tray of corned beef. That was in a garage in an otherwise unassuming house about ten miles away. Eamonn thought it was ten miles. The roads had curved and twisted through the Oxfordshire countryside, so he wasn't entirely sure.

"Assuming it is Oxfordshire."

That settled it. He'd go inside, find out where he was, and use the rest of the daylight to work out exactly where he was going. The gate had a bolt at the bottom, another in the middle, but it also had a lock that clamped the hinges in place. The key had been left in the lock.

The house itself was not what he'd expected. For one thing, it was mostly a museum. From the road, the property had looked like just another grand English pile with turrets and towers, the kind built for an industrialist millionaire during the height of Empire. The 'keep off the grass' signs would have been the clue, but they were obscured by two-foot-long stems, dying off with the approach of winter.

The entire ground floor was filled with mock-ups of kitchens through the ages. He found the seventeenth-century room not much different to the eighteenth, or even the nineteenth. From the ration books on the table of the next room, it was meant to be from the Second World War. However, the fire axe leaning against a chair was distinctly modern.

"Hello?" he called. No reply came, either from the living or the undead.

Beyond the kitchen he found a room that was split in two. One half was Einstein's workspace, the other half Newton's. Beyond that was a hallway with a set of stairs clearly signposted 'down only', with arrows directing visitors to the up-staircase. He resisted shouting out again, and went up.

Upstairs were bedrooms, again from different centuries, but he ignored them. He was looking for signs of more recent visitors. He found them in the tower-room.

The door to it was in a corner furthest from the stairs. It was a small apartment suite with a very modern shower and a not-quite-as-modern kitchen that had four large backpacks dumped on the floor. In a bedroom with wide windows overlooking the countryside were the bodies. Four of them. Two had been children, and they had been undead. The other two were adults, and they had committed suicide.

Eamonn regretted coming into the house. He walked over to the window. There was a cloud gathering in the south. It was dark and angry, rising from the horizon. There was going to be a storm, a bad one, probably bringing torrential rains and flash floods. It was unlikely he'd get ahead of it, but he didn't want to spend the night in this house. At the same time, he couldn't let sentiment get in the way of practicality, not when so many lives were at stake. Without looking at the bodies, he went back to the kitchen. Most of the gear in the packs had been food, and not all of it had spoiled. They must have been out looting when the children were infected. Would they have taken the children with them, or had the kids sneaked away from the safety of the house while their parents were out?

"Don't think about it."

There were enough packets and tins to last him for a month. Not that he needed that much food. Even if he was only in Oxfordshire, he'd be in Wales tomorrow, and on Anglesey two days after that. In three days, five at the outside, he'd be on the island. Even so, there had been too many lean months during this harsh year. He emptied the bags, and then repacked one with all of the food that looked edible.

He went back into the bedroom to look for weapons, but there were only knives, and none were as sharp as his bayonet or as sturdy as his crowbar. As he turned around, his eyes caught sight of the storm cloud. It was heading towards the house, though very slowly. A thread of memory tugged for attention. Something Nilda had said. Something Nilda had seen. Angry clouds approaching Hull. The horde! It wasn't a storm. It was the undead, tramping the countryside to ruin, throwing up a cloud of dirt in their wake.

He watched the cloud, frozen with horror, hoping to see a scar of electric white light up the sky and prove him wrong. The lightning didn't come, and he knew he had to move.

"Greta and the children," he murmured, and turned away from the window. "Greta."

He grabbed the bag of food, and hurried downstairs. He glanced out a front-facing window and saw a wide driveway leading to a car park and more buildings. The museum-house was only one small part of a much larger estate, but there wasn't time to inspect the rest. He slung the bag of food on the crossbar and cycled away from the cloud.

A mile turned to two, and his mind turned to maths. If the undead moved at three miles an hour, and he at eight, but nightfall was two hours away, then they would catch up with him around nine p.m. He cycled faster, and almost fell off the bike when a zombie toppled out of the hedgerow. He swore as he punched at the creature. Its hand caught on his sleeve. He tugged. The material ripped, and he was able to push himself away. There wasn't time to fight.

One foot either side of the frame, he walked the bike along the road until he could mount it and begin cycling again. That was another minute lost. He couldn't work out how much distance that represented, but let the attempt fill his mind until he came to a T-Junction. There was no signpost, but that didn't matter. A small track led northwest while the road curved towards the east. He took the smaller track. It led uphill, and he decided that was good, that the undead would surely stick to the lowland.

The track was muddy and offered little traction for the bicycle's tyres. Earth had washed down from the fields either side, coating the road in a damp, viscous layer. His slow progress was brought to an abrupt halt when he reached a tree fallen across the track. It had been growing in the field, but too close to the embankment. As rain had washed the soil away, and as the ditch had flooded, the wall had weakened. One storm too many had caused it to collapse, and the tree had soon followed. The massive branches, still covered in dying leaves, stretched for thirty feet in both directions.

He wasted five minutes trying to pick a path through the branches and leaves before he took to the field. He staggered through the gluey soil, tempted to leave the bike and food behind, but he knew he couldn't, not if he wanted to live. He reached the far side of the fallen tree, kicked the clods of dirt and soil from his shoes and the bicycle's tyres, and cycled on. The cloud was still there, and he was far slower than before. The track curved from northwest to west-northwest to west, and then it disappeared in a shallow river, forty feet wide, two feet deep. It looked like a stream had burst its manmade banks, returning to its ancient course. Beyond, in the distance, he could see a spire. That meant a church, a road, and better going.

He waded into the river. The water was icy cold. In another time, another life, or simply just another day, he might have found that refreshing, but the cloud behind him was getting closer. Always closer. He slipped twice in the river, and was soaked by the time he reached the far side. The spire didn't appear any nearer, but the cloud behind him did. He tried cycling, but didn't have the strength. After a long few days of little rest and too much tension, his body was giving up, shivering with cold and exhaustion.

A spire meant a town, and that might act as a breakwater for the horde. Get to the other side, find a… a… he had no idea, but he kept moving because the alternative meant death.

The spire belonged to a church, but there was no town. It was simply a lonely church in an empty patch of land. There was a cemetery, a wide willow, a sign offering a service on Sundays, evensong on Mondays, and tours of the crypt only by appointment. Eamonn looked back the way he'd come. He wasn't sure if the cloud was closing in, but night was. The sun was low and soon would set. A crypt would do. It would have to.

The entrance was behind the church, not in it, but down slick steps and behind a wrought iron gate. The gate was locked. He reached for the crowbar, but remembered the undead. He had time.

He found the keys in the vestry, but little else. Eamonn wasn't the first person to take refuge in the church. The previous visitors had made a fire out of broken pews, and left nothing behind but ash.

He unlocked the crypt's gate, took out the flickering light, and shone it inside. There were steep steps leading down to a second gate. He went down and unlocked it.

The crypt was small. It was empty, though he wasn't sure why he'd expected it not to be. It consisted of three chambers, each with a score of stacked sarcophagi. Beyond that a few were adorned with coats of arms, he had no idea whose remains were held within. There would be time to find out. Assuming he stayed. That was the question. The horde might not come anywhere near the church, or he might be able to avoid it if he headed due east or west, or… no, there wasn't time. He could hear a dull rumbling, but night was closer than the horde. He had to rest, and it was here or nowhere.

Taking the bike with him, he retreated down into the crypt, locking the gates behind him. Inside, below ground, he could hear nothing, not the irregular drumbeat of the marching undead, or the wind through the bare branches of the trees outside. He turned off the torch, and waited for dawn.

The horde woke him. It was a low rumble at first, growing steadily in volume until it became a sea of noise. Even the air seemed to be vibrating. It was like being trapped in an earthquake, and it went on forever.

The watch was useless. It had stopped working, presumably when he'd fallen in the swollen river. The light worked, though the beam was weak, but it only showed him the streams of grit falling from the ancient ceiling. He turned the light off. Crowbar in hand, he watched the gate, waiting for daylight.

29ᵗʰ September

The roaring tumult had subsided to a continuous patter. Eamonn had thought being caught by the undead was the worst thing that could happen to him. He'd been wrong. They had stopped overhead. He was trapped. Utterly.

They'd move, he told himself, but only in the privacy of his head. Even though their catastrophic crescendo would surely drown out any sound he could make, he didn't dare speak. He didn't dare do anything but sit and wait.

Dust and dirt cascaded from the vaulted ceiling, and a new fear replaced all others, that of being slowly buried alive.

Thirst finally made him open his pack. He took a sip of water, but nothing to eat. He'd need the supplies when he got outside. He'd lost too much time as it was. He couldn't lose any more searching for food in Wales. Assuming he ever got outside.

There was a loud thump, and a shower of grit rained down on his head. In an attempt to distract himself, he searched the crypt. It didn't take long. In the hope there might be a secret tunnel, he searched again, but there wasn't. The coats of arms on the sarcophagi gave no clue as to whom their occupants had been, though they must have once been famous to warrant this special burial. He'd have to make up an identity for them when he recounted the story to the children. They were knights, he would tell them, the knights of King Arthur, buried in the hillside waiting to be woken when the country was at its moment of greatest need. If the undead didn't count as the greatest need, what would? Quietly, he began to cry.

30ᵗʰ September

Water had joined the dirt and grit streaming from the ceiling. A new fear joined that of being buried alive, that of drowning.

Would they ever go? Would they ever leave?

1ˢᵗ October

No.

10ᵗʰ October

He was out of water and out of food. Half of it had been ruined when he'd fallen in the river. The other half hadn't lasted nearly long enough. The sound from above had changed, diminished, but not disappeared. There was a near constant patter of small impacts above, and a constant rain of mud and dust streaming from the ancient roof.

He was out of batteries for the torch, out of matches, and his family in London were out of time. It was two weeks since he'd left. They would think him dead. Someone else would have left by now. Almost certainly it would have been Greta. Was it fitting that they'd end up facing the same fate, dying the same way though hundreds of miles apart? Was it poetic? Probably not. Death was going to be his fate. He had reconciled himself to that. All that remained was the manner of that death. It could be slow, here in the dark, or quick and painful up in the daylight.

Crowbar in hand, bayonet at his belt, he undid the gate's lock. A small cascade of dirt tumbled about his feet. Above, he could make out the thinnest ray of light. He climbed the steps, but the light got no brighter.

Beyond the top-most gate was a mass of fallen rubble, broken timbers, and twisted metal. He undid the lock, and was prepared for the gate to be blocked, and for there to be nothing ahead of him but a slow, lingering death.

The gate opened. Beyond, the rubble shifted. He grabbed a timber, and when pulling it didn't do any good, he pushed. There was a cascade of brick and dust, and the light grew brighter as the hole grew bigger. He pushed the timber again, working it left and right, making an opening large enough to clamber up, through, and onto a precarious platform of rubble. The church had almost completely collapsed, though grass still grew in odd patches around it. Beyond the grass, where the road had once been, was a desolate expanse of mud.

A raven flew low overhead, landing on the rubble that had been a church. The broken masonry shifted beneath its meagre weight, sending a cascade of dust, tile, and brick down the side of the heap. That was what Eamonn had heard. The horde hadn't passed overhead. It had only travelled close enough to cause the ancient church to collapse. The sound he'd heard, the sound he'd thought had been the passage of millions of feet, was brick and timber collapsing. He could have left days ago.

He wanted to laugh. He wanted to cry. He heard a rasp, turned around, and saw a zombie dragging itself across the sea of mud towards him. The broken, twisted creature must have been left behind by the horde. No, not one, there were a dozen broken wretches crawling towards him. There wasn't time to go back into the crypt for the bicycle. It didn't matter. He'd find another. He had to find water first, and then find out precisely where he was. And then, as before, Anglesey and then London. It would probably take more than five days.

Chapter 16 - Unstill Waters
Birmingham, 20th October, Day 222

Eamonn had been trying to avoid Birmingham, but that was where he'd ended up. It had taken him ten days to travel less than eighty miles from the church, though his sore feet told him he'd covered at least four times that distance.

There were just too many undead, too much rain, and far too little food left anywhere. The dosimeter on his belt said the radiation level was safe, but he no longer trusted it. He trusted the bus sign that told him he was at St James' Church, but only because it was embedded in the pavement. What the sign lacked was an indication of where the nearest railway line was.

He had a vague idea there'd been an express service from London to north Wales that had bypassed Birmingham. That notion came from a dismal Sunday afternoon on a slow train from Glasgow to London. He'd been in Dublin for the weekend, but only managed Friday night and half of Saturday before he'd had to escape. He'd bought the last seat on the first available flight and, ten minutes before landing, been informed the plane was being diverted due to an *incident*. Everyone knew what that meant, and so hadn't grumbled until, an hour later, the pilot had informed them they were landing in Glasgow. By the time his case had come through baggage handling, it was three a.m. and the coach provided by the airline had already left.

Despite the heavily armed police, Eamonn would have vented his frustration at the customer complaints desk, but it was deserted. He'd caught a taxi to the train station, and jumped on the morning's first service heading south unaware that engineering works were taking place on half of the lines. He hated Britain's trains at the best of times. The timetable was never more than a suggestion, and every week they seemed to be ripping up one section of track or another. His phone was out of power, there had been nowhere open to buy a newspaper or book, and a storm cloud followed them south from Glasgow Central.

With rain obscuring the view, he had nothing to distract him except the map pinned to the carriage's far wall. It described the supposedly high-speed lines linking the furthest corners of Britain, and on that map, he was absolutely certain, there had been a line that bypassed Birmingham.

Where that line was, he had no idea, and as he picked his way down the litter-and-leaf-strewn Stratford Road, it dawned on him that the map probably bore little resemblance to geographical reality.

There was a loud metallic creak from his left. Despite the large post-office sign, most of the building was taken up by a convenience store. He suspected it was that which had attracted the looters who'd broken the windows. The creak was followed by a sharp crack, then a cascade of falling shelves. Eamonn didn't investigate, but hurried on. He needed a sign to the train station, or one to the ring road. Birmingham had one, didn't it? Wasn't it famous for it? He needed a sign, but the one he found five hundred metres ahead was entirely unexpected.

The road was blocked by a fallen crane. On the eastern side, a building had been under construction. From the height of the scaffolding, it was going to be a three-storey structure. From the supermarket opposite, and the buildings surrounding it, it was going to be retail downstairs and an office building above. The crane had toppled from the building site to land on, and partially in, the supermarket. On the crane was the sign. The letters were crude, painted on white sheets, but the words were clear, *Safe House*. What wasn't immediately obvious was where the safe house actually was. The wind picked up, the crane creaked. Eamonn found himself looking around, expecting the undead, but the only corpses he saw were near the entrance to the damaged supermarket. There were five of them, and they had been shot. From the leaves on top of the bodies, they'd died some time ago, but whether it was last week or last month, he couldn't tell.

He took a step towards the supermarket's doors. The glass had been smashed. The interior was dark. The corpses suggested the undead had been inside and might be there still. As he turned around, he saw the other sheet. It was similarly marked with those two wonderful words, *Safe House*, and was hanging from the car showroom on the other side of the road and the other side of the crane.

There were four more corpses outside the car showroom. Three had been shot. The fourth's head had been staved in. Had the survivors run out of ammunition? His eyes went to the dosimeter, but then he heard a sound, a familiar dry, rasping mockery of breath. It came from beyond the nearest car.

He raised the crowbar, eyeing the vehicles anew. There were forty, parked at angles across the forecourt, but each was an obstacle between and under which the undead might be concealed. The promise of safety those sheets represented was incomplete, but he was out of food, out of water, and running out of energy.

He clambered up onto the nearest car, and stood stock still, listening. The rasping grew in volume as the zombie drew nearer. He saw it edge out from underneath a dirty blue Vauxhall. Eamonn jumped down, swung the crowbar onto its skull, and then jumped back onto the roof of the nearest car. He waited, listening until impatient terror got the better of him. He clambered down and sprinted for the showroom's entrance. The door was closed, but not locked. He threw it open. Crowbar held in front, he peered around. It was empty of people and the undead, but not of bags.

An hour later, he had an idea of what had happened, though not why. According to Chester, Anglesey had sent teams of people to investigate what had become of Britain. One of those teams had gone to Birmingham, but contact had been lost with them. The assumption, though he wasn't sure if it had been Anglesey's or Chester's, was that they'd died from radiation poisoning. That was why Eamonn had been trying to avoid the city. The dosimeter, still showing the same reading as a week before, didn't offer Eamonn any reassurance that the assumption was wrong. That team *had* arrived in Birmingham, and *had* set up this safe house. There was a tin of paint by the door, the lid off, the brush inside. A barbecue stood, out of place, in the middle of the sales-floor. There was ash inside and an unopened box of saucepans next to it. The packaging had the name of the supermarket on it. Next to that was the discarded plastic packaging for four bed sheets. These people had arrived, cleared the showroom, and gone to investigate the supermarket. They'd killed the undead, taken the sheets, pans, and barbecue, come back and lit a fire, but hadn't had a chance to fill the saucepans before… what? Before they left? If so, they took the half-empty bag of the barbecue charcoal with them.

As to where these people had come from, the contents of their packs confirmed it. One contained an enamel mug with the words 'Vehemently British' painted on one side and two flags on the other, a skull and crossbones and a Union Jack. That had to have belonged to a submariner, and that confirmed the bags belonged to people from Anglesey. That begged the question of where they'd gone. There was no map or note anywhere in the showroom. Nor was there any food. There were other supplies, though *loot* would be a better term. LED light bulbs, fuses, freezer bags, and icepacks. It was an odd collection, of use only to someone with a dependable supply of electricity. It begged the question of how these people had planned to carry it back to Anglesey.

Eamonn wandered back to the windows, and saw the plastic tubing running into the fuel tank of one of the cars. The fuel caps had been removed from three other cars that were within his field of view. They'd syphoned the fuel. That suggested they planned to drive back to Anglesey, or at least to the coast, along with their haul. So why hadn't they? Where was the petrol? Where were the people?

His foot crunched on plastic. He looked down and saw the broken remains of a phone and, next to it, a small pool of dried blood. The people, the food, the fuel, the weapons, they were all gone. The bags had been left along with their personal possessions. The cars outside, though they were covered in grime and dirt, had windscreens and windows that were undamaged. No great horde of the undead had come through here. Why had they so hurriedly fled? Why hadn't they called Anglesey to let them know where they were going? Why had they taken the bag of charcoal? His eyes fell on the broken phone. There was an obvious answer. The purpose of the safe houses was to find other survivors, and those survivors had come here. The team from Anglesey, not expecting danger from the living, had been overpowered and taken away. Where and why, Eamonn didn't know and the car showroom offered no more clues. He went back outside, and headed due west.

Halifax Road led to Shirley Park Road. He assumed that meant a park was nearby. Open spaces might be easier to traverse, but four zombies staggered out of a fire-blackened terrace, and he was forced to turn around. Hurdis Road, then Delrene, and one street looked just like another. The undead were following him now, not on his heels, but he could hear them. So could the occasional undead in the houses ahead. A glass window broke, and a zombie toppled through, landing on a gravel driveway. The creature's legs were twisted at an odd angle, clearly broken, but that didn't prevent it trying to stand. Eamonn kept going, left and straight on, straight on and right, knowing that Birmingham had to come to an end soon.

He didn't stop until he came to a pub opposite Yardley Wood train station. There were three bodies outside, and they had been shot. Had he not gone to the safe house first, he'd have assumed they were the undead. Had he not paused to look more closely, he wouldn't have noticed that they'd been shot in the chest. There were head wounds, too, but each had a neat trio of bullet holes above the heart. One victim had an empty holster at his belt. Eamonn checked around the man's neck. There was an identity disc, but again, that told him nothing more than that the man had once been military.

The doors of the pub were held closed by a bicycle D-lock. He walked a few paces closer. His foot crunched on charred plastic. The doors shook, and opened an inch. Necrotic fingers curled around the edge. Eamonn ran. Straight on and left, right and straight on.

The ragged shrubbery offered little cover, but it was the best Eamonn could find. Birmingham was as endless as London. Thirst was making itself known and the clouds above refused to storm so he'd begun looking in restaurants for soda-syrup. That was something he'd heard Jay talking about. It was more sugar than water, but it was better than nothing. He'd have to make do with nothing because that was all he'd found. When he'd seen the signs for Canon Hill Park, he'd followed them simply to get away from the houses and the undead.

He held his breath. Five feet of dense deciduous leaves, thorny branches, and an inch of railing away, he heard a shoeless foot slap against the pavement. The zombies drifted past, and all was still, at least in the immediate vicinity.

As he thought he was alone, he allowed himself to relax. The park was overgrown, a mixture of dead grass, thriving weeds, and bare trees ringed by giant drifts of leaves and occasional fallen branches. The conifers and pines were struggling, and he wondered if that was a sign of radiation damage. A goose flew overhead, disappearing deeper into the park.

He didn't know what that was a sign of, but he followed the bird. The line of travel took him more north than west, but that didn't matter. An hour here, a day there, he'd already lost so much time that, by now, someone else would already have set out from London. He wasn't giving up his quest. As soon as he was out of Birmingham, he'd find a bike, find the railway that led to Holyhead, and be in Anglesey in two days. Three at most, five at the outside, but, realistically, he would arrive only to find that Greta was already there.

There was an alternative, of course, that he'd be the first to arrive at Anglesey, and that they would return to London to find everyone dead. Or perhaps he'd arrive at Anglesey and find the survivors all gone. He tried not to think of those alternatives. Instead, he focused his thoughts on why a bird might be flying north in the autumn.

He didn't find the goose, but he did find a wide boating lake. There were feathers and plastic mixed in with the leaves floating on the surface, but it was water beneath. It would have to be boiled first, and that would take time, but he'd run out of it today. He'd take shelter in the first house he saw. He'd light a fire, boil the water, and fill himself with that. He took out the bottle from his belt, and knelt at the water's edge.

"I wouldn't do that," a voice said.

Eamonn spun around. Twenty feet from him stood a woman wearing a blue jumpsuit smeared with dirt. In her hands was a crossbow. The bolt was aimed at Eamonn's chest.

"I just needed water," Eamonn said.

"You're Irish?" the woman asked.

"From your accent, so are you," Eamonn said.

"How did you get here?" she asked.

Eamonn wanted to ask her the same question, but she was the one with the crossbow. "I walked. I cycled. I didn't mean to come into Birmingham, but I was lost."

"It's a hard city to miss," she said. "Where did you come from?"

"London," he said. "I left a… a month ago, I think. I've lost track of time."

"A month? It's only a hundred and twenty miles."

"Zombies, you know how it is?" he said. "Do you live here?"

"Where were you going if you didn't mean to come to Birmingham?" she asked, ignoring his question.

"Anglesey," Eamonn said. The woman stiffened, and Eamonn realised that, for some reason, he'd given the wrong answer.

"Why?" she asked.

"It's a long story," he said.

"Find a short version of it," she said.

Uncertain what the right answer was, but knowing that another wrong one might result in a crossbow bolt through his chest, he opted for the truth. "There are a hundred of us in London. About half are children under twelve. Two of our group came through Anglesey. They said there were people there, and they have food, medicine, and a doctor. We need all three."

"They might have it," the woman said, "if they're still there, but if they are, they won't help you. They don't help anyone."

"You know about Anglesey?" Eamonn asked.

The woman looked him up and down, clearly trying to decide whether or not to believe him. Eamonn couldn't imagine why she might think he was lying, not until he remembered the safe house with the discarded bags, and the bodies lying near the pub.

"It's been a long month," Eamonn said. "It's been a long *year*. Right now, I'm tired, I'm thirsty, so if you don't mind…" He turned around and began to kneel.

"There are zombies in the lake," the woman said, almost casually.

Eamonn took a step back from the water's edge. "Seriously?"

"Didn't you see what happened to the bird?" she asked, gesturing at the feathers floating amid the scum. "The undead fell in when they followed me here yesterday. I don't know why they haven't died yet. I suppose they don't breath. You want water? Here." She took a bottle from her belt and threw it to him.

He fumbled the catch, and then drank half of it.

"Thank you," he said.

"Wales is that way," she said, gesturing over her shoulder. "But you won't find help there."

"I've got to try," he said. "I don't think there's any alternative."

"No," she said, "I mean I *know* you won't find any help there. I've been following you, making sure you weren't one of them. Your complete lack of skill almost made me think you were, but you're not. I know you saw the bodies at the pub. They came from Anglesey, and no one came to look for them." She looked at her watch. "Go to Wales if you want, or come with me, but don't stay here. It isn't safe."

She could have shot him without his ever knowing he was being followed, or not warned him about the zombie in the lake, or just left him be. Had she wanted to harm him, she could have. That she hadn't didn't mean she could be trusted. There was something odd about her. Something unsettling that Eamonn couldn't put his finger on. Even so, he needed to rest. He needed supplies.

"Anywhere without the undead would be welcome," he said. "I'm Eamonn Finnegan," he added.

"Sorcha Locke," she said.

They travelled in silence. Sometimes she was at his side, sometimes a step behind but she was always watching him, inspecting him, *judging* him. Against what and why, he wasn't sure. When she stopped, he stopped. Sometimes he could hear the undead moving on the other side of a thin fence, at other times he could hear nothing. After ten minutes, but only a few hundred yards from the park, they came to a smoke-blackened five-storey apartment building. The ground floor windows were broken. Soot stained the walls. At the rear of the building, a zombie staggered towards a row of garages. Locke raised her crossbow, fired, and was slotting a new bolt home before the creature fell.

"Give me a hand," she said, walking over to the corpse.

"A hand with what?"

"We have to move the body. We don't want them to find it." She pulled out a clasp knife and cut the bolt free. "Don't just stand there. Be quick! The red door, open it."

Reluctantly, certain he knew what lay inside, stealing himself against the stench, he heaved the garage door up. The interior was empty, at least of bodies. There was a plastic covered sofa-set, and an odd assortment of lamps and tables, but no undead. Locke dragged the zombie into the garage. They closed the door, and she kicked mud and leaves over the trail of gore.

"Why are we hiding the body?" Eamonn asked.

"Because if they find it, they'll know I was here," she said. It was an answer that explained nothing, before he could ask another question, she pointed at the apartment building. "There's a door behind the bins."

The door led to a fire escape and stairwell. She led him inside, up to the fifth floor, and into a two-room flat. The fire hadn't reached it, but the smoke had, adding an acrid edge to the smell of damp seeping through the broken doors to the Juliet balcony. In the corner of the living room was a crib, with toys kicked against the wall. Three half-packed bags were in the kitchen, suggesting whoever had lived there had fled unwillingly and unprepared. Water stained the wall near the sink. A line of rust ran up the wall from the light switch to a recessed lamp. Mould bloomed on the carpet near the balcony, though it hadn't spread to the leatherette sofa onto which the woman sat.

"Was this your home?" Eamonn asked.

"No," Locke replied. "I found this building last week. I thought it might be a good refuge, but the structure isn't sound. It's a place to watch them, though."

"Watch who?"

"Unless I'm wrong, they'll pass by in half an hour." She glanced at her watch. "Maybe a little longer."

"Who will?" Eamonn asked.

"Tell me your story first, the long version this time." She laid the crossbow on her lap, and though the bolt was pointing outside, Eamonn suddenly felt distinctly unarmed.

"The long version will take longer than half an hour," he said, "but it began after the outbreak at a radio station in London. Things were… they were okay. Three people turned up. A soldier called Tuck, a boy called Jay, and an injured man called Stewart. Tuck made things…" He hesitated. At first, Eamonn hadn't liked Tuck. At first, he'd dismissed her as a burden. At first. "She made things easier. She didn't take over, or take control. It was clear that she could leave at any minute, but she stayed and because of that we thought it could work, right up until it didn't. Water was the problem."

"It always is," Locke said. "How did you solve it?"

"By relocating to the Tower of London," Eamonn said. "Getting it from the river proved to be more difficult than we expected. We spent half our days breaking wood for the boilers. Before we got to the Tower, some of us were trapped in the British Museum, and were rescued by Nilda, Jay's mother. Now, she *did* take charge."

"She wasn't with you at the radio station?"

"Sorry, I'm not telling this in the right order. Jay and Nilda lived in Cumbria. They'd been separated just after the evacuation. Jay had left a note for his mother saying that he was going to London. He'd been born there, and he thought if there was anywhere in the world they might find one another again, it would be London."

Locke gave a snort, more of amusement than derision. "He ran away to London? Some things don't change, even after the apocalypse. The mother came south?"

"Nilda came via Anglesey," Eamonn said. "After they were separated, she ended up on a Scottish— Radiation!" He snatched the dosimeter from his belt. It still showed the same reading as before. Locke looked at him quizzically.

"What?" she asked.

"The radiation! Everyone in Anglesey thought Birmingham was radioactive. I've been carrying this around, but I'm sure it's broken."

"The city's not radioactive," she said. "The nearest crater is outside Peterborough. You don't want to go there. I've suspicions about Leicester, but didn't have time to investigate it properly. We're fine here. Anglesey thinks Birmingham is a glowing ruin?"

"They sent people here," Eamonn said. "They lost contact. I think those are the people who were by the pub."

"Some of them, yes," Locke said. "They set up a base in a car showroom down near Yardley Wood."

"Some of them? What happened to the others?" Eamonn asked.

"I'll tell you when you finish, and your story isn't finished yet. So you knew about Anglesey from Nilda?"

"And from Chester. He'd been with us in London originally, but left, ended up on Anglesey, and came back to England with Nilda. He helped her look for her son."

"And they came to London and rescued you from the British Museum?"

"Some of us, yes," he said.

"And?"

"And then we went to the Tower of London. We were low on fuel and food, and had no ammo or much of anything else. We decided to go to Kent to pick fruit from the trees before it spoiled. We took the boat, Chester, Greta, Me—"

"Boat?" she cut in. "You have a boat? What kind?"

"A lifeboat," Eamonn said. "That's how Nilda and Chester made it to London. They found it on a cruise ship in Hull."

"A cruise ship? Were there any other ships there?"

"I don't know," Eamonn said. "Why do you ask?"

"Look around you," she said. "Look at the ruins. Do you see a future here? So you went to Kent. How did you end up in Birmingham?"

"We found some food, not much, but then we found the children. They came from a boarding school. There had been hundreds of survivors in a millionaire's mansion they'd turned into a farm. Over the months, everyone else had left or died. We managed to get the children back to the Tower, and we brought back some food, but not enough."

"That's why you're going to Anglesey?" she asked.

"Partly. The other part is that someone shot Chester. He's dying, and Hana, our vet, our doctor, is dead. That's why I left. We were out of food and under siege. I should have reached Anglesey weeks ago, but I was trapped by a horde of the undead."

"You won't find help on Anglesey," Locke said. "We came through there earlier this year. They tried to torture the information out of us. A friend of mine died. When did your people go through?"

"September."

"Who was in charge on the island?"

"An old couple, I think," Eamonn said. "I can't remember their names."

"They're still alive? Well, they won't be in charge. I barely made it out, and no one came looking for the people, *their* people, that they sent here."

"Because they thought Birmingham was radioactive," Eamonn said.

"Which is a nice excuse to give as to why no help was sent," Locke said.

"You think there's another reason?" Eamonn asked.

"Of course," Locke said. "Now, keep quiet. Watch."

"Watch what?"

"Shh."

She gestured out of the window. Eamonn walked over to it. Locke grabbed his arm and pulled him down. Even crouching, he could see the zombie in the street. A blue denim hat hid its head, but the sleeve of its green woollen jacket was torn at the elbow, its arm missing just below. Eamonn watched the zombie, uncertain why Locke thought it was somehow special. It looked like every other undead creature he'd seen. And then it collapsed.

A moment after that, a small group ran down the road. Six people, with a seventh following at the rear. Four carried assault rifles, three had double-barrelled shotguns. The front six ran with their weapons raised, almost as if they were trained for it. The one at the rear was moving more casually. He had close-set eyes, greasy black hair, olive skin, pockmarks on one side of his face, and an unlit pipe clenched in his teeth. The group of six ran to the corpse, spreading out, their attention on the surrounding buildings, but they never looked up. The pockmarked man waved them on, and they continued heading down the road. When they were out of sight, Eamonn turned to Locke.

"Who are they?" he asked.

"Do you know about Quigley?" she said. "Did you know he was behind the outbreak, behind the nuclear attacks?"

"I know he's dead. Chester said so," Eamonn said.

"Maybe Quigley's dead, maybe he's not," Locke said, "but those people used to work for him. They're his soldiers. His guard. They killed the people who came from Anglesey. They took their weapons. Before that, they took my warehouse."

"Your warehouse?"

"Let me ask you something," she said. "You said Chester and Nilda arrived in London having been on Anglesey, but when they arrived, you decided to go to Kent. Why didn't one of you set off immediately for Wales?"

"It was Nilda," Eamonn said. "She didn't trust them. It was to do with her son, and how—"

"She didn't trust them, and so now, when the only alternative is death, you're attempting the journey. How long has it taken you to get to Birmingham? You said weeks."

"About four, I suppose," he said.

"It's further to Anglesey," she said, "and there are fewer roads and far more mountains. Do you think you'll ever get there?"

"I've got to try," Eamonn said. "They'll die if I fail."

"There's always an alternative," Locke said. "In this case, the alternative is helping me."

"You? How?"

"I have a warehouse," she said. "It contains enough ammunition, weapons, clothing, and food for about five years."

"Why?" Eamonn asked.

"That's not important," Locke said. "Those people took my warehouse. They haven't taken my supplies. They're in a vault to which only I have the combination. That's why they're hunting me. That's what they were doing out there, looking for me, but they're too arrogant to consider that I'd be hunting them. There were thirty when they arrived, and now there are only twenty-three. In a few days, a few weeks, they'll all be dead. We can take those supplies of mine down to London. Your people will be saved."

Eamonn didn't believe her. Rather, he didn't know what part of that to disbelieve the most. "You want my help killing Quigley's soldiers?"

"Yes and no," she said. She picked up her crossbow.

"They're professionals," he said. "I'm not."

"Clearly," Locke said. "But they're not SAS. They're the rejects, the last pick of a rotten barrel."

Eamonn wasn't so ready to dismiss their ability. "I could be in Anglesey in a week, and back in London a few days after that."

"Ten days? Maybe," she said. "Or you could leave here with supplies two days from now."

"How would I get them to London?" he asked. "It's taken weeks to get here. No, the only quick way back to London is by boat."

"If you go to Anglesey and no one's there, or they won't give you a boat, what then? Will you walk back through England and Wales empty handed?"

Eamonn wasn't a soldier. He knew his limitations. He hadn't, not at first, but he'd learned the hard way what a weapon in trained hands could do.

"You've got a crossbow. I've got a crowbar and bayonet," he said. "They have rifles."

She smiled. "I know, but you won't need a gun and they won't get a chance to use theirs. You can stay with us tonight. Decide after you've eaten."

She led him to a building site less than half a mile from the apartment building. Five bare steel pillars jutted up from behind the hoardings. In front, clawing at the sheet metal sealing the entrance, were two of the undead. Locke whistled. It was an odd little tune, a jaunty shanty utterly out of keeping with the devastation surrounding them. The zombies heard it. One turned around, and then the other. Both were wizened, bent nearly double, covered more in open sores than clothes.

Eamonn raised the crowbar.

"Put it down," Locke said, and whistled again. The zombies staggered closer.

"What if there are more zombies?" he asked.

"You see the northernmost pillar in the building site?"

He wasn't sure which direction north was. "Sure," he said.

"If there were more than five, there'd be a strip of blue plastic hanging from it," she said.

The zombies were fifteen feet away when Locke fired. The bolt sung through the air, plunging through the forehead of the nearest creature. Before it had hit the ground, Locke was working the ratchet, pulling the string back.

Eamonn raised the crowbar to his shoulder, his eyes on the last remaining zombie. Eight feet. Six. He shifted his weight, tightened his grip, but before he could swing, a bolt sprouted from the zombie's eye. It fell, and again, Locke was already reloading.

A section of the metal sheeting covering the building site swung aside. A hand appeared. A small hand. It waved.

"We're clear," Locke said. She slung the crossbow on her back. "Grab that zombie's legs."

Following her lead, he dragged the corpse to the nearest house. The smell hit him before she pushed open the door. It was the smell of London. The house was full of the slowly rotting undead.

"Just leave them in the hall," Locke said. "One way or another, we'll be leaving here soon."

Pausing only to push the door closed, she led him across the street. The metal sheet was still open.

"Phoebe, this is Eamonn," Locke said to the girl on the other side. "Eamonn, this is Phoebe."

He followed Locke inside. It wasn't what he'd been expecting. For one thing, it was a narrow corridor of corrugated metal. The girl, Phoebe, was dressed in a cut-down version of the same blue jumpsuit Locke wore. The girl looked him up and down.

"Where are you from?" she asked.

"Originally? Dublin, I suppose," he said.

"Oh, you're one of Sorcha's friends? That's good!" she said, and before Eamonn could correct her, she'd sidled through a gap far too small for an adult.

It was a murder-hole, a narrow corridor less than three feet wide that bent at ninety degrees, and then again. The top was open, but he could hear the people on the other side. He could imagine them firing crossbow bolts into him. At the far end of the narrow tunnel, a narrower gate was already open. Eamonn stepped through and into a semi-circle of people. There were six of them. Seven if you counted the infant in the woman's arms. An older woman stood next to her, two young girls just behind. A bearded man stood next to them, his hand on the knife at his belt, a young boy at his side. All, except the baby, wore a blue jumpsuit.

"Hi," Eamonn said.

"This is Eamonn," Locke said. "He came from London. He's going to help us."

There was half an hour when he did nothing but answer questions. When food appeared, Eamonn devoured it, and as that gave a pause to their questions, he finally got some answers.

"We'd taken refuge in the library before Sorcha came," the older Isabella said. "She was a gift from God. We had food, we had weapons, we had water, and we had strong walls behind which we could enjoy them."

"Then Barker came," Gavin said. "If Sorcha was a gift, Barker was a curse. That was in the middle of August."

"No, it was the beginning of September," Phoebe said.

"We've got a long-running dispute about what the date is," Gavin explained.

"Barker's one of Quigley's soldiers?" Eamonn asked.

"Their leader," Locke said. "I think that's his name. He's the man with the pipe. I got close enough to hear two of them talking, and heard that much before they realised I was there. That's how we know they came from Quigley. You know Quigley worked in covert operations before he was a politician? One of the reasons for his meteoric rise was his knowledge of the off-the-books missions that the British government took part in. I don't know why Barker came to Birmingham, but he found our warehouse. We weren't cautious enough. We lost most of our supplies, but we escaped."

"Not all of us," Phoebe said. "Micah and Talya didn't. They died."

"Hush, now," the older Isabella said.

"We've been hiding since then," the younger Isabella said. "We've got some supplies, but they won't last forever."

"Why haven't you left?" Eamonn asked.

"To go where?" the older Isabella asked.

"It's the baby," Gavin said. "It is," he added as the children glared at him. "Have I left? No. I stayed, didn't I?"

"Of course you did," the older Isabella said. "He's right," she added, addressing Eamonn. "It *is* difficult travelling with young Bella. She doesn't know to be quiet. It's why we stayed here. In the city, we can kill the undead, and we have plenty of buildings in which to barricade ourselves.

163

Even with Barker and his people, the city is safer than the wide-open countryside."

"We could kill the undead when we had ammunition," Locke said. "Barker and his people have been killing them since, though not as thoroughly as we were. We had planned to drive to the coast. We were syphoning petrol from across the city, and Gavin and I have been venturing out, searching for a route to the sea. That's how we discovered the crater near Peterborough."

"I've never seen the like," Gavin said. "It was—"

"Shh!" the older Isabella said, throwing a glance at the three children. "We've been through that before. Now, why don't you three go and read. Go on. See if you can find some books about London." Grumbling, the children left.

"Before Barker came," Locke said, "we *had* planned to leave. Britain is dead. Ireland is the same. We needed to get to the coast, and get far away. I favoured taking the Grand Union Canal down to the River Thames, and then following it to the estuary. We were worried that we would be chased out of the city, but we thought that the danger would come from Anglesey, not from the north, and so we thought we had time. A canal boat is slow. If the undead heard Bella cry out, we might have been trapped, so Gavin and I went east. We were looking for the shortest route to the coast, and for vehicles that could take us there quickly. We didn't find one, but we found the crater. The canal was our only escape. It would be a dangerous journey, but danger is everywhere, and with guns and ammunition, the danger could be minimised. We began moving supplies out of the warehouse. We started with the food, taking as much as we could, as far as we could. Those supplies are what we've been living on, because Barker came. He took my warehouse, and the supplies we'd brought upstairs. It was a few months of food, and a few thousand rounds of ammunition. I always kept the vault locked when no one was inside. There is a code, and he doesn't know it. The weapons, the ammunition, and at least four years of food are still sealed inside, beyond his reach."

"He didn't seem to have a shortage of bullets earlier today," Eamonn said.

"Those are the guns he took from the group which came from Anglesey," Locke said. "They can't have had more than a few hundred rounds apiece. The people I've killed have never had more than a handful of spare cartridges. They have a few shotguns, a few sidearms, but nothing that counts as an arsenal. He has to be running out of ammo, and of food, but he can't get into the vault. Nor can we as long as he's there. Without the ammunition, it isn't safe for us to travel slowly, and with the child, we can't travel quickly. Your arrival changes that."

"I don't see how," Eamonn said. "It took me a month to get here from London."

"Did you follow the canal?" Locke asked.

"No, I travelled along the railway when I could, on the roads when I couldn't, and the fields when I had to."

"I followed the canal south," Locke said. "I travelled fifty miles, and it was safe and easy. *Relatively* easy. It took three days for the round trip. There is a canal boat ten miles away, and another twenty miles beyond that. There are some gates and locks that require electricity to open, but the mechanisms are simple, and we have a portable generator."

"Do you have fuel?" Eamonn asked.

"A little diesel," Locke said. "Enough to get us to London, but no further."

Eamonn shook his head. "The River Thames is blocked," he said. "The bridges have fallen. Upstream, the locks are blocked with floating wreckage. You might be able to get to the city's outskirts, but no further."

"Presumably someone did," Locke said. "Someone who told you that the river was blocked."

"Jay and Tuck," Eamonn said. "They came through there on their way into London."

"We can do the same," Locke said. "We'll find a way."

"Maybe," Eamonn said. "Even if you managed it, the reason I left London was because we were low on food. That's why we went to Kent. I don't know how much will be left by now, but as soon as we got there, someone would have to set out for help, and the only help we know of is on Anglesey. In which case, better I continue the journey now, and from here."

Locke smiled. "I propose a trade. When we get to London, I'll take all the supplies I can fit into a ship. You can have the rest. The ammo, the food, the clothing."

"I thought that was all in the warehouse?" Eamonn said.

"It is," Locke said.

"In a vault?" Eamonn asked.

"Yes."

"There's a secret way in?"

"No."

"So, to be clear, you want me to kill all of these soldiers first?" Eamonn asked.

"No," Locke said. "We were storing the fuel in the warehouse, and while they've been burning some of the diesel in the generator, they've had no reason to touch the petrol. There's close to a thousand gallons. Here's my plan. They know what we all look like, but they've never seen you before. Tomorrow, when Barker goes searching for us, Gavin will let himself be spotted. He'll lead them to the Bullring. That shopping centre is a ruin. It's an easy place to lose them in. Meanwhile you, Eamonn, will go up to the gates. There will only be six or seven of them inside, and those are the least reliable of Barker's people. You'll spin them a story, and get a few more to leave. While they're distracted, I will sneak in. I'll set a timed incendiary in the fuel store. Gavin will vanish into the ruins, as will you, and I will sneak back out. Barker and his people will return. At midnight, the incendiary will detonate. The fuel will explode. The soldiers will die. The vault, though, will be intact. We will lose the fuel, but we will regain everything else. Getting down to London will be easy when we have more ammunition than we can carry, and no need to stop to search for food. Once there, your people will be fed. Any who wish can return here to collect whatever they need from the vault. I will use your lifeboat to find a larger ship, and then I will return. Anyone who wants to come with me on the next part of my voyage would be more than welcome. I think everyone will. There is no future in Britain. No future for any of us."

There was silence. It seemed like Gavin and the Isabellas were as stunned as Eamonn.

"Do you have an incendiary?" Eamonn asked.

"I can make one," Locke said. "It isn't hard."

"There's another way into the warehouse? A back door or something?" he asked.

"No," Locke said, "there's only one entrance, but I can climb up to the roof if I know they're distracted."

Eamonn shook his head. "I'm sorry," he said. "I wasn't clear. We *had* a boat. We *had* some fuel. We don't even have food. It took me a month to get this far. It might take me another month to make it the rest of the way, but I have to try. I have to go to Anglesey."

"He's right," the younger Isabella said. "It's over, Sorcha."

"Anglesey sent those people here," Locke said. "No one came to look for them. Perhaps they didn't care. Perhaps there is no one left. Can we take the risk?"

"We have to," the older Isabella said. "Your explosive might not work. They might have used up all the petrol. They might not follow Gavin, or catch him, or give up too soon. They might shoot Eamonn on sight, or spy you climbing in. Your plan is fraught with difficulties. Even if it were to succeed, we'd be moving from one ruined city to another. You really don't have a boat?"

"There are some life rafts," Eamonn said. "We looked for boats on our way down to Kent. We looked before then. Anything that could float was taken to sea by those early escapers from London. Yes, Nilda didn't entirely trust the people on Anglesey, and that's partly why we went to Kent rather than sending someone north immediately, but it was also because we knew how dangerous this journey would be. It took Tuck and Jay months to get from Penrith to London. Nilda and Chester made the journey more quickly, but that was because they spent a good portion of it at sea, following the coast. If there was another way, any other option, we would have taken it, but there wasn't. There isn't. Anglesey is our only hope."

"Anglesey won't help," Locke said.

167

"They might," Gavin said. "We've got enough food to last us until Christmas. That's more than long enough for Eamonn to get to Anglesey, for them to return here and deal with Barker."

"What if they won't come?" Locke asked.

"You don't want to go back there," the older Isabella said. "I understand, but you can't stop Eamonn, and you can't stop someone else from going with him. So, instead, go with him yourself, Sorcha. Go with Eamonn, and make sure he gets to Anglesey. How long did it take you to get here from there? Four days?"

"They have electricity on Anglesey," Eamonn said. "They turned the power station back on. In four days, five at the outside, we could have hot water and electric lights, and know that soldiers and sailors were coming to rescue those we care about."

"And if Bishop and the other murderers are still there?" Locke asked.

"Bishop, Barker," Gavin said, "what's the difference? You're ready to deal with one, so why not the other?"

"Will you go?" the older Isabella asked.

Reluctantly, Locke nodded.

Eamonn didn't follow all of the subtext, but he understood the message. He was going to Anglesey. He'd have supplies, and a companion who might be reluctant, but who knew how to move far more silently than he. If they set off at dawn, they should be in Wales before nightfall, and on Anglesey the day after. Three days at most, five at the outside.

Part 5
Search and Rescue

Chester

London and Beyond
November

"That was a nice wedding," Nilda said, "and it was nice to *have* a wedding. Aisha and Kevin looked so happy. It's a shame about the weather, though they say snow on your wedding day is good luck, just as long as the bride doesn't slip on the ice and spend the honeymoon in hospital."

"It was more like slush than snow," Chester said. "I've always said that you have to be crazy to get married in winter."

"Really?" Nilda asked. "How often have you said that? Anyway, technically it's still autumn."

"It's cold enough for winter," Chester said, "and it'll only get colder. I wish Greta wasn't going to Anglesey."

"You don't think she'll make it?" Nilda asked.

"It's not that," Chester said. "I think she stands as good a chance as anyone. Too many people have died, and I don't think there's any need for her to go. We've got food, we've got water, we should take the time to enjoy being alive. If we wait until spring, there'll be far fewer undead. By then, there might not be any need for her to go. If those satellites still work, they're bound to spot the paint on the roof and the smoke from the fires, not to mention us all wandering around. Or maybe they'll send a boat around the coast, just to see whether London is still habitable."

"There's still the danger of a horde," Nilda said. "We may have food and water, but if millions of the undead descend on London, if we have to flee using those rafts, too many will die."

"We can set up stashes of food downriver," Chester suggested.

"Maybe we should do that anyway, just in case," Nilda said, "but the world is too big a place for us to live alone. The people in Wales need to know we're here as much as we need them. Anyway, it's Greta's choice and no one is going to talk her out of it. It *was* a nice wedding," she added, taking his hand. "Let's walk the walls. The air seems fresher tonight. I think the river is finally starting to clear."

Hand in hand, they walked the Tower of London's walls while the sound of laughter carried to them from the castle below.

"I never asked, were you ever married?" Nilda asked.

"No, I'm not the marrying kind. You weren't though, were you?"

"No," Nilda said. "We just didn't get around to it. I regret that."

"I don't regret anything," Chester said. "Not anymore. On which note, I got you something." He took a small package out of his pocket.

"It's too large to be a ring. It's not, is it?" Nilda asked, an air of trepidation in her voice.

"Just open it," Chester said.

She did. "It's a book," she said, puzzled. "About Napoleon?"

"Turn to page one hundred and forty-two," Chester said.

She did. "It's a picture of my sword."

"Probably not your exact sword," he said. "It was the bee etched on the blade that gave it away. That was the emblem of the Bonaparte family. I saw one on a plate in the Fusilier's museum so I asked Fogerty about it. How was it your friend Sebastian described it, his retirement fund?"

"He said it was a replica, but an old replica," Nilda said.

"It was one of five hundred Napoleon had made and which he gave to his generals," Chester said. "The details are all there in the book. I thought... well, just because I don't have any memories I want to cherish, doesn't mean you shouldn't."

"It's perfect," she said, leaning in closer. "If it had been a ring..."

"Yes?"

"I'm just saying— Chester! Coming up the Thames. It's a ship!"

Five minutes later, Chester shifted anxiously from foot to foot, peering at the ship slowly approaching the riverbank. Next to him, Nilda stood stock-still. They were alone. Everyone else had gathered on the walls, and though they were keeping their weapons out of sight, they had them close to hand. In the frantic few minutes since the boat had been spotted, a hubbub of fears and hopes had echoed across the ancient fortress. They all hoped the boat came from Anglesey, bringing the prospect of safety for years to come. Harsh experience told them to fear the opposite.

The ship drew nearer. From above, a trio of bright hand-lamps were shone on the approaching craft.

"It's a sailing boat," Chester said.

"A racing yacht, do you think?" Nilda said. "There's a flag, isn't there? At the stern, is that… is that the skull and crossbones? It is! Oh, hell." She signalled to the walls, moving her hands in the same sign over and over again. They'd all been learning sign language, and though only Jay and Tuck were fluent, the sign for imminent danger was one that they all knew well.

"Wait," Chester said. "Wait, the submariners flew that flag."

"That's not a submarine," Nilda said, but it was too late to retreat to the walls. There was a moment of frantic activity on the ship. It slowed, sliding almost to a complete rest by the fragile jetty.

A young woman with short-cropped red hair jumped ashore, a rope in hand. She stopped, peered at Chester and Nilda, and then laughed. "Chester Carson! It's good to see you, and good to have the ground beneath my feet again," she said cheerfully as she secured the rope. "You wouldn't believe the trouble we had around the Isle of Wight."

Chester squinted into the darkness. His eyesight hadn't properly recovered from when Graham's bullet had scraped along his skull. He vaguely recognised the woman, and the voice was familiar, too. He certainly recognised the next one.

"Give Lorraine a hand, Chester," George Tull called out. "And then give me a hand to get out of this boat. It's been a rough voyage."

"George?" Chester couldn't believe it.

Nilda laughed. "You're from Anglesey?"

"Where else?" Lorraine replied.

"They're from Anglesey!" Nilda called to the tower walls. "They're from Anglesey!" There wasn't quite a cheer. It was more a collective sigh, but it was louder than the wind.

Another sailor jumped ashore, a woman Chester didn't recognise. As she helped Lorraine secure the boat, Chester reached down to help George onto the quayside.

"We saw the flag and thought the worst," Chester said.

"Flag? What flag?" George said. He looked to the rear of the craft where the skull and crossbones hung limp in the chill night air. "Lorraine," he said with a weariness that spoke to a very tiring voyage. "Sorry about that. I knew she'd borrowed it from the *Vehement*, but I'd forgotten to tell her to take it down. And I'm sorry that we're later than we could have been. Things got a little interesting on Anglesey. Nilda? I *am* glad to see you. How many are you here? How are you fixed for food? How safe are you?"

"Safe?" Chester asked. "Safe enough, I suppose."

"We're fine," Nilda said. "We've pushed the zombies back a quarter of a mile beyond the walls and have barricaded the streets. They sometimes get through, but they're not an immediate threat. As for food, why don't you come inside? You can join the party. You've caught us in the middle of a wedding."

"A wedding?" George asked. "Then this is a lot different to what I expected. A lot better than I hoped."

Another woman climbed ashore. "Does any one need medical assistance?" Her accent was American, her back straight, her posture rigid.

"This is Dr Harabi from the crew of the *USS Harper's Ferry*," George said. "She's a trauma surgeon by trade."

"We're fine," Nilda said. "Some of the children could do with a check-up, as could Aisha and Tuck. Chester, too. Actually, we all probably could, but no one's sick."

"That's a relief," George said. "We've got a fuel and ship crisis at the moment in that we don't have enough of either. Hence us coming here in a yacht, and me being the head of this particular expedition, but we do have a helicopter standing by in case an emergency airlift was needed."

"You have a helicopter?" Chester asked.

"And a plane," George said.

"Things have changed on Anglesey, then," Chester said.

173

"That's an understatement," George said. "We should discuss it, but inside, perhaps. Lorraine? Call Anglesey, and tell Scott Higson to stand down. He'll be upset he can't fly all the way from Anglesey, but personally, I'm glad he doesn't have to risk it. When you've done that, unload the aviation fuel. It was to top up the helicopter for the return leg," George added, turning back to Nilda and Chester. "Is there somewhere inside we can store it?"

"I'm sure we can find somewhere," Nilda said, "and while we're—" She stopped as the postern gate opened. Greta ran out and towards them.

"Is he here?" Greta demanded.

"Who?" George asked.

"Eamonn. Is he here?" Greta asked, desperation in her voice.

"I'm sorry," George said. "I don't know who that is."

"One of our people left, he was trying to reach Anglesey," Nilda said. "He didn't get there?"

"No, I'm sorry," George said. "We redirected a satellite over London and saw the message you painted on the roof. We set off immediately afterwards. We would have come sooner, and why we didn't is a long story. They all are, I'm afraid."

"He didn't make it," Greta said. She turned away and walked back to the Tower.

Chester frowned. Happy jubilation at the arrival of their hoped-for rescue vanished as the reality of George's words sank in.

"There's a shortage of ships?" he asked.

"And fuel," George said. "Food and ammunition, too. Why don't you give me a tour?" He turned to Lorraine. "The ship's secure?"

"I don't think Heather would approve of my knots, but since she's not here…" Lorraine grinned. "The Tower? That's cool. Do you have the crown jewels?"

"The children use them for dressing up," Nilda said.

"I'm sure they'll show them to you, *after* you've called Anglesey," George said.

Two hours later, most of the ship's crew and the castle's occupants were in the dining hall, listening to Lorraine and Kevin each trying to outdo the other with outrageously unbelievable stories of daring-do. The doctor had set up a small clinic in the castle's old first-aid station and had begun a slow but methodical examination of the survivors beginning with Chester, Tuck, and Aisha before moving on to the children.

George had joined Nilda, Chester, Tuck, and Jay in the hall's expansive kitchens.

"So, to summarise," George said. "No one needs immediate medical care but Tuck, here, could do with a scan. We can manage that, but you'll need to come back to Anglesey for it. By the way, it is good to see you both, Jay, Tuck. It's because of you that we thought to check London."

"Because of us?" Jay asked.

"Yes," George said. "Do you remember Bran, the man you saved from some soldiers a few months ago in the Pennine Mountains? He'd rescued a group from out of Quigley's clutches, but those renegades had followed them, and they'd caught him. By his account, they would have killed him if you and Tuck hadn't arrived."

"Sure," Jay said. "I remember him." His hands moved as he translated what George had said. Tuck gave a nod.

"We've all led a dozen lifetimes in this past year," George said. "So much of it has been abject horror that it's easier to forget it all rather than remember the few happy moments. We only put the pieces together a few days ago. Credit where credit's due, it's Annette who must take the lion's share. I don't know if you remember her, Nilda. She was the young girl on the boat that rescued you from that barren rock in the North Sea."

"I do, she's the one who found us?"

"She connected the dots, and took it upon herself to move a satellite," George said. "I'm not sure it would have been done otherwise. There's little propellant left, and we don't want to squander it, particularly at this time of year when so much of the sky is shrouded in cloud."

A loud cheer came from the kitchen. George smiled. "So many children. Now that gives me hope."

"What about Rob?" Nilda asked. "What did you do about him?"

George rubbed his shoulder, wincing slightly. "He's dead. Rob turned out to be as bad as you warned us he was. He murdered three people in Ireland and was killed during the pursuit. It all began with Rachel Gottlieb, I don't know if you remember her, Chester? A year ago, Rachel worked for Lisa Kempton, the woman who helped finance Quigley's plans. Rachel had recruited a number of people to her cause, murderers and rapists and the worst examples of humanity, but she was acting through a religious zealot named John Bishop. His people would abduct those Rachel wanted to get rid of. They would be taken to the mainland. There would be a mockery of a trial. The victims would be released into the wasteland where they were meant to be judged by nature or by God. Instead, one of Rachel's people would kill them. She used Bishop and the lunacy of his *trials* so she could keep at arm's distance from the crime, and keep the corpses off Anglesey where they were likely to be discovered. Some of her victims died because they had something that Rachel wanted. Others died because they were in the way. Most died so that she could steal their grain ration, and use that to buy support from strong arms that belonged to saner heads than the zealots. Her goal was to take over. She tried to rig the election, but she was caught. She was stopped."

"And Rob?" Nilda asked. "How did he have a hand in it?"

"He was recruited to her cause," George said. "I don't know if he felt he had a choice. Perhaps he just had an evil soul."

Tuck's hands moved. "She wants to know what happened to the other criminals," Jay said.

"Criminals is right," George said. "Rachel's dead. She died resisting arrest. That sounds far too modern. How it played out was more like the Wild West. She pulled a gun after she was accused. Bishop and most of his acolytes are dead, their lair destroyed. We don't think any escaped, but we can't be certain. Of those on Anglesey, the only evidence we found implicated one man, Gareth Lenetti." He looked at Chester. "Do you know the name?"

"I can't say that I do," Chester said. "What happened to him?"

"There was a trial," George said. "He was found guilty, and he was executed."

"What kind of evidence?" Nilda asked, suspicion clear in her voice.

"An audio recording of him confessing the crime to Paul, he was the man who shot me." George rubbed his shoulder again. "And he was the man who'd taken Rob under his dark wing. There are plenty of other suspects, people who lived on Bishop's farm, those who'd worked for or with Rachel, but we don't have any proof as to their involvement in what happened. We've split them up for now, and have them under as close a supervision as we can manage. There's not much more we can do."

Nilda gave a thoughtful nod.

"Did anyone else make it?" Jay asked. "From Penrith, I mean."

"No, I'm sorry," George said.

"Oh. I kinda wondered," Jay said. He shrugged as if it didn't matter, but it was clear that it did.

Tuck's hands danced. Jay, Nilda, and Chester nodded.

"I'm sorry," George said. "I don't understand."

"She wanted some more details about what you said about the power plant blowing up on January seventh," Jay said.

"I don't think it will blow up," George said. "It might, of course, and that's why we're going to shut it down no later than on the seventh of January. Chief Watts, the engineer from the *Vehement*, thinks there's an eighty percent chance that nothing critical will break before then. If we reach the deadline, we might be able to push it back a few days, or we might have a storm between now and then which causes us to bring it forward. The short version is that Anglesey is finished. We're moving everyone to Belfast, at least initially, and we hope to have that completed long before Christmas. When we shut the plant down, we won't be able to properly decommission it. There will be a leak, and probably a meltdown. The entire island might be contaminated, as might the Welsh mainland, or the Irish Sea. Possibly both."

Tuck's hands moved again.

"She says the problem's going to be contaminated fishing waters and contaminated rain," Jay said. His voice was low, absent of the jubilation that they had all shared when they'd first realised a boat had arrived from the island. "But she also says how much more contaminated can they get?"

"Exactly," George said. "We need the fish. Thanks to Lorraine and the people in Menai Bridge we've got enough seeds to plant a reasonable crop in the spring. It's mostly vegetables, but no potatoes or wheat, so we'll have to find those growing wild. The bigger question is where we plant that crop. We'll get one shot at it, and though Ireland has fewer zombies than Britain, it is far from safe. Can we find anywhere that's safer? I'm not sure. Wherever we plant that crop, we'll be living on fish until the harvest. If the fishing waters are contaminated, if there's no fish, or no fish we can eat, then we'll have lost our seeds and our one chance at keeping our species alive. That's why we're looking for a new home."

"Will you now look in London?" Nilda asked.

George shook his head. "I'm sorry, I don't think so. Britain simply has too many of the living dead. Nowhere on the mainland will be safe while they're still a threat. We might be able to hold Belfast, but it's too early to tell. The reason we're delaying shutting down the power plant until long after all the people have left is to keep the machine shops running. We're stamping out crossbow bolts as fast as we can cut the metal. Even so, we won't have enough. No, we won't be coming to London."

"We've got ammunition," Jay said. "About a million rounds. We've got some explosives, too."

"You do?" George asked.

Nilda closed her eyes. "Yes," she admitted. "Yes, we do. Quigley, we assume it was him, stashed supplies in London. We think he planned to keep an occupation force in the city, but whoever was commanding it rebelled against him. They fought their own civil war here. When they left, the supplies remained behind. We have rations, and we have a *little* ammunition."

"So you don't need to be resupplied?" George said. "That *is* good news. We can focus our efforts on moving people from Anglesey."

"If you're not staying in Ireland, where are you going?" Nilda asked.

"We're not sure," George said. "If the undead die, then everything might change. At present, the focus is on leaving Anglesey. Once that's done, the admiral is going to take a ship across the Atlantic. She'll head for Newfoundland, and then follow the coast down to North Carolina. Perhaps she'll find an empty island, perhaps she won't. She feels she has a duty to take her crew home one last time. I can understand that, and even if the expedition is a failure, it will mean no one else will risk a dangerous transatlantic voyage in search of a haven that doesn't exist. Depending on how long that takes, and what other ships we find, we'll send an expedition to the Mediterranean, perhaps another to the Baltic. That's as far ahead as we've planned." He smiled. "I don't want to give the wrong impression. It's not as gloomy as it sounds. Because of the nuclear power plant, we knew we'd have to leave Anglesey one day. That day arrived sooner than we thought. Things might become a little uncomfortable in Belfast over the next few months, but we've all been through worse. We do have the satellites, though we'll have to be cautious about their use. There are enough seeds for a proper planting as long as we choose the right patch of soil. We still have the oil for the large ships, and now we've found you." He gestured at the door beyond which came the sound of children laughing at another one of Lorraine's impossibly tall tales. "That *is* a wonderful sound. Times are going to be tough, but not as tough as they were. There is hard work ahead, but there is hope, too."

"It's a lot to think about," Nilda said.

"Of course," George said. He rose stiffly to his feet. "We'll talk again in the morning. If you don't mind, I'll have a word with those children. I think I have a story or two that will beat any Lorraine has to share, and ones after which they might find it easier to get to sleep."

"So Rob's dead," Nilda said, after George had left.

"Did you know that Bishop guy?" Jay asked.

"I can't put a face to the name," Chester said. "I think I could pick Rachel Gottlieb out of a line-up, but maybe not."

179

"We'll have to see what Kevin and Aisha have learned from the sailors," Nilda said. "I expect it's the same as George told us. I can't imagine any of that was a lie."

"So what are we going to do?" Jay asked.

"Easy," Tuck signed. "Trade some of our supplies for sailing boats, plan for a retreat but prepare for a defence. We have to hold the Tower against the undead, and against the weather. We've lost our safety net, and that's all Anglesey was. It was an *idea* of safety. We knew that already, didn't we?"

"It's not the news I was hoping from Anglesey," Chester said.

"But it's not what I feared," Nilda said.

"It is what it is," Tuck signed. "It's getting late. It's time the children were in bed." The soldier eased herself to her feet. She was on the road to recovery, but still moved stiffly, relying on her cane as she left the room. Jay followed, leaving Chester and Nilda alone.

"Some honeymoon for Aisha and Kevin," Chester said.

"The wedding seems so long ago," Nilda said. "How quickly things can change."

"How indeed," Chester said. "It's a lot to think about. I suppose we've been here before. We have a few months of grace and then a lifetime of uncertainty ahead of us."

"I think... no," Nilda said.

"What?" Chester asked.

"It's this guy, Bishop. It's Rob. It's that woman, Rachel. There will be others like that. People who didn't like the idea of living in Anglesey, and who like the idea of Ireland less. This would be a logical place for them to come. We don't want them, but how do we know who the dangerous people are if Mr Tull doesn't?"

"One more thing to worry about, and there's always going to be another."

"Isn't there just," Nilda said. She sighed. "The wedding really does seem like a long time ago. I'm going to give Tuck a hand getting the children into bed. I doubt they'll stay there, not tonight, but we should at least try to maintain their normal routine."

"I'll catch up with you in a bit," Chester said. He slipped out through the back door, and went up to the walls, pausing at the same spot he'd stood with Nilda a few hours before. In recent weeks, he'd had many different visions of their future. He'd imagined they'd take a house on Anglesey, or stay all together in their own small village, or they'd stay in London, reclaiming the city one building at a time. The idea that his imagination often returned to, but which he rarely dared believe, was that the undead would die, and there would be no limit to the possibilities ahead of them. Yes, he'd had many different visions of the future, but all were anchored around Anglesey and the society that was developing there.

He could hear the children excitedly chatter through the castle's thick walls. The carrying sound didn't matter. They'd pushed the undead back for nearly a quarter-mile in every direction. Except across the river, of course. He turned to stare south at the bulk of the museum ship, *HMS Belfast*, and the city beyond. A city where he'd grown up, a city he'd left, a city to which he'd returned and, finally, found love, life, and a future. He'd *thought* he'd found a future.

"You're getting maudlin," he muttered. "And it's getting cold."

He pulled his collar up, and made his way back to the stairs. As he did, he saw that a light was on in the Keep.

It was Greta. She was loading a magazine with ammunition.

"Can't sleep?" he asked.

She looked up. "Haven't tried," she said. She returned to loading the magazine. There were six already next to her.

"You're going to look for Eamonn," he said. It wasn't a question.

"If it was Nilda who'd left, wouldn't you search for her?" Greta asked. "Didn't you go with her to look for Jay?"

"Of course," Chester said, "but this is different."

"Because it's me, not you?"

"Because it's been nearly two months since Eamonn left, and we know he didn't get to Anglesey," Chester said. "He took the maps with him, the ones that marked the areas to avoid."

"If he used them, he's dead," Greta said. "Even if he didn't, he still might be dead in a million different ways, but there's still a chance he might be alive."

"Then why didn't he reach Anglesey?" Chester asked.

"He got lost. He got injured. Both. I could construct a thousand different narratives," she said, placing the loaded magazine on the table. "Any one of them might be true, but they're only stories and I find no comfort in them. He didn't make it to Anglesey. He probably is dead. No, he almost certainly *is* dead, but I have to look for him because I know he would look for me."

"Fair enough," Chester said. "You're leaving tonight?"

"I'm not Eamonn," she said with what was almost a smile. "I need to properly prepare. I'll leave at dawn."

"I'll get my gear ready," he said.

"You're coming, too? No, you have to stay."

"I don't," he said. "What's there to do here? I don't know how much you've heard about Anglesey—"

"They're all going to Ireland," Greta said.

"Which means we're not leaving the Tower," Chester said. "For now, we'll keep on doing what we've been doing, and Nilda doesn't need my help with that. I've walked the wasteland before, and it should have been me who set out for Anglesey, not Eamonn. Looking for him is the least I can do."

"I won't try to talk you out of it," Nilda said, when Chester told her of Greta's decision to leave and his to go with her.

"Which is a nice way of getting me to think of all the objections you might make," Chester said. He sat on the edge of the small bed in their small room. The two candles flickered in the wintry draft edging its way under the door. Their dim light cast odd shadows on the drawings made by the some of the younger children, and which they'd pinned to the wall. "Someone has to go with her," he said, "if only to make sure that she gives up the search. Otherwise she'll wander the countryside until she dies."

"I know," she said, "but still, I wish it wasn't you."

"Who else could go? Tuck can't, nor can Aisha. You're needed here, and we can't send Kevin or Jay. No, it has to be me."

"How long will you look before you give up?" she asked.

"A week," Chester said. "I'll have a word with George, find out which safe houses might still have some food in them. We'll go from one to the next, and see if we can get picked up somewhere on the Welsh coast. I'll take one of the sat-phones so I can stay in touch. If we get into real difficulty, they've got a helicopter now. That can pick us up. You don't need to worry, I've done this before."

"When you could properly see, when you could properly hear," she said. "Of course I'm going to worry."

Chester rubbed his scar. "Eamonn shouldn't have gone. It should have been me. A few hours ago, before that ship arrived, it was different. Greta wasn't leaving to search for Eamonn, but to reach Anglesey. When she got there, having found no trace of him, she'd have accepted that he was dead. Instead, now, there'll be no end to her journey. I remember—" He stopped.

"What?"

"Do you remember the journey to Penrith?" he asked. "Before we got there, before we found the note that Jay left in your old home?"

"Not really," she said.

"I do. I remember what you were like. Driven, yes, but purposeless. You were going back to bury your son. Do you know why I went with you?"

"Because you wanted to get to Hull. It was on the way," she said.

"I went to make sure that you gave up the search," Chester said. "I thought Jay was dead and that, when you saw Penrith again, you'd accept it. After we found that note you became possessed. You would have kept looking for Jay in London and then beyond. Nothing would have stopped you."

She sat down next to him. "No, it wouldn't."

"If he'd been dead, or undead, you would never have found his body," Chester said. "We won't find Eamonn, but we can't stop Greta from searching. If I'm with her, then in a week's time, when we're out of food and running low on ammunition, I might be able to persuade her to give up so as not to risk my life. If she's on her own, she'll continue looking until she finds death. Both of us know that she won't have to look very hard or for very long."

"One week," Nilda said. "Then make sure that both of you come home." She stood. "You'll need warm clothes. It might still be autumn, but winter is on its way."

Chapter 18 - The Journey North
Cuddington, 11th November, Day 243

"Assuming that's the Royal Train," Chester said, gesturing at the row of black carriages ahead of them, "then we're exactly where we want to be."

"There are zombies," Greta said. "Five of them close to the rear carriage." She slowed the bike, and then brought it to a stop next to an old concrete signal box. "We're not the first to come here," she added as she dismounted. In the weeds next to the derelict building was a bicycle. A bag still hung from the crossbar. "That's really the Royal Train?"

"I think so. Or I hope so," Chester said. "According to George, there should be a safe house about half a mile further along the tracks. Bran said he chose the spot because anyone coming this far would spend some time looking at the carriages."

"I suppose they would," Greta said, unslinging the submachine gun. It was a suppressed MP5AK from the store of weapons Quigley had left in London. Chester carried one himself, but left it on his shoulder as he squinted ahead.

"Can you see the zombies?" Greta asked.

"Sure," he said.

"Are you lying?"

"No, I can make out the shape, their outline. There are fallen branches on the rails. It looks like the hedgerow was torn apart. They must have come from across that field." He *could* see their outline, but he was unable to pick out any detail.

"I make it about three hundred metres," Greta said. She kicked gravel from the sleeper, knelt, and took aim.

Chester looked back along the tracks, then at the hills either side. It was all a vague blur. He lifted his hat, and rubbed at the scar. Physically, he was as fit as he'd been before he'd been shot. At least, that's what he told himself. His knees were pulsating after a long day's cycling, his feet felt like they wanted to burst out of his boots, and the skin on his hands was weirdly tight. Life in London was hard, and not a day went by that he didn't go to bed exhausted. There was always wood to chop, water to be collected and boiled, clothes to be washed, and the undead to be kept behind the increasingly complex barriers they had in the streets ringing the castle. What there wasn't, but which this trip had in abundance, was the constant tension of the undead about to spring at them from behind every tree or bend in the road.

He peered at the carriages. If that was the Royal Train, then they were near the village of Cuddington, about five miles west of Aylesbury, forty miles northwest of London. The safe house should be somewhere in the hills ahead. Even if it had been overrun in the months since Bran had set it up, they'd find somewhere else to shelter, though they'd have to find it soon. The clouds hadn't opened during the day and the wind had dropped, but the temperature hadn't risen. Night was approaching, and it would be another cold one.

Greta fired.

"Good shot," Chester said.

"I missed," she said.

"Oh."

They'd left the Tower at dawn, and had taken two hours to travel the six miles to Hampstead. That was good time compared to the occasional excursion he, Jay, and Kevin made into the ruined capital. The rest of the journey had been much faster, at least when they'd been moving in the right direction. Dense packs of the undead had forced them off the railway lines twice, and so Chester was only seventy percent certain they were now in the correct place. It didn't matter if it wasn't. One place was as good as another to begin their search for Eamonn, since wherever they began, it was unlikely they'd ever find him.

Greta fired again. "Got it," she said. "Four left. Can't see any more." She shifted aim, and fired.

Chester finally put aside his pride and took out the binoculars. Three creatures slowly slouched towards them. Covered in mud with branches and leaves stuck to their coats, they almost looked like they wore camouflage.

Greta fired again. "Got it. Two left. A hundred and fifty metres."

Chester's hand went to the mace at his belt. The steel head was an antique that verged on artefact, but the shaft was a cut-down shovel-handle wrapped with surgical tape. There was no need to draw it, not yet.

Greta fired again, and there was only one zombie left. Another shot, followed by a muted curse, and then one more.

"It's done," Greta said.

"Good job," Chester said, lowering the binoculars.

"I was slower than I should have been," Greta said.

"It's the wind-chill," Chester said. He picked up his fold-up bike. "The safe house is ahead. We'll rest there."

The fold-up bikes had been an answer staring them in the face. On the journey from Hull, they'd been frequently forced off the road and into the sodden quagmires that had once been fields. During the mad dash through Kent, those fields had more than frequently been washed into the road, turning the smooth surface into a sticky morass. While carrying bicycles through the gluey mud, they were no faster than the undead. The fold-up bikes favoured by London's commuters were the obvious solution. The smaller wheels reduced their maximum speed, but it took only a matter of seconds to collapse the entire bike into a package that could be hauled, one-handed, at quick clip across a field. On balance, they were close to the ideal apocalyptic transport. They wheeled them up the train tracks, and around one undead corpse and then the next. Chester gave them barely a glance.

"These ones weren't dying," he said. "Nor were those that forced us off the road earlier. Makes me wonder whether the creatures in London are the exception."

"Hmm? What? No," Greta said, Chester's words finally cutting through her fog of concern. "No, they've seen some die on Anglesey. Not *on* Anglesey, but in Wales and Ireland. Didn't you hear? I was speaking to the sailors from that boat."

"Ah. George said they've got one confirmed case, and about two hundred possibles. I suppose we'll know, one way or another, before spring. That does look like a crown, don't you think?"

Greta peered at the golden badge stamped to the carriage's side. "It's covered in grime, but I think that matches the crests they have in the Tower. What did Bran say about this?"

"George did," Chester said. "He said that Bran had set up a safe house a little way up the tracks, but there should be a map and some supplies inside the train."

He rapped his fist against the nearest window and heard no sound in reply, but he trusted his hearing no more than his eyesight. The glass was tinted and covered in dirt.

"Can't see anything," he said. "Let's try the door. You ready?"

They moved their bikes a little way down the tracks in case a quick escape was needed. With Greta's gun aimed at the door, Chester pulled it aside. No one, and no undead, were inside the train.

"I have to say, I'm not impressed," Chester said. "This doesn't look much different to the first class on an intercity service. Maybe this carriage is for the staff."

"The note's here," Greta said. "There's a bag of supplies under this table. It's untouched. When did Bran come here?"

"During the summer, according to George," Chester said. "I'm not sure precisely when."

"Four or five months? No one's been here since."

"There was that bike by the signal box," Chester said.

"Exactly," Greta said. "Whoever owned it must have been killed. Why else would they have abandoned their bicycle? Let's find that safe house."

"You don't— Sure," Chester said. He wanted to look at the rest of the train, mostly because it would be a story to tell the children. It came of living in an ancient castle where the old crown jewels had become a children's plaything. But Greta was right, no one had been in the train, and anyone who'd come this far would surely have been as curious as he. He followed her back outside. The wind was picking up.

"Maybe Eamonn came a different way," Chester said. "I mean, if it was me, picking a route that avoided the motorways, I'd go for the railways and the canals, but he might have stuck to the side roads."

"It wasn't just that," Greta said. "Do you know how many survivors have arrived on Anglesey since you and Nilda left there?"

"No," Chester said. "I didn't ask."

"I did," Greta said. "I asked those sailors. They didn't know the exact number, but it's less than a hundred, and that's counting the people they found in Ireland. No one made it from Kent. I mean, if they had, they would have mentioned the children, wouldn't they?"

"Hmm." Now it was his turn to be thoughtful. "So no one from Kent, well, we guessed that, and I suppose if there was anyone left in the Home Counties, they would have made their way to London and the Thames."

"Anglesey is a logical destination for any survivor to try to reach," Greta said. "It's not the only one. Anglesey, the Isle of Man, the Isle of Wight, Orkney, those are the obvious places to aim for. If anyone had enough supplies to last this long, but was worried they'd run out during the winter, the beginning of autumn was the most sensible time to make the journey. The days would still have been long, the nights not too cold. Few people made it. Why? Because there's no one left."

"There probably is," Chester said.

"Maybe a handful," she said. "Maybe a few hundred spread out across Britain, but not a group like ours. We're the exception because we have ammunition for silenced weapons. We have military rations, and without them we would have left the Tower and attempted to reach Anglesey. We would have died, Chester. Don't you see? That's what has happened. We're the last. It's over."

Chester wasn't sure what to say to that, so he said nothing.

"There, up on the hill," Greta said half a mile later. "There's a house with sheets hanging from the windows. Can you see it?"

"Oh, yes," he said. "Sure."

"What colour is the flag hanging out of the left-most window?"

"It's the cross of St George," he said instantly.

"It's a pink bed sheet," she said. "Use the binoculars. Tomorrow, we'll find you some glasses. What was the nearest town, Aylesbury?"

"That's it."

"Then we'll look there," she said. "For signs of Eamonn or…" She trailed off.

There were footprints in the mud leading from the railway and a trio of lines trampled through the overgrown paddock. Chester had the mace in hand long before they reached the house.

They found the zombies outside a barn. Three creatures squatted by the partially open door. Chester had no trouble seeing the stains around the wounds where they'd been infected, the cuts and wheals that had spread as the rotting skin had stretched, the tufts of hair on a balding scalp, or the broken, blackened teeth. He swung the mace low, then high, letting his muscles take over. He slammed the ancient weapon into a knee, then up into the zombie's head as it fell. A small, shiny cube flew from the creature's ear. With a practiced flick, Chester turned the upswing into a sideswipe that crushed the next zombie's arm. It staggered sideways, and he stepped back before he punched the mace into its chest. Ribs cracked, and the zombie crumpled to its knees. He swung down, crushing its skull just as its hands clawed around Chester's boots. He kicked his feet free, bringing the mace back up.

There was a muffled crack as Greta fired. The last zombie fell.

"Feel better?" she asked.

"Better? I feel tired."

"Sometimes you need to feel in control," she said. "You did the same thing in Kent."

"I did?"

"Sure." Greta shrugged. "But so did I. I think we all feel like that. The one thing we all learned from the outbreak, the war, is that we were all utterly powerless to have stopped it."

Chester wiped the mace clean on the long grass, and saw something glint in the sunlight. It was the object that had flown from the zombie's face, a diamond earring. Sometimes it was too easy to forget the living dead had been living people not so long ago.

It took a minute to confirm that the barn was empty of the undead, twenty to confirm that there were no more in the surrounding paddocks, and another thirty to check the house itself.

Chester dropped his pack on the kitchen floor. "That's the map," he said, pointing at the counter top. "It's in Bran's handwriting." He checked the cupboards underneath. "Someone's been here," he said. "There're a couple of empty cans in the rubbish bin. We'd have to check how much food Bran left here before we can tell how much was eaten, but we can do that when we call in."

"There's not much point," Greta said, crossing to the kitchen window. "One person or two, three months ago or four, it doesn't matter. They left because of that map, but they didn't get to Anglesey."

"It's directing them to Llanncanno," Chester said. "That's a beach along the coast."

"It was a mistake," Greta said.

"What was?"

"The maps," she said. "Telling people to leave these safe houses. They should have been told to stay here, and that help would come."

"But help wouldn't have come," Chester said. "This way, they had a chance. What was the alternative? There was a well in the barn. I'm going to get some water. We'll have a wash, have some food, and get some rest."

As a rule, Chester avoided introspection. In his old life, thinking too deeply conjured questions about the morality of his deeds. That was never a good idea for a professional thief. Part of being a professional, and one of the ways he'd avoided incarceration, was to observe his victim prior to a crime. He'd get to know their schedule, their habits, their weaknesses. Of course, back then, he'd thought of them as marks, not victims.

Since the outbreak, and since he was first bitten, he'd found it impossible *not* to think too deeply. He'd tried channelling that into thinking about others, deciding his own future was pre-determined, and that redemption would come through self-sacrifice. Then he'd met Nilda, and he'd read some of Bill Wright's journal. He'd learned what Cannock had done, and confronted the real truth of his own past.

191

Chester had never been as evil as his childhood associate, but he'd never stopped Cannock. He'd had many opportunities to turn the man into the authorities or to do the more normal, human thing of trying to make the man see the error of his ways. Yet how could Chester have done that without accepting the errors of his own? He'd devoted himself to finding Jay, and then to keeping the others alive, but always with the expectation that his own life would eventually be forfeit. He had expected to die, but in the end, he had survived.

In Kent, he'd thrown himself at the undead because he'd not placed any value on his own life. He'd done the same in London and elsewhere. Since then, he'd told himself that he had a blank slate, an uncertain future before the final certainty of death. He had Nilda, he had Jay, and he had everyone else. So was Greta right, did he need to feel in control? Or was there something else?

"How does anyone ever know?" He dropped the bucket down into the well.

As he was hauling it up, he heard running footsteps. A moment later, Greta dashed into the barn.

"It *was* Eamonn!" she said, holding something out.

"What's that?"

"Eamonn's ring! He was here."

"He was?" Chester let go of the rope. The bucket plummeted down into the well. He peered at the ring, but to him it was just a gold wedding band. "Did you give that to him?"

"It was from his first marriage," she said. "His wife died. He wore this around his neck."

"Are you sure it's his?"

"Look at the inscription," she said.

There were letters, and one might have been an *E*, but he couldn't tell. "If you're positive."

"I am," she said.

"Where did you find it?"

"By a window," she said.

"Was there a note?"

"No. I... I'll look again."

"Right. I'll come and help in a moment." He turned back to the well. The rope had slid in, all the way to the bottom.

By the time he'd found another bucket and rope, and had collected enough water to wash and drink, Greta had searched the house twice.

"There's no note," she said. "Should I expect one? No. Eamonn wouldn't have expected to fail, not this close to London." She sounded far more energised than earlier.

"All right," Chester said as he scraped his knife along the edge of the chair. He peered at the splinter. "Looks okay, just polish, not varnish. Shouldn't be any dangerous fumes." He threw it into the grate. "All right, so Eamonn came here for the same reason that we did, for the same reason that Bran set up a safe house here. If you're avoiding the motorways, the railway is the obvious alternative. There're a few lines leading from London, but this was the most logical route to get to Wales."

"The note in the kitchen mentions a place in Wales, but it's not Anglesey."

"Llanncanno," Chester said.

"When was the last time anyone went there," she asked.

"No idea. I'll ask when I call in with our position."

"Maybe he's there," she said. "I mean, he has to be somewhere. He... he..." She trailed off, the excitement fading from her voice. "He made it this far, that's all. He made it far enough out of London that, when something went wrong, he tried to go on rather than go back. That doesn't alter that something *did* go wrong."

"It doesn't mean he's dead," Chester said. "In some ways he survived the most difficult part."

"Oh, Chester," she gave a wan smile. "You're humouring me, and I thank you for it, but the truth is that he's dead."

"If I'm humouring you, I'm humouring myself, too," Chester said. "Let's assume he's alive. So, if he's alive, he's injured, probably with a broken leg or something, but that means he has to be somewhere with supplies. Most likely it's another safe house. When he left here, he would have travelled to the safe house in the Cotswolds mentioned on that map.

That's about fifty miles away. If he made it that far, he would have aimed for Llanncanno. So, that's the route we'll take."

"Do you really think he's alive?" Greta asked.

Chester took out a small bottle of lighter fluid from his pack and gave the wood a generous squirt. He struck a match and flicked it onto the kindling. There was a soft whoosh as the fire took.

"Chester?" Greta prompted.

"Honestly, I don't know," he said. "Part of me thinks that anyone who survived the outbreak stands a good chance of still being alive today. The other part of me remembers all those who I've seen die. I'll give George a call and see when someone last went to that beach."

The call went through, but it wasn't George that answered.

"Chester, yes? Hi, sorry you've caught us in the middle of dinner." The voice was English, male.

"Hi, yes, this is Chester, who's this?"

"Bill Wright. I've been wanting to speak to you for a while, but that particular conversation can wait until we meet. Where are you?"

"Near Aylesbury," Chester said. "The safe house at Cuddington, near the ruin of the Royal Train."

"Ask him if the Queen was in it," a young girl said.

"Sorry," Bill said. "The phone's plugged into the speakers. The whole room can hear you. Is there any sign of your friend?"

"Actually, yes," Chester said. "He came through here, though we're not sure when. Bran left a note here that lists two other safe houses, one in the Cotswolds, the other at Llanncanno. Do you know the last time anyone went through there?"

"No, but I'll find out," Bill said.

"How did you know it was me calling," Chester asked.

"It's caller I.D. of a sort," Bill said. "We're routing all calls through a digital switchboard, one we'll take with us when we go. We're hoping to set it up so people can call each other rather than having all calls coming through here, but that's proving more complicated than we have time for.

194

We've got a boat heading towards Caldey Island, then to Lundy. If you're heading to Llanncanno, they can pick you up."

"I'm not sure if we'll end our search when we reach it," Chester said.

"Of course," Bill said. "I totally understand."

"Ask him about the train," the girl said again.

"There was no sign of the Queen," Chester said.

"Call back in the morning," Bill said. "I'll see what more information I can find. We'll send the boat to Llanncanno anyway. You can get on board or you can resupply."

"Thank you," Chester said.

"Of course. I understand what you're doing, and why," Bill said.

Chester went back to the fire, and watched the flames. Bill Wright might think he knew his motivation, but Chester wasn't sure he knew it himself.

Chapter 19 - Jagged Scars
Oxfordshire, 12th November, Day 244

Even Chester could see the jagged scar ripped out of the landscape by the passage of thousands of the undead, but he didn't raise the binoculars. He had no desire to see the details.

"Zombies did this?" Greta asked. "This was the horde? They came all this way from Hull?"

"*A* horde did it," Chester said. "I don't know if it was the same one as Nilda and I saw in Hull."

"If it was, then it came from the north, and turned west here," Greta said.

"Maybe," he said. "I'm going to call it in. We're not going to reach Bicester now."

"No?"

Chester pointed at the jagged gash leading westwards. "It's over there." Before they'd left the safe house, he'd called Anglesey. They'd been given a list of places that lay more or less on the route to Wales and been asked to investigate them. The first was a vehicle-restoration centre near Bicester. Someone on Anglesey had liberated an old Triumph motorbike from there, and made it to the shadow of Snowdon before the engine had given out. That had been three weeks after the evacuation, but, in addition to a score of other heritage vehicles, they'd found tanks of fuel. It wasn't likely that the fuel had survived the intervening months unlooted, but it had been worth making a slight detour to check. "No," he said again, "we're not going to Bicester now."

Greta jumped the ditch at the side of the road and climbed the dry-stone wall. "Nothing. No, there! Movement. Zombies. Two of them." She climbed down, and sat on the wall's edge. "They're heading south."

"Right," Chester said. He took out the sat-phone and called Anglesey.

"Is that Chester?" It was the young girl who answered.

"It is. Is anyone there?"

"It's just me," she said. "Everyone's packing."

"Is something wrong with power plant?" Chester asked, a new fear piling on top of that of the horde.

"Oh, no. I mean, yes, but there's no change, not that they've told me. We're always packing, now. Where are you? Did you find the motorbikes?"

"We didn't get to Bicester," Chester said. "We're about ten miles west of the safe house. We're… we're looking at a…" He struggled to find words to describe it. "A horde passed this way. They've left a jagged scar through the landscape. Either they came north and took an abrupt turn west towards Wales, or they came from the west and headed north."

"Leaving, like, a desert behind?" the girl asked. "Like there's nothing but dirt and dust and rubble and twisted metal? Hang on, I just need to find the map." She didn't seem shocked. There was the sound of pages being turned. "Is it near Stratford-upon-Avon?"

"Look south of there," he said.

"Yeah, maybe it's the same one that trapped us near Wales," she said.

"Can you get the satellites overhead?" he asked.

"I could," she said, "but I'm not allowed to do it again. I'll have to ask Kim."

"Then you do that," he said. "I'll find out precisely where we are, and I'll call back." Chester hung up.

Greta's eyes were fixed on the desolate expanse.

"It was a girl on duty, a teenager," Chester said. "Everyone else is busy. Not sure it would have mattered who answered, mind you. She said she saw something like it before. Asked if it looked like a desert."

"Deserts don't have arms sticking out of them," Greta said.

"Arms?"

"You can't see them?" Greta asked. "They're moving like branches caught in the wind. It's the buried undead. You see that one, there's ivy growing up its arm." She waved vaguely at the barren expanse.

Chester squinted.

"Just use the binoculars," Greta said.

"Nah, there's no point," Chester said. "Though maybe we should look for a pair of glasses. Come on, we're wasting daylight."

"Wasting? Where do we have to go?" Greta asked.

"Ivy doesn't grow overnight," he said. "It would have taken months. Eamonn would have come this way, he'd have seen the desolation, and he'd have turned around." He imagined the country beyond the horizon. "Due west, more or less, is the Severn Estuary and the southern edge of Wales. On seeing that devastation, Eamonn would have changed his mind about going to Llanncanno. If it was me, I'd go north, up through England, aiming for the northern coast of Wales. I'd follow that to Anglesey."

"You think?"

"Yep," Chester said. "And I'd begin by turning around, and following the railway line. Anyway, that boat from Anglesey will be at Llanncanno in a couple of days. They can check it out while we go north. You ready?"

He chivvied her to her bicycle, and then they set off, heading back down the road. He slowed at crossroads at the bottom of the hill, and pointed north.

"That way," he said.

"Not back to the safe house?"

"No, there's no point. Eamonn might have gone back there, or maybe he found the safe house after he saw the passage of the horde. Either way, he'd have managed at least a few more miles northward. We can take this road and cut those miles off the journey because I think I know where he went."

"You do? Where?"

"Okay, maybe not where he went," Chester said, "but I can guess where he'd head for. Stratford-upon-Avon."

"Why there?" she asked.

"Have you heard of it?"

"Of course."

"Exactly," Chester said. "Eamonn would have seen the passage of the horde, and he'd have put some distance between himself and here. When he thought he was safe, and knowing that he couldn't reach the safe house in the Cotswolds, he'd have looked for a map. He'd know not to go to Birmingham, but he'd see that Stratford lies to the south. Between here and there is the Grand Union Canal. It's not a motorway, and it's not a railway, but it does run pretty straight and has the added advantage of being a water source. The towpath alongside it would be easy to cycle. That's the route I'd take if I wanted to get north from here."

"But Eamonn didn't make it to Anglesey."

"No, but are we going to stand here, or take a look?"

"Chester!" Greta yelled. "Watch out!"

He turned in the saddle just before the zombie tumbled out of the open bus door. The creature toppled forward as Chester swerved. The zombie hit the tarmac, but its hand caught in the bicycle's spokes. Chester jumped from the bike as it clattered to the road, and then had to skip backwards as the zombie squirmed forward, arms outstretched almost as if it was swimming on dry land. Before he could unclip his mace, there was a silent retort. The zombie's head exploded as a bullet smashed into its brain. Greta had stopped twenty feet further back and had her submachine gun in her hands. There was a clatter from the bus. Another zombie appeared in the doorway. The creature was wizened, bent double. Its arms beat against the twisted frame of the bus's doorway as it fell down the steps. Chester swung the mace, splitting the creature's skull.

"I think that's—" He was interrupted by a dry rasp from inside, and a discordant drumbeat of flesh against metal. The bus rocked as the trapped undead struggled to get out.

"Bring up your bike, get ahead, up there," Chester said, giving a wave as vague as his directions, but Greta understood. She wheeled her bike along the road, reaching the end of the bus just as a window shattered. Safety glass tinkled to the ground as a zombie lurched through the broken frame. It landed head first, though the fall didn't kill it. Greta's bullet did. Fired from two feet away. It was followed by three more, aimed at the window.

Chester half turned to look, but caught sight of movement in the doorway. A zombie wearing an overcoat that hung far lower than its feet staggered down the steps. Chester punched the mace into its face. The creature crumpled, and was knocked out of the way by a far more active zombie behind. Chester took a step back, letting the zombie thrash its way outside before he scythed the mace low, pitching the creature to the ground. He hacked the weapon two-handed onto its skull.

He took another step back. Greta had the submachine gun raised, but held her fire.

"I think that's it," Chester said after a long minute's pause.

"No," Greta said. "Can't you hear it? There's at least one more."

They waited, but the creature didn't appear. Chester clipped the gory mace back onto his belt and drew his bayonet. "There's always one," he muttered, and climbed the steps.

Even with the broken windows and open doors, the interior was dark. He heard a soft wheeze coming from the rear of the bus.

"Hey!" he called. There was no response. He took a step. His foot slipped on a rotting suitcase. The plastic crunched, but the zombie grew no more active.

It was hunched in a seat, almost as if it were waiting for the bus to continue its journey. Almost, but it wasn't. It was undead and almost motionless. Its skin was raw, drawn back, split around mouth and cheek. The hair had fallen from its blistered scalp. The clothing had rotted onto its necrotic flesh. Its mouth opened an inch, then closed again. And then it was still. Chester waited to see if it would move again. He counted to five, then ten, then thirty.

"Chester?" Greta called from outside.

Chester drew his hand back and plunged the bayonet into the creature's open eye.

"It was dying," he said as he climbed back outside. The corpses he had to step over to retrieve his bike took away any comfort in that.

"Do you think Kevin's theory is right?" Greta asked as they wheeled the bikes up the road, away from the bus and towards the ridge.

"I think Kevin's terrified about becoming a dad," Chester said. "He's looking for reassurance. No, Nilda has the right of it. We can come up with a dozen stories about what's happening to the zombies, but they're not actual theories because we don't have any real evidence. At night, when we're safe behind our walls, we can allow ourselves the luxury of thinking we might live to see a world without them. Out here, that luxury would—" He stopped.

They'd reached the top of the ridge. Below them was a muddy desert far wider than that which they'd passed earlier in the day. A zigzagging trench cut through the valley and halfway up the hills either side. Nothing grew where the zombies had been. Nothing living could have survived the passage of millions of the undead.

Neither of them said anything. The forced bonhomie of earlier had been a product of desperation. The reality of Eamonn's fate came crashing down on them both.

"It's getting late," Chester finally said, though it wasn't. "We should find somewhere to sleep."

They picked a farmhouse that others had looted before them. It was a mile from the bus, but devoid of the undead as much as of life. Chester thought of calling Anglesey, but didn't see the point. They lit a fire in the wood burning stove, and sat in the kitchen, watching the flames.

Chapter 20 - Acceptance
Buckingham, 13th November, Day 245

"Are you awake?" Greta asked.

"More or less," Chester said.

"Eamonn's dead," Greta said.

"We don't know that for sure," Chester said automatically, easing himself upright and awake. The chair wasn't comfortable, but he'd been tired, far more tired than he wanted to admit. Greta had banked the stove until it roared, filling the small kitchen with heat. On the stove, a large saucepan simmered.

"We do know," she said. "We know, and we knew before we left London. Thank you, though."

"For what?"

"For coming with me," she said. "If you weren't here, I don't know if I'd turn back."

"You're being awfully pragmatic for… what time is it?"

"Night," she said. "Three o'clock, maybe. It's not pragmatism. It's realism. I was holding onto Eamonn because I was holding onto the past. We all have to let go, don't we?"

"I suppose." He was about to rub his eyes before he remembered the last time he'd washed his hands. "Is that water in the saucepan?"

"Rainwater. There's a storm outside. The thunder woke you."

"Did it?"

"Maybe it wasn't the storm." She sighed. "Either the horde caught Eamonn, or maybe he was injured and trapped. If he was, and even if he was still alive now, we could spend a year searching for him but never find him. We can't afford that time, can we? No, he might have died in a million different ways, and I'll never stop imagining them, but the world hasn't stopped. Life still goes on, just not here."

"No, not here," Chester said.

"Eamonn and I talked," she said. "In Kent, after you'd gone back to London. That was the first time we'd properly talked. I don't mean the first time we'd spoken to one another, or even realised we... that I... that we both... that we could, perhaps, grow to love one another. I mean that in Kent, that was the first time we properly talked as two of the last of our species."

"I'm sorry?" Chester asked, still half awake and now thoroughly confused.

"That's what we are, Chester. You, me, Nilda, Jay, everyone. We're the last of our species, and that's how we have to think, how we have to act. All that talk of Anglesey was a proxy for thinking about our own survival, but that's selfish. That was what we discussed in Kent. The future, the children's future, our species' future. That's what we need to focus on. We can't be selfish, and this search for Eamonn is only that."

"Yep, fair enough," Chester said. He stood and checked the water. "I'll get some more and use this for a wash if you don't mind."

"The saucepans are by the back door," Greta said. "I filled them all."

"You did?"

"You must have been tired," Greta said.

"I must have been," Chester said.

"How's your head?"

"My head? Fine," he said.

"Nilda said you sometimes get headaches."

"She did?"

"You mean you don't get headaches?" she asked.

"I do, I was just surprised she told you," Chester said.

"You're surprised we talked? You talk to Kevin and Jay when you go into London on those little expeditions of yours, don't you? I talk to Aisha, Nilda, and Tuck, and isn't that old-fashioned? The men talking to the men, the women talking to the women."

"I talk to Nilda, too," he said.

"About the future?" Greta asked.

"Of course," he said.

"I've been thinking about it a lot," Greta said. "It's better than thinking about the past, as that always leads to thinking of Eamonn. It's Anglesey, or Ireland now, I suppose. None of us wanted to go to Anglesey. Before Mr Tull arrived, it was a place we talked of visiting. It was like London before the outbreak. Or Paris, or Berlin. It was the place with the bright lights, the place where the children might seek their fortune, but it wasn't going to be our *home*. We didn't know where that was going to be. The children thought it would be the Tower, but that's because they *are* children. They like the old castle and playing with the ancient relics. We knew it wouldn't last."

"Who's we?" he asked.

"Nilda, Aisha, Tuck, myself," she said.

"I feel a bit left out," Chester said.

"It's your own fault for leaving the room any time anyone started talking about Aisha's baby," Greta said.

Chester sniffed. "I'm a bit old-fashioned about *some* things."

"Squeamish, you mean," she said. "We need to live where we work, and we're going to work the fields. There isn't enough grassland near the Tower. We could move to Buckingham Palace and plough the great parks. Or we could go to Kent and salvage the orchards, but we can't do either while the undead are a threat."

"Nilda and I were saying much the same thing," Chester said.

"Exactly," Greta said. "London is temporary. We have those supplies Quigley left, but they won't last forever. It was nice knowing that Anglesey was there. Tuck calls it our safety net. In uttermost need, we could reach it by land, though Eamonn clearly didn't, so perhaps it was just the illusion of safety."

"And that safety net is gone," Chester said.

"Precisely, but more than that, without people in Wales, there's no reason for us to stay in London. We can't reach Ireland by land. If we have to sail there, we'll never reach it quickly, so does it matter where we set off from?"

"You don't want to go with them to Ireland?" Chester asked.

"It is not about want," she said. "It is about need. It is about what our species needs, and that is not for every last one of us to be gathered together in the same place. What if there's a tidal wave, or an earthquake, or some other natural disaster? Flu comes from birds, yes? They seem to have survived the apocalypse. Or what if the undead never stop? We might have seen a few that have died, but we've seen so many more that haven't. That American doctor said they were going back to the United States, but how many zombies are there on that landmass? The two continents had close to two billion people before the outbreak. If Britain has too many undead, we'll find no safety on the other side of the Atlantic."

"But if not Ireland, and not London, then where?" he asked.

"Malta," she said. "Or a Greek island."

Chester found the plug and filled the sink with hot water. "A sandy Greek beach? That'd be nice, particularly at this time of year. I suppose the growing season would be longer. That being said, there's an argument for safety in numbers."

"For a community, for a society, for individuals," she said. "Not for the species."

"The islands might already be overrun," he said.

"Would they be worse than Britain? Than Ireland?" she asked.

"Good point. We'd need somewhere with solar power. Or maybe one of those digesters that Kevin was talking about. Malta, Greece, Italy, why not Cyprus? When the zombies *have* died, we'll want to move to the mainland where we can mine all the technology that we, or the children, can't make. Egypt, maybe? I'd like that, living in the shadow of the old pyramids."

"If and when the zombies stop," Greta said. "Then, you agree?"

"Agree with what?"

"That London is over, that we have to leave?"

"I suppose so," he said. "I'll agree that we have to plan for what next, and we can't do that here."

"Are you sure you saw lights?" Chester asked, speaking into the sat-phone, but keeping his eyes on the gap through the curtains. Dawn had arrived, but the four zombies had arrived long before. Their approach had been masked by the storm, and now they stood on the road, almost as still as statues. Coated in mud, they almost looked like them, too.

"I'm looking at the pictures now," Bill replied. "There was smoke there yesterday, and then lights at night."

"It could be an accidental fire," Chester said.

"No one here thinks so," Bill said, "and everyone has taken a look. There's quite a, uh, a buzz about it. There are two fires, about twenty feet apart. We're not too sure of the distance. You know what the resolution on those cameras is like. But the fires don't move, they don't spread."

"This is in Birmingham?" Chester asked. Outside, the zombie furthest from the house slowly turned to its left.

"Not far from the Edgbaston Reservoir," Bill said. "As I say, there's cloud overhead now, and there was a lot of it last night. We've got six usable pictures, the rest are too obscured to make out any details."

"I thought Birmingham was radioactive," Chester said.

"So did I," Bill said. "A team went to investigate it, but we lost contact with them before they could confirm it. No one's been near there since. Do you have a Geiger counter?"

"We do. So you want us to go there?"

"You're near Stratford-upon-Avon, aren't you?"

"Not really," Chester said. "When we saw that devastation left by the horde, we came here instead. We're near Buckingham, and we'd decided to go back to London."

"Ah, and that would explain why we didn't find evidence of the horde on the satellite pictures. Annette put the pin in the wrong place. We were looking around Stratford-upon-Avon."

"Look northwest of Buckingham," Chester said. "Then look about eight miles due west of Aylesbury. That's where we first saw it."

"Right, great. As soon as the clouds have cleared, we'll start our search. As for Birmingham, I can ask Bran to take a look."

"He's near there?" Chester asked.

"Not yet. He's at sea, heading towards Deeside."

"Oh? Is he going to Wrexham, again?"

"Ah, oh, yes, you went there with him once. No, he was actually aiming for a commune that eked out an existence selling handmade pottery. We'd like the kilns and ovens if we can move them, though there's no urgency. They'll be there next year, but we'd like to know that they are still there."

"Give me a moment," Chester said. He turned to Greta. She was watching the undead with an almost mesmerised expression. "Did you hear that?"

"Lights in Birmingham?" she asked. "It won't be Eamonn."

"It might be someone," Chester said. "It's about fifty miles, give or take. We could follow the canal and be in the city tonight, tomorrow at the outside. From there, we can go to Deeside to meet up with the boat that's brought Bran to Wales."

"We'll be walking into the path of the horde," she said. "It won't be as easy as you say. But there are lights. That means people, and while it won't be Eamonn, it is *someone*. Whoever they are, they deserve a chance to be rescued. We'll go."

"Bill?" Chester said into the sat-phone. "We'll check it out. Hopefully, we'll be in Birmingham this evening. We'll call you then. See if you can get us a more accurate location for these lights."

"Thank you," Bill said. "We're the help that comes to others. A help that's unlooked for."

"Let's just hope it's a help they want," Chester said. He hung up. "Fifty miles, call it sixty with detours, and we should manage it in seven hours."

"Not if it rains again," Greta said. She picked up the submachine gun. "And not if we come across that horde."

Chapter 21 - Survivors
Birmingham, 14th November, Day 246

Greta scanned the ruined buildings, and then rubble-filled street. "I think we're safe," she whispered, and crouched down behind the broken wall.

The previous day, they'd managed an almost easy thirty miles along the canal before the storm exploded. Wind and rain had lashed the ground until long after sunset, and they'd set off at dawn under cloudy skies. During an exhausting three hours that was spent walking more than cycling, they traversed flooded fields that morphed into derelict suburbs that seemed as endless as the storm the night before.

Finally, they'd come to a sign for the Edgbaston Reservoir and had left the bikes in the hallway of a tumbledown second-hand bookshop. They'd found a map by the counter, a battered A-Z that would have proved a useful guide if half the streets weren't so covered in rubble that it was often impossible to tell road from house.

"The Geiger counter's normal," Chester said. "Though something destroyed this suburb. I wonder why they targeted it. I can understand why they might drop a nuke on Birmingham, it was a major city, but why launch a barrage of conventional ordnance?"

A cascade of bricks fell from the building next door.

Greta eased herself up. "I can't see anything. Call Anglesey, find out what they can tell us, and then we should move to somewhere less likely to collapse around our ears."

Chester took out the sat-phone. It took three minutes before anyone answered.

"Where are you?" Bill asked.

"Near the western edge of the Edgbaston Reservoir," Chester said. "The last sign I saw was for Mariner Road, but that was a few streets away."

"What's the city like?"

"Ruins," Chester said. A broken tile, warped by the heat of the fire that had swept through the terrace cracked under his feet. "Looks like it was a residential street. The damage is similar to what we saw in London, done by missiles and bombs during the civil war when Quigley was taking over. Not many zombies, mind you. Any update on the building with the lights?"

"We got a few more partial images this morning," Bill said. "There was smoke coming from a U-shaped building a few hundred metres east of the reservoir. It's probably from a cooking fire. We looked back over the pictures we gathered before that team went to Birmingham. There were no lights, no smoke, though we've only got a handful of images. After we lost contact with the team, and with you in Hull, we moved the satellites to take pictures of Ireland, but I think it's pretty clear that these people arrived after we lost contact with our team."

"There's an alternative," Chester said, "that whoever lit the fire is the reason you lost contact with your team."

"Agreed," Bill said. "And there's a third possibility, that they came from Anglesey. Did George tell you about Bishop and Rachel?"

"He did, but I thought you got all their followers."

"We're not sure," Bill said. "It might be that one or two escaped. The lights might be them, in which case there's no connection with our lost people. Be careful. See if you can get eyes on them, and then call back. We'll have someone waiting for the call."

"Give us a couple of hours," Chester said. "If we don't call back before nightfall, send the cavalry."

"The helicopter's fuelled and ready to go," Bill said.

Chester hung up.

"Is that an expression," Greta asked. "Or did he really mean they'll send a helicopter?"

"Let's hope we don't have to find out," Chester said. He pointed at the street map. "We're around here. That's the reservoir. The warehouse is about half a mile away."

A distorted length of plastic guttering was caught by the wind. It tumbled across the road until it landed against a bath that had fallen into what had once been a front garden. Behind them, wood creaked and was followed by a crack of breaking glass.

"There's a lot of noise," Greta said. "You'd expect to see zombies. Living ones, I mean."

There were two, both dead, lying on the pile of bricks twenty yards from their perch.

"Does that bode good or ill?" Chester said. "Either way, it bodes something about the people in the warehouse, but there's little point pondering when we can go and see for ourselves. I say we follow the reservoir until we see smoke."

"I wouldn't do that," a voice said. Chester and Greta spun around. In the ruined doorway stood a woman in a dirty blue jumpsuit with a golden logo across the left breast. In her hands was a crossbow, though the bolt wasn't pointing at either of them.

"You move quietly," Chester said.

"You don't," the woman said. Her accent was Irish, her tone suspicious. "Who were you speaking to?"

"On the phone, you mean?" Chester asked. "We were looking for a friend of ours, though we lost the trail about fifty miles south of here. Our other friends up there..." He gestured upwards, but the woman didn't follow his finger. She kept her eyes firmly on the submachine gun in Greta's hands. "They saw some smoke coming from a warehouse on the other side of the reservoir," Chester continued. "We said we'd come and look. I take it you lit the fire?"

"No," she said. "Where did you come from?"

"Well, now, that's a hard question to answer with a short reply," Chester said with a broad grin and an expansive stretch of his arms that gave him an opportunity to take half a step forward. In response the woman raised the crossbow half an inch.

"London," Greta said. "We came from London."

"London?" the woman said, finally raising her eyes from Greta's gun to her face. She frowned. "What's your name?"

"What's yours?" Chester asked.

"Sorcha Locke," she said, still looking at Greta. "What's your name?"

"I'm Chester Carson."

"And you're Nilda?" Locke asked. "You're not the deaf soldier. Unless… are you Greta?"

"How do you know those names?" Greta whispered.

"Eamonn told me about you," Locke said.

"He's alive? He's here?" Greta asked, her voice cracking.

"Oh yes," Locke said. "He's alive, but it's not safe talking here. Come." She walked sure-footed and silent across the rubble, disappearing into what had once been a back garden, and then into the house beyond.

"Wait," Greta said, and hurried after her.

"Oh, hell," Chester muttered.

The woman hadn't taken shelter in the house, but had continued through it. She seemed to have memorised a route that took her through the unsafe ruins of homes and partially flooded streets.

Greta had almost caught up with her when they reached Reservoir Road. Outside a broken-doored newsagent was a zombie wearing a red fleece stained brown from a savage gash in its shoulder. Before Locke took another step, Greta raised the submachine gun and fired. The zombie collapsed.

"Damn it," Locke snapped. "You shouldn't have done that."

"Where's Eamonn?" Greta asked.

"If they see the corpse," Locke said, "they'll know I was on this road."

"Who's they?" Chester asked.

"Where's Eamonn?" Greta asked again.

Locke ignored them both and went into the newsagent. Greta threw Chester a look of confused concern. Chester shrugged, as unsettled as she. A moment later, Locke reappeared, grabbed the zombie by the legs, and dragged it inside. She paused in the doorway.

"Are you coming?" Locke asked.

"Enough," Greta said. She pushed Locke away from the corpse. "Tell me about Eamonn. Where is he?"

211

"Being held hostage in my warehouse," Locke said. "Five of the soldiers came out this morning to inspect the reservoir. They should be coming back soon. I don't think they'll come here because there's nothing left to loot, but if they see the zombie, and they see that it's been shot, they'll know that someone new has arrived in the city. You don't want that, not if you want Eamonn to live. Grab the legs, and help me get this corpse inside."

Greta stared open-mouthed, but only for a second. She took hold of the creature's legs. Together they carried it behind the ransacked counter. It wasn't a large shop, truly there for the convenience of the nearby residents for whom the extra few pence on a bottle of milk was a fair price to pay for the minutes saved on a Saturday morning.

Chester took up a station in the shadows near the open doorway. "I think we could do with a few more details about who these people are," he said. "And who you are, too. You've certainly got the advantage of us."

"The warehouse where you saw the smoke," Locke said, "that's mine. That's my warehouse. They took it."

There was something about Locke that was familiar to Chester. He was certain he'd never met her, but she had a manic calm that he'd come across too often in his old life. She was the kind of person to be kept beyond arm's length, and an unarmed one at that.

"Who are *they*?" Chester asked.

"Soldiers," Locke said. "They used to work for Quigley. You know about him, don't you? You know what he did? These soldiers are the last survivors of Quigley's little empire, but we didn't know who they were when they arrived. They took over my warehouse, and we barely got out with our lives. Eamonn arrived about three weeks ago. I had a plan. We were going to— It doesn't matter. We were in a building site, but they must have seen us, they must have followed us. They came at dawn. Not all of us escaped. They took Eamonn and Isabella hostage."

"Eamonn only arrived three weeks ago?" Greta asked.

"Three weeks. Maybe four. Who keeps track? He was trapped by a horde somewhere to the south," Locke said dismissively as if it was an unimportant detail.

"Hang on," Chester said. "A hostage usually means that you've got something that they want. What is it? Why haven't they killed Eamonn and… what was the other one's name?"

"Isabella. They're still alive because I have something they want. There is a vault beneath the warehouse. It contains ammunition and food, enough for five years. That's what they want."

"They can't open it?" Chester asked.

"Not my vault, no. I have the codes, and they have the prisoners. They think that gives them the upper hand." She gave a dark smile.

"Then just give them the codes," Greta said.

"If I do, they will kill Isabella and Eamonn," Locke said.

"Hold on, both of you," Chester said. "How many soldiers?"

"Thirteen," Locke said. "There were thirty when they first came to Birmingham, twenty-three when Eamonn arrived."

"Thirteen?" Greta asked. "That's not too many. What do you think, Chester?"

"I think we need some more information," Chester said. He needed some more time to think.

"There are five buildings that offer a clear view of the warehouse," Locke said. "I can take you to one I've not used before. You can see for yourself."

"Then let's go," Greta said.

"Just a minute," Chester said. His instincts told him not to trust this woman, but they also told him that she wasn't lying. His instinct had been tragically wrong in the recent past, but he didn't think it was this time. Nevertheless, he could ask the woman all the questions he wanted, he still wouldn't believe the answers. "I guess seeing is believing," he said. "After you." Only when her back was turned did his hand slide around to the submachine gun on his back. He slid the safety off.

Locke crawled across the roof to the edge of the seven-storey apartment building. Greta followed, clearly eager to get a view of the place Eamonn was being held hostage. Chester hung back, uncertain whether the woman's story was some kind of elaborate trap. The apartment block was just another mid-rise building in a city infrequently dotted with them. With the binoculars, Chester could see the reservoir to his left. He could see the centre of Birmingham to his right, and see that the devastation extended deep into the city, with collapsed buildings often obscuring the line of the old canal.

"Chester!" Greta hissed.

He knelt, and crawled to the building's edge.

"There. You see," Locke said.

Chester didn't, not immediately. Then he saw the wisp of smoke rising from a large U-shaped building a few hundred metres from the eastern edge of the reservoir.

"Where is he?" Greta asked.

"Inside the warehouse," Locke said.

Chester stared blankly into the distance. "How do you know he's still alive?"

"Up until two days ago, they would bring them both outside," she said. "It was always at noon. You know why?"

"So you'd know they were alive," Greta said.

"No," Locke said. "So they could try to catch me. They sent people out before dawn. They would lie in wait, but I never went to sleep, and now there are only thirteen of them."

Yes, she was mad. Mad and dangerous. In some ways, she reminded Chester a lot of McInery.

"So Eamonn got trapped by a horde for a few weeks, then he came here?" he said.

"The soldiers came the night Eamonn arrived," Locke said. "He wasn't very good at walking quietly through the city. The soldiers must have seen the zombies that had been following him. They found us. Gavin died getting the children outside. He sacrificed himself. Isabella and Eamonn did the same, just so Isabella could escape."

"Sorry?" Chester asked. "I thought you said they caught Isabella."

"No, they caught the other Isabella," Locke said.

Now she was sounding more like Stewart, not making sense to anyone but herself.

214

"That was three weeks ago?" Chester asked. "Did Eamonn tell you he was on his way to Anglesey?"

"Yes," Locke said.

"He told you there was help there?" Chester asked. "That there were people with boats? That there were soldiers?"

"He told us that was what he thought," Locke said.

"So why didn't you go to Anglesey for help?" Chester asked.

"Because I couldn't," Locke said. "I came through there months ago, and barely escaped with my life. My friend wasn't so lucky. Do you know a man named Bishop?"

"I know he's dead," Chester said.

"He is?" Locke seemed surprised.

"Yeah, apparently he was killing people," Chester said. "There was something to do with a religion and taking people's supplies. I didn't get the full story, but I do know he was killed, along with his supporters."

"Like Rachel Gottlieb?" Locke asked.

"Yeah, and a few others," Chester said. "I wasn't too interested in the details. We were told this by people from Anglesey. They came by ship up the Thames."

"How did they know you were in London?" Locke asked.

"Satellites," Chester said. "They got some working."

"They did?"

"Eamonn didn't tell you that?"

"No, though we didn't have long to talk before he was captured. Maybe Anglesey *has* changed. Eamonn seemed to think so. To leave here, to take that chance, would have meant leaving the others alone, undefended."

"You mean the children?" Greta asked. "How many?"

"Four," Locke said. "And there's Isabella as well."

"Hang on," Chester asked. "Another Isabella."

"Isabella the grandmother and Isabella the granddaughter are safe. Isabella the mother is the one who was captured," Locke said testily. "Since then, the soldiers have been trying to capture me, and since then, I have been setting my own ambushes, but mine have been successful where theirs have been abject failures. That's why they stopped coming outside, and that's when I blocked the water pipe. It leads from the reservoir to a pump room in the warehouse basement. I had to find scuba gear, of course. That was an interesting experience. For forty-eight hours, they stayed put. This morning, at dawn, the soldiers came out. Five of them." She smiled. "When they go out tomorrow, they will be less watchful. In a week, I will get them all."

Every answer begged a dozen more questions, so Chester stopped asking. He took the binoculars from Greta, and scanned the building. It was shaped like a 'U', with no windows on the ground floor and only small ones on the upper level. The entrance was blocked with a bus around which barbed wire had been wrapped. Beyond the bus, two thin wisps of smoke rose up from the courtyard.

"Is that a deckchair?" he asked, passing the binoculars to Greta. "On the roof, to the left of the entrance."

"That's where Barker comes to sit sometimes," Locke said.

"Barker?" Chester asked.

"Their leader. I think that's his name. I heard some of them talking," she said. "That was just before I killed them."

"What are they armed with?"

"A few rifles and shotguns," Locke said, "but not much ammunition, not any more. The first I killed had three spare magazines in his belt. The last only had two loose rounds. I've been using my crossbow since, but I'm still more than a match for them. They took some of my guns and ammunition when they stole my warehouse, though I'd only brought a few thousand rounds up from the vault. They got more ammunition from a group that arrived from Anglesey. No one came looking for those people."

"We came," Greta said.

"What happened to the people from Anglesey?" Chester asked.

"They hung a flag on a car showroom, declaring it safe. Barker killed them. He took their guns."

"How much food do you have in that vault?"

"It's not just food," she said. "Ammunition and guns, tools and clothing, and all the supplies to last ten people for ten years. Or it should have been ten years. Half was gone when I arrived."

"Why do you have a vault of ammunition and food in Birmingham?" Greta asked.

"Because we were preparing for the end of the world," she said.

Yes, each answer only begged a dozen more questions. Ten people for ten years, though with half of it gone, it would resupply London for six months. Spread across all the survivors now heading to Belfast, it would last a couple of days. Did that make it a priceless treasure, or did it make it a worthless albatross that had only brought more death into the world?

"What do you think, Chester?" Greta asked.

"How many ways in are there?" Chester asked.

"Just the front entrance," Locke said. "That's why I moved the bus there. The vehicle's windows are sealed with wood and cement."

"What about the roof? Is there a skylight or something?"

"No," she said. "I designed it like a castle. A few can hold off an assault by dozens."

"Do you know where Eamonn and Isabella are being held?" Chester asked.

"No."

"Why should we believe Eamonn's in there?" Greta asked.

"Why would I lie?" Locke said.

Greta frowned, seeming to weigh the woman's words. She gave a decisive nod. "Chester, can we rescue them?"

"If Tuck was here," Chester said, "I might say yes. Set a thief to catch a thief, but these aren't thieves, and this isn't London. I did some work in the city, sure, but it's not my stomping ground. Thirteen soldiers? Even without much ammo they're still soldiers." He turned to Locke. "If the food is locked in the vault, how are they still alive?"

"We'd carried some upstairs before they arrived," Locke said. "They brought some with them. I don't know how much food they have left, but their stock of water must be running low, despite last night's rain."

"Chester?" Greta prompted. "We're not walking away. We have to get Eamonn."

"I know," he said. He scratched his scar. "We've run out of time."

Greta hadn't seen it. The possibility that her beloved was still alive was blinding her to the obvious. Whoever these people were, whether they were Quigley's soldiers or renegades from elsewhere, they would have made Eamonn talk, and he would have told them about London. If the renegades had come from Northumberland, they would have assumed the old capital had been destroyed. Now they knew it was whole.

If Locke was to be believed, she'd killed seventeen of the soldiers. By now, the remaining thirteen would be eager to leave. Once they did, London was their only possible destination. Eamonn had been unlucky to have taken so long to reach Birmingham. They couldn't trust that a similar misfortune would delay these renegades. They could be in London in four days, perhaps sooner, but certainly before any help could arrive in a sailing boat from Anglesey.

Once again, the Tower would be under siege. This time, it would have to be abandoned. Even then, it wouldn't be over. The thirteen renegades would have Quigley's remaining supplies. They would have the Tower and all the gear that Chester, Nilda and the others had collected. The renegades would be safe, secure against anything but a horde. They stood a good chance of outlasting the undead. There might only be a few hundred other survivors in the British wasteland, but once the zombies died, they would go to the capital. People from France, Belgium, and further afield might try to do the same. They would find the renegades and have no choice but to join their ranks. A new evil empire would be created, an echo of all that Quigley had wanted, and it would be a very real threat to all future generations. Fight them today, then, because the alternative was leaving them for the children to fight tomorrow, and that was a worse legacy than a land of the undead.

Chester took out the sat-phone. "Set a thief to catch a thief, but these are soldiers, so I think it's time we got some professional help."

Chapter 22 - Bran's New Recruits
Rossett, Wales

Bran pulled the trigger, but the hammer found an empty chamber. He slammed the rifle-butt into the zombie's face, then swept his leg low, knocking the creature from its feet. He stepped back and ejected the spent magazine, loading in a new one while the zombie thrashed to its knees. Before Bran could fire, an arrow sprouted from the creature's eye. Bran could guess who'd fired it, but didn't check. Instead, he scanned the rest of the battlefield.

Dermot was on the ground, a zombie on top of him. He'd managed to get his machete lodged so the flat of the blade pushed against its throat, and that was holding the creature back, but only just. As its hands clawed and its legs kicked, the zombie's mouth inched closer and closer to the fallen man. Dermot screamed, in fear not pain, but the zombie's head was now too close. Bran didn't dare risk the shot. He let the rifle fall to its sling as he dashed across the intervening ten yards. He grabbed the creature's rotting leather jacket. The cloth tore, but Bran dragged the zombie from the recruit. He hurled the creature to the ground, and drew his bayonet as he leaped onto the zombie. Pinning the creature's flailing arms beneath his knees, he slammed the blade down into its eye. As he sprung back to his feet, his hand had already grabbed the gun's stock. He brought his weapon up as he scanned the car park and saw that the only movement was from the living.

From her perch on the low roof, Lena gave a whistle. Bran waited for her to signal the all-clear. She didn't, but she did lower her bow.

"We're fine," Dean called out. There was a chorus of muted agreement from the rest of the squad.

Bran bit back an automatic reproachful command. His volunteers weren't soldiers, not yet. He'd spent many an evening discussing that with Dr Umbert. The psychiatrist had been one of the few people in whom Bran had felt comfortable confiding. In some ways, it was because they agreed on so little, but they had reached common ground on one thing. The survivors weren't soldiers. He wasn't sure if this group would ever become them.

"Lena reckons we're clear for half a mile around," Dean said, sauntering over.

"What do *you* think?" Bran asked as he retrieved his bayonet.

"I always trust her," Dean said. "She's got eyes like an eagle."

"Trust is good," Bran said. "You need that, but not blind trust. The brain's an odd thing. Sometimes it can miss what's right in front of it. What's your opinion?"

Dean frowned. He looked up and down the road that led to the agricultural supply business, and then at the fields either side. "I think we should hurry," he said.

"Good. Take Akeem, Dermot, and Patricia to check that warehouse. You know what we're looking for?"

"Fertilizer and hand tools," Dean said. "We take photos of everything we find."

"Good," Bran said. "You've got five minutes."

No, they weren't soldiers. Not yet, and most of them never would be, but Dean and Lena both had the makings of it. Partly it was their age, and partly it was that they'd spent the last eight months in the harshest of training grounds. Fighting their way up and down Ireland had forged them into something far tougher than the survivors who'd spent those months on their ships. But, like he and Dr Umbert had often discussed, fighters weren't soldiers.

"Andy, Jane, Rashad, you're with me," he said. He glanced up at Lena who was watching the road and the fields beyond. She'd warn them if danger came. Yes, he could trust her. He'd have to.

Silently, he signalled for Rashad to open the door and then step back for Jane and Andy to enter, flanking left and right while he took the centre. Their blank expressions told him they hadn't understood. He held up three fingers, then two, then one, and then opened the door. The warehouse was empty, at least of the undead. The shelves had been untouched for months. Bran shone his torch on a row of oddly shaped scissors he assumed were wool-shears. Next to that was a rack of wide-toothed combs. Against the left wall was a rack of plastic buckets, troughs, and oddly square ramps next to a wide selection of plastic tubing.

"I think it's all gear for livestock," he said. "It's mostly plastic and metal. It'll last a few years. Maybe, by then, we'll have a use for it. You've got those phones? Take photographs of everything. You've got five minutes. If you get your thumb over the lens, you'll be coming back here on foot and alone. Move!"

Leaving them fumbling in their pockets for their phones, he went back outside.

There was a third building on the site, a two-storey cottage with plastic furniture outside, a *closed* sign on the glass front door, but an assortment of child's stickers on one of the upstairs windows. It was a home for the owners, but also a small cafe and shop. They probably made as much profit serving tea and coffee to local farmers who stopped for a chat as they did selling farm supplies.

He looked up at Lena. She was watching the road. Yes, she and Dean would make good soldiers, eventually. The others wouldn't. Perhaps that was for the best. Bran had noticed something that no one else had. Something that no one else *could*. This was his second trip into Wales in as many weeks, but he'd been through the area a month before, and again a month before that. What he was sure of was that there were fewer undead. There were still the odd two or ten gathered inside the walls and fences ringing the rural properties, but there were virtually none on the roads or in the fields. He'd counted a grand total of two since they'd left the pottery that morning, and none between the boat and that odd little commune. Even accounting for the creatures he'd killed on his previous trips, there were fewer than he was expecting. He wasn't going to share that with anyone.

As far as he was concerned, not seeing many zombies only meant he'd not seen many zombies. It didn't necessarily mean that they'd all died, their bodies now rotting in some ditch, covered by leaves and mud where they would never be discovered. No, it didn't necessarily mean that, but it might. It might mean that, once winter was over, they'd find spring's first dawn shone on a land full of green shoots and empty of unnatural decay. It might mean there was nothing to fight but nature and themselves. The elements couldn't be fought with rifle and bayonet, and there were too few people for them to war among themselves. No, hopefully, maybe, possibly, there'd be no need for soldiers in the future.

He smiled. That was a sentiment that had echoed through the ages and had always been proved wrong. Besides, first they had to get through the winter. Everything had changed on Anglesey. He wasn't sure how he felt about it. The election had been as disastrous as any political contest in the old-world. That calamity had swiftly been forgotten with the news of the power plant's imminent demise. Ireland was to become their temporary home. Whether it would become a permanent one, he didn't know, but it wouldn't be his. Britain was his home, and if the undead were dying, then he would return. Perhaps he'd return anyway, if only to hasten their end, one zombie at a time.

He crossed to the small house. The front door was intact. He went around to the back. The door was open. He raised the rifle, pushing the door inward. He didn't expect to find any undead inside, and he wasn't disappointed, but there were bodies. Probably three. They'd been torn apart, their remains feasted on by whatever wildlife had avoided the undead. He rapped the silenced rifle barrel against the battered water-heater. There was no reply. That wasn't good enough, though. Not for him. He checked the small cafe and convenience store downstairs, and then the bedrooms upstairs. A couple and a child had lived there, but he left their belongings to the ghosts and returned outside.

Dean's group had finished and were gathered near the road. The young man had found a shepherd's crook with which he was jabbing and waving, demonstrating how he'd use it to fight the undead. Bran gestured that they should assist those in the other warehouse.

They'd come ashore on the River Dee, not too far from where he'd made landfall when he'd gone looking for the brigadier. Chester had been with him then. Bran smiled a grin of genuine relief. The thief was still alive. That was the first piece of good news they'd had in a long while. A hundred survivors had taken over the Tower of London. They'd also provided an idea so obvious he was embarrassed he'd not thought of it himself. The fold-up bicycles were lined up on the road outside. Thanks to the scant few undead, they'd not had to take to the fields on this exploratory mission, not yet. Knowing that, if they did, they wouldn't be making the rest of the journey on foot had given his recruits confidence.

On leaving the boat, they'd gone to the potters' commune and found it mostly intact. After taking photographs, they'd come here to the agricultural supply business. Bran had remembered seeing it on one of his previous journeys. He'd been hoping to find fertilizer or seeds, but not every mission was going to be a success. Touch wood, everyone who set out was going to make it home alive. That was success enough.

He took out the sat-phone to report their position and saw there was a blinking light. He'd missed a call. He redialled.

"Hello?" a young voice answered.

"Is that Annette? It's Bran. I'm reporting in. Is anyone else there?"

"They're in a meeting. Hang on."

He heard a chair being pushed back, footsteps on bare wood, a door opening, and a sudden hush.

"It's Bran," Annette said.

"I'll take it," Bill said. "Bran? Are you in Wrexham?"

"A little to the south of Rossett," Bran said. "An agricultural supply warehouse. There are some tools, some—"

"Okay, listen, there's been a change in plans," Bill cut in. "There are survivors in Birmingham, and some of them are being held hostage."

"Hostage?" Bran asked. "Held by whom?"

"This is where it gets complicated," Bill said. "Does the name Sorcha Locke mean anything to you?"

"You wrote about her. She was in Elysium, wasn't she? Worked for Kempton, made it to Anglesey. Didn't Rachel kill her?"

"Apparently not," Bill said. "We know Kempton had redoubts and refuges dotted across the world, there for her people to use when the apocalypse happened. One of those redoubts is in Birmingham. Locke, on escaping from Bishop, went there. That must have been in the early summer, and she found other survivors in the city. Civilians all, from what

I gather. The supplies are locked in a vault to which she alone has the code. Around the beginning of September, some soldiers arrived. They took over her warehouse and captured some of the civilians."

"And they're the hostages?" Bran asked.

"Right. The soldiers want the code for the vault. Locke won't give it to them, since she thinks, once they have it, they'll kill the hostages."

"Probably. How reliable is this information?"

"Chester Carson told it to us," Bill said. "He was looking for one of his people who left London a couple of months ago in search of help. That man, Eamonn, is one of the hostages."

"Chester? That's interesting," Bran said. "So how many hostages, how many soldiers?"

"Thirteen soldiers, two hostages. Eamonn, and Isabella, she's from Birmingham. That's the next complication. Isabella has an infant daughter, born just before the outbreak. The infant is the reason they didn't leave the city. There's an old woman and three other children, two ten-year-olds and a twelve-year-old. They're still in the city. They're safe, for now, guarded by Locke."

"Anything else?" Bran asked.

"Chester doesn't know who Locke is," Bill said. "George mustn't have said, and I didn't want to risk telling him. The soldiers in the warehouse are possibly the last of Quigley's praetorian guard. Locke seems to think so, and the timeline fits with the destruction of Caulfield Hall. The warehouse that they're in was built like a fortress. They killed the team we sent to investigate the city, and they took their weapons."

"So thirteen of Quigley's renegades have a fortress, two hostages, and are sitting on enough weapons and supplies to fight a war. There's one old woman, three young children and one infant trapped in the city, currently being protected by a woman we know had a hand in the apocalypse. Sounds like a hard choice. What do you want me to do?"

There was a moment's pause. "Go to Birmingham," Bill said. "Find out how much, if any, of that is true. We can't let Quigley's people run loose in England, nor can they get access to those supplies. Chester said there was enough for ten people for five years. It won't make much difference to us, but it would be enough to let these people become warrior-barons."

Bran looked over at his recruits. He'd served with the best of the best, but Quigley recruited the worst of the worst. These civilians would be no match for them.

"Where're the French?" he asked.

"In the North Sea," Bill said. "There were four ships drifting towards Belfast, full of the undead. The Marines are in the Shannon Estuary. The *Vehement* is towing the *Harper's Ferry* towards Elysium with some of the British submariners and American sailors. The rest, not counting those we can't afford to risk, are in Belfast. I'll need about seventy-two hours to get them back here, and then we can send them in on the helicopter. So, go to Birmingham, take a look at this place, and…" There was another pause. "Find out how much of it is true, and whether we can rescue the hostages. If not…" Another pause. "If not," Bill finished wearily, "we'll have to destroy this warehouse."

"I understand," Bran said. "And Locke?"

"Just because Rachel and Bishop tried to kill her doesn't mean we can trust her," Bill said. This time, the hard order now given, he sounded more certain. "But there are some questions we'd like answers to. Getting those children out of Birmingham is the priority, then rescuing the hostages and stopping those soldiers. Locke is last. A distant last."

"When did Chester call you?" Bran asked.

"About an hour ago. He arrived in Birmingham about two hours before that. How long will it take you to get there?"

Bran checked his watch. "If today is anything to go by, I could be there tomorrow. I'll send everyone else back to the ship, and call this evening. Out."

Bran hung up. He hadn't asked exactly what he should do if Locke was lying, nor what to do with the renegade soldiers if she was telling the truth. He didn't need to be told.

"Battles finish, but the war never ends," he murmured. "All right," he added, loud enough for his voice to carry. "Finish it up, fall in!"

The recruits scrambled back to their bikes as Lena nimbly dropped down to a ledge and then jumped to the ground.

"What's going on, Sarge?" Dean asked.

"You're going back to the boat," Bran said. "I'm going back to England."

Chapter 23 - Old Friends
Birmingham, 15ᵗʰ November, Day 247

Chester had the mace in his hands and his good eye on the zombie crawling through the inch-deep, twenty-foot-wide puddle. Chester had chosen the petrol station for the rendezvous because it offered a clear view of the road into Birmingham, but it was completely absent of anywhere comfortable to sit. Glass from the shattered window had worked its way into the padding of the solitary chair behind the counter. There was nowhere comfortable to lean, either, not without risking bringing down the rest of the partially collapsed roof. Instead he stood by the shattered after-hours sales window and watched the zombie crawl across the flooded tarmac while he waited for Bran.

It was a truly pitiful specimen, with mangled limbs and moss growing on the remains of its clothes. Its shoulders rose then fell with a feeble splash as it pivoted its hips. Chester had seen the zombie before he'd gone into the petrol station, but it had moved less than a foot in the time it took him to hang the looted beach towel on the field-side of the building. That was more than signal enough for Bran, but it would also be a signal to Quigley's soldiers if they'd followed him. If they were Quigley's soldiers.

The zombie thrashed a little more violently, and that caused it to roll onto its back. Chester's hand went to the submachine gun slung on his back. He'd barely used it since leaving London, but if Quigley's soldiers *had* followed him, he'd need it soon enough. Yes, he wished he'd found another rendezvous, because he doubted the walls of the forecourt shop would stop a bullet. Then again, if they had followed him, it would make things a lot easier. He'd let them pin him down while he called Anglesey and they called Bran, and, together, they caught the renegades in crossfire. However, despite his poor hearing and worse eyesight, Chester was reasonably sure he hadn't been followed. The partially submerged zombie was confirmation. When Chester had entered the petrol station, the zombie had seen, or heard, or sensed him. That was when it had begun its slow crawl through the puddle. If it changed direction Chester would know there was someone else in the area.

Greta had counted five soldiers leaving the warehouse that morning, and they'd been carrying buckets. They'd gone in the general direction of the reservoir, and walked as if they'd had no care in the world. That was odd, because they weren't that well armed. Unlike the previous day, only one had a rifle. From its over-long suppressor, it was a weapon from Anglesey. Another carried a shotgun, and the other three had fire-axes. Did that mean that they didn't have enough assault rifles, or ammunition, for everyone? Possibly. No doubt they all had an assortment of other sharpened tools about their persons, and possibly sidearms at their belts. Those would be more than enough to fight the undead, but Chester was confident that, with the arrival of Bran and his squad, they would be able to defeat Quigley's soldiers in a pitched battle. What he wasn't sure about was whether they would be able to get Eamonn and Isabella out alive.

That was a dilemma to which he had no simple answer. When facing Graham, it had been easy to sacrifice himself in order to save a greater number, but now the equation had been turned on its head. How many lives were two hostages worth? Eamonn was one of his people. Risking his own life for Eamonn was one thing, but could he risk anyone else's?

Isabella was a new mother, and it was a miracle her child was still alive. Then again, it was a miracle that three generations of the same family had survived. Of course, the other way of looking at it was to count the number of survivors with living relatives. That was a ridiculously small number considering that most people had begun their quest for survival with one or more members of their family.

The infant was sick, though. Time was running out for her. The months-old powdered formula, the poor air, the damp, the cold, the fear, it was taking its toll, but the baby's survival was now assured. It was Eamonn and Isabella whose fate was in doubt.

From the way that the renegades had left the warehouse, they were going to collect water. From the way that they'd showed no concern for danger, they must think Locke had left the city. In which case, there was no need to keep Eamonn and Isabella alive. It was possible that the hostages might already be dead. If they weren't, then how many lives was their rescue worth?

It was an impossible question to answer, so instead, Chester watched the zombie. It began to thrash and roll a moment before he heard a very human whistle. A second later, the whistle came again. Chester wasn't sure how to reply.

"Hello?" he tried.

"Good to see you don't go anywhere without your towel," Bran said. He stepped around the broken wall, less than eight feet from Chester. "It's good to see you, Chester. What happened to you?"

Chester raised a hand to his scar. "I got shot," he said. "I suppose the bullet couldn't find any brain to harm. Lost my eyesight for a bit. More or less lost the hearing in that ear, but I'm alive. Where's the rest of your squad?"

"I sent them back to Anglesey," Bran said. "They were raw recruits, barely skilled at fighting zombies. I couldn't risk them on this."

"Oh. I was hoping for a squad of Special Forces."

"You've got me," Bran said. "Are you here alone?"

"I left Greta watching the warehouse. Five of the soldiers are on the loose. I think they're gathering water."

"You told Anglesey that you'd found a survivor named Sorcha Locke," Bran said. "She's not here?"

"No, she's with Greta."

"What did she tell you about herself?" Bran asked.

"Not much," Chester said. "She came through Anglesey from Ireland but barely escaped with her life. She said it had something to do with that bloke, Bishop."

"You know about Bishop? George told you?"

"Yes, what's wrong?" Chester asked.

"Clearly George didn't tell you about Sorcha Locke," Bran said. "She used to work for Lisa Kempton. Locke was her deputy in Ireland, the UK, and who knows where else. She knew about the apocalypse. She knew about Quigley. As Kempton was financing Quigley's plans, we have to assume Locke knew about them, too."

229

"So that's why she's got a warehouse full of a ammunition and survival supplies," Chester said.

"We can't trust her," Bran said. "You know that expression, the enemy of my enemy is my friend? When the last bullet has been fired, your enemy is still your enemy. We need to be careful. What do you know of the people with her?"

"Three children aged ten to twelve, a grandmother and her infant granddaughter," Chester said. "The mother's the other hostage."

"I meant, do you think they knew about the warehouse? About Kempton?"

"They're Birmingham locals," Chester said. He thought back over his brief conversation with the older Isabella. "I don't think Isabella, the grandmother, knew Locke before the outbreak."

"And there are thirteen hostiles?"

"Not too heavily armed, either," Chester said. "With a few more people, I think we could take them."

"I doubt we have time to wait for reinforcements," Bran said.

"Nor do I," Chester said. "When they went out for water this morning, they left as if they didn't have a care in the world. I think they reckon either Locke has left the city, or she's dead. In which case, why keep the hostages alive?"

"What about the undead?"

"It's not too bad," Chester said. "In fact, it's better than London. It's far, far better than Kent. You'll see one on every other street, if that. Locke and her people, and then these soldiers, have been killing them."

"That's something," Bran said, "but it's more than just in the city. On my way in, I counted fewer than thirty on the roads. There were a few more inside buildings. In northeast Wales, it was much the same. I think they're dying, I really think they are, and in a month or two, they'll all be gone. Then these soldiers will be able to go anywhere they want. We have to deal with them now so we don't have to do it later."

"Agreed," Chester said. "You really think the zombies are dying."

Bran gestured out of the window at the creature splashing through the water. "I think it's a possibility, but they're not dead yet, and until they are,

I'm not going to bank on it. We've a helicopter on Anglesey. It's a search and rescue machine, and it's ready to collect the children. That's the only safe way to get them out of here. When it comes, the sound will summon the undead. Even if some are dying, there will be too many for us to fight. So when the helicopter comes, we'll all have to leave."

"You mean we're not going to try to rescue Eamonn and Isabella?" Chester asked.

"Right now, I don't know," Bran said. "It's more a question of whether or not we can."

"This is Greta, and this is Sorcha Locke," Chester said.

"Sergeant Branofski," he said. "People call me Bran. Chester said five of them left this morning. Any sign of them?"

"They came back an hour ago," Greta said. "They had buckets. They were full."

"Where are the rest of you?" Locke asked.

"For now, it's just me," Bran said, "but we've got a helicopter that can come in and collect the children."

"I see," Locke said. "A helicopter? Then things are looking up for the people of Anglesey."

Bran knelt down and crawled to the edge of the roof. Chester hung back, not looking at Sorcha Locke, but reassessing his opinion of the woman. Chester had heard of Lisa Kempton, but so had everyone on Earth. He'd not heard of Sorcha Locke, but then who knew the number-two of any billionaire? Cannock and McInery had played a part in Quigley's ascension, but neither had expected an apocalypse. Considering how events had played out, not even Quigley could be said to have properly prepared for the end of the world.

By their deeds ye shall judge them, and this woman's deeds spoke a very dark tale, albeit tempered by her escape from John Bishop, and her actions with this small group in Birmingham. Again, he thought of McInery. She'd saved the lives of survivors. That hadn't been out of any great love, though, but because a ruler needed subjects.

231

There was a lesson in that. As long as they had a common enemy, Locke was an ally. After the helicopter arrived, it was going to be a different story, but one battle at a time.

Bran eased himself back from the edge of the roof, rose to a crouch, but didn't stand until he was in the shadow of the fire escape.

"Please," Greta said. "Just… please?"

Bran gave her a smile and a brief nod, and then turned to Locke. "There're thirteen of them?" he asked.

"Thirteen, yes," Locke said.

"No secret escape routes? No tunnels? No hatches?" he asked.

"No."

"What about a sewer?"

"There's a septic tank under the vault and a compost-toilet," Locke said.

"So, no manhole covers? Where does the water come from?"

"From the reservoir, through a five-inch pipe that I blocked."

"So the only way in is through the gate or onto the roof." Bran turned back to Greta. "They have soldiers on Anglesey, Special Forces and a few Rangers, but they're deployed in Ireland. It will take at least another forty-eight hours to get them back to Anglesey. Overland, it would be another two days before they would get here. If we could wait that long, I'd set up an overwatch position on this roof, and another sniper in the building facing the gate. I'd send one team up onto the roof at the rear, and then send another in over the bus. We'd need an explosion first, a distraction to draw as many of them out into the courtyard as possible. We'd mark our targets, and take out all that we could, then move inside hard and fast. Unless we knew where the hostages were, there would be no guarantee they'd survive. If there's a jailer, he might use a prisoner as a human shield. If so, he'll kill the other because a spare would only get in the way. I've seen it happen. Fifty-fifty are the best odds I can give you for a frontal assault, and that's the not the odds of success, but which of the hostages would live. Casualties on our side would be low, but not zero. That's if we had the time to wait. We don't." He turned back to Locke. "You blocked the water pipe. Today, five of them went out to get water. You are no

232

longer viewed as a threat. Either they think you're dead, or they think you've gone. Either way, they have no reason to keep the hostages alive. No, we don't have time to wait. We need to act, and we need to act now, but not from up here. You've used this position before? They might think to look. Where are the rest of your people?"

"It's not far," Locke said.

"Show me," Bran said.

Chapter 24 - Older Foes
Birmingham

"This'll do," Bran whispered. The collapsible ladder clinked as he extended it, but it was barely audible against the background sounds of a dying city. "Do you want to do the honours?"

Chester took the spray can out of a bag that was otherwise filled with dry paper and kindling.

"This takes me back to my youth," he murmured as he scrawled a message on the doors of the three garages while Bran climbed up the ladder onto the roof.

The garages, more for the storage of goods than vehicles, were at the edge of an industrial unit to the south of the warehouse. All that lay between were three hundred metres of road, ruins, scrub, and one of the building sites that Kempton had purchased, levelled, but never developed. Chester took a step back. If he could read the message, then one of the renegade soldiers would easily manage it. He followed Bran up onto the garage's low roof. It was sagging in the middle, and coated with a thin pool of foetid water. Insects buzzed around the surface, taking flight as Chester crawled over to Bran's position. The soldier had his rifle aimed at the warehouse, but the binoculars raised to his eyes. He passed them to Chester.

"Keep watch," he whispered.

"You should have asked Greta to do this," Chester muttered, "and not just because the stagnant rainwater's seeping deep into my clothes. I don't have the eyesight to be a spotter."

"Greta's already at the limit of endurance," Bran said. "Thinking someone she loves is dead, then discovering they might be alive but suffering the worst torments evil can wreak on this world. No, I don't want to add to the pressure."

"Fair enough, but even so, and even with the binoculars, I doubt I'll see anything."

"You'll see movement," Bran said. "Dusk is approaching. Someone will come up before dark to inspect the perimeter."

"You've done this before, then?" Chester said.

"Something like this," Bran said.

"You were in the Special Forces, the SAS?"

"The entire British Army is a special force," Bran said.

"Tuck said much the same thing when I asked her," Chester said. "Will this work?"

"No plan can ever be guaranteed a success prior to implementation," Bran said. "No action is without risk. A frontal assault would mean up to four deaths. This way, it's only the two hostages who are in danger, and they are already close to death. There's a slim chance we might all get out of here alive, and that's the best answer I can give."

Chester wasn't happy with the plan even though he'd come up with the initial idea. They'd returned with Locke to where her people sheltered in a cinema near the centre of the city. After a few minutes of discussion, it became clear there was no easy way to get inside the warehouse.

Bran had his rifle and sidearm, Chester and Greta their submachine guns, Locke her crossbow. They had a few hundred rounds of ammunition. Against people, that wouldn't last long. Chester had said they'd faced a similar problem when dealing with Graham. As he'd recounted the story, he'd realised that he had it the wrong way around.

The warehouse was the fortress. In its way, it was as formidable as the Tower. A frontal assault wouldn't work, so they had to get the renegades to bring the two hostages outside. Since they were only being held captive so the renegades could gain access to the vault, they needed to be persuaded that the real treasure *wasn't* inside the warehouse. Bran was going to provide the evidence of that by wasting an entire magazine shooting at the bus blocking the warehouse's entrance. As Chester and Bran ran, they would set light to the bag of kindling to guarantee that the renegades realised where the shots were coming from. They would investigate, and find the message spray-painted on the garage doors: *You can have Britain. I want my people. The real vault is one mile from here. Bring the hostages to St Mark's Church, north side of reservoir, tomorrow, noon. I'll give you the location of the vault and the codes.*

"Do you think they'll believe the message?" Chester asked.

"It depends on what the hostages have told them," Bran said, "and how much of that they believe. At least some of them will come to the rendezvous. Between a rifle and two submachine guns, we'll catch them all in the crossfire."

"But will they bring the hostages?"

"Possibly," Bran said. "Maybe only one."

"So what do we do if there's a hostage still inside the warehouse with half of the soldiers."

"I'll worry about it when it happens."

"I don't know how you do it," Chester said. "Go to war, I mean. In my line, in my old life, death was a risk at times, but it wasn't this ever-present angel."

"Focus on the mission," Bran said. "Never its end."

"What if, tomorrow, they don't leave the warehouse?"

"I'll revise the plan accordingly," Bran said.

"Did they teach you that in the Army?" Chester asked, as he raised the binoculars.

"What?"

"How to sound so calm. There's movement," he added. "People. Two, no, three of them. They're coming to stand on the bus."

"Let me see." Bran took the binoculars. "Damn."

"What?" Chester asked. "What is it?"

"Barclay," Bran said.

"I think his name's Barker," Chester said. "Wait, Barclay? You mean the guy who killed the people near the aqueduct? I thought you shot him." It seemed like a lifetime ago. It *had* been a lifetime ago.

"I shot him," Bran said. "I didn't kill him. He's got more lives than a cat. He made it to Northumberland, I saw him there." He took aim.

"If you shoot him now, they'll kill the hostages," Chester said.

"I know," Bran said. "Get off the roof. Quick."

Chester hesitated, but only for a second. He knew he could trust the soldier to make the right choice. He crawled back across the roof, and down the ladder. His head was an inch below the rooftop when the firing began. The soft crack-crack-crack almost made him fall the last few steps. The firing lasted for twenty seconds, and then he heard Bran crawl along the roof. The soldier jumped down.

"Time to go," Bran said.

"Did you shoot him?" Chester asked, as he dropped a match into the kindling. There was a soft whoosh as the lighter-fluid-soaked wood and rags caught.

"I shot an X into the bus," Bran said. "I'll settle the score with Barclay tomorrow."

Chapter 25 - The Night Before Battle
Birmingham, 16th November, Day 248

Eamonn

The door to the underground cell opened. Eamonn tried to open his eyes, but his lids were too caked with blood to part.

"One minute past midnight!" Barclay called from the doorway. "And you know what that means, but there's good news of a sort. You have a reprieve. A message came earlier today. I didn't want to trouble you with it at the time, but it seems that Locke is alive. She wants to trade for you. Where I'm a little confused is that her message says that the vault isn't in this building. So, what do you think, should I believe her?"

"Why would you believe *us*?" Isabella replied, utterly defiant.

"A valid point," Barclay said, "but I thought we'd established that I'm the one who asks the questions. Do you really want that lesson again, because we have time? I thought not. So, can I trust her? If her supplies aren't behind that door downstairs, then where are they?"

Eamonn spat blood onto the floor. He wanted to spit it into Barclay's face, but he'd done that before and knew what the man would do. He'd flip a coin. Heads was Eamonn, tails was Isabella, and she would have to endure a far worse torment than a beating.

"I don't know," Eamonn said, the words a guttural hiss through his broken teeth.

"That's honest, at least," Barclay said. "Locke has ammunition and a gun, and she didn't have those last week, so where did it come from? London? She disappeared for a couple of days, so is that where she went?"

"It took me a month to get to Birmingham," Eamonn said for the hundredth time.

"But you are a singularly useless specimen," Barclay said.

"Aye, I'm useless," Eamonn muttered.

"She didn't tell you everything, did she?" Barclay said. "She didn't tell you what she knew, how she was involved in the outbreak, how she paid for the virus to be created. Do you think she told you about her real vault?"

Barclay wasn't sure, Eamonn realised. Up until now, the thug had been certain of everything. Certain which fingernails to pull out, which teeth to extract, where to cut, where to hit. Barclay knew how to cause pain without leaving Eamonn too incapacitated to spend his days pumping water from the reservoir. When the water pump had stopped working, Barclay had announced Eamonn was going to die.

"You don't know," Barclay said. "What about you, Ms Garcia?"

"I told you," Isabella said. "There was nothing inside the basement. Lots of empty boxes and crates. Locke said someone had stolen her supplies. She said they'd sold them on the black market before the outbreak."

Despite all they had put her through, Isabella had repeated the same line over and over, and so often than even Eamonn thought she was telling the truth.

"So was she lying to you?" Barclay asked. "Is there a real vault somewhere in this city?"

"All I know is that she will kill you," Isabella said.

"That's what I think, too," Barclay said. "Not that she'll kill me, she hasn't managed it yet, but I think it's a trap. She's not shot at us in weeks, and we've seen no dead zombies with bullet holes in them. I know she took ammunition from the people of mine she killed. I think she's been hoarding the bullets, and it's those she used to shoot the wall. Yes, it's a trap. She's good at those, but I'm better. I'll set one of my own. So you two have a reprieve. Until tomorrow, then." He grinned, and left.

Bran

Bran didn't need to check his watch to know that they were nearer to dawn than sunset. The delay had been caused by the infant Isabella. They'd been minutes from departure when the baby had begun to cry. Finally, she was sleeping, but it had been a reminder of how precarious their position was. Bran would give her another twenty minutes to properly settle, and then they would depart.

It was less than a mile from the cinema to the car park near the library. He'd walked the route at dusk, after confirming that Barclay's people had all returned to the warehouse. Bran knew Barclay of old, and his brief observation of the warehouse and its lack of a permanent sentry had confirmed that the man hadn't changed. The renegades wouldn't leave the warehouse at night, but they almost certainly would leave at dawn to set up an ambush at the church where the hostage exchange was meant to take place. That was fine with Bran. He planned to set up his own ambush close enough to the warehouse that those soldiers who remained inside would hear the shooting. As soon as the hostages were brought outside, Bran would attack. If some of the soldiers had already gone to the church, all the better. Though it begged the question of whether, after freeing Isabella and Eamonn, he should concentrate on finishing those in the warehouse, or those who'd already left. Once the hostages were safe, his priority had to be Barclay. Wherever he was, Bran would go. The man had to be stopped.

First, though, he had to get the civilians to the roof of the car park where the helicopter could collect them. Anglesey had it ready to leave, but it was going to fly light. It was a hundred and fifty miles from Birmingham to Anglesey in a straight line, but the chopper was going to fly over water until it reached England so as not to disturb the undead in Wales. That would add fifty miles to the outbound leg. Assuming that they flew back the same route, it would be at least four hundred miles. The helicopter had a range of five hundred and fifty miles, though a lot depended on the wind and exactly how much time the chopper spent in the air between collecting the civilians and the hostages. There was a margin of error, but it wasn't as large as he'd told the older Isabella and the children.

He smiled. The helicopter wasn't his problem. Getting the civilians a mile through the night-time city was. One mile? That was easy enough.

Locke

Locke stared at the blank cinema screen, her mind lost in a memory of Sean O'Brian, a heat wave in New York, and a midnight screening of

240

Serpico. That had been a good night. There had been many like them. Odd moments snatched from the frantic chaos of preparing for the apocalypse. There hadn't been a chance for a life, for romance, or even friendship beyond their inner circle. Sean *had* been a friend, a *good* friend, the brother she'd never had. So many had died in Elysium and elsewhere, but his was the death she regretted the most, the life she missed, the memory she couldn't forget.

Greta looked anxious. Well she might. Eamonn was probably dead. The two of them had known love, for however brief a time. The woman would grow to appreciate that if she lived long enough. Locke knew that her chance at that variety of happiness died long before the outbreak.

It was over. It had been over the moment that the infection had escaped the hospital in New York. Lisa's preparations had been a last resort, a desperate contingency if all other plans failed. Those plans had failed with spectacular swiftness. Those desperate contingencies had collapsed soon after. Locke had clung onto them, onto Lisa's dream, beyond the point where any hope remained of it being realised. No, it was over. She should have accepted it when Elysium had fallen. If she had, Sean might still be alive. It was over, which meant it was time for a new plan, and there was only one that was possible. Assuming, of course, that she survived the day.

Chester

Bran looked tense. Greta was anxious, knowing that by the end of the day, Eamonn would be dead or in her arms. Locke was quiet. It was left to Chester to be cheerful.

"Think of this as a race on sports day," he said to the children, "but one where the prize doesn't go to the fastest, only to those who complete the course."

Hazel, the oldest of the children, nodded.

"I didn't like sports day," Damian said.

"Me neither," Phoebe said, a fraction of a second later.

"Yeah, okay, that was a bad example," Chester said. "Actually, thinking about it, I don't think my school ever had a sports day. Or if it did, I never went. Then again, I did miss quite a lot of school. When I should have been in lessons, I was running through the streets. When I was bit older, I wasn't in school because I was asleep having spent the previous night running around the railways and rooftops. Now that was in London, but the same principle applies here. We've got about a mile to travel, back to the library."

"We know the way," Phoebe said.

"Hush," the older Isabella said. "Listen to the man."

"You know *a* way," Chester said. "It'll be different at night. We're going to travel quietly, and together, and for most of it, we'll be moving in the dark. In daylight, this would take twenty minutes. Tonight, it's going to take longer, and seem far longer than that, but even if we have to stop, we'll be safe at the library long before an hour is up. Now, first things first, we don't want to make any noise. There are no loose straps?"

"Just this one," Damian said tugging at the rope around his wrist.

"Hsst!" the older Isabella hissed. The children went still.

"Check your shoes," Chester said. "Make sure there are no loose stones in the treads. No metal keyrings liable to knock into a button? No loose change in your pockets?"

"Why would anyone carry loose change?" Phoebe asked.

"Good point," Chester said.

They were leaving almost everything behind. Chester checked his water bottle and weapons, and then the straps loosely tied to his left wrist and which were each attached to a separate child. He could drop them if he needed to fight, and the children could pull them free if they had to. The pack on his chest contained the last of the children's worldly possessions. It was a motley assortment of keepsakes that Chester would have left behind, but the children hadn't wanted to, and he didn't want to risk them attempting to return for them. With Chester carrying those, the three children were carrying nothing. Isabella was carrying the infant, but the baby was now thankfully silent. As long as she stayed asleep until they reached the car park, they would be safe. The children were scared. If Chester was honest, so was he. Before the outbreak, he'd loved the night.

Ever since, he'd tried to stay behind thick doors and thicker walls after the sun went down.

"I think we're ready," Chester said.

"Ms Locke," Bran said. "If you would lead the way."

Chester mentally ran through the route as they left the cinema. They had to follow the side roads to Upper Dean Street, then Hill Street to the Town Hall. It wasn't the shortest route, but it involved the fewest turnings and it avoided travelling through the ruins of the Bullring shopping centre. Travelling at night under the open sky was one thing, under ground was something else entirely. After the nightmare that had been the Tube in London, Chester never wanted to venture below ground again.

Large clouds scudded quickly across the sky. Their speed spoke of a new storm on its way. For now, the more immediate concern was that stars and moonlight were blocked.

Bran turned on his torch. Everyone else followed suit. The light from the children's weak beams shook. Chester had pinned his to his chest, otherwise he was sure it would have been just as unsteady.

"Lights on the ground," Bran said. "Never up, and never into anyone's eyes. Ms Locke?"

They began their slow journey. Beneath their feet, leaves rustled, plastic split, metal crunched, and then, from somewhere to their left, glass tinkled to the ground.

Bran hissed, and swung his rifle up. The torch attached to the barrel shone on a zombie just before he fired. The zombie crumpled to the ground.

"We're fine," Bran said calmly. "But we can pick up the pace."

It was easy to say, but their speed was determined by the three children, and by the older Isabella carrying the infant in her arms. Chester wanted to offer to carry the baby, but he needed his hands free for the fight that was coming, and it came just after they reached an unhelpful road sign. One arrow pointed to the ring road, another to the railway. There was no mention of the Town Hall or the library, but just beyond the sign were the undead. Chester counted three before Locke fired. He had given her his silenced submachine gun, and she made good use of the weapon. A zombie with a jagged gash running from lip to empty eye socket collapsed as a bullet smashed into its forehead. The other creatures staggered on, their arms raised, their mouths open, the torchlight glinting on rusting zips and exposed bone. Bran fired. Locke fired again. The creatures fell.

"It's over," Phoebe whispered.

"Not yet," Hazel said.

She was right. From somewhere in the ruins, glass cascaded onto brick in a torrent that lasted five seconds but seemed like five hours.

"Keep moving!" Bran said, less calmly than before. They moved, but not nearly quickly enough. Their lights danced from one patch of rubble-strewn road to the next, from one long-dead zombie to another, and that creature raised its head. Chester raised his mace. Before he could hack it down, a bullet smashed into the zombie's temple. Greta lowered her submachine gun.

"Almost there," she said. "Almost there."

Ahead Bran fired one shot and then a second. Chester couldn't see what he was aiming at.

"Don't stop!" Bran said, firing again. "Keep moving!"

"Come on," Chester said, pulling at the ropes attached to the children's wrists. He turned his head to the left to look at them. When he turned it back to the right, he saw Greta, her rifle raised, firing back behind them. He followed the beam and saw the undead. One fell, and then another, but in the moving beam of light he saw a dozen more sepulchral faces barely twenty feet away.

"Move!" he hissed.

"Right!" Bran called. "Go right! Down there!" Bran flicked his torch to shine on a side road, before returning his aim to the creatures in front. Locke ran down the road first, her light disappearing for a moment. There was a dull crack as she fired.

"It's clear!" Locke called.

"Almost there," Chester said, as he pulled and chivvied the children along.

"We're almost there," the older Isabella echoed as she followed them into the alley. Chester heard Bran and Greta's feet behind him. He hoped it was theirs. He didn't turn to look. The children had their lights shining every which way and he found it disorientating. He had to close his left eye just to keep his balance, but taken with the stroboscopic illumination, staying upright and moving forward was as much as he could manage. Locke ran, paused, fired, moving as professionally as Bran, sweeping broken windows, alley mouths, and open doorways as she took the lead.

A narrow street. A wide road. An alley blocked with bollards at either end. Chester looked for signs, but saw none when his light, and then the children's, struck battered sheets of reflective metal. Light bounced up and away, shining on a monstrous expanse of ruins.

"The Bullring," Isabella murmured. "We're almost there."

"Almost there," Chester echoed.

"Almost," Hazel said.

Phoebe whimpered. Damien moved closer to her, and that tugged on the strap attached to Chester's wrist. As he turned around, he saw the zombie, barely three feet from Isabella and her granddaughter. Chester dropped the straps as the zombie lurched out of the darkness. The older Isabella thrust out her hand, warding it off, while moving the infant to her other arm. The creature's mouth snapped down. Blood arced from Isabella's hand. She hissed, but didn't scream. Chester punched the mace into the zombie's face. The creature staggered back with the impact. Chester drew the mace back, but it was too big a weapon for such close quarters. The zombie lurched a step forward, and Chester wasn't going to raise the mace in time. There was a muffled crack. The zombie fell.

"Almost there," Greta said, lowering her submachine gun an inch.

"Almost there," Chester echoed, repeating the words that were becoming their mantra. "Isabella, are you okay?"

"I'm fine," Isabella said, though through gritted teeth. Metal clattered across brick somewhere in the distance. "Can you take her?"

Chester clipped the mace to his belt, and took the bundled infant from Isabella. The child was thankfully warm, but whimpering quietly.

Locke fired. Something heavy fell to the ground.

"There's two more," Locke said. "Two more in the shadows." A louder clatter came from the ruined Bullring.

"Move!" Bran said. Following Locke, they ran through the streets. Their passage marked by the sound of one shot and then the next.

Chester thought he caught the word *library* on a road sign, but didn't want to believe it.

"I know this road," Phoebe suddenly said. "We *are* almost there. We are!"

Chester didn't want to dare believe she was right.

Bran and Locke suddenly stopped. Chester and the children staggered to a halt behind them. There was a trio of shots from Bran and three more from Locke. Chester followed the beams of light and saw the undead streaming out of a gaping hole in the side of a box-shaped building.

"Greta, watch the rear," Bran said without looking away from the sea of undead flowing into the street. "Chester, you have the sat-phone? When I say run, take the children find somewhere inside, anywhere you can barricade. Call Anglesey."

"Understood," Chester said. He shifted the infant to his left hand side, getting ready to fight his way through the nightmare streets. He let his mind go blank, thinking not of the future, nor of the past, but only of the present threat as the undead lurched towards them. He ignored the shots as one, then the next, fell. He ignored the rattle of spent casings hitting the road. He ignored the whimpering of the children, and the bubbling fear in his own chest.

"Greta? What's the rear like?" Bran called, slotting a fresh magazine into place.

"We're clear," she said.

"Up to the front!" Bran called.

Greta ran forward to add her submachine gun to the volume of fire being aimed into the building.

"It's the library," Isabella said calmly.

"That building?" Chester asked, keeping his tone just as nonchalant.

"That's where we were sheltering," Isabella said. "It was a good home. I don't think they have anything similar on Anglesey."

"I… uh… I don't think so," Chester said. He couldn't think of anything else to say. Too much of his mind was concentrating on Bran, waiting for the man's command to run. It would come soon. Very soon. Before it did, there was a different warning shout.

"There! Behind us!" Isabella called.

Chester spun around. The creature was barely ten feet away.

"Here!" He thrust the infant into Hazel's arms as he drew the bayonet. As the zombie lurched forward, Chester launched himself at the creature. He knocked its arms out of the way, grabbed the back of its neck, and plunged the knife up through its mouth and into its brain. With a twist, he wrenched the blade free. As the zombie fell, he decided it was over. It was time to run. He was about to lead the children somewhere, anywhere, when he realised that it *was* over. The firing had stopped.

"Clear! We're clear!" Bran said. His voice was low and as calm as ever.

Five minutes later, they were on the roof of the multi-storey car park, huddled between an abandoned car and the low exterior wall.

"Can the helicopter land here?" Isabella asked.

"Easily," Bran said.

Chester slumped against the wall, but then remembered Isabella's injury.

"Let me see your hand," he said.

"It's fine," Isabella said. "It's just a scratch, that's all. It's nothing serious, though I could do with a bandage."

"Here," Bran said, taking one from the pouch at his belt.

"Are you immune?" Chester asked.

"Of course," Isabella said. "I've never had a day's sickness in my life. No Isabella Garcia ever has."

"Except that cold you got in September," Phoebe said.

"That was hayfever," Isabella said. "It's entirely different."

Bran finished tying the bandage. Isabella barely flinched, though her expression hardened.

247

"You've lost a lot of blood," Bran said. "You need rest, and you'll have it soon. I make it about three hours until dawn, about eight until the helicopter arrives. Keep an eye on them, Chester, I'll be back."

He headed for the ramp. Chester didn't ask where he was going, nor did he volunteer to help. For once, he was happy to let someone else do the work.

As adrenaline wore off, the cold set in. Chester broke the lock on the car door, and the children huddled in the back, Isabella in the front with her still-sleeping granddaughter. He stayed outside with Greta and Locke, and then with Bran when he returned.

"The car park is empty," the soldier said. "There are no zombies inside, or in the stairwell. I think there might be a few still moving in the library, and others in buildings nearby. As long as you're quiet, you should be fine. The ramp leading up here worries me, but there isn't anything to block the entrance. I looked at the cars down on the ground level, but their tyres are flat. Moving them would take too much effort and make too much noise."

"We'll stay quiet, then," Chester said. "We can manage that."

He looked over at Greta, she was the quietest of all, but there were no words of reassurance Chester could offer. Soon, it would be over. Soon, they would know whether Eamonn was alive. Soon.

"There's light on the horizon," Bran said. "We need to leave. Chester, when there's enough light to see the numbers on the phone's keypad, call Anglesey, confirm your location. We'll see you this afternoon."

"Good luck," Chester said. There wasn't anything else to add. Leaving Isabella and the children in the car, he crossed the short distance to the wall. He listened to the soft sound of quickly moving footsteps as the three humans ran into the city. He kept listening as they were replaced with the slower, dragging, lurching sound of undead feet staggering along the road. When those feet, too, had disappeared, he placed the call.

It was answered immediately by Bill Wright. "Chester? Where are you? How many are with you?"

"We're on the roof of a car park, next to the library," Chester said. "There's one infant, three children, two adults."

"And we're collecting five adults later?" Bill asked.

Hopefully, Chester thought. "That's right," he said.

There was a moment's pause at the other end. "That'll be fine. We'll have more than enough room, though not for baggage. The helicopter will arrive at noon. If there's a change in your situation, call. Otherwise, I'll see you tonight."

"Yeah, yeah, I suppose you will," Chester said. He hung up. Above, the clouds were gathering. He shivered, pulling his coat close around his neck. He didn't think there would be snow, but there might be rain. Would that affect the helicopter? Presumably, but precisely how much, he didn't know. That wasn't his problem. He went over to the car.

"You're smiling," Isabella said.

"It's almost over," Chester said, "and the hardest part is already done. We just have to wait and help will come to us. This evening, we'll be back among the electric lights."

"On Anglesey?" Damien asked.

"That's right," Chester said. "You can have a hot bath, and a hot meal, in a centrally heated house. That's what I'm going to do."

"Sorcha said that Anglesey wasn't a nice place," Hazel said. "They killed her friend."

"I don't know about that," Chester said. "I know there were some bad people, and I know the good ones dealt with them."

"But you're from London," Damien said. "Is that where you're going back to?"

"Me, Greta, and Eamonn, yes," Chester said. "At least for now."

"What's it like?" Phoebe asked.

"London?" Chester looked at the skeletal frames of the buildings jutting up into the grey sky. "It's not as bad as this, though it's not too different. The Tower's all right, but it can get a bit cold. The river smells a bit, though it's not as bad as it was. We've got the crown jewels. The kids like to play with them, taking it in turns to be princes and queens."

"There are children there?" Hazel asked.

"Of course, didn't you hear what Eamonn said?" Phoebe asked. "So we're agreed? That's where we'll go. Not to Anglesey, but to London."

"We'll see," Isabella said.

Chester wasn't sure if it was his place to say yes to their coming to London, though he saw no reason to say no. Sorcha Locke was a different matter entirely. After a few more hours in the woman's company, he'd already decided that she wouldn't be welcome in the Tower. It wasn't that he entirely distrusted her, but that he knew he'd never be able to trust her entirely.

"So that's the library where you used to live?" Chester asked, pointing at the metal-clad building adjacent to the car park.

"That was a good home," Isabella said. "It would have been perfect if it wasn't for the undead."

The infant whimpered. Everyone went quiet, listening for the sound of the approaching living dead.

Dawn properly arrived, the day truly began, and the seconds slowly ticked away. There were five hours until noon, and that soon became four. Chester sat on an upturned oilcan by the edge of the wall and watched the road. Below, a zombie drifted towards the car park's entrance, but didn't venture inside. It lurched onwards. Only when the creature had staggered another twenty yards along the road did Chester relax.

The plan had worked so far, but so much could still go wrong. With no way of blocking the entrance to the car park, there was nothing to stop the undead from slouching inside and up the ramp to the roof. On the other hand, as long as they were quiet, there was no reason for the living dead to venture inside. He found himself looking at the infant Isabella.

They should have found a better place to wait for the helicopter. Somewhere without a ramp at the very least. Somewhere indoors, perhaps. Somewhere that could be secured. Neither Locke nor the older Isabella had been able to think of anywhere else that was relatively clear of debris and overhanging obstacles, and which had enough flat space for a helicopter to set down.

Below, another zombie drifted into view. Chester didn't let his expression change as the creature limped along the road. One leg was injured, and it moved in a series of short circles, maintaining its momentum more by the swing of its arms than the movement of its legs. It had heard something. Whatever it was, it wasn't from the car park. The zombie disappeared into the city. As long as they were quiet, they were safe.

The children sat in the back of the car, huddled together, not quite asleep, but exhausted from terror. As long as they were quiet, they should be safe, but what if the infant woke up? What if the undead heard the child and came into the car park. He needed a backup plan.

"I'm just going to take a look at the stairwell on the other side of the car park," he whispered.

"Why?" Hazel asked.

"I want to see if the door's locked or not," Chester said. "Best to know that there's only one way in or out."

"Are you going downstairs?" Phoebe asked.

"No. I'll be there and back, and you can see me from here." He nodded to Isabella. She had the infant swaddled her coat, the crossbow in her lap, loaded. "I won't be long," he said.

Chester crossed to the stairwell in the far corner of the car park. The door was unlocked. After a moment's hesitation, he went through and down. The stairwell was dark, filled with the stench of death caused by two corpses near the first-floor door. They had probably been undead, and had certainly been killed long ago. He kept going down. At the bottom were two doors. One led into the car park's ground floor, the other led outside. If they had to escape, it would have to be out there, but where they would go then, he had no idea. He went back upstairs.

"You said you weren't going through the door," Hazel said.

"I thought I heard something in the stairwell," Chester said. "There was nothing there. We're safe. I'm getting a bit restless, that's all. I never had the patience to sit still. That was always my problem when I was your age. I always wanted to be out and doing."

Three hours became two. Thunder rumbled in the distance. The storm was coming. The infant Isabella whimpered. Chester forced a smile through gritted teeth. The rain was holding, for now, but in many ways that was the worst weather they could have hoped for. The dense clouds meant no satellite images of the area, and while a lack of rain meant the helicopter would have no trouble landing, it also meant there was nothing to muffle the sound of the child's cry. The other children watched the infant, and looked as worried as Chester felt.

"You know, I flew on a helicopter once," he whispered. "It was for my birthday, let me see, four years ago. I was feeling a little flush at the time, but temporarily without any friends. They, uh…"

The job had been off the books, and done without McInery's knowledge. The target had been a betting shop that ran a side line in gambling on no-rules prize fights. In one of those ironic twists of fate that was amusing only to those who hadn't been caught, Chester's gang hadn't been the only people who'd noticed the betting shop's owner's ostentatious display of wealth. The tax authorities had taken note, and the police had been conducting an investigation. They'd seen Chester's gang go in through the back, and had quickly organised a cordon. Chester had slipped away with the haul, but the others had been arrested. To ensure that his name was never mentioned to the police, Chester had foregone most of his share. He'd been left with a meagre two thousand pounds. It hadn't been worth laundering, so he'd spent the money instead. A helicopter flight over London was the first thing he'd bought.

"My friends were all too busy to come with me, so I took the helicopter flight alone," he said.

"Did you like it?" Phoebe asked.

"Oh yes," Chester lied. "It was one of the most exciting things I've ever done." It wasn't, and he'd hated every minute of it. He had no problem with heights, but being confined to a small box had felt too much like being in a cell. "It was amazing what you could see from—" He was interrupted by a jarring clank from below.

He eased himself up, and peered through the railings at the top of the wall. Two undead drifted down the street. They'd been a man and a woman by their clothes. Brightly coloured clothes, too. She wore a pink jacket, rainbow scarf, and blue thigh-length boots into which tartan trousers were tucked. He was in a white leather jacket, red combat trousers, and leopard-print trainers. Either they'd found the clothes in the bargain bin of a charity shop or in the private catwalk-collection of a world-famous designer. There was little mud or dirt on the clothes, though a few dark stains and jagged rips indicated how they had become infected.

The infant Isabella gave another whimper. The undead woman jerked her head left and right. Her lank hair whipped across her face as she looked for the source of the sound. She stopped when her eyes were level with the car park's entrance.

"Give me a moment," Chester whispered calmly.

And he did feel calm as he crawled back along the roof for a few paces, then ran, doubled over, to the ramp. It was the calm that came in the middle of the storm when fear of the impending tumult had been replaced with certain knowledge of what the worst was and how far away safety yet lay.

On the ground floor, the undead woman had taken two steps towards the entrance. The other zombie was a step behind. Chester stood in the shadow of a pillar, watching, waiting, but knowing that he couldn't wait for too much longer. The undead woman took another step inside, and it was time to act. He unclipped his mace, and stepped out of the shadows.

"Morning," he said, mostly to get the creature's attention. "I'm sorry about this. I really am."

The undead woman growled and lurched towards him, her gnarled hands punching the air. Left, right, left, right. There was almost a rhythm to it.

Chester rested the mace on his shoulder as he strode to meet her. The shadows were deep, the light was poor, making her face nothing but an empty silhouette. He was glad of that as he swung the mace up. The tip clanged into the low ceiling.

"Damn it!" He skipped back a pace, changed his grip and drove the mace horizontally into the woman's chest. Bone crunched, cloth tore, and she staggered sideways. The undead man was only two steps behind. Chester let momentum turn him around, pivoting a full three-hundred-and-sixty degrees, crouching as he turned, putting his entire weight into the next blow. The mace smashed into the zombie's knee. Bone shattered, sinew tore, decaying muscle fell apart as the zombie toppled forward. Chester rolled out of the way, and then to his feet. He flipped the mace, and drove it down onto the back of the fallen creature's skull. Turning around, he looked for the undead woman. She'd collapsed, and lay near the booth by the exit. Her left side was a ruin. The fingers on her right hand dragged across the concrete, but her left hung limp. Her legs twitched, and her mouth jerked up and down, but she was unable to move.

"I really am sorry." He slammed the mace into her face, crushing it. She went still. He checked the road outside. It was empty, at least of the moving undead. Further down the road he could see the corpses they'd fought during the night. He looked at the dead woman.

When he'd left the Tower with Greta, he'd thought that this trip would be his farewell to England. A footnote that would provide stories for future generations, stories like the discovery of the Royal Train. That was an indulgence, the same kind of distraction he'd used in his last life when he'd told himself that he'd make one last score and then retire. The truth, the real truth and his real future, was that the war was never going to end. The undead might. They might truly be dying, but that would not be an end to danger, simply a harbinger of the next one. People had always been the real threat, just not always the most immediate one.

Barclay might have been one of Quigley's lieutenants, and his interest might be in a warehouse built by a co-conspirator, but the reality was that they were fighting over supplies. They might get distracted by the undead, the weather, or by hunger or disease, but ultimately, their foe was other people, just as it had been throughout history. To Chester, Anglesey had represented the dream that it could be otherwise. It was the myth that he could lay down his weapons. His past would become a collection of amusing anecdotes, stories of rooftop chases, of outwitting dim police officers and canny canines, told to the children and their children as he grew old. It was a fantasy. *This* was his life. Ultimately, it would be his death. It was humanity's endless struggle, the war that would never end, the battle from which there would be an occasional rest but no respite.

He walked back to the ramp, and went up to the roof.

"It's all fine," he said. "It looks quiet out there. Not long to go."

"Quiet except for the storm," the older Isabella said. "But there's no lightning yet, that's a blessing, and Isabella's settled."

Chester crossed to the wall, and saw that the sat-phone was blinking. "Hello?" he said.

Chapter 26 - Hostage and Misfortune
Birmingham

Bran stood statue still, his eyes on the warehouse, his ears on the zombies stumbling along the road outside the terraced house. There were many routes the renegades could take to reach the church so only two possible locations to ambush them. Either at the church itself, or close to the warehouse where the renegades would least expect trouble.

Behind him came a squeak as Greta moved a fraction in her chair. Bran raised a warning hand. The squeaking stopped. He knew it was Greta. He'd been keeping one eye on Locke all night, and learned the woman could move more silently than a ghost.

It was that constant observation of Locke which had almost spelled their doom as they had walked from the cinema to the car park. Bran had been paying too much attention to her and not enough to the undead. More than once, Locke had risked her life to save the children. Bran felt he could trust her up to the point where the hostages were rescued. After that, he expected she would vanish into the ruins. Anglesey wanted her alive, or at least wanted confirmation that she was dead. Bran had made up his mind on that. He'd known many evil people in his life, people like Barclay, and Locke wasn't like him. When the woman vanished, Bran wouldn't stop her.

The end-of-terrace house offered a view of the bus parked across the warehouse entrance. When the hostages came out, Bran would go downstairs and then through the front gardens, looping ahead of Barclay's people. As to precisely how and where they would ambush the renegades would depend on how many guards the hostages had.

It was ten o'clock. He'd been watching the warehouse since just after dawn, and so far, no one had left. It was possible that some of the renegades had departed before sunrise. It was more likely that no one had and that no one was going to. An hour ago, two figures had climbed onto the building's roof. Not wanting to risk them catching light reflected from the binoculars, Bran hadn't given them a close examination, but he was sure neither was Barclay. Those two had been sent up to the roof as bait for a sniper. They'd stood there for five long minutes before they'd retreated back down into the warehouse. In the hour since, Bran had seen no one.

There was another near silent squeak behind him. Again, he raised a warning hand. There was no chance the soldiers would hear, but he was more concerned with the undead in the street outside. There had been a lot more during the night than he was expecting. It might simply have been that those zombies had been trapped inside the ruined Bullring, but it might not. It might mean something else. It might mean they were in more danger than they realised. He couldn't do anything to confirm it, not now.

"Another hour to go," he whispered. He wasn't sure what he'd do when that deadline was reached. He wasn't going to delay the helicopter, but didn't think Greta would leave Eamonn behind. He wasn't sure that Locke would leave Isabella. Bran knew himself, and he knew Barclay, and he knew that he couldn't leave the two hostages to that thug's scant mercy.

The best option was to wait until the helicopter arrived, hope that Barclay heard it and came out to investigate. They could kill some of the renegades in the open, and then launch an assault on the warehouse. Perhaps. It was unlikely to work. It certainly wouldn't work without casualties. Still, Chester, the children, and the grandmother would survive. That was something. The crook had survived and truly reformed. Bran smiled, glad to have been proved wrong.

Ten minutes later, a figure climbed onto the roof of the bus. A second joined him, and then a third, and Bran was sure that man was Barclay. There was something about the man's stance Bran had always been able to spot from a distance. In Somalia, Afghanistan, and Iraq, in training when they'd both been recruits, and before when they'd been children.

Barclay climbed back down into the warehouse, while the other two renegades cleared the barbed wire from the bus's roof.

"It's happening," Bran whispered. "Get ready."

There was a too-loud shuffle behind him, and then Greta was as quiet as Locke.

Bran kept his eyes on the bus. With the wire cleared, a ladder was dragged up from the warehouse-side, and propped on the road-side of the vehicle. The two renegades climbed down. One gave a shout. The words were inaudible, but the meaning was clear when more figures climbed up onto the bus's roof. One, then two, then three and… no, that figure wasn't climbing, he was being hauled up and then unceremoniously pushed over the bus's edge. One hostage, male from the ragged beard. Another figure was hauled up. Like the man, her hands were tied at the back, but that didn't stop her from trying to kick at her captors. Bran thought he heard a laugh as she, too, was pushed down into the road.

"Two hostages," Bran whispered. "A man and a woman."

"Eamonn," Greta whispered.

Bran hoped so, because all the other figures climbing onto the bus and then down into the road had their hands free. It was a ragtag group, dressed in more civilian clothing than military, armed with as many shotguns as rifles, and with some only carrying axes. With surprise as his multiplier, Bran had no concerns about the coming fight, even though, from the look of it, they were going to fight them all. He counted ten, then eleven, then twelve, and then thirteen renegades gathered in the road.

"They're all outside," Bran said.

"All of them?" Locke asked.

"I count thirteen plus two hostages," Bran said.

Barclay was talking to his men. Something was wrong. Bran couldn't work out what until the group broke into two.

"Okay. We're up," he whispered. "It looks like four are leading the hostages towards us."

"What about the other nine?" Locke whispered.

"They're heading east," Bran said. "Barclay's with the larger group. I think those four with the two hostages are to keep us distracted while the other nine loop around and encircle us. We'll have to strike quick and fast to get the hostages clear. Okay? Move."

Bran spared no thought as he shot the stray zombie loitering outside the damp terrace. The time for subterfuge was over. He ran sure-footed down the road, two strides ahead of Greta. He let her set the pace, but he set the direction, following the memorised map rather than personal knowledge.

Left and left again, and then right, running along the edge of the reservoir. One glance at the bubbling blanket of white foam covering the water was all he needed to be glad that he hadn't had to swim in it. His respect for Locke grew a notch. Even with scuba gear and a wetsuit, he would have thought twice about venturing into its depths. In a flash came a memory of Australia and the promise of a very different type of rendezvous. He pushed the distracting thought away, raised his rifle, and shot the zombie staggering along the path. The creature collapsed. They ran on, slowing when they reached an access road that led to Icknield Port Road. From the direction the four renegades had taken on leaving the warehouse, they would have to travel along that street. Opposite the access road was a row of two-storey low-rise flats with an alley between them. He marked that alley as a possible escape route.

"Wait here," he told Locke and Greta, and edged forward. Trees and bushes had been planted in a plot not quite large enough for a house. The overgrown shrubbery obstructed his view without offering any real cover. He inched forward until he had a clear view of the road. There were more houses, then what was possibly a row of shops, and there, coming towards him, were the two hostages and four soldiers. They'd been too slow. There was no time to set up proper angles of fire. How good a shot was Greta? They would find out.

Turning around, he raised a finger to his lips, and then motioned for the other two to approach. Again he marvelled at how quietly Locke could move. Greta was a lot worse, though no nosier than a zombie. Bran turned back to the road, watching the soldiers, waiting for any sign that they had heard Greta. He saw a soldier at the front looking around warily. And then he saw Eamonn fall. The closest guard kicked him. The renegade at the rear hurried forward and grabbed the soldier's arm. Any momentary flash of concern that not all these soldiers deserved their imminent fate vanished when that second guard smashed the stock of his rifle into Eamonn's arm. Eamonn moaned. Isabella yelled and lashed out with her feet. The guard closest to her slapped her across the face. It was a vicious backhand that sent her spinning across the street. The soldier at the front barked at them, an inaudible command that was obeyed when they dragged the hostages to their feet, and pushed them along the road.

Bran glanced at Greta. She was beside him now and must have seen some of the confrontation. Locke was next to her, submachine gun raised.

"Greta," he whispered, "shoot the man at the front. Locke, take the man at the rear. I've got the two either side of the hostages. Fire only when I say. Not before. One shot. No more."

He waited. The group drew nearer. A hundred yards. Fifty. Bran heard glass break in the distance. A can clattered along the road behind them, rolling closer. The lead renegade slowed, watching it. He didn't stop, but the others slowed, too. That lead soldier was armed with an assault rifle fitted with an over-long suppressor that could only have come from Anglesey. The man at the rear had a shotgun. The other two had axes. One was an ancient weapon with a butterfly-blade, the other a more modern firefighter's tool.

As the soldiers slowed, they bunched together. Bran's second shot was going to be difficult. They were thirty yards away, close enough to make out their uneven stubble and hacked-short hair, their stained clothes repaired with tape and smeared with mud.

Twenty yards, and another rattle of metal, and this one came from the alley on the other side of the wide road. This time, the soldiers stopped. The lead renegade raised his rifle. Bran took aim.

"Now," he whispered.

Greta fired. So did Bran. The lead soldier fell, as did the guard next to Isabella. A moment later, the one at the rear collapsed. As Bran shifted his aim to the last renegade standing, Eamonn charged sideways, knocking the man to the ground. Isabella spun around, launching a kick at the man's head. Bran had lost his shot.

"Move!" he barked, and pushed his way through the undergrowth and down into the road.

The renegade grabbed Isabella's raised foot, twisted, and pulled her to the ground. Eamonn was on his knees, clearly already beyond his limit of endurance. The thug grabbed his axe. Still running, Bran raised his rifle, but before he could fire, the renegade collapsed, a trio of bullets in his chest.

Bran glanced around. He saw Locke lower her weapon. Then he saw the zombie ten feet behind her. He spun, fired. The zombie fell. Locke, seeing the rifle pointed in her direction, raised her own weapon, aiming it at him. Bran ignored her and headed for the hostages.

Greta reached them first, rushing to Eamonn's side.

"I'm here. I'm here," she said, sobbing with relief as she cut the ropes. "You're an idiot, Eamonn, an absolute fool. You should have told me you were leaving."

He mumbled something indistinct in reply as Bran ran to Isabella's side.

"You're safe. Your baby's safe," he said, cutting her ropes. "Can you stand?"

"Who are you?" Isabella asked. "Sorcha? Sorcha!"

"They're friends," Locke said. "Friends of Eamonn's, anyway."

"The children are safe? Where? Where's my baby?" Isabella asked.

"In a car park near the library," Locke said. "A helicopter is coming."

"She's not safe, then," Isabella said. "Not yet. They've gone looking for them. Barclay has gone to find the children. He thought you were alone here in the city, so if you were coming to get Eamonn and me, the children would be unguarded."

"They're not unguarded," Bran said as firmly as he could manage. He took out the sat-phone to call Anglesey.

"It's done," Bran said. "We've got the hostages. They're safe."

"They're not," Bill said. "I was trying to reach you. The clouds have cleared to the northwest of Birmingham. There's a horde. It's heading towards the city. It's about four miles from the reservoir at the moment. It'll be in the city in an hour, two at the outside. It's big, Bran, bigger than anything we've ever seen. At least one million strong. Maybe ten times that."

"Ten million? Are you serious?" But he knew Bill was. Bran had wondered why he'd seen decreasingly fewer on his trips to that same corner of northeastern Wales. He'd hoped the zombies were dead. They weren't. It explained why so many of the undead had appeared in the city overnight. They were the outriders, the orbiting undead that hadn't yet been sucked into the horde's dark, dense mass. He looked up at the low clouds, but they offered no hint at the nightmare on the horizon.

"Can you get any images of us, or of the car park?" Bran asked.

"Not at the moment," Bill said. "The city's still covered in clouds."

"Fine. Greta, Locke, and the two hostages are going to Handsworth Park. Get the helicopter to pick them up there after they've collected the children. Four of the renegades are dead. The other nine are searching for the children. Get that helicopter here as fast as you can." He hung up and handed the sat-phone to Greta. "Go to the rendezvous. Call Anglesey when you get there. If you can't make it to Handsworth Park, call Anglesey, arrange to be collected somewhere else." He turned to Locke. "Make sure they get on the helicopter. All of them. Then you can do what you have to do, but get them there first."

Locke crooked her head to the side, suddenly thoughtful and knowing.

"Understood," she said.

Bran ran to the corpse of the soldier with the assault rifle. The briefest of searches turned up one spare magazine with nine rounds. He took that and the magazine from the fallen weapon, and ran east, into the city.

Chapter 27 - Stand Off
Birmingham

"Hello?" Chester said, answering the sat-phone.

"Chester, they've all left the warehouse," Bill said. "Four took the hostages west. The hostages are alive and safe. The four renegades are dead. The other nine are looking for the children. The clouds are too dense to get a satellite image, so I can't tell you where they are."

"Looking for the children?" Chester said. It made sense. If Barclay thought that Locke was alone in the city, then he would think the children were only guarded by the older Isabella. Suspecting that Locke might lie to them about the vault, Barclay planned to trade Eamonn and Isabella for more valuable hostages. "Well, he can look, but he won't find us. Where's the helicopter?"

"Travelling as fast as the winds allow," Bill said. "It'll be there in under an hour."

"An hour? Fine. We'll be fine. We'll be here."

"Wait, there's—" Bill began, but Chester's finger had already pressed the button to end the call. He thought of calling back, but silence was their best friend now. He put the phone away.

"Is there a problem?" Isabella asked in a tone that suggested she knew there was.

"Your daughter's safe," Chester said. "So is Eamonn. The bad news is that nine of the soldiers are loose in the city, looking for us. It's a big city, the helicopter is on its way. In a couple of hours, you'll be with Isabella again, eating hot food somewhere nice and warm." He forced a smile. The older Isabella did the same.

"Two hours and we'll have a hot meal, that'll be nice," she said brightly. "Though I think I might have a hot bath first." As she spoke, her hand curled around the loaded crossbow.

"I'll go and keep watch," Chester said, and returned to his perch by the wall.

Eamonn was alive. It was hard to believe. Good news had been rare over the past nine months, and in this case it was tempered by the renegade soldiers searching for the children. Birmingham was a big city. Finding the children would be like finding Graham in London. Of course, they *had* found Graham in the end. No, that was only because Graham had come to the Tower. Barclay had no reason to search an empty car park. He'd look for buildings that were fortified.

Except…

Except that Barclay had found this group once before, when he'd captured Isabella and Eamonn. Chester hadn't asked how the man had managed it, but Barclay was one of Quigley's people. Bran hadn't rated the man, but perhaps finding people was Barclay's speciality. Perhaps, but that didn't mean he'd be able to find the children.

Except…

Except, Chester and Greta had found Eamonn. Out of all the towns and cities in the world, they had found the one that Eamonn was in. Technically, it was Locke who'd found Greta and Chester, but even that wasn't a coincidence. The satellites had spotted smoke and lights. Chester hadn't asked precisely what Anglesey had been looking for, but Birmingham couldn't have been the first place above which they'd moved the satellites. Out of all those places, from Anglesey to London, they'd seen lights and smoke in one place. The reason that life was here was because of the vault that Locke had built. Locke had stayed here because of that vault. Had Barclay come here for the same reason? Had he learned of it from Quigley? No, it was no coincidence that Locke and Barclay, and he and Greta, had all come to Birmingham, so what? That didn't mean Barclay would find them now.

Except…

Chester's gaze lingered on the corpses lying in the road outside. Barclay *would* find them. Prior to tonight, Locke had been careful to hide the corpses of the undead. The bodies they had left during the night-time skirmish were a trail leading right to the car park.

Chester took the sidearm out of his pocket. It was a silenced nine-millimetre, given to him by Bran in exchange for the submachine gun that

Chester had given Locke. He would have preferred something with a greater volume of fire. The pistol would have to do.

He crooked his head to the side, listening with his good ear. All he could hear were the sounds of tiles falling, of leaves blowing, the slowly approaching storm rumbling in the distance, and... and of feet, running.

His mouth went dry. He checked the safety on the pistol, and glanced at Isabella. Her face was stern. Her jaw was set. He had no advice to give her, so he shook his head, and lowered himself behind the cover of the wall.

He heard the running feet draw nearer.

"Sir!" a voice said.

"I see it," a second voice said.

"She said they lived in the library before they moved to the warehouse," a third voice said. "Those must be the zombies they killed back then."

"Then tell me why that blood is still wet," the second voice said. "Fan out."

Chester wrapped his fingers around the pistol's grip more tightly. How long until the helicopter arrived? Half an hour? Forty minutes? Fifty? He had two spare magazines, plus the one in the gun. Sixteen rounds in each, and it didn't add up to enough, not with his eyesight. The only glimmer of hope was that the renegades couldn't have much ammunition, either. Time, that's what he needed, and he wasn't going to buy it on the rooftop.

He gave Isabella as reassuring a grin as he could manage, and rose to a crouch. Doubled-over, he ran back to the ramp, and eased his way quietly downward.

By the time he reached the ground floor, the renegades were already inside. Chester stopped behind the massive supporting column around which the ramp was wrapped. He eased around its edge until he could see the shadowy outline of the renegade soldier. He was examining the undead woman by the ticket booth. In his left hand was a long-arm. The interior of the car park was too dark, the figure was too blurred for Chester to tell if it was a shotgun or hunting rifle, but it didn't look like an assault rifle.

"Hurry it up," another man called, walking into the car park. In his hands was the unmistakable silhouette of a fire axe.

"It's recent," the crouching soldier said. "Very recent. Died today."

Chester eased the safety off. He closed his bad eye and took aim.

"They're not going to be in a car park," the axe-man said.

"Do you want to tell the boss that?" the other said. "Search the place."

"Fine," the axe-man said. He walked a few more paces into the car park. His outline blurred as he stepped into the shadows, and away from the light. In two more steps he'd no longer be silhouetted by the daylight outside.

Chester pulled the trigger, firing two suppressed shots at the axe-man, another two at the man with the gun. Both fell, but the axe-man wasn't dead. He crawled out into the daylight as Chester shifted his aim.

"Boss! Bo—" the axe-man managed before Chester fired again, his bullet forever cutting short anything more the renegade had to say.

Two down, seven to go, but any hope that the sudden death of those two would cause Barclay to retreat or even pause were dashed with a shotgun blast. Pellets skittered wildly across the near-empty car park, burying themselves in concrete and abandoned cars. None came near Chester. He didn't move. Another shotgun blast roared. A glass windscreen shattered somewhere below and to his left.

"Give up!" a man called. Was it Barclay? Probably. "We've got all day. You haven't. The zombies are coming." There was another blast from a shotgun, and this time, Chester thought the gun had been fired into the air. Certainly, it hadn't been fired inside the garage. "In ten minutes, the zombies will be here. You and those children are going to die. Give up, or die."

Chester grinned. The man was either an idiot or he was desperate. Probably both. Let the undead come. Chester knew how to fight *them*. Barclay thought he was only facing the older Isabella. Chester decided to let him think that for a little longer.

Outside, a shadow moved to the cover of the ticket booth, another ran to the other side of the car park's entrance. Barclay wasn't waiting for the undead after all, but just until his people got into position. Time, that's all Chester needed, and there was one way to buy a few more minutes.

"What children?" he called out.

There was silence for a moment, and Chester hoped it would stretch to a full minute, but after twenty seconds Barclay replied.

"Who are you?" the renegade called out.

"That's a long story," Chester said, trying to think of a plausible lie. "It began in Wandsworth nick. I was doing ten years for a bank job. Now I'm a free man, and I plan to stay that way. I've survived nine months on the road, and you ain't going to change that."

Outside, someone hissed something to Barclay. Chester couldn't hear what, though he heard Barclay tell the man to shut up.

"You robbed banks?" Barclay called. "Not much call for that these days."

Chester grinned. It was working. "I dunno," he said. "You'd be amazed what people stored in safes. Not food, sure, but I've found a gun or three since my release. Still got them, and plenty of ammunition. What have you got? Shotguns and axes? You're outgunned, mate, so why are you shooting at me?"

"Because you just killed two of my people," Barclay said.

"Only because you shot at me an hour ago," Chester said. He could feel the thread of his lie slipping between his fingers. Each second counted, though. Each second meant the helicopter got just that little bit closer.

"Someone shot at you this morning?" Barclay called. "Where?"

"Down near the Bullring," Chester said. "That wasn't you? Hell, I think we've got a case of mistaken identity here. Why don't you go your way, I'll go mine, and we'll call it square."

"You killed two of my people," Barclay said. "We're far from square. I need payment."

And then there was a cry from above. A wail, loud and clear.

Barclay laughed. "Oh, very good. I don't know who you are, but we'll take the children now."

A hail of gunfire came from the left of the entrance as an assault rifle's magazine was emptied on fully automatic. The bullets were aimed at the dark shadows to the right of the ramp, but a ricochet pinged past Chester's good ear as he ducked lower. He'd bought a few minutes, but he'd need a few minutes more.

He swung around the pillar and fired at the ticket booth until the gun clicked empty. Ten bullets came back in reply as he took cover again. He loaded a fresh magazine. He was already running low on ammo and he was completely out of ideas. He heard feet running and getting louder, nearer. He edged around the pillar and saw a shadow sprinting towards the ramp. He fired two shots. The figure collapsed, screaming. Chester sprinted back up the ramp, and onto the first floor.

There were more abandoned cars than on the ground floor or the upper-most level. Most had their fuel caps, boots, and doors open, evidence of being searched by Isabella and her people when they'd lived in the library. From below, the gunfire had ceased. They knew he'd retreated.

Chester took cover behind a field-green four-by-four, aimed at the ramp, and waited for the next soldier to appear. At first he was relieved. After a minute, he began to worry. What were they waiting for?

He realised they weren't waiting for anything when the door to the stairwell opened. Chester stood, swinging the gun around firing at the shadows. He heard bullets hit wood, and thought he heard a heavy object falling to the ground. All hope that he'd killed the man was dashed when there was a roar of a shotgun. The bullets hit the car's chassis. Chester fired back as he ran to the ramp and up to the top-most level. He ran out into daylight, saw Isabella with her crossbow aimed in his direction, and then saw her abruptly change aim. He spun around to face the stairwell in the far corner. The door was opening. Chester fired, emptying the magazine into the renegade. The man collapsed, and Chester dived for cover behind the low wall.

"You all right?" he called to Isabella, as he ejected the magazine.

"We're fine," she said. "You?"

"There're five or six of them left," Chester said. "Barclay!" he called. "Barclay! Are there five of you left, or is it six? How many more have to die?"

"There are more than six of us," Barclay called back, and his voice came from close below. He was on the ramp. Chester eased himself around the wall, listening for footsteps while keeping his eyes on the stairwell. The corpse stopped the door from properly closing.

"Barclay? Barclay! We've got Isabella and Eamonn," Chester yelled. "They're safe. Your people are dead. It's over. Walk away. Leave now or you'll never leave this place."

A shot came from the stairwell, a single bullet that slammed into the car behind which the children were sheltering. Chester fired at the door, but another shot came, and again, it wasn't aimed at him.

"Surrender," Barclay said. "I won't ask again."

This was the hard choice, the one he'd been dreading having to make in London. His life might buy the children a few minutes, but would that be enough?

He fired at the stairwell again. Again a shot came in reply. Again it was aimed at the car. The windscreen shattered. There was a cry of anguish from the children as broken glass rained down on them.

"Give up!" Barclay called.

Chester reached over the ramp's low wall, and fired blindly down the other side.

There was a laugh from below. "Not even close," Barclay crowed.

Chester was out of options, and out of time. He whistled. Isabella peered from around the side of the car. Chester slid the safety on, and threw the gun to her. His death should make the renegades incautious, and if Isabella could kill another one or two, that might make the rest hesitate. Hopefully, for long enough.

"Sorry, Nilda," he murmured, and unclipped the mace from his belt. "Tell you what, Barclay," Chester called. "How about—"

There was a scream from below, abruptly cut short. Then a yell of surprise, terminally ended.

"He's below us!" someone called, but it wasn't Barclay.

Chester heard shouts of fear, cries of pain, the sound of a shotgun blast, and then there was silence.

"Chester?"

"Bran?"

The soldier ran up the ramp, gun raised. He swept the car park, finishing with his weapon aimed at the stairwell. "Everyone all right?"

"You took your time, mate," Chester said, grinning. "Yeah, we're fine."

"My daughter?" Isabella asked. "Is she really alive?"

"She's alive," Bran said. "She and Eamonn are alive and safe. Greta and Locke are moving them north. Wait here."

"Where are you going?" Chester asked.

"After Barclay," Bran said. "I let him live once before, and look what he did. Stay here, the helicopter is on its way."

Bran ran to the stairwell, and disappeared down it.

Chester eased himself upright.

"You're bleeding," Isabella said.

There was a stain on Chester's sleeve. It was only a shallow wound. Isabella ripped a length of material from her shirt, and wrapped it around his arm.

"Thank you," she said.

"Save the thanks until we're on that helicopter," Chester said.

"It won't be long," Phoebe said.

She was right.

"Do you hear it? Is that it? Is that it?" Damien pointed at the sky. "It's coming! See!"

Chester didn't. Not at first, not until all the children had, and were jumping up and down and waving.

Chapter 28 - The Chase
Birmingham

The helicopter flew in low, circling the car park once before settling to the tarmac. The door was already open. A woman jumped down. Short with dark hair, she carried a sniper's rifle. She was followed by two, far bulkier figures. A man and a woman, both wearing body armour over fatigues emblazoned with the Stars and Stripes.

The woman called out something, but Chester couldn't hear her over the sound of the spinning rotors. They weren't slowing, and it was clear that the helicopter wasn't going to linger. Chester grabbed Phoebe and Damien as Isabella, carrying the infant, hustled Hazel into the helicopter.

The dark-haired woman yelled something again. Chester shook his head. He pointed to the SA80 in the U.S. Marine's hands. The Marine frowned.

"I'm going after Bran!" Chester yelled. He didn't think they'd heard him, but the woman seemed to get the gist. She motioned for the Marine to hand over his weapon. Chester took it and a spare magazine, and checked he still had the sat-phone in his pocket. Head low, he ran away from the helicopter, and towards the stairwell.

Since Bran had come up the ramp from the road, that left the rear exit to the stairwell as the only direction for Barclay to have gone and for Bran to have followed. Outside, there was a corpse with blood still oozing from the pair of bullet holes in his chest. It was one of the soldiers, but it wasn't Barclay.

Chester jogged away from the car park, pausing when he heard a change in the drone from the helicopter. He watched it rise up, and fly away.

With its absence, he heard the woken-undead claw at doors, smash glass with fists and face, and kick through the drifts of litter and debris as they lurched along the rubble-strewn streets. Ahead lay a creature recently shot in the head. The wound still oozed brownish-black gore. Chester was on the right trail.

He heard the sound just before he reached the alley. He raised the borrowed rifle to his shoulder, and pulled the trigger just as the zombie staggered into sight. The weapon was set to fully automatic, and Chester fired ten shots into the creature's head before he released the trigger. The zombie crumpled. He slung the gun and drew his mace. He'd save the bullets for the living and keep the steel for the undead.

Following the trail of recent corpses, he jogged along Lionel Street to Livery Street and across a bridge over the rubbish-strewn canal. At a junction with a wider, nameless road, he caught up with a zombie travelling the same direction as he was. He swung the mace into its legs, but didn't stop to finish the creature. Another road, and then a dual carriageway, an alley, and onward. He followed the bullet-riddled corpses northeast until he reached a junction absent of zombies, moving or dead.

It was as nondescript a junction as he might have found in London. Even the shops were the same. A newsagent, a chain-bakery, a fried-chicken shop, a down-market deli with up-market prices still advertised on the chalkboard in the window.

Perhaps he'd been unwise to chase after Bran, but it had been an automatic response. Whether it was wise or not, he wasn't going to find the soldier now, nor would he find Barclay. Instead, he would go home. He took out the sat-phone, with the intention of finding out where the helicopter was going to collect Eamonn and Greta. The light was already blinking.

"Hello, Chester?" Bill answered immediately. "Where are you?"

"I'm not too sure," Chester said.

"Is Bran with you?"

"No."

"Okay, listen. We got cut off before I could tell you earlier, and Kim tried to tell you when she landed, but you couldn't hear her. There's a horde. It's massive. Somewhere between a million and ten million strong. We think it's the horde that you saw in Hull, the one that we saw in Wales, and most of the rest of the undead that were in this part of the world. It was heading towards the city before the helicopter flew over it. The main mass will swamp the reservoir in under an hour. There's a swarm of thousands ahead of it, and they're already in the city."

"Ten million?" Memories of Hull came back to Chester in a flash. There wasn't a sea to jump into here.

"Probably less than that," Bill said, "but there are so many that the exact number doesn't matter. The helicopter is about to pick up the two hostages, Greta, and Locke. Can you make it to Handsworth Park?"

"Dunno," Chester said. "Where is it?"

"Northeast of the prison," Bill said.

"If I could find the prison…" Chester murmured, looking for a street-sign. "No, I'm not going to find it in time."

"If you can locate somewhere the helicopter can land," Bill said, "and if you can do it in the next forty minutes, the helicopter can collect you. Otherwise, head east. Keep running. Outpace the undead. We'll refuel the helicopter, and send it to get you later this afternoon."

"Understood," Chester said. He hung up. The compass he usually kept strung to his belt was gone. He'd lost the water bottle, too. Probably during the fight in the garage, though he didn't remember when. No matter. Absent of any better idea, he continued the way he'd been going.

His knowledge of Birmingham wasn't great, though it was better than it had been before the outbreak. Where Jay had taken to spending the evenings watching TV shows and bad movies, Chester was reading more. Old stories about the construction of the Grand Union Canal were among his favourites, but that wasn't a place for a helicopter to land. There was Spaghetti Junction, of course, and that was to the east of the city. The motorway would be signposted, but it would also have been fenced in during the evacuation. He walked a little faster. What he needed was a park. London had plenty of those, surely Birmingham was no different. He looked for a sign. Instead, he saw the zombie.

It lay in the road, its feet in the flooded gutter, but its torso on top of a mass of rotting leaves. The wound in its head was neat, and it was fresh. There was a rustle, then a bang of a bin falling over somewhere behind the houses.

273

"Bran?" Chester called.

He got a reply, but it wasn't from Bran.

"Don't reach for that gun," Barclay said. "Slowly, turn around."

Chester did. Barclay stood twenty feet away in the doorway of a two-storey house, a rifle in his hands.

"I don't know you," Barclay said.

"I know you," Chester said. "Your name's Barclay. You worked for Quigley. You held my friend hostage."

"Do you mean Eamonn or Isabella? Eamonn? So you're from London?"

Chester's fingers tightened around the handle of his mace. Anger bubbled up from deep inside. It was a rage that had been festering for years. At times it had masked itself as fear, at other times frustration, but now it was just raw fury. Bran had once told him that stopping power was a myth. He was going to put that myth to the test.

"You worked for Quigley. Did you know Cannock?" Chester asked.

Barclay smiled. "You know him?"

"He was a—" Chester hesitated. "I grew up with him. It is one of my deepest regrets that I didn't get to kill him myself. You knew him, then? You're one of those people. One of Quigley's acolytes?" His eyes on Barclay, he bent his elbow so the mace began to swing back and forth.

"Cannock's dead?" Barclay asked. "We all thought he might be, but I honestly didn't dare believe it was true. Well, that is a good piece of news to end a bad day. Where's Web?"

"Who?"

"Sergeant Branofski, where is he?" Barclay asked. "I saw him chasing me. You don't know?"

"I know this," Chester said, as he dropped his shoulder low, spun his arm up, and threw the mace at Barclay's face. The renegade soldier pulled the trigger once as he ducked, but Chester heard three shots. He felt something tug at his arm. Barclay felt nothing as the two bullets hit him, one in the head, one in the neck. He fell, dead.

Bran stepped out of the alley opposite.

274

"You stepped into my sights," the soldier said. "I had to work my way around the building."

Chester laughed.

Bran frowned. "You didn't see me?"

"Hadn't a clue you were there," Chester said. There was the sound of glass breaking further down the street.

Bran shook his head. "We can talk later. There are zombies coming. Let me see your arm."

"You mean the horde? I heard on the sat-phone," Chester said. "If we can find somewhere a helicopter can land in the next half hour, they can collect us. Otherwise we've got to keep running east until they have time to refuel."

"It's just a flesh wound. You'll be fine. East is that way." He pointed ninety degrees to the direction Chester had been travelling.

"Hang on," Chester said. He walked over to Barclay's body, and picked up his mace. "Say hello to Cannock when you see him," he said to the corpse.

"How many did you get in the car park?" Chester asked, as they jogged through the streets.

"Four died two streets from the warehouse," Bran said. "I got two inside the car park, one immediately outside, two more a couple of streets from here."

"Add Barclay, and the four I got, and that makes… fourteen."

"Thirteen. You winged one, didn't kill him," Bran said. "And thirteen is all there were."

"Unlucky for some," Chester muttered, "but not for us."

A zombie staggered out of the broken door of a narrow terraced house. Bran brought his rifle up. The weapon clicked. Chester swung his mace, slamming the ancient metal into the creature's skull. As it collapsed, he saw the other zombies behind. "There are four of them."

"And no time," Bran said. He pushed Chester on and away, pausing after fifty yards. "Give me your rifle. Mine's jammed." Chester handed it over. "Now run."

They came to a halt when they reached Frederick Road. It was full of dozens of stalled cars, but more than twice that many of the undead. There was no access to the motorway a hundred yards to the east, so it was possible the vehicles had been trying to reach Aston Park whose southern entrance was to their left.

"I count thirty zombies on the road," Bran said. "There's more behind them. At least a hundred. They must have come from the motorway. We're not going to be able to cross it here."

"So we can't go any further east," Chester said. The zombies were drawing nearer, though the closest from that pack was still sixty yards away. "The rumbling of the horde's getting closer. I can feel the vibrations through the soles of my feet. Either we head southwest and find a route around the motorway, or get air lifted from Aston Park."

"Call Anglesey. Find out if the helicopter is still in the city," Bran said. He raised the rifle to his shoulder as Chester made the call.

"We're at Aston Park," Chester said the moment the call was answered. "Can we be collected?"

"Stay on the line," Bill said.

Chester could hear the background noise of Anglesey, and what sounded like an infant laughing, an exasperated woman asking *why,* a kettle boiling, and music playing. He heard a deathly sigh from far closer. He spun around, and saw the zombie crawling out from underneath the abandoned Volvo. He stepped forward and was already swinging the mace one-handed before he'd time to properly register the creature's torn yellow and brown uniform. The mace slammed into the zombie's skull. He knew that uniform. It was from a fast food place, wasn't it? All restaurants were shut during the weeks of rationing, so how come the young man was still wearing it when the country had been overrun? He must have run out of anything else to wear. That was depressing. Bran fired again. Chester raised the phone back to his good ear, almost blocking out every other sound.

When he'd killed that zombie, he'd had to step close to the car. Close enough that the second crawling zombie was able to reach out from underneath and claw its hands around Chester's boots. The creature pulled as its grip tightened. Chester almost fell over, dropping the phone as he dragged his foot free of those necrotic hands.

"Get off!" he yelled punching the mace down at the decayed arm still caught around his left leg. He stepped back, and looked for the phone.

"Time to move!" Bran yelled.

"I dropped the phone," Chester said. He couldn't see it. "It must be under the car." As he bent down, the zombie with the wrecked arm kicked its way free of the vehicle.

"No time!" Bran said, pushing Chester towards the park. "Run!"

They did, for a hundred yards until they were on a wide avenue surrounded by partially flooded grassland dotted with massive bare trees. Even the evergreens seemed to be dying.

"You told them where we were?" Bran asked. He had the rifle raised to his shoulder, and was pivoting to the front, back, left, and right. "They're following, but I can't see any ahead. There may be some behind that screen of bushes. You told them where we were?"

"Yeah, yeah, I told them," Chester said. "I said we were in Aston Park. I asked if we could be picked up from here. They didn't have a chance to reply."

"This way," Bran said, pointing away from the entrance through which they'd come. "If the helicopter is still in the city, we'll hear it before we get to the park's far side. If we don't hear it, we'll keep going east. We'll have to find a way across or through or under the motorway. Watch the left." He raised the rifle, but didn't pull the trigger. The zombie was thirty feet away. The creature slipped in the mud, splashing to its knees.

"East it is," Chester said.

The grassland was frequently flooded, occasionally overgrown, but often withered and dead. The wide pedestrian thoroughfare was carpeted with a thick blanket of leaves and fallen branches, interspersed with pecked-clean, off-white bones.

"Do you have any spare ammunition," Bran asked.

Chester checked his pockets, his pack. "Just the one magazine." He looked for the sidearm Bran had given him earlier in the day, but then remembered he'd given it to the older Isabella.

"How are your legs?" Bran asked.

"My legs are fine, it's my knees that are the problem," Chester said. "You're limping a bit."

"I know," the soldier said. "We should hear the helicopter soon."

Ahead of them was the centre of the park and Aston Hall, a seventeenth-century wide-windowed mansion that had become a museum. Parked outside were a score of heavy-duty vehicles. Trucks, lorries, vans, flatbeds, all were civilian, and explained where the abandoned cars outside the park were trying to reach. The boards nailed to half of the exterior ground-floor windows explained *why* they were trying to reach here. That only half of the windows were boarded-up told him what they'd been doing when they had been overrun. It had happened quickly, and a long time ago, judging by the decaying skeletons lying in the open doorway.

"We need a few minutes," Bran said. "Somewhere to catch our breath." He looked around. "One zombie behind us. Two in the grassland heading this way."

Chester couldn't see the distant living dead. He was grateful for that. There was a clatter from inside the mansion's open doorway. A figure lurched out of the shadows and into the courtyard.

"We can't rest here," Bran said. He fired. The zombie collapsed.

They walked on in silence. Beyond the main part of the house was a one-storey extension. Its steep, sloping roof was only ten feet above the ground.

"Up here," Bran said.

"You sure?" Chester asked, looking back and around.

"After this, we won't be able to rest for at least two miles." Bran raised the rifle to his shoulder and fired a shot towards the grassland, then another, and then two back the way that they'd just come. "I think we've got five minutes."

Chester reached up, and grabbed hold of the gutter. He hauled himself up, then reached down, and helped Bran onto the roof.

"Five minutes? The helicopter's not coming, is it?" he said.

"No," Bran said. "We'd have heard it. We're on foot, and that means we've got to run through or under the motorway. We'll have to—" He stopped. A sound had come from the far side of the roof. The extension was ten metres wide, but fifty metres long, creating an open space on its far side. That space was full of the undead. The zombies had heard their voices and were slowly rising to their feet.

"Back the way we came," Chester said wearily.

Bran shook his head. "They're coming across the grassland. I count ten in sight. There were more in the ground floor of the house coming out of that door." He ejected the magazine from his rifle and checked the load. The first of the undead had reached the wall of the low extension. Its hands slapped into brick.

"I've got forty rounds," Bran said. "We'll need them."

Another creature had reached the wall, then a third, a fourth. The building began to shake as fists and faces, feet and legs beat and kicked against the brick. In the distance, Chester was now sure he could hear the rumble of the approaching horde.

"The worst part of this," Chester said, "is that even if we were to make this our desperate last stand, killing these zombies won't make a blind bit of difference to anyone."

"They're starting to spill around the side of the building. Ten seconds," Bran said. "Then we jump and run." He pointed southeast. " One hundred yards that way, then turn and sprint northeast."

Below, glass shattered and wood splintered as a window broke.

"Are you ready?" Bran asked.

Chester closed his eyes and fixed Nilda's face in his memory. He wanted that to be the last thing he'd think of. "I'm ready. It was a pleasure knowing you, Bran."

"It's not over yet."

The building shook. Bricks tumbled from around the broken window frame as the undead pushed and clawed at the masonry. The roof sagged.

Gripping the mace tightly, Chester crossed to the edge of the roof. He could see two zombies that had made it around the edge of the extension, and four more indistinct figures approaching across the grassland. He was glad he couldn't see the rest.

"Here we go," he said.

"Wait!" Bran grabbed his arm just before Chester jumped.

"What?"

"The helicopter!" Bran said. He twisted the silencer free of the rifle. "You don't have any flares? Matches?"

"Nothing," Chester said, turning to look into the sky.

"Then wave your arms," Bran said, as he fired the rifle into the mass of the undead. "I don't know if they'll hear the shots over the sound of the rotors, but they should notice the zombies."

They did. Twenty seconds later, Chester heard it. Ten agonisingly long seconds after that, the helicopter appeared from over the ancient house. It hovered fifty feet above.

"Now what?" Chester yelled. The helicopter edged to the left, then to the right, slowly getting lower as it moved away from the mansion.

"Further along! To the edge of the extension!" Bran said.

Hearing the sound of the helicopter, the undead below had grown furiously active. The roof shook. It sagged above the broken window. With a thunderous crack, five feet of roof collapsed.

"Run!" Bran yelled, but Chester didn't need the encouragement. He was already sprinting along the collapsing roof. The two men staggered to a halt three feet from the building's edge. The helicopter hovered, thirty feet above.

"Do they want us to jump?" Chester yelled, eyeing the landing gear. It was an impossible distance away.

Before Bran could answer, the helicopter's door opened. An orange bundle attached to a rope fell. The soldier grabbed it as it hit the roof. It was a harness. As soon as Bran took hold, someone above began working the winch, retracting the rope.

"Hold on!" Bran said, dropping his rifle. Chester let his mace fall and wrapped his arms through the straps.

"This can support the weight of two people, right?" Chester asked.

"I guess we'll find out," Bran said.

The rope went taut. With a lurch, they were wrenched upwards. The helicopter began to rise even as the rope slowly ascended. Chester didn't look down, not until the rope stopped moving, arms reached out, and hauled them inside the helicopter.

Chester collapsed into a seat, closed his eyes, and didn't open them until there was a tap on his arm. It was the dark-haired woman. She handed him a headset. He put it on.

"Hi, I'm Kim. We've not properly met, though I think I know you already."

He wasn't sure what to say to that, so he smiled.

"We're coming up on it, if you want to see," she said.

"See what?" he asked.

"The horde," she said. "We've got five minutes' margin of fuel, and we're going to use it take some pictures. It's the satellites," she added at his clearly confused expression. "With this cloud cover, they're useless. We need to see what we're facing."

"Right, sure, of course," he said. "Out there?" He turned to look out the window more to forestall any further conversation than out of curiosity. Now that the immediate danger was over, his body was reacting to the activity of the last few hours. He was getting too old for a night without sleep, and he'd not had a proper night's rest since he'd left London. His knees were screaming in agony worse than after that skirmish by Tower Bridge. Had that only been two weeks ago? He'd lost track. His arm ached. For some reason it was bandaged, and he couldn't remember why or when that had happened. His ears were ringing, though that might have been the thrum of the rotors. His eyes were refusing to focus on the window. Then they focused on what was outside. It was a sea of mud, mercifully indistinct, flowing up and over the city.

"I'm glad I can't see it," he murmured.

"Here, I've some binoculars," Kim said.

Chester hadn't realised the headset's mic was still on. "That's okay," he said. "I don't need to know the details."

"There's not much to see, not really," Kim said. "The reservoir is just below us now. Or it was. It's gone. I don't know if they've filled it with corpses or with dirt or mud or what, but they've obliterated the warehouse, the reservoir, everything. I think they're moving in an almost circular pattern, spinning anticlockwise, almost like a hurricane and just as destructive. Roads, houses, hills, even towns, they've left nothing in their wake. Since we know Bran came to Birmingham from the west, and you arrived from the south, we think it came from the north. It's levelling the city. That's what I wanted you to see." There was an edge of desperation in her voice.

He turned away from the window and looked at her. "Why?"

"It's barely over a hundred miles to London," she said. "We think it came from the north, which means it was heading south. If it can utterly destroy Birmingham, it'll do the same to London."

Now he understood. He closed his eyes again. Searching for Eamonn had been an indulgence, despite that they'd found him. Locke and Barclay had been a distraction. It was the undead that were the immediate threat. They couldn't simply hope the zombies would beat and mill themselves to death in that massive throng. They couldn't hope that the zombies would die. They had to plan for the worst, and that was the horde reaching London. He and Nilda had talked about it, of course, but it was always framed as simply another danger like starvation or illness. It hadn't seemed so real, so imminent.

When he opened his eyes, Kim was gone. He looked about the cabin. It was a larger helicopter than he'd realised, with seats for over twenty people. The children were huddled between the pair of Marines, chewing enthusiastically on bread rolls. The three Isabellas sat together. Mother, daughter, granddaughter, reunited. The younger Isabella was battered and bruised, but her eyes sparkled as she held her infant child.

Eamonn was on a stretcher. Greta was next to him, holding his wrist not his bloody hand. He looked terrible. Chester knew he should go and speak to him, but he needed a few more minutes to collect himself. Behind them sat Bran. He looked as if he was asleep. Next to him was Locke. Chester was surprised to see her. Then again, had she stayed in Birmingham, she would have died. There would be no other escape from that city.

Epilogue - Before the Storm
Anglesey, 17th November, Day 249

"You're going to be fine, mate," Chester said. "A few weeks of rest, and you'll be as good as new."

Eamonn gave a thin smile borne mostly of morphine, exposing a mouth almost empty of teeth.

"They're going to make you some dentures, which'll be a lot less bother in the long run," Chester said. "No more risk of toothache, for one thing."

Greta's smile was fixed and fake. "Are you going back to London?" she asked. Her tone was as brittle as her smile.

"As soon as they can organise a boat," Chester said. "Maybe tomorrow or the day after."

She nodded. "You'll pack up our things?"

"I'll send them to you when the boat returns," Chester said. "When you get to Belfast, you can pick out a nice house, big enough for all of us. Not a hotel, though. See if you can find a mansion like the kids had in Kent."

Eamonn and Greta weren't going back to London. Yesterday, as soon as they'd reached Anglesey, Eamonn and Isabella had been rushed to the hospital. While an initial examination of Eamonn hadn't showed any internal damage from which he couldn't theoretically recover, there was still a good chance that he wouldn't. Aside from blood loss, malnutrition, scurvy, and the damage to his mouth, he had scores of paper-thin cuts across his entire body. Three ribs were fractured, his kidneys were on the verge of failure, and he had an infection on his left hand where the nails had been pulled, the bones crushed. And those were only the findings from the *initial* examination.

"What if you don't come to Belfast?" Greta asked.

"We won't leave you behind," Chester said. "We're family, aren't we?"

Eamonn gave another morphine-induced shallow smile.

"I, uh, I've got to have a word with the doctor," Chester said. "I'll come and see you later. Keep strong, mate. Get better quick. We're going to need you in the days to come."

Chester didn't need to speak to the doctor, but if he stayed much longer, he knew he would snap. They'd learned what had happened more from Isabella than Eamonn, and she had told them more about what had happened to him than to her. Barclay was a man who enjoyed causing pain, and liked to see that pain displayed on his victims. Chester's anger wasn't in regret at the swiftness of the renegade's death, but in the familiar way that the U.S. doctors had treated the two hostages. They had seen those types of injuries before, and often enough not to be shocked by them. Barclay wasn't the first. He wasn't even the first since the outbreak. Would he be the last? Chester wouldn't bank on it, but he forced the fury from his face because the small hospital wasn't entirely empty and Eamonn wasn't the only patient.

In the corridor, the three children from Birmingham were drawing on the walls with marker pens and wax crayons. The older Isabella sat in a chair outside the room in which her daughter and granddaughter were being treated. Her hand was thickly bandaged, her eyelids heavy, and the smile on her face looked oddly false.

"Hello all," Chester said cheerily. "That's a nice house, Hazel. You've got a real eye for perspective."

"How's Eamonn?" Phoebe asked.

"Oh, he'll be fine," Chester said. "It's mostly bruises, and they'll heal quickly enough. He's got to rest, though. And how are you finding Anglesey?"

"It's strange," Phoebe said.

"It's wet," Damien said.

"I don't like it here," Hazel added. "Sorcha was right. Where is she?"

"I'm not sure," Chester said. "I can ask around."

"When can we go to London?" Phoebe asked.

"I'm not sure about that, either," Chester said.

"You know what's best on a cold wintry day?" the older Isabella said. "Hot chocolate. I heard them say there's some in the nurse's break room. Why don't you three go and see if the rumour is true."

"You want to get rid of us so you can talk, don't you?" Hazel said.

"Yes," Isabella said, "but I'd also like some hot chocolate, so be a dear and see if you can find some."

"Do you know where Sorcha is?" Isabella asked when the children had grumbled their way out of earshot. "I haven't seen her since the helicopter landed yesterday evening."

"Not yet," Chester said. "I washed, ate, slept, and woke up about an hour ago. I can ask around."

"One of the doctors told us that she's infamous," Isabella said. "That she was part of the conspiracy that created the zombies."

"I don't know about that," Chester said.

"*I* know that she kept the children safe all these months," Isabella said. "She could have left us when Barclay arrived. She stayed. She kept us alive. I think someone needs to be told that."

"I'll make sure they know."

"Thank you. Will you go back to London?" she asked.

"For now," he said. "I don't know how long we'll stay there."

"Because of the horde?"

"Partly, but I think we were going to leave anyway," Chester said. "We hadn't really talked much about what we'd do in the spring, but there's not enough land around the Tower to plant a crop. If the undead were dying, we might have moved into Buckingham Palace and turned the Royal Parks into farms. Some might be dying, and the rest will in a year or so, but I don't think we can wait for it to happen. Yes, it's that horde. It's a roiling cauldron that could spill south and drown us all. No, the Tower's not going to be safe."

"So you'll come to Ireland?" she asked. "That's where they want us to go as soon as they've cleared Bella for release. They're more worried about her than my daughter."

"I didn't realise. Is that why it's taking so long?" he asked.

"Bella was born three days before the outbreak. She seemed healthy enough." Isabella shook her head. "Sometimes it's easier when you don't have a doctor to tell you that there's something wrong. Will you come to Ireland?"

"Greta and Eamonn certainly will," Chester said. "They won't be coming back with me. As for the rest of us, I don't know. Stay close to Greta. I'll make sure she knows our plans. There'll be a place for you and yours wherever we go. As to where that is, I suppose I better find out."

She smiled. "Thank you," she said. "For everything.

He returned her smile, uncertain what to say.

Anglesey was very different to how he'd remembered it. When he'd left, not long after the power plant had been turned back on, the island had seemed a place of hope. It had bustled with promise as people stripped shops to their floorboards and talked of opening new ones, new restaurants, new farms. It had been more talk than work, but there was the prospect of something good being forged from the ruins. It had seemed as if the best parts of the old world could be rebuilt and the worst parts consigned to history. Now, the streets were virtually deserted. According to one of the doctors, only a thousand people had so far been relocated to Ireland, with most of those now living around Belfast Harbour. He wondered where everyone else was.

His feet took him to the terrace where Bill Wright lived. Chester had gone there with Kim after the helicopter had arrived, principally so that he could call Nilda. They had offered him a bed, and he'd gladly accepted, but he'd gone to the hospital first, and there he had fallen asleep. He wanted to call Nilda again. He wanted to hear her voice. After that, like all the other people on Anglesey, he wasn't sure what he'd do while waiting for the ship that would take him away.

Inside the house, a score of people huddled around a row of screens. Some showed the partially cloud-covered satellite images, others the slightly blurred pictures taken from the helicopter. All showed the horde.

"Was it really as bad as that?" Annette asked, detaching herself from the group as Chester entered.

"I don't know," Chester said. "How do you measure bad?"

"That's what we're trying to work out," she said. "How many there are, and where they're going. Do you think they'll go to London?"

He was too tired to lie, but before he had to tell the truth, a door opened on the other side of the room.

"Chester?" It was Bill Wright. "Can you come through? I was about to look for you."

The small kitchen was empty, the table covered in papers, and two laptops.

"Please," Bill said, "take a seat, we've a lot to talk about." He leaned against the counter as Chester took the more comfortable padded chair close to the window.

"You look like you've had some bad news," Chester said.

"So do you," Bill said. "You stayed in the hospital last night?"

"I fell asleep the moment I sat down," Chester said. "Eamonn's probably going to recover, as will Isabella. I'm not sure about the baby."

"I got a report this morning," Bill said, picking through the sheets of paper. Unable to find the one he wanted, he quickly gave up. "We'll have to move them to Elysium. It'll be a longer journey than to Belfast, but that's where the *Harper's Ferry* is being towed by the *Vehement*. The *Harper's Ferry* has the medical equipment, and Elysium has an energy supply. It'll mostly be wind turbines this winter, maybe supplemented by solar if the clouds ever clear, but that's more than we'll have in Belfast. The ship's a few miles east of Cork at the moment, but they should get there in another four or five days. Once it's safely moored, we'll send them there."

"Where's Elysium?" Chester asked.

"Near Kenmare Bay on the southwestern corner of the Atlantic coast."

"About as far from Belfast as you can get," Chester said.

"Pretty much," Bill said. "It was one of Kempton's retreats, and originally run by Sorcha Locke until it was overrun by the undead. I can't promise that your friends will be safe there, but they'll be with medical personnel, and protected by Marines. If the walls break again, they can retreat to the *Harper's Ferry*."

"This isn't what I was hoping my return to Anglesey would be like," Chester said.

"And it's not how I pictured this meeting," Bill said. "I often thought about it. You know that our paths crossed in Sydenham a few months after the outbreak? I was trapped in a house. We communicated with bits of paper stuck to the window. I was angry at first, when you left your house and walked past mine. I waited for you to come back, and you didn't."

"I wanted to," Chester said. "I was trapped in a cafe a few miles from there. When I managed to get out, I went back for you, but you'd gone."

"Bran told me," Bill said. "It was part of the story that caused Annette to move the satellites over London. Although, if I'm honest, I think she was looking for an excuse to see what her old home looked like."

"She's a Londoner?" Chester asked.

"She is," Bill said. He shook his head. "I never really thought I'd be a parent. Now I have two children and responsibility for so many more."

"Tell me about it," Chester said. "I've acquired a few myself. Every minute is a new worry."

"Isn't it, just?" Bill said. "Yes, after you didn't come back to rescue me, I was angry for a time. I cursed your name and blamed you for every ill that befell me. Eventually, the anger faded as I came to realise who I was and who I'd been. I was a different person back then. Arrogant, selfish, self-centred. I suppose I still am, but at least I'm aware of it." He smiled. "In the end, I hoped you'd survived and that, one day, we'd be able to sit and chat over a drink." He waved a hand at the counter. "Herbal tea is the best I can offer. We're out of the proper stuff. Out of coffee, too. The hospital has a stash we seized when we raided the Inn of Iquity, but they say it's only available on prescription. I don't begrudge them. Not too much."

"Anything hot will be fine," Chester said. "When you say raid, what do you mean?"

"That was the pub where Rachel Gottlieb worked. Have you heard of her?"

"A little."

"She's dead, but we didn't get all of her supporters. Rather, we only found evidence that pointed to one. Gareth Lenetti." The kettle clicked. Bill poured water into two mugs and brought them over. He sat opposite Chester. "Lenetti was found guilty of murder. There was a jury trial, and an appeal, and then there was an execution." He was silent for a moment. "No, when I imagined the two of us meeting, I didn't expect the future to be like this." He shook his head. "We'll have that conversation another day, perhaps. For now, I need to warn you that strangers arriving in London might not be friendly."

"George mentioned that," Chester said. "But we've had troubles of our own, we know to be suspicious."

"I'd like to hear your story," Bill said. "I think everyone would, so if you don't mind, I'll write it down and have it printed. Not right now, though. There are more pressing worries. Even more pressing than some of Rachel or Bishop's followers still being alive. Despite that horde, my biggest worry isn't the undead. It's not finding fresh water in Belfast, or coping without electricity, or even our dwindling food supplies, though those are all contributing factors. My greatest concern is that law and order will break down. We're maintaining a paper-thin veneer of civilisation through a newssheet, through holding elections, but mostly through fear that the power plant will melt down before we've all left. That veneer will crack during the long winter months ahead of us. If it breaks, any hope that we might create something new and better than what we had before will be dashed. Even maintaining something that's the same might be beyond us."

"I don't envy you," Chester said. He took a sip of tea as he formulated how to best ask the question. "That's disgusting."

"I know," Bill said. "We're down to what we're happy to leave behind."

Deciding there was no circumspect way to ask, Chester went for the direct approach. "Are you running things now? I thought it was Mrs O'Leary and Mr Tull."

"I would say," Bill said carefully, "that she is the head of state, and that I am currently heading up the civil service. Officially, I am her chief of staff. In practice, I'm organising our departure from Anglesey and the search for a new home, which may or may not be in Ireland, but certainly won't be on the British mainland. I've been reading a lot about Churchill and his wartime cabinet, and I tell myself it could be a lot worse." He took a sip of tea. "You're right, that is foul."

"I don't think any people will reach London overland," Chester said. "The horde will see to that. That's going to be *our* biggest problem."

"I've been up all night, trying to find a solution," Bill said. "I even considered a nuclear strike. The *Vehement* still has its arsenal. We've no GPS, and can't use the satellites for navigation, so we'd have to plot the trajectories the old-fashioned way. With a target as big as the horde, we'd hit it, but I don't know how many zombies we'd destroy. Even if it was all of them, there's no reason to think that another horde might not coalesce. The question, though, is whether Mister Mills would refuse to launch. He did when Quigley gave the order, and he refused to even countenance it during the summer when the idea was even more theoretical. He has a point, of course. We're the survivors of a nuclear apocalypse. Launching a missile would do untold psychological damage. It would take us a step away from democracy and one step closer to despotism, and all for what? Everything we do now isn't just about staying alive, but it's about how the method of our survival will determine the shape of our future."

"All for what? Exactly," Chester said. "It wouldn't change much for us in London. We can't plant in concrete so we'll probably have to move come the spring. Our best hope is that the horde grinds itself to dust against Birmingham's bricks. If it doesn't, if it turns south, we'll have to flee far sooner. For that we'll need some ships."

"And that's where I can offer you some more practical help," Bill said. "George and Lorraine, and their yacht, are staying in London until we know whether the horde is continuing south. If it is, they'll transport your people downriver. Over the next few days we'll put together a flotilla of sailing boats with sound hulls and strong rigging. If it comes to it, you can move far enough from London that you'll be safe until a large ship can collect you. If you're still there in a month, we might be able to give you a larger, powered ship with enough oil that you can reach Ireland as and when you need to."

"If we're there in a month?" Chester murmured. "The power plant, the horde, do you think it will ever end? Will there ever be a time when we can look about and say that this land is ours, that it's where the children can live and grow old?"

"I hope so," Bill said. "But there's something else I wanted to discuss. Sorcha Locke."

"Where is she?"

"Under guard," Bill said. "It's more for her own protection than anyone else's. After the business with Bishop, I put out a brief account of our trip to Ireland. In all honesty, it was a way to distract people for a few hours, because we were that desperate for breathing time. I might have made a bigger deal out of Sorcha Locke than I should have, but mostly because I assumed that she was dead. Everyone on the island knows the name and knows her as Kempton's right hand, and so as complicit in the outbreak as Quigley or Kempton herself."

"Did you ask her whether she was?" Chester asked.

"She won't talk about it," Bill said. "You know the rule here, no one will be judged on what they did before they arrived on the island because we all did things we wished we hadn't just to survive. I am the walking precedent. The evacuation was my idea. Quigley might have turned it into a mass cull of the population, but I devised the original plan. All we really know about Sorcha Locke is that she held a senior position in Kempton's organisation. That's not enough to convict. It's not enough to even come up with a charge."

"Are you going to let her go?"

"I'd like to," Bill said. "She arrived here on a sailing boat that Bishop took from her. We offered her a new yacht, a little bigger but small enough one person could pilot it. We offered her a gun, ammunition, and food. She didn't want it."

"What *does* she want?" Chester asked.